ENCAMPMENT.

a novel of race
and reconciliation

To Bill,
Hope you like it!

Carl Eeman

ENCAMPMENT.

a novel of race and reconciliation

CARL EEMAN

Mélange press

Round Lake, NY

This is a work of historical fiction. Apart from the well-known actual people, events and locales that figure in the narrative, all names, characters, places and incidents are the products of the author's imagination or are used fictitiously. Any resemblance to current events or locales, or to living persons, is entirely coincidental.

Published by
Mélange Press
a division of Word Alchemy, Inc.
5 Albany Avenue
PO Box 696
Round Lake, NY 12151
www.melangepress.com

Library of Congress Control Number: 2009937614

ISBN 978-0-9824337-3-7

Printed in Canada

Thank you to Boyd Printing

Book design by Kimberley Debus

Cover design by Jeremey Bingham

Maps drawn by Carl Eeman

Dedication

To the 600,000 who came from 1861 to 1865
From farm and shop, across lane and stream
For cause and home, country and freedom.

To the 160,000 of these who came in 1863
To offer the last full measure of devotion
On Gettysburg's fields and hills.

To the 54,000 of these who came in 1913
For handshakes, long talks, a great embrace
In Gettysburg's fields and under her trees.

To the 1,800 of these who came in 1938
In wheelchairs, with wispy voices
Giving Gettysburg one more look.

And to us,
who live in the land they loved.

Acknowledgements

While the first words of *Encampment* went on paper in 1999, the roots of this book go back to Bruce Catton's Civil War trilogy and his war biography of Grant, which had me learning names like Shiloh and Spotsylvania in time for the centennials of those battles. Harold Keith's *Rifles for Waite* told a long, intricate tale that kept me up reading under the covers with a flashlight. American Heritage's *Civil War* coffee table book gave me Matthew Brady's searing images and a sense of place and time. Before I knew it, I was a Civil War buff.

My interest smoldered for a couple of decades, but the end of the 1980's saw my interest in the Civil War flare up again. Edward Zwick's amazing film *Glory* reminded me of a forgotten angle of the War, the presence and courage of black Americans in uniform. Then PBS aired Ken Burns' stunning series on this American convulsion, with running commentary by Shelby Foote. Christmas brought a present of Foote's massive three-volume *Civil War: A Narrative*. Foote's captivating prose took me through the struggle from the New Mexico sands to a war related Vermont bank robbery. Having sailed the *CSS Shenandoah* around the world and reached the death of Jefferson Davis in 1889, I laid down his work convinced I need not ever read anything about the War again.

And yet… something lingered. The last episode of Burns' series showed the veterans of the War gathering in ever-diminishing numbers for reunions. Watching these scenes, I began thinking of a story of reunion and reconciliation, perhaps set at the largest ever of these gatherings, the 1913 Encampment at Gettysburg. I discovered Catton's old article on this reunion from *American Heritage* magazine, entitled "The Day the Civil War Ended." Despite his declaration, Horowitz's *Confederates in the Attic* showed that even 130 years later, some found it vitally important to keep the memory of the Confederacy alive and active.

Taylor Branch's documentary *Eyes on the Prize* and the much darker *Mississippi Burning* pointed me to the 90-year gap between the end of the War and the full (albeit halting) realization of equality and civil rights. Could the realization have been accelerated? Why had equality been so opposed and so delayed?

I was intrigued by the odd overlaps of history from these years. Harriet Tubman died in March of 1913, just one month after a baby girl born in Alabama would one day take up her cause. I saw a newsreel of the premiere of *Gone with the Wind* in Atlanta in 1939. One scene showed aged Confederate veterans entering the theatre. An earlier part of the newsreel showed a photo of a children's choir that had sung a selection of 'plantation' songs for a carefully integrated audience during the prior week; one child pictured was a 10-year old boy named after his father, Martin King, Jr. As I thought about a northerner and southerner meeting at Gettysburg for reunion, I kept adding a third major character, a former slave, who in his person could bring to the fore the issue of race and the cause of freedom.

David Blight's pivotal work *Race and Reunion* provided insights into this gap. He writes of the bargain struck among white Americans regarding the Civil War that carefully excluded black Americans, a bargain still operative today: the Civil War is a military cataclysm of tactics and technology, suffering and victories that can be talked over and even re-enacted in perpetuity. However the causes and outcomes of the clash are ignored or suppressed. Common phrases from the 1870's still in use today expressing this bargain include "The War was never about slavery" and "Reconstruction was a serious mistake." This bargain effectively silences the place, contributions, and claims that a tenth of the country has in American life. I suppose as a son of refugees from Estonia, a nation that was erased from Europe's map, I feel keenly any attempts to erase other people's history.

After Blight, Donald Shaffer's *After the Glory*, and Jim Week's *Gettysburg: Memory, Market and an American Shrine,* were instrumental in strengthening the story, as did J.W. Johnson's *Autobiography of an Ex-Colored Man* and portions of W.E.B. DuBois' *Souls of Black Folks.* The National Park Service provided a wealth of on-line information about the 1913 reunion, supplemented by Colonel Lewis Beltier's official 1914 report on the gathering to Governor Tener of Pennsylvania. Malcolm Gladwell's excellent article in the August 2009 *New Yorker,* "The Courthouse Ring: Atticus Finch and the limits of Southern Liberalism," arrived just in time in the editing to greatly strengthen the third section of my tale.

Family and friends generously read earlier drafts of the manuscript. While several others read, Vera Eeman, Wanda Hammond, Keith Olstad, and Laurie Eaton were particularly helpful and detailed in their suggestions. The story is much clearer and smoother because of them. A two-day lecture by screenwriter Dara Marks at the Midwest Writer's Conference in Madison in March 2008 led to yet another complete re-write and helped me make friends with my three heroes and the people in their lives. Sue Hageness sat through late drafts with endless curiosity, asking for clarity and explanations, leading to yet further revisions. Daughter Annelise and son Marcus were patient with Dad's intensity over all things 1913 and cheered me on with their smiles and their delightful teasing. To all of you, my thanks.

Then there is my boundless gratitude to the people of Mélange Press, who have again proved their worth in bringing this author's passion to life on paper. Jeremey Bingham patiently shuffled cover ideas until this combination of manly and wistful emerged. Julayne Hughes offered dozens of comments as she copy-edited the work. Thanks also to Irene Michelitsch and Laurie Boyce.

Finally, great praise goes to Kimberley Debus, who incessantly changed hats at Mélange Press as publisher, editor, scold, confidante, cheerleader, writer's provocateur, and patient friend. Her unwavering dedication to seeing this book through, her insistent care for historical accuracy, and her delight and engagement in exploring the "what-if" premise of the story made her a joy to work with. Along with those noted above, her sage advice has helped produce as good as story as I can tell.

C.G.E.

October 2009

A Note to Readers

Three matters may help readers enjoy this story:

First is the use of the English language. The novel is set in early twentieth century America, when travel was more limited and local speech patterns were stronger, so American regional differences were sharper than today. My Southerners will often use "y'all" and greet the day with "G'Mawnin." Before noon my New Englanders wish each other "G'mannin'" and in the evenings warm their hands over a "fiyah."

Second is racial language. I have used terms common around 1912 to refer to people of color and these terms, with the opening exception, had different weights than today. Starting at the bottom, "nigger" was and is a vile term for insult and denigration. "Negro" was only marginally better but usually was a synonym for "slave," so freed people avoided it while racists usually relished it. "Darkie" and "dusky" could be fairly neutral but were typically used in a casually or deliberately negative way. "Black" was quite rare, usually paired as a simple opposite of "white" and rather neutral, seen in W.E.B. DuBois' *Souls of Black Folks* (1903). "Colored" was by far the broadest, most acceptable term. James Weldon Johnston's *Autobiography of an Ex-Colored Man* (1912) and the organization National Association for the Advancement of Colored People (NAACP, founded in 1909) are representative. "Ethiopian" was the most positive term typically used in educated circles, like "Slavic" or "Oriental," but has virtually disappeared today. In social conversation it was complimentary, positive, and considered descriptive.

Finally, my story is one of historical fiction, of history re-imagined and taking a different path. I try to describe the events, people, ideas and assumptions of the time, and then change one thing, to then see how history could have run differently. That is perhaps the most intriguing aspect of the this genre, but when I read historical fiction myself I am somewhat frustrated not knowing where the history leaves off and the fiction begins. One must become a researcher to hunt down some of the facts of a given period, which seems an unfair burden to the curious reader. I have therefore included a chronology of dates and historical facts at the end in order to save the reader this chore. Whether I have used the facts presented well and moved them around occasionally as needed to make a better story is for the reader to judge.

Part One

THREADS

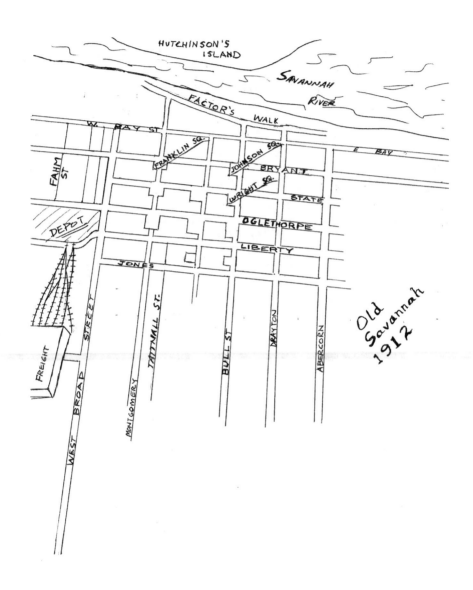

Old
Savannah
1912

Sunday, May 26, 1912

Savannah

A scowl scraped under the words, "What you doin' in this part o' town...
boy?"

No answer.

From inside a loathing came, "Iffin' this was a ratt run country you'd be
showin' me yo' massa's pass."

He echoed back, "Iffin' this was a ratt run country..."

He noticed the pavement was pretty warm, even when it clawed his palm
and smeared itself with his blood. That hurt.

The toe of the black, worn-down brogan hurt too when it kicked his ribs.

Another pair of worn brogans came up, brown this time, and pulled the
black pair around. "Hold on there, Dooley."

"You niggah-lovin' Longstreetin' bluebelly!"

Now came two pairs, some handsome men's half-boots under brown
pinstriped cuffs, and a black pointy toe peeking out from under a dark green
hem just above the sidewalk.

Brown brogans shifted back and forth. "Simmer down, Dooley. Ain't fitten'
pushin' anybody 'round on the Lord's Day, 'specially with a lady present."

Black brogans turned toward green hem. A single word, "Ma'am," floated
down; then the black brogans stomped away, the heels grinding the pavement,
the left one worn down at an odd angle.

Half-boots and green hem passed by together and brown brogans trailed
after.

He pulled out an old green kerchief and with black fingers pressed it against
the pale, bloody palm. After he left, the rest of his blood turned dark on the
pavement.

കൈ

The Atlantic breeze ballooned the cigar-fumed drapes toward Zachariah,
and he sneezed. It stunned him for a moment, but his headache was only
grumpy. He bent over again and finished tying his shoes. Then he stood,
buttoned his fly, and pulled his suspenders over his shoulders. In the open
armoire opposite him hung a gray tunic with three gold chevrons on the sleeve
and matching pants.

He took a deep breath and pulled his door open, but there was no one to face.

"Mawnin', Mistah Hampton," Alma said, coming in from her backyard visit. She was tying on a blue-checked full apron over her puff-sleeved blouse and long, bell-shaped navy blue skirt.

"Mawnin' Alma."

"Would you like a cup o' coffee *today*, suh?" she asked, moving toward the stove. Zachariah wondered at her stress on "today." "Yes, thank you kindly."

He took the enameled tin cup out onto the front porch and dropped into the rocker. He heard a far-off church bell chime, then another. "Sunday?" He took a sip. Too hot.

He blew on his coffee and got down a slurp, staring at the white uprights of the porch railing. White. Evenly spaced. Ribs? What? No. Back porch steps... white, wet. Went down them. Up them. Minié bullets drumming on...the roof... and his shoulders...his slicker.

He got down a full gulp and closed his eyes. His stomach protested and he tasted bile in the back of his mouth. Almost gagged. Gagged after the steps... after a backyard crossing. There'd been a gray door...a gagging smell...cool air blowing on his bare backside...a bit of gray light from a crescent moon cut out. Squinting up the street he faintly heard horse hoof clops and motorcar clatter from Jones Street.

Emily and Lee rounded the corner at the end of the block onto Tattnall. Lee Thompson looked dapper in his brown, pin-striped Sunday suit and matching brown derby. He was a lean, angular man nearly six feet tall with short, black hair over pale skin. His dark, calm eyes set over angular cheekbones missed little. His wife Emily's dark green skirt brushed her toes, while her white blouse rose chin-high at the collar. Her flower-trimmed hat shaded both her face and shoulders. Behind them, Zachariah could see the bobbing hat of a third figure. Occasionally Lee would say something over his shoulder. Meanwhile the clank of porcelain and silver through the dining room window announced Alma was laying out Sunday dinner.

Zachariah went to his room, slipped on his dark jacket and watched his fingers in the small shaving mirror loop on his tie. The face in the mirror showed flowing eyebrows over gray-green eyes, a hawk nose between medium cheekbones and a full silver beard, second-button long.

Back in the kitchen, he found Alma peering into the oven. "Alma, I see Lee and Emily comin' up the street and someone else with 'em. I 'spect they'll be four fo' dinner today."

"Thank you, suh," Alma said. "I've already set an extra place."

"Bully, Alma," approved Zachariah, moving to the door. "Say, did it rain some yesterday?"

"In the mawnin' it sure did, Mistah Hampton. Thunder n' lightnin' and the rain beat down fierce for a time and lingered on past noon."

He passed through the hall to the parlor and pulled a Bible off the bookcase. He and St. Matthew were settled in a stuffed chair when the iron gate squeaked open. A moment later, Lee held open the front door to let Emily pass. Glancing over the top edge of the page, Zachariah saw Peyton Colby's profile floating over the words, "Blessed are the poor in spirit."

"Mmmm! Smells like dinner's 'bout ready," said Emily. "Lee, why don't you and Peyton go in the parlor? I'll send Alma in presently." She turned and called, "Alma? We're home. Come take my hat. Is everything ready?" Her voice faded toward the kitchen.

Lee hung Peyton's nondescript bowler on the hat rack next to his own brown crowner. They came in the parlor and stopped short when they saw Zachariah.

"Hello, Zack," Peyton said, stepping over with an outstretched hand as Zachariah moved to rise from his chair. "Oh don't get up. Sunday ain't *that* formal."

"Hullo, Peyton," Zachariah shook his hand. "Hello to you too, Lee."

"Readin' the Good Book I see," Lee commented as both he and Peyton took chairs.

"Yes, I am," Zachariah responded. "Sermon on the Mount. Who's blessed and how they're blessed. Always gives me a restful feelin' when I read it." Then he turned. "Peyton, what brings you here today? Were you at First Baptist?"

"Actually, I was walkin' home from Independent Presbyterian when I came 'cross that Dooley Culpepper pushin' 'round some blackie."

"Emily and I saw it too, coming up the street," Lee chimed in. "We were still humming 'Blest Be the Tie that Binds' and came across these three old men who should know better. Two of them shoulda had enough fightin' to last 'em their whole lives."

"What was it about?" Zachariah asked, although having heard Dooley's name he had a fair guess.

"Nigh on as I can make out," Peyton answered, "Dooley said somethin' 'bout how when things was right, white folks wouldn't ever need to see dusky faces 'cept workin' the fields or keepin' house. He said, 'Iffin this was still a ratt-run country...'"

Zachariah heard the rest and began to offer, "Well Longstreet would say..." when Alma broke in from the doorway. "Gentlemen, dinner's ready." Lee gave silent thanks being spared another quote from General James Longstreet, Zachariah's long-ago commander and hero. He hoped this dinner they could stay in the twentieth century.

"Oh, do say it a bit more grandly, Alma," Emily said from behind her. "Gentlemen, dinner is served!" She started a bit when not only Lee and Peyton but also her father rose and moved to the dining room. As Zachariah passed behind her heading to a side chair, she turned and said evenly, "Glad you could join us, Daddy." He nodded back but dared only look up as high as the cameo brooch standing between her chin and collarbone on the stiff collar. Her dark brown hair was up off her neck and framed her spare, engaging face and hazel eyes.

After grace, Colby ventured, "So what was your preacher's theme today and what did he say about it?"

Emily turned back a harsh thought about her father's morning absence and said, "Reverend McWilliams preached on 'Blessed are the peacemakers' from Matthew chapter five."

"Do you think he was aiming that at anyone special in the church?" Lee asked, sipping his iced tea. Emily arched an eyebrow. "If you mean that set-to in the altar guild and Libby Pocklington...well, he was very careful not to look at any one of them."

"Libby Pocklington is a hard case to look in the eye," Zachariah remarked casually to Peyton, never looking left.

"She happens to be right in this case," Emily answered, glancing at her father's profile. "There's no reason for wax paper under the altar candles. That Rachel Collins just doesn't want to stay after and scrape off the drippings."

"So how would you be a peacemaker between Libby and Rachel?" Peyton asked carefully.

Emily eyed the men. Peyton was all innocence, but both Lee and her father were uncommonly attentive. They both knew Emily was trying to stay on both women's good sides and move up into their circle. She looked back at Peyton thoughtfully and said, "I'd take it to Reverend McWilliams and suggest First Baptist spend an extra dollar a month on those new, dripless candles Pauline saw last winter in Boston."

"Bravo," Lee exclaimed, spearing a couple of sliced carrots. "Make peace by taking away the cause of contention." As soon as he said "cause" he groaned inwardly. Zachariah missed Lee's wince as he spoke on.

"You know, the way Libby and Rachel square off is like a Lost Cause hothead havin' to shake hands with a Yankee."

Peyton chimed in. "Old Dooley goes off like a sulfur match 'bout the Lost Cause anytime."

"Them Lost Cause fellers and the Reconstruction men between 'em almost murdered Longstreet in New Orleans after the War," Zachariah said earnestly to Lee and Peyton.

With a sigh, Emily looked down at her plate. "And how was that, Daddy?"

"Longstreet walked out into the middle of a New Orleans riot when the secession boys were shooting every colored they saw. Longstreet was tryin' to make peace and he was almost shot by some Confederates he'd once commanded."

Lee and Emily hadn't heard this one before. Their eyes met, exchanging the thought that Zachariah was tracking this conversation rather well.

"Miz Emily," Colby answered, "I think yo' idea of them dripless candles is a much safer way a-bein' a peacemaker." Emily smiled.

Lee piped up. "You know, Zack, given what Longstreet was up against, maybe that's why the good Lord *blessed* the peacemakers, because He knew they'd catch it from both sides."

"Could be," Zachariah answered, while everyone waited for him to chew down the last of his pot roast. "Never know with them Yankees. Hard enough hearin' 'em 'round town these days in the shops and along the docks, let alone puttin' up with them bluebellies from my day."

As Alma cleared the dishes and brought in cobbler, Emily said with a sweet malice, "Thank you again, Peyton, for…helping Daddy home from the regimental dinner Friday night."

Zachariah eyed the centerpiece, remembering the flasks littering the tables. He frowned, remembering pools of sidewalk lights, some stairs, and…his room. But that had been Friday…and this was definitely Sunday. So Saturday had…

Emily's voice broke into his staring. "Peyton, do you think after forty six annual regimental dinners the drinking might ever start easing off? Or are some of the men too much in the habit?"

Peyton gulped. "Well, Miz Emily I don't rightly see how the 8th Georgia could keep its hard fightin', hard drinkin' name if we ever did. Not sayin' some fellers like Dooley don't indulge a bit too often, but, uh…" Now *he* couldn't look at Emily either, or Zack for that matter, and the pause grew awkward.

"You know Emily," Lee broke in, "Sunday bein' a day of rest I wonder if old Peyton and Zack might feel like an afternoon nap today?"

Peyton stretched and allowed how he really needed to head for home for just such a nap. After he left, Zachariah headed for his room and missed the sound of Emily's quick steps heading across the hall into the parlor under her skirt swish. Lee heard and went after her, knowing from her walk she was upset. Emily greeted him from the settee with, "Why? Why always the old soldier talk? It's been fifty years!" A tear slipped past her poise.

As he sat down next to her he said, "Maybe he misses…"

"Misses?" she snapped. "Every month there's some bourbon-splashed, regimental something. He lives under our roof, but how can that galoot Bob Bidwell or that four-flushing rascal Dooley Culpepper see him as much as we do?"

Lee tried again. "I meant maybe he misses some of those who didn't come back."

Emily's frustration and temper brought her to her feet. "He'd rather be with a dead one of them than with Mama when she was dying." Her self-control crumbled and Lee took her in his arms as she sobbed.

"Now, Emily, you know that's not fair. It was unfortunate but not his fault."

"But he should have been here; at least...my heart says he should have been."

"I expect his heart says the same. He loved her...and he loves you."

She turned around in his arms so he wouldn't see her face as she choked out, "He loves those flasks most of all."

West Side, Savannah

"Ow!" yipped Lucius Robinson.

"I'm sorry, Papa," Beulah said, gently daubing with a wet cloth over a bowl of water. "But that's a nasty scrape on yo' palm and we gotta clean it."

"I know dat, hunnybun," Lucius answered, "but it still smarts." He hissed through his teeth as she blotted the red-raw skin dry with a towel.

"Hannah gal," Beulah called, "you found that salve yet?"

Eleven-year-old Hannah came scampering into the kitchen, all pigtails and Sunday shoes. "Here it is, Momma."

"Now take a dab of salve and spread it gentle as you can on Grandpop's palm where it's all red." Beulah tucked Lucius' brawny forearm under her own ebony arm and pulled him snugly against her side.

Hannah popped the cover off the metal can. She gingerly dipped two fingers into the gooey mass, wrinkling her nose at the camphor aroma. She turned her earnest, dark brown eyes to her grandfather. "I'll try to be as easy as I can."

"I know you will," Lucius said. Hannah gave him a small smile, then spread the salve. Lucius winced but held his hand steady, then sighed. "Ooo, that's nice an' cool."

"Good," Beulah said. "Now Hannah, hand me that folded kerchief, and put a bit of salve on it too." Beulah gently landed the cloth squarely on her father-in-law's palm, then took another handkerchief and draped it over both sides. "Turn yo' hand over, Papa," she said, loosening her hold. As he did she snugged up the handkerchief and tied a firm knot below his knuckles, trying to keep a gentle pressure.

"How's that?" she asked.

Lucius flexed his creaky fingers cautiously. "Pretty fair. You and yo' nurse here do ratt fine medicine. I'm 'bliged."

Hannah lifted her chin and crowed, "The Momma an' Hannah Colored-Folk Clinic is proud to be of service to our fellow man." Beulah giggled as Hannah finished, "That'll be one cent or two eggs, payable by Friday. We cain't run this here clinic for charity 'cept for poor folk, which you ain't."

Lucius wiggled his tightly curled eyebrows at her, then dug his good hand into a pocket of his overalls. He pulled out a new penny and expertly mounted it on his thumb. "Mistah Lincoln," he said to the coin, "you keep company now with Hannah." He flicked his thumb. She caught the coin and slapped it onto the back of her left hand.

She lifted her right and exclaimed, "It's haids, Grandpa. That's good luck. Thank you." She stepped up and gave him a quick peck on the cheek, then skipped off to find her cigar box of treasures.

"Put the lid back…" Beulah began, while Hannah's pigtails scampered out of sight. "…on the can of salve," she finished. She shook her head. "Oh I'll do it."

Lucius picked up the washbowl with his good hand, bumped the screen door open and heaved the cool, slightly bloody water into the back yard.

Beulah wiped her hands dry on her apron. She was lean, with shoulder-length black hair falling in wiry locks that framed an angular face. Her warm, brown eyes were darker than her mahogany cheeks and were large for her narrow nose. Her mouth was wide with delicate, often-smiling lips. "You shouldn'ta given Hannah that penny. It's gonna spoil her into thinkin' she'll get paid for' doin' what she ought."

"One penny ain't goin' ta spoil that girl," Lucius answered. "An' don't start with me 'bout principles and 'zamples neither. Grandpops get to swap small kindnesses with their granchillun, don't they?"

"I s'pose," Beulah answered, turning back to supper. "Well the rice and beans are gettin' done and everybody'll be here soon. You go out on the front poach an' set a spell with Rufus. There's a nice breeze tonight."

Tree shadows were slanting across the street as Lucius stepped onto the porch. He resumed his usual humming, crossed over the spongy boards to the far corner, and sat down in his rocker. With an airy cane seat and back it never felt sticky or sweaty even on sultry days. The cane-weaving was a bit slack near the top, encouraging dozing. The hickory runners had worn a faint pair of tracks in the porch floor. This was his usual spot, in the shade of the big camellia bush where he watched life go by on Savannah's west side.

Rufus was sitting in a ladder-back chair tilted back against the house between the door and the rocker, eyes closed and letting the breeze work over his face, listening to his father hum.

"I know what yo' thinkin' 'bout tonight," Lucius said rocking briskly.

"I know you know," Rufus answered, opening his eyes. "It's been so long comin' I can hardly b'lieve tomorrow's the day."

"Think you and Beulah'll get any sleep?"

"I won't. I'm 'bout as keyed up as a seventeen-year locust lookin' for love."

Lucius struggled hard to muster up his excitement to match Rufus' as he asked in an edgy way, "Now, you sure you got everything covered?"

"Far as I can make out, we got it down to the penny," Rufus answered.

"Goin' over it again tonight?"

"Probably another ten times out loud."

"I'm hopin' for you, Rufus," he said with his eyes watery. Lucius' spirit was a wet log on a fire, steaming and sputtering instead of burning bright.

"Thanks Pop," Rufus answered intently.

About the time Beulah had finished bandaging Lucius' hand, Alma was walking home from the Thompson's. Sea gulls were feasting at the rail yard garbage dump as she came up Broad Street. The crossing gate clanged down at Liberty with warning bells. The Atlantic Coast Line 5:22 rang its bell in reply and blew a long note on its whistle. The gulls rose in a cloud of squawking flappery, roundly protesting the interruption.

She walked another three blocks by their short ends and then turned onto Fahm Street. After a block and half of jaded houses the long way north, she turned in at her gate and came up the path to a sagging front porch.

After twenty-four years of scavenging for bits and pieces, the house had risen to "dilapidated." It rested on cinder blocks, some permanently charred black from a fire. Scraps of tarpaper quilted the roof. A too-thick board bulged into an accidental sill on the south side, unable to hide under a weather-beaten coat of pale green paint. An ugly pair of high-mounted square windows flanked a six-panel front door that looked salvaged from the hall of a seedy hotel. The rotting base of the far porch post made it lean toward the camellia bush at the corner, but the old man sitting in a rocker seemed unworried as he talked gravely to a younger man.

Alma had often seen the two of them talking like this, although usually not looking so serious. The stocky one, well worn by the years, with a full, silver-white beard that reached down to armpit level, was obviously good friends with the rocker and the big bush at the porch corner. He had a kerchief tied as a bandage around his hand, and his dark, lively eyes with easy-going smile lines were damp tonight.

The other man was sitting in a kitchen-ordinary brown chair. He was three decades younger, taller and leaner, and his sleeves were rolled up, showing off sinewy forearms in a chestnut shade and long muscular fingers. This man's mouth and jaw were more jutting, and not just because the other was getting old-age jowly, although the two had similar eyes and matching noses. His eyes were brown, in a slightly-creamed coffee hue that was very appealing.

Alma bounced up the jouncing steps and gave them a big smile. "Hi, Daddy," she said, pecking Rufus's cheek, her eyes a perfect match for his. "Hello

Grampa." She gave him a matching peck and smiled an extra notch.

Lucius scratched her chin and his eyes twinkled. "My beard still makes you giggle, don't it?"

"Always has," she answered warmly. It was true. In the crib Alma had giggled endlessly for the chance to play with "gampa's" face fur as a game between them and as a tuck-in routine.

"Ever'thin' all right at work today?" her father asked.

"Well we did see old Mistah Hampton," her eyebrows arched in humor.

"Oh? And how did you see him today?" Lucius asked.

"Well, like you put it, Friday night he was slanticular, hangin' between Mistah Thompson and a Mistah Colby. Yesterday he didn't make it past horizontal. But today he was actually vertical. Polite, too."

"Well, you go yo' horizontal-vertical-slanticular way inside an' help Mama get ready for suppah," Rufus said.

"Yes, Daddy," she piped. "We'll call you when we're good an' ready." She pushed in the door on the second try. As she tried to close it, the door bottom bound tightly the last six inches.

"I'll get it," Rufus said. He rose and gave the door a long pull with all his weight but the humidity-swollen door would not squeak across the doorsill.

As he sat back down, Lucius said, "I can help you plane it down again if you think it'll help."

"Oh I don't know, Pop. If everything goes like it should, it won't matter.."

Lucius hummed, staring off. "You're ratt about that. With any luck at all, in a few more weeks…"

The front door opened suddenly and four smallish feet landed with a thump on the porch. "All right, its time fo' suppah," came two excited voices. Hannah Marie and her nine-year-old brother Sherman seemed to bubble with delight at having surprised the men. Rufus's head snapped around, followed by a grin, but Lucius gave his rocker an extra push and almost knocked himself over backwards. At the last minute, he caught himself, reaching a hand back against the house wall. Rufus saw his fright was not just from the near spill, but the children missed it.

"C'mon, c'mon, let's have suppah," they implored, pulling the men to their feet. Hannah proclaimed like a prophet bringing the Word. "Mama said, 'Now go get that Rufus Saxton Robinson and his old man Lucius right away. Iffin' you get 'em here before I count ten you'll each get a piece of penny candy for the walk to church.' So hurry up, hurry up! Mama's countin'!'"

They led the grinning, mock-protesting men inside. As Rufus carried in his chair he said, "How come we don't get a piece o' penny candy for walkin' to church?" With a hard push, the door squeaked shut.

Later that night Alma couldn't fall asleep. Through the thin wall by her bed came the sound of Lucius's sleep noises. She frowned in the dark. His snoring, whimpering and mumbled words were a dead ringer for Mr. Hampton's on Saturday.

Saturday, June 1, 1912

Rutland

Spring had overcome the stubborn Vermont winter. Even east of Rutland, Pico Peak no longer wore a grey-brown coat, but now flaunted a green cape.

Calvin Salisbury came north along Main Street's east sidewalk. The worn tip of his cane landed a regular eight inches wide of his right shoe, but his step was still springy for being in his mid-seventies.

Ahead of Calvin across the street, a heavyset man lumbered south past a row of shops to the streetcar stop where Terrill became West Street. His hair was plastered down with Brilliantine, and a full gray beard rode under a squat pug nose. Calvin was suddenly fascinated by a handbill nailed to a wooden utility pole. He read the notice several times, keeping the pole between his face and the chunky fellow until a streetcar came clanging up West Street. As the car squealed to a halt, Calvin crossed the street behind the car. He heard a familiar wheezy voice from the open door saying, "You'd think after sixteen years they'd just give up their seats without a reminder."

The conductor's loud voice said to someone in the car, "You'll either have to stand or get off the car." A moment later, two lanky black men dressed as bellmen and wearing scornful expressions stepped onto the curb, griping loudly. As the car pulled away, they shook their fists after it.

Calvin walked past them and turned down a small row of shops and let himself in the fourth one. The bell over the door jingled while aromas of soap, camphor, and bay rum met his nose.

From behind the high leather and chrome chair, Randolph stopped snipping his scissors. "G'mannin, Calvin." The checker players by the window paused too. "Hello, Calvin." "Mannin', Judge." The stranger in the chair nodded and said, "How air ya, sarr?" His lilt rolled from the Irish countryside to the barbershop window, still a bit surprising for Rutland.

Calvin nodded toward them all. "G'mannin, gentlemen." He carefully hung his coat, hat, and cane on the usual third hook, crossed to the barber's chair and held out his hand to the stranger. "How do you do? I'm Judge Calvin Salisbury, retired, from here in Rutland." His tangy New England vowels ricocheted off his crisp consonants.

Flipping the barber's sheet off his right hand, the newcomer shook Calvin's hand. "Playsure t' meet you, Judge Salisbury. M'name's Tom Boyle from South Boston. I'm the new manager at the Paramount over near Merchant's

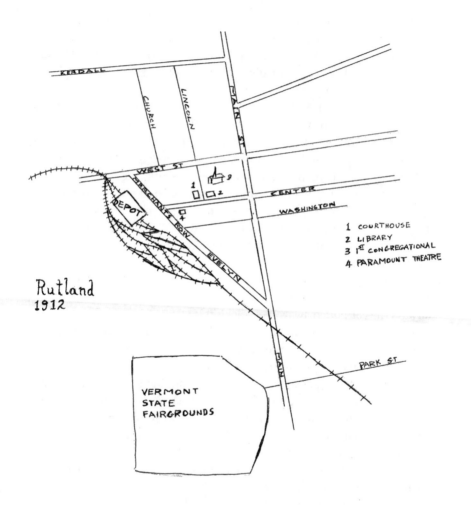

Rutland
1912

1 COURTHOUSE
2 LIBRARY
3 1ˢᵗ CONGREGATIONAL
4 PARAMOUNT THEATRE

VERMONT
STATE
FAIRGROUNDS

Row," which sounded like "roo" to the others. "My staff recommended Mister Randolph's shop here."

"I'm sure," which struck Boyle's ear as "shah," "Randolph will give you his finest cutting," Calvin said, chuckling, as he took a chair by the wall. "He'll want you as a customer to replace us old fogies that have been here since before the War."

Randolph grinned and went back to his snipping. Soon he swung Boyle around to face the large wall mirror.

"Very handsome, I'm sure," Boyle said, quite pleased. Randolph scattered the clippings with a small brush, unbuttoned the sheet collar, and brushed the nape of Boyle's neck. "Tonic for you? Only five cents," he asked, wide, dark brown eyes blinking over a heavy, black moustache, the only hair above his neck.

"Ooo, not this time," replied Boyle, his jowls fluttering. Randolph nodded and worked the chair lever. Boyle lumbered down, reached in his vest pocket, and handed Randolph two dimes.

"There's fifteen for the cut, and five for your trouble," he said.

"Thank you," Randolph answered with a smile, his teeth bright in contrast to his walnut-colored skin. "Hope to see you next Saturday."

"I just might," said Boyle, slipping on his coat. "A good day t'all, gentlemen."

The bell jingled over Boyle, and Calvin took his place. Over at the checkerboard old Sam Wentworth doubled-jumped Tom Cockburn, leaving the middle-aged clerk of courts miffed. Sam had grown his hair mountain-man long in his cow-punching and prospecting days out West after the War. Now in his mid-seventies, he wore his salt-and-pepper hair in collar-length locks and faintly resembled a bearded Ben Franklin. He nodded after Boyle and imitated, "Thar's fifteen for the coot an' five for your trooble. Ha! A full chisel Boston Irishman here in Rutland."

"If he brings good shows to the Paramount, its fine by me he's Irish, or from Boston, or even Catholic," Calvin answered over the *shika-shika* of Randolph's scissors. Something about the barber's mood led Calvin to ask, "Everything going well, Randolph?"

"Guess it shows, huh? Well, it's just that Josiah Trimble who was here before Mr. Boyle. Got a haircut and beard trim but didn't want to pay me the five cents for the Brilliantine. Said since I had a lot of colored customers I didn't need to order it as often and so he should get it free."

"Cheapskate," the men agreed.

"Piker."

"Scrooge."

"He likes to show off his money without parting with it," Randolph growled. "Has he always been like that?"

Calvin shrugged but Sam piped up, "Ayup. Has been since the War, but before then the Trimbles were pretty hard up. I wonder if he got an inheritance or something."

Randolph's scissors went back to normal until Calvin sensed him finishing. "Randolph, this mannin' I'd also like a shave of my cheeks and a trim of my beard. And I'd like a tonic, the Bay Rum please."

"Yes, sir!" said Randolph eagerly. After squaring off Calvin's goatee he reclined the chair fully. Over the *chocka-chocka* sound of the shaving brush stirring in the mug Randolph asked, "What's the special occasion, Calvin?" He lathered up Calvin's cheeks, stopping where the edge of his moustache connected to his goatee. "Beard, shave and tonic is quite the haircut for you." He stropped his razor as Calvin answered, "It's Decoration Day, or Memorial Day as some of the younger folks call it. Tonight is the regimental dinner." He continued through barely moving lips as Randolph began shaving. "I'm giving the address this year."

"Congratulations, Calvin," Randolph said as he shaved.

"Quite an honor for you," Tom said to Calvin. "King me," he said to Sam.

Randolph finished the shave and applied a steaming towel. When Calvin came up from under the terry cloth, Sam asked, "All set for the speech?"

"I've got it written, if that's what you mean," Calvin said. "But I'll admit I'm nervous," which he pronounced "navvis."

"Why's that, Calvin?" Randolph asked.

"I gave orders in battle and made rulings in court," Calvin sighed, "but speaking to comrades about sacrifices... what the War meant... is a hard thing for me. Some of them were wounded, some didn't come back." He swallowed hard. "Why were some blessed to survive when others gave so much?"

A somber mood crept into the barbershop. For Randolph and Cockburn, the war had been schoolboy stories and tight-faced looks from neighborhood women. For Sam, something tightened his guts and dried his mouth. Out loud he said, "I'm sure you'll do just fine, Calvin."

"And I'll make sure you look fine," said Randolph abruptly. He poured a splash from the white, conical bottle of Bay Rum and began rubbing it into Calvin's scalp. Smiling, he added, "I'll make sure you even *smell* fine," combing Calvin's plastered hair into place. Talk turned to idle topics.

A few minutes later, Calvin stepped down carefully and pulled out his snap purse. "How much I owe you, Randolph?"

"Well let's see. Haircut and shave, twenty-five cents, and another five for trimming your beard."

Calvin sniffed. "You forgot the Bay Rum, so that makes thirty-five."

Randolph looked at him steadily. "Thirty. No charge for the Bay Rum for the dinner speaker."

Calvin gave him a small smile, then handed over a quarter, a dime, and five pennies. "Then this is an extra tip, Randolph. Thank you."

Calvin headed west on West Street, crossing Lincoln and Church on the long slope down until he came to Merchant's Row. The shops were open and the sidewalks crowded. Calvin thought of the old days when a Rutland Line and a Hudson train almost arrived together and all the passengers would spill out onto Center and Evelyn streets. But this was Rutland's own population, shopping, jostling, laughing, hurrying, and generally ignoring the crisply bearded gentleman walking carefully with a chestnut cane and Bay Rum air.

Calvin passed Trimble's jewelry store, but there was no sign of the crusty, heavyset owner. He thought again of what Sam had said about Trimble's change of fortune at the end of the War. Sam had wondered about an inheritance, but now as Calvin pondered, he couldn't ever recall any of Josiah's or Abigail's relations having any particular wealth.

Calvin turned off a few doors later at Abernathy's. They had done a fine job – no dangling threads, a fraying cuff touched up with dye, brass buttons and insignia polished to a gleam. He paid twenty-five cents for the touchups and the new dry-cleaning process. The brown paper sheets crinkled softly as he carried the suit over his left arm. He decided to walk up Center Street for the exercise rather than take the streetcar. Just shy of Court Street, he eyed the courthouse, his second home for over thirty years. Centered on the double front doors, across the street to the south, was a statue in a small park.

A pair of light green eyes stared south, not noticing Pico Peak off to the left, unblinking despite the gusty breeze. The sun was high enough so the cap bill shaded the eyes. Ever southward stared the eyes, nearly twenty feet off the ground, framed by squared-off sideburns and wisps of greenish hair. Weather-stained, lifeless, yet kindly, for nearly five decades those eyes had stared south. Pedestrians, carriages, motor cars, the eyes missed them all and did not see the cane-steadied walk of the eastbound man on the sidewalk carrying a freshly cleaned suit over his arm.

The cane-wielding old man knew those eyes and their stare, and the cheekbones, brows, forehead, mouth, and chin that attended them. But Calvin rarely looked, either into those green copper eyes, or south for the menace. Today he did not see that the bird serenading the morning was perched on the cap bill that shaded the eyes of the statue as he walked home to East Washington Street.

Later in the morning, Eleanor asked, "Calvin? Would it help if you tried out your speech on me?" Her marvelous blue eyes looked at him from her V-shaped face under a coiled crown of snow-white hair. Calvin valued her mind and her love but also this chance. The weight of wifely conventions had sunk heavily upon her, but being his sounding board for important speeches and rulings was a lasting reminder of her daring spirit and keen thoughts. Unconsciously, he hoped the effect of talking over his speech might last at least the rest of the day.

"Well, all right, I suppose," he stammered, not himself. He stood at the dining room table while she listened. Her face was a mask as he finished and asked, "What do you think?"

As she thought for a long moment he admired the passionate concentration nearly glowing from her, a passion he'd fallen in love with and married. "It's good Calvin. You cite history, quote Lincoln, and ask them to consider the causes of the War. But I think it's a little too Judge Salisbury and not enough Calvin."

"How do you mean?" he asked, sitting down next to her.

"It's almost a court ruling. You avoid hardships and you're hiding your smiles and humor."

"Ah, but the men..."

She finished, "...wouldn't mind some mention of their pains or something light-hearted from their soldier days. Show a bit of yourself and your own burdens and it will help the men with theirs."

"You think so?"

"Calvin, I've seen it in you when you've come back from reunions. You've talked up a storm with the other veterans and somehow that's helped you. The effect lasts for several weeks, so I'm glad you get to go so often."

"Really!" he exclaimed, still amazed how well she knew him.

"Maybe you could note their pains in the War and their pains now. This is 1912, and I think the men need to pay attention to that." Calvin nodded while scanning his manuscript. He began scribbling in the margins. Eleanor reached into her sewing basket and pulled out a pair of scissors. "These could help you move around some of the pieces."

He grinned as she snapped the pair in the air. "Ayup, I'll get it."

"I know you will," she smiled back in the way that always made him blush slightly.

Calvin finished reworking the manuscript and tried out some lines and paragraphs on Eleanor. She nodded vigorously. "That's it. That's a speech!"

"Thanks," he said, feeling drained. Indeed, lunchtime was at hand but he felt weaker than just from hunger. "I think I'll lie down for a bit." She saw him pale and shaky.

"Don't try the stairs. Go right into the back room and draw the shade. Lie down on the guest bed and I'll bring you a compress. Maybe we can head off an attack."

Calvin wobbled around the back room, loosed the drapes' tie-backs and lay down, small lights flashing in his closed eyes and a pang behind his right eyebrow. Ellie hurried in with a dishcloth and an enameled tin bowl of ice she had chipped off the block in the icebox.

"Take your shoes off," Ellie said softly but with a certain crispmess as well. "Loosen your collar and your shirt cuffs." With an effort Calvin managed, then whispered, "Sorry to be a burden, Ellie."

Ellie chuckled back. "Well this is no burden. Heat, biting bugs, storms, and poor colored folk coming into camp at Port Royal by the dozens every day; that was a burden. Unruly soldiers making fun of us trying to teach reading and writing; that was a burden."

Calvin winced as his shoe slipped from his hand and thumped the floor. The sound bumped through his head like a book falling off a high shelf. Ellie saw his pain and bit her lip as he lay back on the pillow. She wrapped the ice chips in the wet dishtowel and spread the compress across his forehead. She stroked his cheek as relief washed his face, and she whispered again, "No burden. Port Royal and missing you was a burden. Not this. Not you."

Calvin fell into a deep sleep. Eleanor pulled an afghan over him and tiptoed out.

She wrote him a note in case he woke while she was gone. She made herself a sandwich and cut up an apple and tucked them into a basket. She cut a few spring flowers from the side garden and tied them with a ribbon. Then she went to the Rutland Town Cemetery for the Decoration Day ceremonies. She laid flowers from Calvin and herself on the grave there. She hoped the rifle squad volleys and especially the three blank cannon rounds would not carry to East Washington Street. If he could sleep, he might make it to the banquet.

After the men had recited the Gettysburg Address, Calvin rose, aligned the creases in his pants, and walked deliberately to the podium. He was not quite himself but was much improved. He leaned lightly on his cane with the brass ring at its neck. The spiraling inscription in the freshly polished brass read,

> *To Maj. Calvin Salisbury, 14th VT, Army of the Potomac,*
> *for heroism, duty, and service to God and country.*
> *From his men, May 30, 1876.*

A compactly built, small-boned man of angular features, his cheekbones stood out in sharp relief above his surprisingly smooth cheeks. Thanks to Randolph, his neatly trimmed moustache rode white and crisp above a wedge of beard. He pulled on his steel-rimmed glasses and scanned the room, seeing old friends, but missing Ashton Melo. Ashton was from the gallant 54th Massachusetts, a regular attendee, but tonight the oval African face was absent. Calvin was crestfallen since he hoped Ashton, in particular, would like his speech.

Calvin spread out his manuscript, written in small, clear script on several sheets of fine linen paper. When he spoke, his voice was classic New England nasal in a tenor pitch often called boyish. His light voice made him take extra pains choosing words and phrases for their authority. He nodded to John Franklin.

"It is from a solemn obligation to duty that I accepted our post commander's request. We meet tonight for the forty-sixth time to honor our comrades, recall our sacrifices, and reaffirm the principles of liberty and democracy which we defended.

"Not every generation is called on to defend the nation. Not every generation suffers as we have suffered." Calvin glanced at the empty sleeves and mask-like faces of several men at their tables. "My friends, we are such a generation. We were called, we answered, and we suffered and died so that those who live after us might have peace and opportunity.

"But was our sacrifice of limb, life, blood, and treasure worth the ideals of America? After all, those who fought against the Constitution also gave their treasure, their blood, and their lives. They fought nobly and courageously. If there was equal valor and equal suffering on both sides, can't we stop there? There are many who do so. Many veterans and Civil War enthusiasts want to debate tactics, celebrate old soldiers being old together and leave aside the meanings of the War." His blue-gray eyes slowly swept across the room like it was a jury box. "Of all Americans, we cannot do that."

"What if the South had prevailed? Suppose Lee had broken our Army and taken Washington City? What if Bragg had beaten Buell in Kentucky? What if Halleck had stayed in the field scratching both elbows and standing in Grant's way?" A snorted chuckle ran around the room. Men recalled the old photograph image of Henry Halleck, Grant's superior in the War's first year, performing an odd self-hug as he scratched.

"We would hear much less about valor and honor. Instead, another nation would taunt us about states' rights, the superior white race and Negro inferiority, and justify slavery by Biblical appeal. Indeed we hear much of that now.

"But my friends, because of the North's victory we have given the whole nation a new birth of freedom. Our struggles were the birthing pains of a deeper liberty for all Americans and a beacon for the nations of the earth. That is why we require our school children learn Lincoln's Gettysburg Address and what our fight accomplished.

"You see, freedom has been born and defended many times. Freedom was born in the Magna Carta of 1215. Freedom was defended by the men of Sir Francis Drake against the Spanish Armada in 1588. Freedom was reborn on our shores at Plymouth Rock in 1621. Freedom was defended in Boston in 1689 when royal governor Andros and his state bishop were overthrown. Freedom was reborn in 1776 in the immortal words of Jefferson's Declaration. And my friends," Calvin said in a measured pace, "four score and seven years later we defended freedom and brought freedom to millions.

"Our national shame was preaching and denying liberty at the same time. It fell to our generation, led by President Lincoln and his mighty generals Grant and Sherman, to pay this national shame. We bled, fought, starved, and died so our national sin might be atoned for in our flesh. For this, we have earned the praise and thanks of our countrymen.

"Yet has liberty taken root? In the South, colored people are barred from schools, jobs, parks, even from cemeteries. Every year dozens of lynchings..."

A heavy thud boomed against the double doors at the back of the hall and the doorknobs rattled. Through the cigar smoke haze, Calvin saw someone get up and pull open the door. He looked down and started violently. Then a strong but shaky voice said, "It's Ashton Melo, bleedin' bad."

The banquet dissolved into a hubbub of chatter, scraping chairs, and clumping feet. One cook was dispatched to fetch a doctor, and another to bring a constable. Calvin pushed through the chaos and saw a blood smear congealed on the brass "54" on Ashton's kepi. Melo's whimpering made his heart sink and his stomach turn over. He even had a stab of pain behind his eye like from earlier in the day. He had forgotten, because he never wanted to remember again, how blood stained a dark blue Union uniform.

The ambulance horse beat an easy, fading clip-clop on Rutland's street bricks. The crowd began fading away with the clang of the ambulance bell. A policeman had questioned many but learned little. The veterans stood in knots, mourning this sour, nasty finish to their Decoration Day banquet.

By the blood-smeared door jamb, Calvin stood talking with Detective Higgins, Sam, and Commander Franklin. As he overheard post Junior Commander Josiah Trimble holding forth nearby with a small group, he set his jaw and narrowed his eyes. Trimble had big bones crammed into little height, his double chin unsuccessfully hidden by a "Grant"-style beard. A fat, gaudy ring on his left pinkie winked in the glow of the gaslights in the hall. He shook his jowls in apparent sadness. "Looks like he'd lost a button off his uniform. Don't know if the blood'll wash out. It's a real shame that an old man like Ashton should get hurt like this."

The others muttered sympathetically while inspecting their own threadbare and often straining jackets with fifty-year-old trousers. One vet, whose pants' outseams showed the red ribbon of the artillery, said, "Have we become so insignificant?" A tiny, leathery veteran sporting the crossed-sabers pin of the cavalry answered, "This is just mean. I've been to reunions and shaken hands with old Rebels. Not one of them would do anything like this even though they were on the other side. What would possess someone to attack a vet'ran in uniform?"

Josiah stroked his beard backhandedly. "Maybe someone objected not to the color of the uniform so much as the color *in* the uniform." A strained group chuckle encouraged him. "President Lincoln could not have foreseen putting freed slaves in uniform also put ideas in their heads: voting, or living where they want rather than where they belong, or working in respectable lines." Two men nodded, but two others scowled slightly as Josiah continued. "Just because Ashton joined the army and played house boy on a colonel's staff doesn't make him a soldier. We didn't need his kind to beat the rebels then and we don't need his kind to not know their place now."

Josiah suddenly said "oomph" and stumbled forward as Calvin lurched from the milling crowd into the group. "I'm so sorry, Josiah. Are you all right?" Calvin's hand caught Josiah's shoulder from behind. The hand arrived quickly from its visit to the ribs over Josiah's kidneys.

"Ah, ooh, yes, I'm fine Calvin," Josiah said, apparently wondering at him.

Calvin sighed theatrically. "Such a shame anyone in Vermont would attack one of us. Constable said whoever did it used a knife. The cut didn't go too high on Ashton's arm because of his volunteer veteran's chevron. Good thing he reenlisted in 1864. That chevron might have saved his life tonight." Calvin tapped the heavy, V-shaped appliqué on his own sleeve, issued to "volunteer veterans" who re-enlisted, and who were rewarded with substantial federal and state government bounties and bonuses for doing so. In this group, Calvin and two others had a chevron while Josiah's sleeve was blank below his corporal's stripes. He glared at Calvin and said, "Re-enlisting for garrison duty wasn't very heroic."

Calvin held his matching glare to Josiah's a bit longer than usual before he broke it off. "Re-enlisting like Melo did for Cold Harbor and the Crater earned him that chevron." A round of nods, a couple of them reluctant, quietly applauded Calvin.

Determined to lighten the mood, Calvin said, "Gentlemen, supper's over and so is my speech, but could you help me settle everyone? We have news about the Fourth of July parade and about next year's Encampment at Gettysburg."

As Calvin moved back to the head table, Post Commander Franklin began gaveling for order. Even the hard of hearing quieted quickly.

"Gentlemen, please be seated," Franklin directed. "As we find out more about Ashton's injuries, the Post secretary" – he nodded at Calvin – "will write you. I want to inform the post of two items.

"First, members of the post and visiting veterans are asked to assemble at the train station by nine o'clock on the Fourth of July to march in the parade."

Ordinary nods greeted this routine reminder.

"Second, we have received a letter from Alfred Beers, Commander-in-Chief of the GAR, I mean, the Grand Army of the Republic. Calvin?"

Calvin rose and read, "All veterans, regardless of army of service, are invited to a national Encampment at Gettysbaag in July, 1913. The state of Pennsylvania is paying rail fare of every vet'ran living in that state. Members of the GAR are invited to ask the same from their home states.' It's signed by both Commander-in-Chief Beers and Irvine Walker, General-Commanding of the United Confederate Veterans, the UCV. So this will be a true national, North and South, Encampment."

A rumble of conversation rose amid approving nods.

Commander Franklin gaveled for order. "Men, the U.S. Army has already been at work for a year preparing for this Encampment. They will work the coming year to make ready for maybe 40,000 men from both sides. Imagine it, men! Two years' work for an eight day event – and for us, the men of the blue and gray. That will be an Encampment worth attending." He sighed, his eyes far away in imagination for a moment. Then he sobered. "Now let us stand and bow our heads as Chaplain Rupert leads us in prayer."

Monday, June 3, 1912

West Side, Savannah

Rufus and Beulah turned the corner onto Savannah's Bay Street and headed east toward Bull Street. Beulah's burnt-orange skimmer rode level on her head. She walked carefully since her Sunday shoes under her long brown dress weren't as comfortable as her everyday shoes.

Rufus' feet also protested the extra walking in his best pair of shoes. He felt conspicuous in his Sunday suit this Monday morning. The high glassine collar tacked to his shirt dug into his neck at the least provocation, and the black homburg made his scalp sweaty.

They said little, excitement alternating with fear. Even Rufus' teasing Beulah about fussing earlier with bottles of hair fixings made by Madame CJ Walker, and then hiding all her work under her hat, had not brought forth her usual giggle.

After several blocks and the clanging bell from a passing streetcar, they came to the store where a clerk was just cranking out the awnings. They avoided eye contact with him, stepped inside, and gave a wide berth to three white women shopping at the fabric counters. Beulah held her chin a bit high for "race etiquette" as they headed to the catalog counter.

The wizened clerk with the dark blue armbands over his shirt biceps eyed them curiously. "Sumpin' I can do fo' y'all?" he asked in a nasal voice more bored than hostile.

"Good mawnin', suh," Rufus answered. "We're lookin' fo' Mr. Henry Batiste?"

Surprised, the clerk blurted, "Oh. Uh, I'll fetch him."

He disappeared through a curtained doorway and returned with a handsome man in a dark blue suit. His piercing eyes over a thin, trained moustache seemed to confirm a certain Gallic ancestry. He said coolly, "I'm Henry Batiste. What seems to be the trouble?" He was slightly jarred when Beulah pulled an envelope from her purse and piped up, "There's no trouble Mistah Batiste. Yo' letter here said to ask fo' you special."

Batiste took the letter and saw it was limp at its creases. Rufus and Beulah saw him note the date of May 1909 and glance at his signature at the bottom. With a slight smile, he said, "Y'all been holdin' onto this letter for three years?" He quickly skimmed the contents and his eyes clouded. "I'm afraid the price for this has gone up."

"Yes, suh, it surely has," Rufus answered. "We been keepin' track in the newer catalogs. Mistah Batiste, we're ready to pay the new price."

Batiste shifted uncomfortably under his clerk's side glance. He took a deep breath and said, "I'm 'fraid we cain't allow folks like you to pay over time. If I'da known, uh, who y'all were, I woulda' put that in this letter," he said, handing it back with a shrug. "That's just the way it is."

"Mistah Batiste," Beulah said evenly, "we didn't expect no different, so we're ready to pay today."

Batiste forgot to be condescending. "You have $850?" Beulah smiled as Rufus moved discretely behind her and undid two buttons on her dress. She reached under the large back bow and pulled an uncomfortable lump from her corset. As Rufus nimbly redid the buttons Beulah splayed the fat wad of bills toward Mr. Batiste, then quickly slipped them into her purse.

Amazed, Batiste said with unconscious cruelty, "Well yo' money's the ratt color." He turned to the clerk. "Percy, get one of the number fourteen order forms an' sharpen yo' pencil. Soon as we get this all wrote up I'll take it over to the Western Union." Turning to Rufus and Beulah he beamed. "Folks, on behalf o' Sears, Roebuck and Company of Chicago, Illinois, I would like to say that kit house number 156 is one of the finest homes you can buy anywhere."

Unlike their earlier, nervous walk Rufus and Beulah chattered and grinned all the way home. Not even a run-in on the street with a beefy, bare-armed white man who called Rufus "an overdressed popinjay" and spat at Beulah could dampen their joy for long. The receipt signed by Henry Batiste, the thirty-day delivery guarantee, and the $1 rebate for the set of floor plans rode in the place of honor in Beulah's corset.

Zachariah wiped up the last of his fried egg with a bit of toast, then crooked a pudgy finger through the dainty handle of one of Emily's china cups. "Coffee's good this mawnin'," he said, toasting toward Emily, his eyes locked on the cup.

"It's the real Rio," answered Emily pleasantly. "Coffee's one thing the Yankees do well."

Zachariah grinned back and glimpsed her eye for an instant. "Well, even a blind squirrel finds an acorn now an' again."

Lee likewise finished his coffee. "I'm dressed for work, Zachariah, but I see you're all turned out as well."

"That's ratt," said Zachariah. "Saturday was the fust so I'm pickin' up my check at the post office an' visitin' the bank."

"Daddy," Emily said, "Alma could run over and see if the Ratzingers could take you in their motorcar. You know Hugo likes to show off his new toy."

Zachariah waved his hand. "I'm chary o' motorcars. 'Sides, it's just a nice walk for me."

Both men rose. Lee bent down and gave his wife a peck. "I'll be home the usual time."

"See you then, Lee," Emily responded. "Greet Mr. Howard for me." John Howard was Savannah's city engineer and Lee's immediate supervisor. Lee walked to the hall and plucked a hat off the rack. Alma anticipated him and swung the front door open for him.

"Thank you, Alma." Lee's smile was a trifle embarrassed. While Emily found Alma's gestures and demeanor passable, Lee never knew quite how to take these little courtesies. He crossed the porch and took the steps slightly flustered.

Zachariah came out of his room wearing the wide-brimmed straw hat he usually wore for yard work. As he passed through the hall, Emily flinched at his shabby dignity. "Oh Daddy, do you have to wear that old hat?"

"Coolest one I have, darlin'," he answered, pausing at the dining room archway. Adjusting the hat to a more rakish angle, he winked at her and said, "Iffin' I find a plume feather fo' my hatband, some of the ladies will take me as the second comin' of Jeb Stuart. Baited for widow, don't ya think?"

She giggled in spite of herself and muttered, "Impossible" under her breath.

Zachariah passed Alma with a nod, crossed the porch and yard and headed up the east sidewalk keeping a steady pace. Pine and chinaberry trees overtopping the tan brick walls on his right provided good shade. Overhead in the oaks, gray beards of Spanish moss rippled and fluttered.

After a time, he came up Whittaker Street and turned toward Bull and the post office. He closed up on a chunky white workman who might have been a dockworker, judging from the anchor tattoo on his bicep. A well-dressed colored couple chattering excitedly tried to squeeze by along a yard wall at the same time Zachariah moved to pass him along the curb. The colored woman modestly turned her eyes away from the man's bare arms. Her husband was gesturing heartily and accidentally brushed his hand against the stevedore. He shoved the colored man back and called him "an overdressed popinjay" and for good measure he spat a stream of tobacco juice at the feet of his wife.

Zachariah stepped past the three of them gingerly but the incident was still on his mind a few minutes later as he took a flight of granite steps. He swung back the heavy brass door and rested in the marble-cooled lobby, fanning himself with his hat. Having caught his breath, he wiped away the sweaty sheen on his brow and joined the line of customers. An old woman in yellow ahead of him buying stamps erupted.

"Don't give me none o' them Lincoln pennies," she spat out. "Gimme the real Indian haids." She counted her change out loud, gave the clerk a hawk-faced glare and moved away.

The bored clerk had obviously endured worse. "Next," he said to the bewhiskered gent with the grey-green eyes.

"Gen'ral d'livery please. Zachariah Hampton."

The clerk nodded and ambled to the back room. He returned and slid two letters across the counter.

"Much 'bliged," Zachariah nodded. The clerk's expression held steady as he called out, "Next." A skinny farm lad in overalls and straw basket hat was gaping at all the marble. "Next," the clerk called again, breaking the country boy's reverie. His bare feet splatted up to the window.

Zachariah eyed the return addresses. One he expected, from the Georgia Bureau of Veterans. The second was from Robert Bidwell. He wondered why Bidwell was writing him just after the regimental dinner. He moved to the postmaster's window and opened the first envelope. He pulled out the money order, signed his name on the back, and slid it under the window's brass bars. The postmaster studied the order, then counted out three $5 bills across the marble. Zachariah put the bills into the Veteran's Bureau envelope.

Zachariah walked more slowly up Bull Street toward Johnson Square. Along this stretch, his bench appeared. It was a "whites only" city bench by a shady streetcar stop, but he often sat here on his expeditions to watch Savannah, or like today, to read his mail.

As he pulled out his spectacles from an inner pocket, his fingers touched the flask there, but he left it alone. Hmm. Bidwell. Fragments of the regimental dinner floated by. The food had been good. He recalled men munching; their worn and missing teeth needing a long time to get each bite down to swallowing size. The tables… had been glittery, that's right, with all the glass or pewter flasks of the old vets. Yep, the flasks, Zachariah's shiny pewter one engraved "ZH", an older Christmas present from Emily, among them. Reach, raise, uncork, gulp, re-cork, back to the table – all done with a smooth rhythm formed by years of repetition.

Peyton Colby had sat next to him, yes. Good. Dooley Culpepper had sat across from them. Not so good. Even draining his "cigar" flask during smoking time hadn't helped much with Dooley there. Dooley's cackling laugh and hoots of support at speechmaking time had rung Zachariah's head that night. Even his half-pint "safety" flask, inside his breast pocket, hadn't completely blocked out Dooley or the speaker.

Or had it? Zachariah knit his brow to remember the speaker's name. "Only three nights ago!" he said to himself, annoyed, but there was nothing there. There were phrases stuck, "lost cause" and "beloved South" of course, but also "natural order" and "sacred way of life." Something about that speech was tetched, both Friday and now. Dooley's cackle said something about rather spitting on a Yankee than shaking hands with one while Peyton gripped his hand to pull Zack to his feet. The word "popinjay" kept circling his mind, chasing "natural order", but he couldn't make sense of them. He shook his head.

He opened Bidwell's letter. His mind saw Bob Bidwell's blunt nose and pockmarked face reading some sort of announcement. At eighty, Bidwell's hair still showed some streaks of the copper red he used to sport in full. After all these years, he still tried to wear a square cut "Lee"-style beard even though his face was narrow and long-chinned.

> *Dear Zack,*
>
> *I'm writing to remind you about the 8th Georgia's invitation from Irvine Walker, General-Commanding of the UCV:*
>
> *"All veterans of the War Between the States are invited to a national Encampment at Gettysburg next July for the fiftieth anniversary of the battle. The state of Pennsylvania voted to pay their veterans' rail fare and invited other states to do likewise."*
>
> *Just dropping you this note so you'll write Governor Joseph Brown and see if Georgia might help out all us Georgia vets re-visit the high watermark of the Confederacy. Oh, and put something in about keeping those black GAR vets out so the Encampment's all white. Do you know anybody from your conducting days on the railroads we might right to as well?*
>
> *See you at the Fourth of July parade.*
>
> *Bob*
>
> *P.S. The UDC will also be raising funds for veterans to go starting on the Fourth of July.*

Zachariah put the letter down and smiled briefly. Oh the United Daughters of the Confederacy would be at the parade all right; would hardly count as the Fourth of July without the UDC ladies doing fund-raising for one thing or another. Then he stared off, musing. Gettysburg. Fragments from the dinner circled the word in his mind. Bob Bidwell saying, "The United States Congress has voted over one million dollars to help the Army finish preparing for the veterans' encampment." Zack whistled low at the memory. A million dollars? Whew.

And then he smiled, remembering Jim Calhoun had said the Army would need two years to get ready if they were going to feed the veterans more than hardtack crackers and a quarter pound of bacon a day. Dooley had growled that since the Encampment would be in Pennsylvania, it was likely the Confederate veterans would have to sleep on the ground, but he had been hooted down by others saying Northern hospitality would prove better than that. And what had Luke Simpson said? Oh yes, his son was editor of the *Savannah Tribune.* Even a year in advance, the young Simpson was planning to send along two reporters just to send in daily stories about the Savannah men.

Gettysburg, huh?, he thought, unconsciously flexing his left hand. A dull pain ran up his forearm from wrist to elbow. For a time, Savannah's sights and sounds became a dreamscape to him, while his memories of black powder gunsmoke, screaming wounded, and the pounding of his heart seemed much more real.

With a long sigh, he dismissed the gloominess, folded the letter and his spectacles, and slipped them both into his coat pocket. He took a couple nips, then walked with an old man's stiff, short stride toward the bank.

West Side, Savannah

Monday morning, Lucius walked north on Broad Street, unruffled among three boys nearly dancing with excitement. All carried bamboo poles and Lucius also gripped a battered pail holding dirt, water and worms.

"Jes' settle down," Lucius called. "We'll be there soon 'nuff. The fish'll wait."

"You think we'll catch some big 'uns?" his grandson Sherman asked, scampering back and matching Lucius' pace.

"Don't see why not," Lucius said, grinning. "I'm goin' 'long with you, an' grandpops know 'bout fishin'. 'Sides, I grew up by the Savannah Rivuh. We's old friends."

Sherman's pals Ralphie and Abner let the other two catch up.

"Were you born along Bay Street, then?" Abner asked.

"Nope," Lucius replied, "I's born near Port Wentworth, 'bout nineteen mile uprivuh."

"Was you on a plantation there?" Ralphie asked carefully, dropping his voice as two bony white men in bib overalls lolled by them.

"Yep," said Lucius. "I's born on a plantation called Mulberry Grove, ratt on the rivuh."

"I've heard-a strawberries an' blueberries an' blackberries," Abner piped up, "but I ain't never eaten no mulberries. What they taste like?"

Sherman giggled as Lucius answered, "Mulberries ain't for eatin', leastwise not by people. But there's a worm – not like a fishin' worm but mo' like a caterpillar – called a silkworm. They loves to eat mulberries."

"Well whyja grow mulberries to feed to worms for?" Ralphie wondered. An awful thought struck him.

"Didja eat the worms?" The boys made faces and Abner stuck out his tongue.

"Naw we didn't eat no worms," Lucius said, marching on. "Silkworms spin themselves a wee bitty house and after they spin it you's can un-spin it. The bit that unwinds is silk. It's real soft and lacy, and ladies like it." The boys nodded. "It's like what you do with cotton boles. You gin out the cottonseed an' unwind the bole to make cotton cloth."

"Mams and Pawpaw both talk 'bout pickin' an' ginnin' cotton," Ralphie and Abner agreed. "Did you ever pick cotton?" Abner asked.

"Lawdy, yes," said Lucius. "The silkworms ne'er did keep the plantation goin'. Just the name was old and some mulberry bushes was still 'round. But we growed cotton, chopped cotton, picked cotton, ginned cotton and baled cotton 'til the War came."

"Did Gen'rul Sherman's men stop the cotton growin' at yo' plantation, Grampa?" Sherman asked.

Lucius nodded. "Yep. His men burnt the whole plantation and there ain't much left."

"Is that when you went free?" Sherman persisted.

"No, I went free befo' dat."

"Can you tell us how?" the boys asked.

"Sure. 'Smatta fact, iffin' you'll follow me I can show y'all part of it ratt here in Savannah." The boys trailed Lucius as he turned east across Broad Street onto Broughton Street.

"It was Novembah 1861. Massa Winkler had me drive a wagon load o' rice an' cotton down the Augusta Road here to town. Massa had dinner an' haggled over prices. Took a coupla hours. Then came the panic."

"Who's that?" Sherman asked.

"A panic ain't a who but a what. While Massa was on Factor's Walk hagglin', I was waitin' with the team an' wagon. A ferry boat came over from Hutchinson Island. They hadn't but dropped the plank on the wharf when a Confederate fella mounted up his hoss and came a-ridin' down an' crossed the wharf over to Bull Street like the debbil himself was after him."

"An' that's a panic?" Ralphie wondered.

"Naw," said Lucius, "the panic come next. That Confederate brought word from Fort Walker an' Fort Beauregard at Hilton Haid. The Confederates had figured them forts would make matchwood outta any Yankee ships that come close. But instead, them navy ships blasted the forts an' the Union Army was all in Hilton Haid and Port Royal. Then all the white folk in Savannah figured the Yankees might come here the next day so ever'body wanted to leave. Hosses, wagons, carriages, an' buckboards was all a-jammin' on Bay Street and Bull Street. Women folk was screamin' an' fussin'. Menfolk was a-pilin' everythin' they could from their houses into the wagons. Soljahs an' constables was runnin' 'round talkin' loud. Went on the rest o' the day an' all night."

Lucius and the three boys had turned up Montgomery Street and reached Franklin Square. The city market bustled at the east end. The Second African Baptist Church stood guard at the west side. Lucius led them to the foot of the church stairs. Checking for nearby whites, Lucius went on in a lower tone.

"I runned away in all dat an' came down thisaway." He pointed across the square to where Bryant fed in from the east. "They wasn't no market 'cause all them sellers had lit out. When I got to this Square ratt over there" – he pointed to the northeast corner where Jefferson crossed Bryant – "I seed two things. One was this brick church with three o' four colored folk bein' waved inside."

"The other thing was some Confederate fellas runnin' at me on Jefferson Street from Bay. They was a-callin', 'Hold it ratt there, runaway' An' 'Where's yo' massa's pass?'"

"What's a massa's pass?" Abner asked.

"Slaves had to be off the city streets aftah dark, 'lessen they had a pass writ out from their massa sayin' they was on massa's business."

"What if they catched you with no massa's pass?" Ralphie asked wide-eyed.

"Theys could beat you or whip you, an' make yo' massa pay money for not controllin' his slaves."

All three boys wondered with fright at the edge of their eyes.

Lucius continued. "I was scared an' I runned into the church. I went thru this door an' somebody puts a hand over my mouth an' says, 'Iffin' you's runnin' away keep quiet an' follow 'long.' I looked 'round at a sistah carryin' a shade lantern. She told us, 'Follow me,' an' she led us in the church 'round to some small crawly places. 'Bout ten or 'leven of us laid down in a funny, dark little room, too small to stand in, with just' a little bit o' light from above. The lantern lady said, 'Y'all be safe here iffin' you don't make no sound. Soljahs an' constables gonna look for' to catch you but they never found no one in this room. When they's gone I'll come fo' y'all. When you hear me callin' you, whisper back.'"

The nineteen-year-old corporal with a starter moustache and a peach-fuzz beard pounded on the church doors. The steel butt plate of his pistol dented the wood and made the door boom.

"Open up," he yelled, his voice cracking with excitement and his own importance. "The city watch wants to search the church." Soon, faint footfalls and then a clacking signaled the opening of the heavy door. Corporal Calhoun, three militia privates and two nightwatch constables mobbed through, nearly knocking over a black teenager.

"Boy," Calhoun snapped, although they were hardly a year apart, "boy, show us where y'all keep lanterns. Then latt all the candles in the church, you hear me?"

"Yes suh," said Pastor Campbell's son, wide-eyed at the crowd of armed men. "Ratt over here's some candles and some lanterns," he said, leading them to the deacon's closet and pulling out a candlelighter. "I'll get ever'thin' lit, suh."

As he hurried off, the posse rifled the closet, then scattered in a determined hurry. Doors opened and slammed shut, with mutters or calls of "nuthin' here." A couple men lay down in the sanctuary, not in prayer, but to spot anyone lying under the pews. Occasionally they all stopped and hushed one another, but each time the faint sounds turned out to be panicky passersby in the Square urging each other on ahead of the imminent Yankees. One triumphant "Aha" melted into disappointment as a terrified dark face turned out to be the pastor's son returned from his candle lighting. Sanctuary, sacristy, two chapels, balcony, basement, and every room under the church roof were empty.

"All ratt boy," boomed one of the constables through his walrus moustache, "take us to the manse."

"Yes suh," Samson replied. "Ratt through here."

After a time of utter quiet, Samson and his mother returned. Priscilla said, "Samson, go 'round an' save some these candles. Now that the Joja Malisha," she said with a clipped air and a mocking toss of her head, "an' the nightwatch is gone to spend the night watchin' white folks leave town, we can do some good." Samson hurried off with his candle snuffer.

Priscilla paused, listening down a certain hallway. Like the posse, she heard only the seeping sounds of white disorder. Satisfied, she lit her shade lantern and passed in a turn or two to the hidden room under the chapel.

"They's all gone," she said in a smiling voice to the listening darkness. "Whole lotta watt folk takin' trains to-natt. Time fo' the Freedom train to take on some colored folk. Any riders here?"

The silence sighed. A few smiles showed in the pool of lantern light, mixed with soft chuckles. "I'm ready." "Yeah, let's go." "Amen to dat." came voices, and then an old woman's crackly voice, "The jubilee is come. Praise da Lawd!"

"Now," said Priscilla quickly, "this ain't no revival meetin'," and the group was instantly still. She went on. "Them hunters walked over your airholes in the one chapel when you heard them close but I told you they wouldn't catch you. Now I'm a conductor on this Freedom train, so y'all mind, ya hear? Stick close but in a line, not a bunch all together. We'll go a bit at a time to da rivuh."

"Where we goin' to?" came a voice as they flitted down the corridor.

"Fust we gets you to Hutchinson's Island. Then the next conductors gets you 'cross Back Rivuh. Aftah dat, I'ma thinkin' with them Yankees at Hilton Haid, some o' the conductors is gonna send you there. Thirty miles is a whole lot less'n six hunnert, doncha think?"

The two or three who could count a bit nodded hard. The others took their cue from them and agreed thirty miles sounded much better than six hundred. Creeping out a door, Priscilla led her charges in a string that stretched and shrank through the alleys and backyards of Savannah.

Lucius and the three boys walked nearly the same route by daylight. After they crossed Bay Street, the odor of salt mud mingled with dead fish. As they turned left along the bank, Lucius pointed out a couple of stumpy pilings awash a few yards offshore.

"Just' keep walkin' boys, but do you see them fat poles pokin' up?"

"Yes, suh," they answered. "What are they?"

"Them's all that's left of a shipbuildin' yard dat goes back to colony times. This is where the lantern lady brought us. Two men in a boat rowed us 'cross to Hutchinson Island. Then a conductor brought us 'cross to a swamp by Back Rivuh and hid us in the scrub trees an' cattails. Then the two men with the boat had it on Back Rivuh an' rowed us over to the Carolina side."

"And that's how you got free, huh Grampa?" said Sherman with a touch of pride.

"Mo' o' less," Lucius replied as they came under a stand of trees. They passed through where the trees shaded the water.

"This would be a pretty good spot," said Lucius. "Let's get comfortable an' see if y'all can catch sumpin." The four settled down to the serious joy of fishing.

Tuesday, June 18, 1912

Savannah

The night shift of railroad roustabouts unloaded freight trains into Tuesday's dawn. The overnighters slept odd hours, but they got a bit of extra pay, and nighttime was about fifteen degrees cooler. The livestock cars went first so Savannah's slaughter houses could get to their grim work. After the barnyard sounds faded, flatcars came next. Their awkward, oversized loads needed trackside cranes and portable hoists. Finally came the boxcars with endless crates, kegs, and pallets, moved by handcarts or arm hefted, then sorted by customer. Tonight, an entire boxcar was filled with crates for one customer, an individual.

Several heavyweight wagons were loaded from this boxcar, so when the drivers and teams showed up by half past seven, a string of well-taxed drays stood by the track ready to roll. Two black men in overalls, hobnailed work boots, and flat caps came into the yard leading four draft horses. The man in the dark red shirt began hitching up the first wagon while the other went into the office. He came back out with a sheaf of papers in his back pocket and helped finish hitching the lead team. They both climbed up on the driver's box. The lead man, sporting a dingy white neckerchief, checked the papers again and took the reins. His partner manned the hand brake. With this morning's weighty load, his job meant heavy shoulder work on the steel brake bar, keeping the lumbering payload from rolling into the wheel team.

"Any slopes or hills?" the brakeman asked as the driver flicked the reins.

"Not this time," the driver answered, "and it's not that far from here, but we'll have go on Broad Street fo' a few blocks."

A slow walk by the horses brought them out from the yard and past a couple blocks' worth of warehouses. The Central of Georgia Railroad owned these and also manned the intersection with Broad. The crossing guard at Broad Street timed his traffic stop just right so the team and men made an easy, wide left turn straight into the right lane. As traffic resumed, single riders, carriages, farm and delivery wagons, and various motor cars passed the slow-grinding mass.

Coming up to cross Jones, the Savannah policeman gave them a stop signal early on. The brakeman strained on the brake bar, followed a few seconds later by the driver calling, "Whoa" and reining in. The wagon paused nicely short of the intersection behind a mover's wagon marked "Brown & Sons Cartage."

Something was annoying the railroad wagon horses and they were restless. The lead team tossed their manes repeatedly, and the right side wheel horse stamped a rear hoof twice. The driver made a series of clucking, humming, and other calming noises, but these did not have the usual effect.

The Brown & Sons men were having similar troubles with their two-horse team. A single rider crossing east on Jones looked to be a good horsewoman, but her jet-black mount was skittish. She snapped at the reins and scolded "Smoky," but the horse champed his bit and whinnied. "There be an ambulance cummin'?" the brakeman wondered out loud, "or maybe one o' them fire wagons? They gettin' spooked by a sireen?"

The driver called to the team trying to settle them. He muttered, "I don't hear nuthin', but hosses can hear bettah than we can. I wonder if a navy ship's givin' off a toot on the rivuh?"

"Don't hear nuthin'," the brakeman answered, keeping a good double grip on the lever and bracing his feet.

The policeman whistle-stopped the Jones Street traffic, then waved the left turn traffic from both directions of Broad Street onto Jones. Then he whistled for the straight and right-turn traffic to move along. Brown & Sons got their rig rolling and the dray wagon brakeman let up on his lever as the driver chivvied his four. As the horses strained back into a slow walk, they seemed calmer, but the driver wondered.

A few small cross streets rolled by until Liberty Street. The traffic patrolman here waved them on through with the rest of the northbound flow. As they gained the north side of Liberty, several pedestrians on the east sidewalk gave second looks to the high-piled, double-teamed heavy wagon. The driver sighed in relief, feeling the worst – especially Liberty Street – was behind them. Up ahead, a little street fed in from the right. A lamppost marked the outside corner. Across the sidewalk a brick-walled yard lined the inside corner. As the long rig's tailgate cleared Liberty Street, the left lead horse whinnied again and flinched to the right. The right lead showed his big yellow teeth and made a bite toward his left. "Gimme a brake," the driver called sharply and snapped the reins to settle the lead team. The brakeman levered hard but the load crept ahead.

"What's goin' on?" the wagoneers said in unison. The outsized wagon under them was swaying hard enough to make their stomachs queasy. Now both wheel horses stamped the pavement. The driver redoubled his grip on the reins and fought the spooked team.

Onlookers began looking away from the troubles of the double-teamed wagon and toward each other. Fear washed over faces. On Broad Street, motorcars stopped randomly and people jumped out. A southbound streetcar ground to a halt and passengers spilled onto the street. Single riders fought for control or dismounted awkwardly. A riderless horse galloped down from Oglethorpe Street to the cries of "runaway." The traffic policeman back at Liberty Street staggered drunkenly, and pedestrians in every direction swayed and stumbled. Several women screamed and the right lead horse of the Central of Georgia wagon whinnied, its eyes white with fear. He reared up on its hind legs and boxed the air. The towering draft horse with hooves the size of dinner plates terrified a young couple on the sidewalk.

"Hepp me get him down," the driver gasped, standing at his bench and using all his strength on the reins. The brakeman didn't dare let up on his lever, but he reached over with his left arm and got a grip on the leather, adding a bit more pull. Another pedestrian staggered from behind the wall on the little cross street. A bearded old man, he was saucer-eyed and reaching desperately for the lamppost to catch himself. A screaming whinny from far overhead jerked his head up and he cried out. He flung up his left arm, lost his balance and missed the lamppost. The three-handed hauling at the reins finally brought down the right lead horse. His right fore hit the old pedestrian square on and drove his head hard into the lamppost, killing him instantly. He was eighty-two years old, a veteran of the War Between the States, and now a casualty of Savannah's earthquake of June 18, 1912.

Saturday, June 22, 1912

Savannah

Independent Presbyterian filled comfortably without crowding. The Reverend Cavanaugh stepped into the chancel and said, "Thank you fo' comin' to pay yo' respects with the family and friends of Peyton Colby. Please join in singin' numbah 309, 'Rock of Ages.'"

The organist began a verse of introduction. Reverend Cavanaugh walked down the center aisle to the vestibule and joined various members of the Colby clan behind the coffin. The congregation sang, the pallbearers bore their burden, women in the procession and pews wept softly, and the funeral began. Cavanaugh preached a tribute.

"Peyton Colby, born March 6, 1830, baptized July 17, 1830, and died four days ago on June 18, 1912, aged 82 years, 3 months and 12 days. Peyton Colby answered the Lord's calling as a faithful member of Christ's church. He answered the calling of his state when foes had risen. Like David the shepherd boy called to Saul's army, Peyton answered the call in 1861 to be a soldier. Proud was he to join with the men of the South in defending the sanctity of his home and Georgia's rights. Honored was he to serve under General Lee in defense of liberty and a sacred way of life. Stalwart was he in rebuilding his state after invaders had laid waste.

"At the Seven Days, at Manassas, at Gettysburg, or in all the glorious fights of the Army of Northern Virginia, Peyton and his comrades went into battle with hope. Hope for victory of course, but also the soldiers' hope, and the soldiers' prayer, that they would live through the battle. For Peyton that hope and those fervent prayers were answered, and he lived through the war.

"In his later days, Peyton Colby answered a call like the prophet Jeremiah. When ruin had come, Jeremiah gave a word of hope. Peyton Colby spoke hope in his years of honest labor at the Savannah depot. Think about it. Why do folks of all ranks go to a train station? They get on a train with some sort of hope. Peyton Colby sold tickets to wealthy folk heading for the highlands, hoping to get away from the summer heat. Peyton sold tickets to ordinary folks hoping to find a job, a new place, or a fresh start at the end of their train ride. He sold tickets to the poor, the no-account, the colored, the country crackers, and even for these, his tickets were some sort of hope.

"Now Peyton Colby has passed on, struck down in the earthquake this past Tuesday. Yet as a believer in our Lord Jesus Christ, he died in hope. 'So then whether we live or whether we die, we are the Lord's,' wrote St. Paul to the Corinthians and to live or die in the Lord is to live and even to die in hope.

"My friends, we gather today to pay our respects and to offer one another our consolation. That consolation consists of hope, a hope rooted in the Lord. Peyton is gone, but hope is not gone. The hope Peyton Colby lived in and died in is the hope of all believers. It is the hope we are baptized into, the hope we receive in the preachin' of the Word of God, the hope we receive in the Lord's Supper. It is the hope of the Christian faith, the end of death, the hope of everlasting life, the hope of glory everlasting.

"Peyton Colby had his share of earthly glory. Serving as a soldier for a righteous cause – that is earthly glory. Now this old soldier rests in the hope our Lord gives us, resting in the glory of a well-lived life of a believer, resting for when the glory of the Lord shall be revealed."

As the pallbearers carried Peyton's coffin down the front steps of the church, six members of the Longstreet Post, United Confederate Veterans, joined alongside, Zachariah Hampton among them. Age and ailments had weakened the veterans so they could no longer carry the coffin, but they could march, wearing once more the gray and butternut of well-worn uniforms. Two matching gray horses slowly pulled the hearse flanked by the double set of pallbearers. A band played dirges and hymns for family and friends on the mile-long walk to Laurel Grove.

About a half hour later, coffin and mourners were assembled next to a freshly fresh dug grave. An honor guard of six veterans was waiting with rifles. Reverend Cavanaugh offered final blessings as the mortician's assistants lowered Peyton Colby's earthly remains into the ground. When they finished, the band struck up "Abide With Me" in a mournful tempo. Then the honor guard came to attention, aimed their rifles up at a forty-five-degree angle and fired a volley of blanks. Heavy-hearted, Zachariah ran the men through the manual of arms to reload, using the old paper cartridges and black powder. He tried hard not to flinch as a second volley cracked, and, after a decent pause, a third. Then members of Colby's family – nieces, nephews, cousins and such, for Colby had been their bachelor uncle – stepped forward, stooped by the mound of fresh earth, and each tossed a handful onto the coffin lid.

People tossed their own handfuls, then moved away and spoke softly. Men exchanged strong handshakes. Women offered each other their sympathy with a two-hand clasp of down-turned palms. The veterans swapped stories about the careful little man with wistful hazel eyes who had always seemed at home behind his brass-barred window at the depot.

"He was always so nicely turned out at the depot window," Bob Bidwell said. "But today I keep thinking 'bout Peyton at Spotsylvania Courthouse, standin' behind a log breastwork with his mouth all black from powder grit bitin' off the ends of them paper cartridges." The men nodded heavily.

"I'm gonna miss him," Dooley said with a sigh, "even if he did shake hands with that Yankee surgeon at the Richmond Reunion back in '09."

"Hard to see that," Jim Calhoun agreed. "Took me a while to get over it."

"Aw, he was jest lettin' bygones be bygones," Zachariah said. "Ain't no big deal."

"Yeah, it is," Dooley said evenly. "It was shakin' hands with a Yankee."

By the iron fence enclosing the hallowed ground stood four colored men, leaning on shovels. They averted their eyes and talked in whispers, waiting for the white folks to take their leave so they could fill in the grave they had dug earlier.

Lucius Robinson had lucked out and been hired for the day thanks to a friend of a friend. The other gravediggers had wondered at the bearded old man but had seen him work his shovel with a will. One man asked him, "You know who dat being laid to rest?"

"Don't know," Lucius answered, his eyes misty and faraway, "but dat rifle squad with the three shots says it's one of the War soldiers."

"Yo' ratt. That bunch is wearin' gray" the man answered.

"Blue or gray, don't matta to me."

"How come?"

"Well son," Lucius said softly to the gangly man who was thirty-four, but truly looked barely out of his teens, "whatever these men had 'gainst each other, if it's a bluecoat, he fought so we's could be free. If it's a Johnny Reb, ain't no reason to hold a grudge 'gainst a man who lost a fair fight." He stared off and swallowed the lump in his throat. "Time to move on. And," in a lower tone, "iffn' I can hepp some of them 'Lost Cause' men move on this way, well that's okay too."

Dooley Culpepper stood leaning on his rifle and like most of the honor guard chatted awkwardly about small things in a solemn way. He saw Lucius at this moment and growled to the rest, "What them niggas smirkin' 'bout anyhow? This is serious bidness here 'bout Peyton. Somebody oughta teach 'em some respect."

Zachariah, Jim Calhoun, and the others looked over now, but saw only solemn faces and downcast eyes. "Cool down, Dooley. There's no disrespect bein' shown. They just' waitin' to finish bein' grave digga niggas." Bald, bush-bearded Turner Hawkins grinned at his own wit.

Dooley was not diverted, but was also in agreement. "Well gravediggin's fit enough work fo' that inferior race," he said, bearing down on 'inferior'," but still, some o' Peyton's kin are payin' money fo' 'em to do it. In the old days they'd just be doin' it."

The others were unsettled. They shared most of Dooley's racism, but not generally his fierce seriousness about pre-War slavery.

"Oh come on, Dooley," Turner said, "let 'em draw water, hew wood an' dig graves and suchlike fo' the pennies they make. Don't bother most folk iffn' they buy their own food, water, clothes, even houses, long as white folk can sell it to 'em and get the pennies back. Some white folks in Chicago got a whole lotta colored folks' money fo' that kit house on the wagon Tuesday when Peyton died."

"What you talkin' 'bout, Turner?" Dooley asked.

"Well" Turner replied, "a big ol' dray wagon on Broad Street was piled up with pieces of a kit house when the earthquake came. Spooked the hosses an' they started rearin'. Peyton came 'round a corner, staggerin' 'cause of the quake. He stumbled into the street an' the right lead hoss was just comin' down from rearin' up. Hoof hit Peyton and knocked him into a lamppost head fust." Turner paused, then added, "Colby passed quick."

"You sayin' the house on the wagon was fo' a pack-a niggas?"

"Yep, that's what I heard too," beefy Jim Calhoun added through his walrus mustache. "Sears & Roebuck was deliverin' it to a colored family on the west side."

"Damn!" Dooley snapped, shocking the others by using the rare swear word. "Iffn' it hadn't been fo' a pack a niggas Peyton'd still be alive. Damn!" Only a few mourners, along with the honor guard, heard Dooley as he turned and called out, "Damn y'all to hell, you shiftless, no-good…" Before Dooley could really get rolling, Hampton, Calhoun and the others cut him off.

"C'mon, Dooley, lets get goin'. They ain't worth it nohow. Don't be cussin' over Peyton's grave."

Dooley subsided and he moved off with the others, grinding his heels angrily, the left one at an odd angle. But his eyes still shot malice at the digging crew whose race had now added to their sins.

Friday, June 28, 1912

West Side, Savannah

Like much of west-side Savannah, many of the shabby Fahm Street houses had quake damage, especially the lightly built porches. Quake day and the next were a swirl of salvage and clean up. The *Savannah Colored Tribune* printed extra editions all week heavy with photographs of west side neighbors at funerals, cooking in back yards and sleeping out.

There were signs of normality. Carpenters worked everywhere and glaziers had followed, so residents inhaled the odor of fresh caulk around new window panes. Temporary steps let folks get in and out, although a week later a lot of folks still preferred sleeping in their yards under soft canvas.

At 305 Fahm, the front porch had sheared off cleanly behind the camellia bush, but roof, window, and siding damage appeared severe. At first glance, strangers might have thought the house was the hardest hit in the area, but the yard was clear of debris. A second look showed six rectangular masses spotted around: three were mostly lumber, a square stack of shingles, a cluster of window and door frames, and a gathering of barrels. Only a heap by the curb had broken or rotted bits and pieces, while the six piles were all new.

In the middle of all the settling down and pulling together, the Central of Georgia Railroad decided to finish deliveries. So Monday, Sears & Roebuck Kit Home "Magnolia" model #156, was delivered to 305 Fahm Street. An entire boxcar load of every item needed to build the house, right down to the large, soft-leather-bound construction manual, was stacked up around the property. A large tarp was piled with the Robinsons' furniture, clothes, cookware, a wood stove, a bathtub, mattresses, and more, all under a second tarp acting as a roof.

Lucius, Beulah, Alma, Hannah, and Sherman toiled dismantling their old house. Beulah decided early on she was the only one of the five who would do ladder work, but a long skirt was completely impractical. Passersby gawked as a woman in Rufus' overalls emerged from the old house the second morning. She left Lucius amazed as well, and he chuckled.

"My stars! If my Beulah could see you now – a woman in man's pants!"

"You don't think she'd be just as practical?" Beulah jibed back.

Lucius held his smile as he thought back a moment. "You know, to build a house, I believe she'd 'a joined you." A tear popped out of his eye as Beulah took his leathery hand. "No need to be all manly, Papa" she whispered gently.

Lucius gave one gasping sob and then shook his head. "No. No." He looked up at his daughter-in-law. "It's all right somehow. My Beulah died when the Kluxers burned down that rickety shack, but she saved Rufus." He gallantly kissed her hand. "Now Rufus and this Beulah get a house for livin'. Squares things up somehow. Old Beulah and an old house gone. New Beulah and a new house."

Rufus helped in the evenings, but the quake's silver lining was an instant demand for carpenters. Rufus had plenty of paid work, and the family insisted he rack up as much money and overtime as he could. "It's one o' them 'seven fat years' like fo' Joseph in Egypt, son," Lucius told him one night. "Make hay while the sun shines." Still, Rufus would come home toward sundown and put in a couple hours of hand demolition. By lantern light he would study the manual until he fell asleep.

Hannah and Sherman worked with excitement. Sherman in particular found demolishing an entire house to be a boy's dream. One morning he woke up and found a new eight-ounce claw hammer next to his pillow. The weight, hickory handle, and the shiny head were just right for his hands and arms. When he got dressed, he found a ninety-degree stiff leather loop had been expertly stitched onto his belt at the hip. He slipped the handle of the hammer through and strutted proud as a jaybird to the breakfast table.

Lucius stopped humming his rather upbeat tune and said to Beulah at the stove, "Bettah give Sherman an extry rasher of bacon today. A junior carpenter needs his strength." Beulah beamed as Sherman hugged her. "Daddy an' I hope you like it. He stopped by the Sears store the other natt on the way home. Grampa did the leather loop fo' your belt." Lucius got a hug and a double "thank you."

Hannah looked crestfallen at Sherman's luck, but not for long. Beulah slyly slipped a flat box onto Hannah's plate and set it in front of her with a flourish. "Time for breakfast," she said laughing while Hannah stared. "Go ahead. Open it." Hannah pulled off the lid to uncover a set of new overalls and a small pair of leather work gloves. "When yo' Daddy was at Sears for a hammer, he also found a pair o' lady carpenter overalls and gloves just yo' size." Hannah squealed with delight as Beulah announced, "We'all gotta have the tools for buildin' this kit house." After breakfast, passersby noticed an extra energy flowing at 305 Fahm Street.

Beulah eyed Lucius as he worked. He looked satisfied, and the sad cloud that usually clung to his shoulder was gone. "Silver lining," she thought to herself, hearing him hum as he cleaned nails from boards pulled from the house.

Sherman had just dragged several bad boards to the curb when he looked up into the bearded face of an old white man staring at him. The man was watching the activity up and down the street, but took an interest in the extra work happening at 305. "Say boy," he rasped to Sherman, who had dropped his eyes. He was trying to be friendly but lack of practice gave him an edgy tone. "You fixin' up or tearin' down or what?"

Sherman gulped. "Well, suh, a bit o' both. We's tearin' down, but savin' the better bits. Makin' way fo' our new house."

Under the canvas fly in the yard, Beulah looked up from the manual and saw Sherman and the old man. She tucked the book under her arm and walked over.

"Sherman, you run 'long now. May I hepp you, suh?" she asked the stranger.

He saw the name and logo on the cover of the manual and shook his head. "Nope. Just passin' by, seein' how ever'body's gettin' on after the quake." He moved off in a bandy-legged, mincing way. Beulah looked after him, not liking his air or manner. Soon, she was breaking loose plaster and lath in the front bedroom with real zeal.

Thursday, July 4, 1912

Savannah

Savannah's Fourth of July parade formed along the river on Factor's Walk, a conglomeration of wharves, warehouses, and an old slave auction building that shared an open-air space for freight handling. Busybody parade marshals struggled with an ever-growing mass of paraders, motorcars, floats, bands, and horses.

White spectators starting spreading along both sides of Bryant Street before eight o'clock in the morning. Ignoring the "whites only" and "colored only" signs, the street car benches filled quickly. Many outdoor wooden folding chairs and ladder-back chairs fresh from breakfast duty filled the sidewalks while boys squatted somewhat uncomfortably on the curbstones.

In Reynolds Square, the space around the statue to Confederate Vice-President Alexander Stephens was a thicket of Stars and Bars, Georgia state flags, and the same annual cluster of rough-voiced young men. They gibbered devotion to the Lost Cause with Rebel yells and read out the words on the plaque at the tops of their voices:

> *Our new government is founded upon exactly the opposite idea; its foundations are laid, its cornerstone rests upon the great truth, that the negro is not equal to the white man; that slavery – subordination to the superior race – is his natural and normal condition...*

The parade display of white supremacy meant colored attendance was thin. Those who did come typically gathered on the west side of Franklin Square where the parade turned from Montgomery onto Bryant. Despite the blatant display of mounted police power on constant patrol at the "black corner" but nowhere else, the Robinsons took the day off from house building. Lucius insisted. "This is our country an' it's our day of celebratin' too." Both he and Rufus wore suits, and Beulah's hair carried the aroma of Madame C.J. Walker's hair treatment, marking the importance of the day.

In each square along Bryant, the city built temporary wooden viewing stands. Admission to these was by ticket and municipal officials of all ranks did a brisk barter trade at Franklin, Johnson, Reynolds, and Warren Squares, west to east as the parade would pass. Assistant city engineer Lee Thompson had such an excellent seat, but this year he sat alone in the Johnson Square bleachers. Not only would his father-in-law march by, but Emily too. She had been happy but secretive about details, but she had confirmed that the United Daughters of the Confederacy would feature two floats rather than one in this year's parade. The floats and some Forsyth Park events commenced the UDC fund-raising for the Gettysburg Encampment.

At exactly nine o'clock, a cannon boomed from atop the Cotton Exchange building, and the parade stepped off down Montgomery to Franklin Square. A fife squealed "Yankee Doodle" as three men appeared: the fifer, a young drummer boy, and a gaunt older man carrying a flag. They all sported ragged uniforms and the three-cornered hats of Washington's soldiers, a living representation of Archibald Willard's popular painting, *Spirit of '76*. The tattered flag with the circle of thirteen stars was the real thing, kept at Fort Pulaski and brought out only for such occasions.

All the colored folk rose as this flag passed, and all wearing hats uncovered. A few new members of Savannah's mounted police and their horses were startled when the whole mass rose suddenly. For an instant some thought this was the kind of racial revolt they had been raised to fear and trained to crush. But the hats coming off and the reverent stares at the old Colonial flag calmed them. As the *Spirit of '76* passed down the street, the black spectators sat back down while the first wave of white folk rose and uncovered respectfully.

A marching band of Navy sailors was followed by a team of horses pulling the day's first float. A group of white men dressed in Colonial garb and wearing obviously itchy powdered wigs were using large quill pens to "sign" a large, pale yellow paper curling off a table. Then they smiled, shook hands, slapped each other on the back, or pointed out something on the paper. Applause rose at the old-fashioned lettering on the back wall:

The Constitution

125 Years

1787-1912

Next came a single file of men, accompanied by a teenage boy wearing a sandwich sign, each carrying one of the "Flags of History over Georgia." Spain's ensign and the French monarchy's lilies led the way. The seventh flag bearer carried the Confederate "Stars and Bars" battle flag and he shook the flag staff at the silent colored folk as he passed. Beginning with the Franklin Square bleachers, an enormous roar welcomed the colors of Davis, Lee, and Longstreet.

The next float's rear wall read, "Cotton: Georgia's White Gold." The deck was knee deep in gleaming cotton surrounding a cotton gin. Four barefoot white men dressed in rags were made up in blackface. They beamed with pretended joy as one turned the gin's crank and cotton bolls fell out. Another man filled a basket with these, hoisted it on his shoulder and circled the deck rim back to reload the gin. The quartet alternated between singing the opening lines of "Dixie" – "I wish I wuz in de land ob cotton" they bawled – and choruses of "Da Camptown Races." One of them pitched a few bolls at the crowd near Lucius shouting, "Remembah? Remembah?"

Most black folks looked down in the approved manner, but this year Lucius bobbed his head with a scowl, and a few of the young men muttered curses. But before these attracted the horse police, Lucius covered his mouth, deflecting his voice down and behind him. "Let it go. Look what's comin' next. Let it go."

Coming next were several close ranks of men mostly in their thirties dressed in blue tunics over khaki trousers with slouch hats. A wide banner across their front rank proclaimed "Spanish-American War" and "Veterans of '98." Their gaitered boots crunched together, sounding like one very large, very loud set of footsteps.

Further down Bryant after the "Vets of '98" and the Wesley Monumental Church choir float, Lee Thompson craned his neck at a flock of white-clad suffragettes. Under a banner, "The Vote for Women," and hats festooned with silk, lace, feathers, ribbons, and fruit, perhaps eighty women were clapping in rhythm. They alternated chanting, "Give us the vote!" and, "Women should vote!" with the chorus of a ballot song from California:

> *A ballot for the Lady*
> *For the Home and for the Baby!*
> *Come, vote ye for the Lady,*
> *The Baby, the Home!*

A couple of elderly women stumped along on canes. Several younger ones ignored the severe, narrow skirted look of the day's fashion and walked in free-swinging, uncorseted Battenberg or even tea dress styles. Some of these women were apparently mail order customers of immigrant Estée Lauder as certain cheeks, eyebrows and lips had color beyond the exertion of walking.

Lee looked carefully, but Emily was not among these women, and he sighed in relief. The suffragettes were receiving white-gloved applause and soprano and alto calls of "Yes, the vote!" but many more offered catcalls, scattered boos and hisses, and matronly tossing heads. A few men along the route uncovered politely, but many more kept their hats on their politics.

The suffragettes were frequently drowned out by the next two parade units. The Savannah Fire Department came with its pumper and ladder trucks behind the walking women. Their banner, "The first fully motorized Fire Department in America," brought cheers of civic pride. Their engine clatter and howling hand-cranked sirens drew ear-covered shrieks of delight from boys and girls.

Behind the creeping, chain-driven emergency trucks came the combined musical forces of the Savannah Police and Fire Departments. Lee looked past the band for Zachariah or Emily.

Back at "black corner," West Savannahians had seen these units, followed by a small group of khaki-clad boys in broad-brimmed campaign hats reading "The Boy Scouts of Savannah." Two floats were coldly received, the first showing "Confederates" pointing bayoneted rifles at surrendering "Yankees." The float listed the golden anniversary of victories from 1862 from Stonewall's Valley Campaign to Chickasaw Bluffs.

The next float urged "Vote Wilson," "Vote Democratic," and "Follow Virginia again," referring to Woodrow Wilson's home state, rather than his recent life as president of Princeton University. A walking escort of well-dressed men carrying buckets full of campaign buttons had few takers at "black corner." One little boy scampered delightedly to his family crying "Lookie what I got," but the middle-aged adults were glum. By contrast, the slave-born grandparent generation refused to drop their gaze to the white bucket men, but rather stared at them eye to eye with a silent, smoldering defiance that left the marchers dry-mouthed and worried.

As the next float approached Franklin Square, Savannah's mounted police formed up. Long-handled billy clubs were unsnapped from their holsters and a police lieutenant made a show of checking his revolver. Lucius was just turning his head from saying something to Beulah when a police mount passed broadside. The policeman randomly flicked the end of his long stick toward the crowd and caught Lucius on his right ear. As he yelped and the crowd around him looked over, a following police sergeant called down from the saddle, "Let that be a lesson to all you niggas!" Lucius' kerchief sopped up the blood from his ear as the float swung by.

The float was familiar, built for the United Daughters of the Confederacy a few years ago and re-assembled again this year. It was a giant's staircase rising five levels from front to back, drenched in flowers. Benches on each step held several elegantly dressed, beautiful young white women. The back wall held three huge letters: "UDC," and below, "Protect us," "Save Us," and "Remember the South." Each beauty held a bouquet on her lap while she waved to the left; to the right was a wall of the Savannah Mounted.

The policemen inwardly congratulated themselves on their show of force. The young women behind them called out sweetly, "Thank you, officers. Thank you." The street expressions were a mix of scorn and exaggerated boredom, just beyond police earshot: "Hope they get sunburned." "Nuthin' to see here." "We don't have to look at horse rumps." The float passed and the mounted men dispersed, believing they had saved white womanhood from a possible rush of sex-crazed black rapists.

Now a middle-aged woman marched at the right end of a thin line of nervous teenaged girls. The woman's skirt was flared at the hem and loose-flowing, so short that at every step her entire shoe was visible. The girls' "health" skirts matched the free flowing movement and exposed shoes of their leader. They wore matching, long-sleeved blouses with V-collars buttoned at their collarbone notch. Two slightly younger girls led them, carrying a banner reading "Mrs. Juliette Low and the Girl Guides."

The girls were in a wavering line, looking to their smiling leader on their right. Their shy smiles warmed the crowd. "Hurray for the Girl Guides" came Beulah's voice as she rose clapping. Another female voice chimed in, "Amen! Hurray Girl Guides!" Children took their cue and began applauding and merrymaking. The marchers were surprised but delighted. All at once, the men at "black corner" stood, tipped their hats and cheered heartily. Juliette kept marching, but she beamed, saying repeatedly, "Thank you kindly." The mounted police were alert, but things looked far too friendly for them to stay concerned.

In the Johnson Square viewing stand, Lee overheard very mixed reactions to the Girl Guides troop, with most of the negatives pitched in feminine tones. "Well I nevah!" "That is not lady-like." "That Juliette Low is lookin' to make more independent women." "Makin' more suffragettes."

Assorted dignitaries came by riding in a flotilla of motorcars. Model T's, Stanley Steamers, Thomases, Underslungs, a couple of Cadillacs, and even a French Renault all chuffed and clattered, although the ghost-quiet Rauch & Lang electric only honked, as drivers grinned and waved. As the cars passed, Lee smiled. Male voices talked roadsters, but female voices still commented about "a woman's place" and "shamefully short skirts" while the Monitor and the Merrimack float slid by. But the comments faded as an enthusiastic band and a cavorting group of singers drew up.

The band was playing the jaunty, Irish-tinged strains of "The Bonnie Blue Flag" and sure enough in the last rank was a color bearer holding an enormous blue flag, fringed in gold, and sporting a huge white star. The singers massed in front of the viewing stand and sang out the first verse as the crowd clapped in rhythm:

> *We are a band of brothers,*
> *Native to the soil*
> *Fighting for the property*
> *We gained by honest toil.*
> *And when our rights were threatened,*
> *The cry rose near and far;*
> *Hurrah for the Bonnie Blue Flag*
> *That bears a single star!*

When they came to the chorus the singers urged the crowd, "Now you sing! Join the chorus," and they did so eagerly. The band continued passing as the singers serenaded the stands with the next verse.

> *As long as the Union*
> *Was faithful to her trust,*
> *Like friends and brethren,*
> *kind were we, and just;*
> *But now, when Northern treachery*
> *Attempts our rights to mar,*
> *We hoist on high the Bonnie Blue flag*
> *That bears a single star.*

A huge banner carried by a half dozen young men stretched curb to curb. "Veterans of the War Between the States" in letters over six feet high floated a good fifteen feet in the air. Cheers, roars, and Rebel yells arose as the spectators came to their feet in prolonged greeting. Women's handkerchiefs waved furiously. A mass of old Confederate veterans tramped along, nearly all bearded, and often bulging out of their tired but patched uniforms of gray and butternut. A few marched in a tiptoed bounce, trying to match rhythm to one of the South's great marching tunes. Most carried their old long-barreled rifles with fearsome-looking bayonets. Some in the ranks, like Dooley Culpepper, had the butt of a revolver sticking out from his belt while others, like Turner Hawkins, displayed serrated bowie knives. Captain Robert Bidwell wore his dress sword.

Zachariah was on the right end of the 8th Georgia, sergeant stripes gleaming, calling cadence. His eyes caught Lee's in the stands and he grinned broadly. Lee almost didn't recognize this hearty, zealous sergeant as his father-in-law. Lee grinned back, standing and waving his hat.

The singers were reaching the end of a verse. The leader cupped his hands into a megaphone and called, "Sing them the chorus." So as the first ranks passed, the Johnny Rebs were nearly bowled over by hundreds of voices belting out Harry Macarthy's roaring chorus.

> *Hurrah! Hurrah!*
> *For Southern rights, Hurrah!*
> *Hurrah for the Bonnie Blue Flag*
> *That bears a single star!*

The cheers mingled with called out names and shouts of "Daddy!" and "Hi, Grandpa!" Then came two ranks of veterans in wheelchairs being pushed along by some of the smartly dressed Boy Scouts. The crowd choked as the amputees rolled by, then redoubled their volume. Admiring eyes followed the old men and many handkerchiefs ceased waving and went on tear duty. With full hearts the watchers turned to the following unit, and the spectators' pride now blossomed into gale force nostalgia.

A double-length float approached, hinged in the middle, the pride of the United Daughters this year. Its rear wall was a two-story plantation mansion, with white columns, a deep porch, and a second floor balcony, draped with a large Confederate flag. Huge letters at the top roof line spelled "UDC." In the "front yard" under potted trees, a handsome man dressed in the antebellum suit of a wealthy planter and wearing riding boots was sitting in a rocking chair enjoying conversation with several men in gray perched on benches, all elderly veterans who were unable to march. A woman in plantation finery was upon the "grass" in the shade of one of the trees, with several younger girls similarly dressed and equally posed.

On the front half of the float, a half dozen white men made up in black face and dressed in slave rags were smiling as they pretended to hoe in a "field" of cotton plants while singing plantation songs. One man was not only in black face but also dressed as a woman. "She" had a bandanna tied on her head and a water pitcher in her hand. "She" moved barefooted from field to planter to veterans to lady and back again, filling cups and glasses. Occasionally "she" would flutter a hand fan toward a white face.

On either side of the float walked a dozen or so women, their hair done up in the vertical curls of War days and each dressed in a hoop skirt. These were a dazzling collage of colors, styles and fabrics that had been lovingly kept for years. Each lady twirled a parasol over her inside shoulder and carried a flat basket in her curbside arm. They smiled sweetly, calling, "Help send a veteran to the Encampment." After a basket filled with various coins and the odd bill, the lady would sashay to the float and empty the contents into a horse trough in the "plantation's" front yard.

Emily ambled up from the float to the Johnson Square viewing stand. She was in a deep maroon dress with a black lace bodice and bows knotted at intervals about a foot up from the hem. She saw Lee staring in amazement a few rows up. She called out in her best Southern belle voice, "How about you, suh? Would you be so kahnd as to help the Cause?" She smiled coyly, flashed her eyes and extended her basket. Several neighbors and friends now recognized Emily and laughed, both at her fine air and at Lee's astonishment. Lee had enough presence of mind to dig out a silver dollar from his vest pocket. His coin toss landed squarely in her basket. She pretended to be taken aback, and then curtseyed dramatically.

"Thank you, suh. Yo' kindness is most becoming." She smiled at him again, this time not play acting but with real warmth. Lee caught the emotion and blushed as Emily strolled away.

The spectators were awash in swords-and-roses memories. The final unit of the parade brought them back to 1912. People stared in wonder at a long wagon holding a thirty-six-foot wide modern apparition. Two parallel canvas beams, connected to each other by a maze of rods and struts, seemed to float from curb to curb. The canvases were stiffened into a delicate curve that ran their length, bowed up toward the sky. A pair of wood beams, sculpted in a delicately twisted shape, hung vertically behind and between the upper and lower canvases.

A man dressed in a high-collared white jacket, wearing a skull-hugging leather helmet and what looked like massive, oversize spectacles sat on the contraption's front end. A short boom stretched ahead of his feet while a long boom ran back behind him, overhanging the rear of the wagon by several feet.

The crowds buzzed with excitement as the words "flying machine" leapt from mouth to ear. The buzzing turned to applause as watchers read the sandwich boards of several men walking alongside the wings of the Wright Flyer: "Exhibition Today" and "See a man take to the skies!"

"Where will it be?" people asked.

"All over Savannah," came the answer. "Keep your eyes on the skies!"

Applause, waving handkerchiefs, and cheers followed, and the sound washed over the Savannah Mounted Police that came in a line of horseflesh about twelve riders wide. The lieutenants at either end of the line kept saying to the crowds, "Thank y'all fo' comin'. Have a great Fourth o' July!" The spectators headed home and on to various parks around town for picnics and games.

Lee made his way among the happy crowd of picnickers at Forsyth Park looking for Zachariah and Emily. Lemonade, popcorn, and pretzel carts were everywhere, along with the snap and pop of small firecrackers set off by young boys. The occasional constable strolled by while sack races, firemen's tug-of-wars, and a carnival air prevailed. Indeed, there was a bit of a carnival going on with a ring-the-bell concession, a pie-eating contest, and a kissing booth.

Lee overheard a surprising number of snatches of conversations among Savannah's well-to-do about "Next Fourth of July in Gettysburg" and "Pennsylvania vacation next summer." He bumped into his boss, city engineer John Howard, who said, "Well, hello, Lee. Quite the parade and picnic today, isn't it?"

"Definitely well done, John," Lee answered while shaking hands.

"I wonder if Gettysburg will measure up to this next year."

"Are you going?" Lee asked with a slight start.

"Wouldn't miss it, Lee, wouldn't miss it. To see those old gents have a chance for a last hurrah, while the country watches by way of all the newspaper reporters..." he trailed off wistfully, then came back. "But your father-in-law will be going I'm sure. Are you and Emily going along too?"

"We haven't really talked about it," Lee said thoughtfully.

"You might consider it," Howard replied. "No only are these men living history, but they have a chance to point the way to the future, too. They can heal the breach between the sections like no one else." He poked Lee with a finger like he often did at the office. "Mark my words. If thirty thousand Gray and Blue veterans from across the country make peace publicly and set an example, then nobody younger, North or South, will be able to stir up the hurt anymore. If Johnny Rebs like Zachariah and the blue bellies say it's over, then it really will be."

Mr. Howard wandered off in search of hard lemonade, and Lee found Zachariah with Bob Bidwell and other vets at the tail of the line for the kissing booth. A table here held a petition to the Secretary of the Army to keep the Gettysburg Encampment an all-white affair. The men chatted casually about their mutual honor and the dastardly idea of putting freed slaves in the military in the first place.

"An insult to any man who evah wore a uniform," Turner Hawkins proclaimed as the others nodded along.

"The Yankees have no pride as men even askin' to have them black boys in blue at Gettysburg," Bob Bidwell chimed in as Lee joined the booth line and nodded to Zachariah.

"Any of them show up in Gettysburg," Jim Calhoun chimed in, "we'll give 'em a different kind of black and blue." A chuckle ran around the group.

"C'mon Zack," Lee called over, "come get a kiss from your daughter."

Zachariah first pretended he hadn't heard. When the others looked at him expectantly, he said awkwardly, "Oh, she wouldn't think that'd be proper." Bob tried too, but Zack hung his head. "I don't want to embarrass her." After a bit, they all drifted away, leaving him alone on a bench.

The booth was a gazebo hung with Confederate colors and trim. Two of the antebellum parade ladies were perched on chairs with hand fans fluttering and eyes flashing invitingly. Libby Pocklington and Rachel Collins held baskets and stood by neatly painted signs proclaiming "UDC Kissing Booth, five cents a smooch," "Veterans free," and "Help send the boys in gray to the National Encampment."

At the head of the line, Dooley Culpepper puckered up, leaning his grizzled chin toward Emily. She gritted a smile as the liver-spotted face with the mole northwest of the upper lip drew close. A mix of scents tapped her nose and stung her eyes: tobacco juice, the sweaty tang of unwashed skin, and an alcohol whiff that could be medical, rotgut, or hair pomade, but in any case, cheap. As soon as she felt the wet smack on her cheek she drew back, grinned, and exclaimed, "Oh mah! A kiss from a genuine Confed'rit soljah. How ever shall I get over it?" She fanned herself in mock passion but in real discomfort.

Dooley grinned and winked. "You never git over bein' kissed by the best." He made a lunge across the counter to peck her again but Emily was too quick for him. Side-stepping, she called out to the line of civilians behind Dooley, "Gentlemen! Help... send a Confederate to Gettysburg. Kisses five cents apiece. Step right up, won't you please?" This last was said earnestly, misted with desperation. Lee said a quick, "Pardon me" to the two men ahead of him, stepped to the counter, produced a nickel and said gallantly, "For the South!" He pecked Emily on her left cheek as she eyed Dooley through her slitted right eye.

"Why, thank you sir," she said, smiling warmly and carefully moving another step away from Dooley. A middle-aged man sporting a sandy, handlebar moustache had also seen Emily's distress. He stepped up smoothly, nickel in hand. He stood so as to pin the string-tied Lee to the counter, thereby forming a human blockade against Dooley. Emily thanked him with her eyes and submitted to his bay-rum scented buss.

As he pulled back, he could see Emily was still concerned about Dooley. He turned to the seedy veteran, lifted his Panama straw hat in salute, and said loudly, "Sir, would you do me the honor of a tale or two of yo' service in the War?" He gently steered Dooley away from the kissing booth toward a vacant bench. "Did you serve under General Lee, suh?" came the gentleman's fading voice. Emily sighed in relief, gave a quick smile to Lee and then went back to offering her cheeks for the cause.

Rutland

"Ellie, this pie is simply delicious," Calvin exclaimed.

"Absolutely," echoed Anna Louise. "You haven't lost your touch."

Eleanor smiled sweetly and nodded her thanks as her mouth was full.

Anna Louise McCloud, Eleanor's great friend from Montpelier, had come down by train yesterday. Like Eleanor, Anna Louise had a heart-shaped face, but her hair was still salt-and-pepper despite her years. The pepper streaks matched her lively, chestnut-brown eyes. Defying fashion, Anna wore her hair down, shoulder-length, and often with a wide-brimmed, pale bolero hat that gave her a Southwest look. "Practical and comfortable," she would state, "two concepts lost to women's fashion." She was taller than Eleanor and had a poised, muscular way about her, like a dancer or even an acrobat.

"This dessert just tops off the day," Calvin said. "The parade, the bands, the picnic and Mayor Howe's speech. And now Ellie's raspberry custard pie and a trip to the fairgrounds."

"It was sweet of Mayor Howe to mention Port Royal," Eleanor remarked. "Most Fourth of July speeches sound like the whole War was about battles and shooting."

"It's no more than our due he spoke of it," Anna Louise replied. "We had the right idea, trying to show what the nation would be like if we won."

"Just so, Anna," Calvin put in. "We men marched and fought for a cause. You women at Port Royal with your copybooks and blackboards and McGuffey readers turned that cause into reality."

"Well, we tried," Eleanor said modestly, scooping a fresh raspberry with her spoon.

"I have to admit I had my doubts," Anna offered, "when Reverend Dalrymple asked us to go to South Carolina, right in the heart of the rebellion. No white folk there would like the idea of educating former slaves and teaching them to make their own way in the world. But Amanda insisted they could learn and we could teach them."

"I tell you, that Amanda Fairchild was worth a division or two of Union troops all by herself. And all of you were so brave," Calvin said with real admiration, waving his spoon like a baton. "It had to have been a challenge, going in only six months into the War."

"Not a good six months for the Union," Eleanor chirped.

"Ayup," Calvin nodded. "After Fort Sumter, Bull Run, Ball's Bluff, and Wilson's Creek it didn't look like the North even knew how to fight, let alone win. Yet there you went, teaching the runaway slaves before Mr. Lincoln even freed them."

"That's what Mayor Howe said today," Eleanor said earnestly. "What he didn't say was how often our own troops acted like those slave owners, calling our old men 'boys' and the children 'pickaninnies.'"

"Those Union soldiers accused our women students of impropriety and loose morals," Anna Louise added grimly. "Then they'd come around at night hoping to force impropriety and loose morals. Thank heavens our commander Amanda had the ear of their commander, Colonel Higginson."

"Sounds like he was a good man," Calvin said.

"Yes, quite a good man," Eleanor answered. "A lesser man would have let it go, saying some claptrap about 'boys will be boys' or soldiers needing relief or some such. That Thomas Higginson was a prince. I was grateful to him for posting those standing orders against drinking and abusive language and enforced them."

"I imagine it gave the colored folk some peace of mind," Calvin mused.

"It helped," Eleanor replied, "but the real sea change was after January first, 1863...Emancipation Day. The white soldiers were very surprised at how many young colored men joined up. They came up to us with real apologies."

She tried a plantation accent. "'Miz Ellie, I'm wantin' to take my spellin' book with me when I go soldierin'.'"

Anna chuckled at a memory. "The sergeants of drill found the young colored men to be no more block-headed than white soldiers, and that actually surprised the sergeants."

Calvin snorted in turn. "A sergeant's view of a recruit is always someone who doesn't know left from right, front from back, up from down or his..." he checked himself and then went on carefully, "...ah, his wrist from his elbow."

Anna Louise gave him a sharp look with a smile. "I remember it as elbow and another body part."

"Oh, Anna," Eleanor protested, "how can a lady even think words like that?"

"It's what they said," Anna answered, rising with Eleanor to clear the dessert dishes to the kitchen.

Soon afterwards in the kitchen, Eleanor peered closely at Calvin. "Are you sure, Calvin? Anna Louise and I will be just fine going by ourselves." Normally she'd have just urged they all stay home and pretend she actually didn't want to go, but having Anna Louise around raised Eleanor's courage, even to going out in the evening without a man.

"Yes, I'm sure," Calvin said, putting away the last dish from supper and hanging up the towel. "I'd like to see them this year. Why don't we head down now and take in some music and treats?"

"Sounds tasty," Anna agreed. "I'll buy the first round of lemonades."

"Oh, Anna, don't be silly," Eleanor said. "Calvin will treat."

"If you're going to give me bed and board for a few days, it's the least I can do. I insist," she said with a warm smile and a glint in her eye. Both Eleanor and Calvin smiled back. They knew that glint.

Calvin shook his head in feigned despair and quavered his voice. "Once again I'm sold down the river, the poor, hen-pecked man being led around by the apron strings of two headstrong women, force-fed lemonade, custard, chocolate..."

"Oh, go get your hat," Eleanor mock scolded, waving him toward the front hall. "At least that way you can actually talk through it. Apron strings indeed."

A few minutes later, Calvin locked the front door behind them and steadied Eleanor down the porch steps in her long skirt. He was going to do the same for Anna Louise, but she had already reached the walk on her own, sporting her bolero hat and free-swinging riding skirt.

"Anna that is quite, um, an unusual way to carry a purse," Eleanor remarked. Anna's leather pouch rode on her right hip, held in place by a thin leather strap buckled over her left shoulder.

"She's wearing it like a soldier wears a bandolier," Calvin said lightly. "I'm feeling safer already."

Ellie smiled. "Oh stop it. Next you'll be telling me Anna's carrying a Derringer in there."

Anna's flashing reply, "Not tonight," set them chuckling, and yet there was something in her tone that made both the Salisburys glance at each other in wonder. When Anna had been out West *had* she carried a Derringer some nights?

They walked down Washington Street to Main and caught a southbound streetcar. The sun would be up for about another ninety minutes, but it was blocked occasionally by some thunderheads building up toward the New York line. As they got off at Park Street and passed through the State Fairground gates, Anna's "frontier" look set off much female comment, which she ignored. A bearded version of Benjamin Franklin emerged from the crowd.

"Sam!" Calvin and Eleanor exclaimed together.

"How are you?" Eleanor added.

"Fine, thanks," Sam said, all smiles. But his eyes strayed to Eleanor's right.

"Sam, you remember my friend Anna Louise McCloud from Montpelier? She visiting us for a few days and…" her voice trailed off as she watched both Sam and Anna's eyes light up.

"Umm, why yes," Sam stammered. "I do remember Miss McCloud."

"And I remember you, Mr. Wentworth," Anna said sweetly. "But please, call me Anna."

Sam gulped. "Of course. Will you call me Sam?"

So as dusk came on and the sound of the calliope drifted from the carousel, the four went about the fairgrounds, one pair a small-boned couple married over a half century. The other pair strolled too, the lifelong bachelor and the vigorous, sprightly woman whom most men found fascinating and whom no man had found the courage to court, let alone wed. As promised, Anna bought lemonade, but Calvin and Anna decided to have theirs differently. That half-frozen, lemon-and-sugar wonder called "Italian Ice" was the rage this year, and Eleanor and Sam both agreed, after small tastes, that the other two had picked a winner. As the sun met the landline, they all climbed into the veterans' reserved seats in the grandstand and waited for nightfall.

"Hello, Judge Salisbury. Mr. Wentworth." Both looked up to see Ashton Melo standing in the aisle with a handsome, middle-aged couple. Both men popped to their feet and Calvin reached over for a handshake. Sam lifted his hat from beyond Eleanor and Anna.

"Ashton!" Calvin said with pleasure. "You're looking well. And you made it in time." Looking at the couple he asked, "Are these some of your relations?"

"No sir. Actually this the Reverend Homer Stanton, pastor of my church over in West Rutland, and his wife Dahlia."

"Delighted."

"My pleasure" and other pleasantries filled the introductions all around.

"Calvin?" Ashton asked. "Could we get past you to those empty spots?"

"Of course, of course," and the four stood to let the three pass into mid-bleachers. As he sat back down, Calvin pondered the similar glint in the eyes of Eleanor and Anna and now Mrs. Stanton. Was it really the same look? He was staring off for a moment when his eyes focused on a familiar but frowning face. Josiah Trimble from two rows ahead across the aisle glared disgust toward Calvin. He noticed Abigail Trimble staring over her shoulder at them and shaking her head while she said something to Josiah with a scornful look on her face.

Suddenly there came an enormous boom. All heads turned to see the orange trail of a firework rocket rising in the air, then ending in a brilliant flash and an immediate boom. Eleanor sat close to Calvin and held his hand tightly, but after the first two bangers he did well, and even enjoyed it. The display and the crowd's delight went on a good half hour. When the black powder aroma drifted over the stands, the civilians didn't mind but the veterans' memories stirred hard or sad thoughts. Once in a while to the west, nature added her own glitter with lightning bolts flashing inside the thunderclouds slowly approaching from Albany. Vermonters told each other their thunder was "just New Yorkers arguing."

The quartet all made it on the fourth jammed streetcar leaving up Main Street from Park. Sam bade Anna a gallant, hand-kissing goodbye at Center Street as he changed lines for home. Calvin, Eleanor, and Anna walked up Washington and all turned in while the weather was still mostly distant rumbles and heat lightning.

It was after midnight when a thundering crack woke Eleanor. She sat up and gasped "oh." She looked over to Calvin, but his side of the bed was empty. Rain drummed the bay window and lightning flashed again. In the ghastly glare, Eleanor saw Calvin sitting rigidly in a chair, his knuckles white, gripping the armrests, his eyes shut and tears streaming down. She hauled back the sheet, moved over to him and stood holding his head in her arms.

She could feel him trembling and knew he was back in the War, feeling the fear he couldn't show at Gettysburg, at Spotsylvania. But now, decades later, still the cannon boomed, the wounded screamed, and Eleanor could only hold him until one storm or the other spent itself or passed over.

Tuesday, July 9, 1912

West Side, Savannah

A lean, handsome man of forty-eight with close black hair, a dashing moustache and small goatee, Elijah Porterfield had been pastor of Second African Baptist on Savannah's Franklin Square since 1901. On Tuesday morning he slid a long sheet of paper covered with signatures out from under a pasteboard bucket holding a few pennies and nickels. He checked the church's front doors and turned to walk down the hall when he heard humming from the sanctuary. Following the sound to the front, he found a toolbox of well-used carpenter's tools. Lucius Robinson was lying on the floor looking up where the second pew seat joined its aisle end piece.

"Hello, Lucius." Robinson jerked and the humming broke into a "waaah." His eyes went wide and his body went rigid.

"Oh, easy, easy, Lucius. I'm sorry. I didn't mean to startle you," Porterfield said anxiously. "Are you all right?"

"Yeah, Reverend, I'll be fine. Jes' gimme a minute," Lucius answered, taking a deep breath and closing his eyes. When he opened them, Porterfield could see the haunting gone, so he started again.

"What you workin' on?"

"Oh, last Sunday, Ruby Talmadge told me her seat was squeakin' and felt mushy, so I told her I'd have a look at it."

"What do you think?"

"It's loose all right. Glue joint's comin' apart and a coupla nails are gone."

"Give you a hand?"

Porterfield passed Lucius a hammer and crow iron. Lucius cleaned out the joint as best he could without removing the entire elm end piece with the carved rosette. He used a bit and brace to drill some countersink holes for screws to replace the nails. He took a piece of scrap wood from his box and sat down on the front pew to whittle three wedge shims to tighten the joint. Porterfield joined him on the pew.

"Thanks for doin' this, Lucius. I appreciate it, 'though not as much as Ruby, I'm sure." Lucius smiled as Porterfield studied him closely. "How you doin', Lucius? How's the house comin'?"

"House is comin' along nicely. You know, I always wanted to build a house for Beulah and in a roundabout way now I got the chance. And this Beulah is as good for Rufus – and me – as my own Beulah was."

Lucius whittled, the soft smell of pine mingling with the faintly sweet smell of beeswax candles. The quiet grew. Shavings hitting the floor sounded loud.

"Something else on your mind?" Elijah asked.

Tears welled in Lucius' eyes, and he winced them shut. Porterfield noticed a scabbed-over bruise near his right ear as Lucius said in a strangled voice, "It was the Fourth of July parade. Same old Jim Crow after fifty years. I thought it'd be different by now. Maybe not right aftah the War and 'Mancipation. President Johnson ended Special Field Order 15, but then," a tear rolled down his cheek. Another shaving tapped the floor "...we got the vote." Even for church his tone was angel-holy. "The vote."

"President Grant put down the Klan so hard they've stayed down. By now I figured ever'body woulda settled down, live and let live."

A bitterness scrunched his face as his knife stopped. "But they don't!" he wailed. "I cain't take a night walk or I'll get run in fo' curfew. I pay my nickel same as a white man for the streetcar and gots to stand out on the runnin' board, rain or shine." He looked up at Porterfield. "Rufus and Beulah went in their Sunday best to buy the kit house and got treated ratt at the Sears and Roebuck. But on the way home, some cracker hauled off and called Rufus an 'over-dressed popinjay' and spit at Beulah, just 'cause he could. Or 'cause he was, or they were..." His words fell apart.

Porterfield leaned over and put a hand on his shaking shoulder, searching for what to say. As Lucius wound down, Elijah closed his eyes with a deep breath and said, "Lord God, we have passed out of Egypt and left slavery behind. How far to the Promised Land, O Lord? Lord, it's been forty-nine years since leaving slavery and even Israel only had to wander forty years. How long, O Lord? How long?"

Lucius sobbed from the heart, then calmed as Porterfield continued. "Lord, hear your servant Lucius, lamenting for his people. Hear, O Lord, a cry for justice. Listen, O God, your people cry to you for justice. We have waited with patience, O Lord, and still justice is delayed. How long, O Lord? Let justice be no more delayed, O God, so none believe justice is denied. Let your people cross over Jordan. Cross over soon, O Lord, into the Promised Land."

"Soon Lord," Lucius echoed. "I ain't got that much time to see it, Lord, so let it be soon."

"Yes, Lord, let it be soon," Elijah continued. "Let it be soon."

Lucius gave off a long, rich sigh. In the silence, he painted a mess of glue into the joint, tapped in the wedges and drove home several screws. He wiped up the drips and used a little broom to collect his shavings, then packed up.

They finally stood inside the doors leading onto Franklin Square.

"Signed this letter yet?" Elijah asked, breaking the silence of the last several minutes. "It's going to W.E.B. DuBois at *The Crisis* magazine in Chicago."

"Oh that's ratt," Lucius answered. "'Bout havin' the USCI vets at Gettysburg next summer. Here, lemme have that."

Elijah handed him a pencil and Lucius signed. Porterfield read the signature and said quietly, "You ought to add 'Mister' in front o' your name. They'll print it that way you know: mister, missus, miss."

Lucius sighed. "Yeah, but so what? Won't get us any respect with white folk. They won't read *The Crisis*. And look here." He picked up the pasteboard bucket marked "Gettysburg" and shook the few coins in it. "You really think house servants, street sweepers, and grave diggers scratching for every cent are gonna fill this up? Ain't no way we'll even raise enough to send one of our USCI men to Gettysburg. And even if they'd go, where would they stay? What would they do there? Who'd pay the United States Colored Infantry veterans any mind at all? Jes' treat 'em like a bunch of old coots in blue and expect 'em to hand out blankets, cook and clean, or jes' put on a vaudeville song and dance fo' all the watt folk."

Porterfield waited until they were both outside. "We're just gettin' started. Who knows? These pennies might be the seed and the letter could be the water. If so, God'll give the growth. I believe the men will get a chance to go." He paused and sighed. "But you may be ratt 'bout where they'd stay and how white folks might look at them." He shook his head at the thought, then shook Lucius' hand. "Anyway, thanks for fixin' that pew."

"You're welcome, Reverend. Thanks for the prayer."

"See you Sunday."

"That is such a preacher thing to say."

Thursday, August 8, 1912

Boston

Although it was a mournful crowd in the Tremont Street church in Boston, underneath the prelude, ripples of whispers swept the sanctuary around Calvin. Mayor John Fitzgerald and fellow mayors from Roxbury, Concord, and Lexington touched off a wave. An elegant man in a top hat – Civil War Governor Andrew's son, said the whispers – entered with Governor Eugene Foss. Several retired military officers entered together, their uniforms and medals colorful against the black-suited civilians.

When the prelude ended, the congregation rose and faced the rear. The skirl of a bagpipe was accompanied by muffled drums. The procession entered, Reverend Whittington first, followed by the casket, which was draped with an old, well-worn flag. The casket was unusually attended. Each pallbearer was accompanied, one step behind and one step wide, by a woman. While the pallbearers were all middle-aged, every one of the women was in her seventies or better. Two of them leaned on canes for support. The piper and drummer came next, followed by the family. Finally came two dozen uniformed old men in Union blue. All were retired members of the USCI, the United States Colored Infantry, who had enlisted after Emancipation. "Amazing Grace" floated out the windows into a perfect August sky.

Reverend Whittington found his text in Proverbs 31.

> *She opens her mouth with wisdom and the teaching of kindness is on her tongue. She looks well to the ways of her household and does not eat the bread of idleness. Her children rise up and call her blessed; her husband also, and he praises her: 'Many women have done excellently, but you surpass them all.'*

"'You surpass them all.' Amanda Fairchild surpassed them all.

"Amanda did not eat the bread of idleness but said, 'Let us go down and teach.' Many said to her, 'They are unteachable.' She answered firmly yet with a womanly smile, 'I will teach them.'

"Many said to Amanda, 'A woman ought not go.' But it is also written in the book of Proverbs; 'She girds her loins with strength and makes her arms strong.' So Amanda said, 'I am strong enough to go.'

"Others said wisely, 'You ought not go alone.' Amanda took wisdom, took counsel, and took with her other excellent women, some of whom are here today and walked alongside her once more. I see Catherine Simmons and Eleanor Salisbury. Anna Louise McCloud walked alongside Amanda both then and today, and so did Prudence McKenzie. We name Dorothy Swanson and Mary Ashbaugh as part of her company.

"Amanda's goal was helping the newly freed live as free people. The enemies of freedom are fear and ignorance. Our gallant men in blue warred against the fear, the fear of the whip, the fear of overwork, the fear of a slave-owning man attacking and even outraging a slave woman, the fear of families being separated by the slave auctioneer's gavel.

"Gallant Amanda Fairchild and her companions battled the ignorance. Frederick Douglass once said the slave owners' greatest cruelty was denying their slaves education. To heal that cruelty came the women to Port Royal, South Carolina.

"*Port* Royal. What a perfect name for the battle against ignorance to take place. In God's providence, He arranged for the fleeing slaves, the contrabands, the emancipated, to find a port, a harbor, an anchorage. In Port Royal they would be safe while the storms of war thundered around them.

"Port *Royal.* Amanda and her dauntless band brought the royal gift of education, the queenly grace of letters, the princely power of numbers to the freedmen, the freed women, and the freed children. By her efforts Amanda fulfilled the words of St. Peter when he wrote, 'Once you were no people, but now you are God's people.' By bringing the newly freed out of ignorance into understanding, Amanda was God's instrument of fulfillment."

It was a long funeral, matched by a long processional to the cemetery. Once she got over the surprise of being an honorary pallbearer, Eleanor had relied on her very best lady manners during the services. She knew by heart all the expected graces of a lady grieving publicly so she could do them automatically, while inwardly she could lament undistracted for Amanda.

But the wake was different. As a pallbearer and a Port Royal woman she was something of a heroine, and playing the celebrity was something her Victorian manners simply didn't cover. New England manners were ignored as people kept breaking in on each other's words. Handshakes kept sweeping up to Eleanor and the other Port Royal women. She looked on as professional politicians Mayor Fitzgerald and Governor Foss took this all in stride. Eleanor marveled at Anna Louise at ease in a ring of star-struck men. It took her while, but as the wake continued, she not only caught on to saying charming thank yous, she also found the core meaning of a wake – bringing together grieving hearts so the tears of the mourners would water the celebration of the departed.

And it was a celebration of Amanda, a long, good, and noisy wake at Faneuil Hall in the heart of Boston, full of memories, stories, and singing from

Port Royal days. The Port Royal spirit of liberation lived on as well. There was a petition to the Secretary of the Army to invite the USCI to come to the Gettysburg Encampment. Calvin and the other veterans were all asked to sign with their rank and units from the War. Anna Louise and Eleanor and the others were all urged to sign on too, and after their names add the rank "Company ABC, Port Royal Brigade," and they all did so to cheers. The hall rang as of old with talk of liberty and justice, with tidings of rights and opportunity, with curses upon oppression and prejudice. The very room, full of maple-ribbed descendants from the Puritans and newly-arrived Irish Catholics, slave-born and free-born colored folk, the powerful and the poor, veterans and civilians, gave mute evidence of the success of the experiment.

The train's whistle shrieked as the engine tightened the car couplings, then gripped the rails and began pulling out of the station. Calvin and Eleanor had made themselves comfortable in the compartment, each lost in thought. Calvin saw, yet didn't see, the farmsteads passing by the window at twenty-five miles an hour. Trim, clapboard farm houses and stout barns crouched behind stone walls that lined fields and marked neighbors.

After a time, Eleanor shifted in her seat, the folds of her black dress rustling. With a trembling sigh, she said, "Calvin, you know I love you with all my heart." Startled at this public declaration, Calvin stammered, "Ah... yes, I know Ellie," and gently took her hand.

"So I know you'll understand," she continued, "when I say I have lost a dear, dear love. I will miss Amanda so much." Her tears rolled down her wrinkled cheek and dripped onto the edge of her veil. "She was such a dear friend, with a heart of gold... a heart of gold, and a will of iron. Yes, that's it, a will of iron. How well she bore us up, bore up her students, bore the heat and the bugs. None of us who went with her could have imagined our trials and our triumphs. We taught so much and learned so much...". She trailed off, musing.

Calvin stroked her hand as she poured out her lament. Most of the trip back to Rutland was spent reminiscing. Late that night, Calvin noticed an oddity. Often it was he who tossed and turned in his sleep, haunted by vivid dreams of battle and suffering. But tonight he held Eleanor as she sighed, mumbled, kicked, and cried out. He held her in his arms, and when he stroked her cheek she was able to sleep quietly, and soon, so could he.

Friday, October 18, 1912

Savannah

Hugo Ratzinger's Thomas motorcar pulled up his in front of the Green-Meldrim House. Zachariah gave off a deep sigh and unclenched his white knuckles from the seat and dashboard.

"How do you like it so far?" Hugo asked with oblivious enthusiasm.

"I don't care much for bein' carried along by somethin' not livin'," Zachariah answered as he opened the right door and stepped out. He turned and pulled the seat forward and gave his hand to Emily.

She took it gratefully while thinking about her father and the unliving Thomas. After all, she thought, he was a railroad conductor for over thirty years. Wasn't afraid of 'unliving' trains. He had been in the War and had plenty of courage. Why was he such a nervous Nellie at motorcars? Yet her annoyance at his uneasiness with modern devices softened at his old courtly ways. He not only handed her out of the car, but he walked her elegantly to the gate. He opened it with a flourish and held it like an old manservant for her to pass into the yard. Suddenly the quietly idling Thomas gave off a sharp backfire as Hugo fussed with the choke knob.

Emily flinched but Zachariah instantly closed his eyes, ducked into a crouch and called out, "Sniper!" Emily watched her father slowly straighten, open his eyes, blush and look down.

"I, ah, hope you have a nice tea with the ladies," he mumbled under her mortified look, then scooted back through the gate. "Hugo. Thanks fo' the ride. I'm gonna walk home, but I'd be obliged iffin' you could still pick up Emily at four o'clock like we said earlier. I'll be seein' you." He waved to Emily and then Hugo and walked off in a hurried stride. Hugo clattered away in his Thomas and Emily moved through the wonderful October cool to the door. She shook off her embarrassment at her father and put on a lady's face and airs as the door of the Green-Meldrim House opened.

"Please come in, Mrs. Thompson," the white woman said in a voice a trifle loud. "I'm Juliette Low and I'm helping out Pauline today. Won't you please come this way?"

"Thank you so much, Mrs. Low," said Emily with real enthusiasm, delighted by today's tea. It not only marked her rising position, but she had longed to see inside the house on Madison Square. Juliette led her with an easy familiarity to the archway of a sumptuous dining room. The long table against the far wall was arrayed with cakes and treats. As Juliette returned to the door, Pauline Meldrim greeted Emily and led her to the table. French doors opened onto a rear verandah topped by a pergola and set with chairs and small tables for two or three. A soft breeze waved the garden's autumn flowers without disturbing the hats of any of Savannah's elite.

As Emily sat down with her plate, Rachel Collins, two tables away, said to their hostess, "Pauline the food is wonderful. I can't remember the last time I had a spread like this. But I suppose because the cost of everything has jumped these last few years is why you don't see it very often. So thank you."

"You are welcome, Rachel, and indeed all of you ladies. Sometimes I think you need to ignore the expense and just do things right. But I suppose that's why all the political talk is about the cost of everything and how to bring down prices."

Libby Pocklington chuckled and said, "If it's one thing all the parties agree on, its lower prices for everyone. It would be very hard to win an election calling for higher prices for everything." She giggled at her own joke.

Juliette Low came onto the verandah and sat down as Pauline said, "You're quite right about that. The only other thing they have in common is keeping women from voting."

"If women had the vote," Rachel Collins offered, "the prices of everything would take a turn for the better because women simply wouldn't stand for them."

"There is no need for women to have the vote," Libby pronounced. "Mr. Pocklington can handle everything like that so I don't even need to trifle with the Alaska Territory or Cuban bandits or even Chinamen voting in San Francisco."

Juliette chirped up, "Surely the men haven't solved everything. So a woman's vote and point of view might help." The group looked at Juliette with raised eyebrows. Suffragettes were not considered ladies in this circle. Pauline looked to steer the talk into safer waters as she turned to Libby and said, "Now Libby, are things harmonious once more in the altar guild at First Baptist? Is all forgiven and sisterly love prevailing?"

"Well, dried flowers on the altar still strike me as wrong somehow," Libby said.

Rachel answered charitably, "You may be right, Libby, but the deacon's board agreed to only an experiment for six months." At First Baptist, Rachel's proposal for dried altar flowers instead of fresh-cut every week still stirred feelings. Emily tried to avoid catching either Rachel or Libby's eye to avoid taking sides. She was relieved when Pauline moved into yet safer waters when she asked, "Libby? What news do you have about the UDC fund drive for Gettysburg?"

Libby brightened at the chance to lead again. "I suppose the vexing news is from Governor Brown. The Legislature won't vote any funds since the state is strapped for money and unwilling to tax or borrow any." Heads shook at the news, although state politics rated far below church, fashions, and family.

"On a happier note, my last letter from the Georgia UDC showed our Savannah chapter is almost even with Atlanta in fund-raising. The parade and kissing booth gave us a great start. Baked goods sales are picking up now that autumn has given menfolk a sweet tooth."

Various bits of UDC business and gossip passed around until Rachel asked the circle neophyte, "Emily, how is your father these days?"

"Pretty much the same," she replied, setting off a round of comments. Most families had a veteran among them and the women mostly cared for them. "They don't appreciate all we do for them," some said. They agreed the grizzled survivors were often sad, detached, fond of the bottle, subject to severe headaches, or touchy about loud noises. "They just want their bourbon and their War talk, like their regiments matter more than what happened to their families," someone else remarked.

Rachel Collins answered. "That's why Robert and I won't be going on vacation next summer to Gettysburg. If you think the regimental meetings are bad, imagine armies of men chattering on like that for a whole week." Emily nodded along, the thought of seeing Zachariah sodden and maudlin for days on end giving her a chill.

The circle's hearts went out to Helen Chestnut who was still in black; today was her first outing. She recounted the sudden death of her father, Luke Simpson. Her cook had dropped a large pot from a top shelf just as Luke was entering the kitchen. The noise had made him jump, then he clutched a hand to his chest and fell. "The doctor said he passed in that moment," Helen finished. "Even though I fired Rebecca the day after his funeral I still miss her cobblers." Helen had everyone's support, but for some reason today Emily felt unsettled by what had happened to a colored cook for merely dropping a pot.

Pauline then led the ladies' tea in a more unusual direction. "Juliette," she said, smiling, "you lived here when it was General Sherman's quarters. Do you remember him?"

"Yes, I do, one day in particular." The women hung on Juliette's tale. "It was late December. I remember it for two reasons. We were coming up on Christmas and with the Union army occupying Savannah, my sister and I were worried they wouldn't let us have Christmas. And second, this particular day more black men came into our house here than I had ever seen at once in my whole life. I didn't believe it when mother said they weren't slaves or even workmen but clergymen, and they actually were."

A few ministers fumbled their hats in their laps, but the whole flock shifted uneasily on their hard seats. Two Union soldiers sat opposite them at a long table strewn with ink wells, pens, and various papers. They occasionally looked up from their careful copying at the row of black men. A pair of sentries, members of Howard's XI Corps, guarded the far double doors and also wondered. These two, derisively called "paper-collar Easterners" by others of the Western army, snapped to attention as the doors abruptly opened.

The clergy were startled as a gaunt, red-haired man with a close cropped beard, hollow cheeks, and the double stars of a major general pounced into the room. Other blue-uniformed officers trailed in as the general puffed furiously on a small cigar, smoke streaming over his shoulder like a human locomotive. Before the ministers could react he had reached the first one, hand outstretched.

"Thank you for comin', Reverend. I'm General Sherman. What's your name?" Astounded at this vigorous greeting, Reverend Preston Langely forgot to stand, but rather dropped his eyes and mumbled something inaudible. Sherman stopped short and sized up the situation. Snatching the cigar from his mouth he said to the awed civilians, "Gentlemen, as commander of an army of the greatest government yet devised, I am here...with 60,000 men...to end rebellion and slavery. This I have done and you are free. I would be honored if you would look me in the eye like free men do." The men stood gulping with blinking eyes and broad smiles, as one officer later put it, "displaying an amount of ivory terrible to behold." Sherman came down the line pumping each man's hand and introducing himself eye to eye.

Generals Howard, Slocum, Logan, Davis, and various staff officers were introduced. Then Sherman took the floor, pacing from sheer nervous energy.

"Gentlemen, as of January 1, 1863 President Lincoln declared all of you free. I would like to make a public reading of his Emancipation Proclamation. I require your help in two ways. Can you bring as many colored folk as possible to Franklin Square for the reading?"

"Yes, suh," "Of course, Gin'rul" filled the air.

"Good, good. Second, I know most of your people have very little education. When I read the Proclamation I would like you to be among your people." He pulled out a wrinkled sheet of paper from his pocket, and smoothed it out. "In the book of Nehemiah, chapter 8 it says,

> *"And all the people gathered as one man into the square before the Water Gate; and they told Ezra the scribe to bring the book of the law of Moses which the Lord had given to Israel.... And he read from it facing the square before the Water Gate from early morning until midday, in the presence of the men and the women and those who could understand it..."*

Sherman interrupted himself. "There's a list of jaw-breakin' names here, who are called the Levites," he said, then continued.

"'The Levites helped the people to understand the law, while the people remained in their places. And they read from the book, from the law of God, clearly; and they gave the sense, so that the people understood the reading.'

"I would like you to be explaining the Proclamation. President Lincoln put in some grand words and your people deserve to understand every one of them. I've asked these officers to read through the Proclamation with you so you too can grasp its meaning."

Turning to the somewhat surprised group of officers, Sherman scooped up a sheaf of papers the two clerks had spent the last hour copying out. "Here you are, gentlemen. Each of you take a sheet, then pick your man. And that's an order," he finished, arching his eyebrow at Davis and a couple of others who looked balky. Then Sherman took one sheet himself, put the cigar back in his mouth and crossed to one of the pastors. "Reverend Langley, isn't it?"

Langley nodded, beaming glassy-eyed. "Let's you and me step over to the window and go over this together," Sherman said, guiding his charge by an elbow. A hum of conversation rose. The sentries watched amazed as black and white, uniform and motley civilian paired off around the room.

Nearly an hour later, Sherman sauntered toward the kitchen to scrounge a bite. As he swung into the warm, good smelling room, five-year-old Daisy Gordon and her sister said, "Boo!" and popped into view from the dining room. "Ha, ha, general. Got you that time," Daisy said grinning.

Though Sherman had started slightly he just grinned broadly and turned quickly toward the girls. "And now I'm going to tickle you!" he said.

With shrieks of laughter and pretended fear, the girls scampered through the dining room with Sherman in long-striding pursuit, deliberately tramping the floor for extra noise. Katy, the stout colored woman stirring the stew, shook her head. She anticipated the tea circle by fifty years as she said, "A gin'rul playin' tag. Who'da thought?"

Conversation chirped among the tea ladies and several chats broke out. They tried reconciling stories about the terrible Sherman, destroyer incarnate, with his earnest concern for the ministers and his playfulness with two little girls, one nicknamed Daisy, but whom they knew as Juliette.

Election Day
Tuesday, November 5, 1912

Savannah

"Not too warm this mawnin', Lee," Zachariah said over his second cup of breakfast coffee. "Jes' a little crisp, like fall oughta be."

"That's just what I thought when I opened our window getting up," Lee replied, offering a coffee cup salute. "Oh thank you," he added as Alma sidled up with the pot to give him a refill.

"So do you two really think Mr. Wilson can win?" Emily asked. "He would be only the second Democratic president in my lifetime."

"Count on it, honeybunch," Zachariah said gaily. "Them black Republicans are split like a smashed pumpkin after Halloween. Roosevelt may even get more votes than Taft."

Lee nodded earnestly. "If Roosevelt does, the Republicans will disappear like the Whigs or the Know-Nothings."

"Won't Mr. Wilson be too progressive for your tastes, you two?" Emily teased. "Who cares about settling the Alaska Territory or chasing raiders in the Philippines for these last ten years?"

"Oh, now Emily," her father answered, "no need to trouble yourself about America bringing civilization to the Eskimos or to our little brown brothers around Manila Bay."

Emily didn't care much for his dismissal. A bit tartly, she went on. "What if Mr. Wilson really backs that amendment for an income tax? What if he sets up a Federal Reserve Bank, even if J.P. Morgan doesn't like it? Suppose he's a secret suffragette? Or maybe he'll sign a national law against lynching?"

Lee hadn't realized how closely Emily had followed the contest. He waited until Alma passed out of earshot into the kitchen with the breakfast dishes before he said thoughtfully, "On these shores the country can probably only stand one big social upheaval. Wilson will have to choose between advancing the women or advancing the races. I think he'll choose the women."

Zachariah stared at him while Emily beamed. "You really think?" she said. "The vote? I might get to vote?"

"I think so," Lee said calmly.

"Not in my lifetime," Zachariah said, perturbed. "Women voting? Oh, pshaw! Might see a nigger doctor in Savannah before women get the vote."

"Daddy!" Emily snapped. "Your language."

Zachariah blushed and stammered, "I'm sorry. Jes' slipped out. But look. A woman votin' jes' ain't natural. Her place is in the home. Her husband should handle worldly things outside the home." He nodded to Lee, hoping for support.

Emily remembered Helen Chestnut from last month's tea. "And what about widows then? Or independent working women?"

Zachariah subsided into a grumpy silence just as the hall clock chimed. "What do you say, Zack?" Lee said, pushing back his chair. "Time to go vote?"

"I reckon it is," he answered, getting to his feet. "Guess we'd best get on to the courthouse." As Lee stepped into the front hall, Zachariah turned to Emily. "Didn't mean to offend. I'm jes' not used to talkin' politics with a lady, let alone a smart lady."

She gave him a small smile and said, "It's all right, Daddy."

She was pleased as she saw Zachariah move to the hall hat rack and ignore his yard hat for the soft gray planter's hat she'd bought him last year for his birthday. She noticed for the first time he was nicely dressed today – not his Sunday best, but his second-best gray suit.

Zachariah posed the hat against his arm and said to her, "I think these go together ratt fine. Thank you for my hat." He hesitated, then added, "Honeybunch."

"You're welcome, Daddy. You look like a real gentleman today."

A faraway look misted his eyes as he said, "Gotta beat them durn Republicans, but ballots are better'n bullets."

"Yes, they are," she said, her throat suddenly tight.

"Well said, Zack," Lee exclaimed, clapping him on the shoulder and donning his own dark blue homburg. "C'mon. Let's go beat 'em." Emily looked after them a bit wistfully as they crossed the yard.

"Hope you don't mind dawdlin' for an old man's pace," Zachariah said as they reached the sidewalk.

"Not at all," Lee replied. "It's good for me to take a different pace. Too much rushing around in my life as it is."

Waiting to vote at the courthouse, Zachariah ran into Turner Hawkins, who always explained his bald head and full beard as his head hair "just changin' places." They joshed a few minutes about voting for Taft or Roosevelt just to aggravate the Republican schism.

"Oh I'd never vote for Roosevelt even to cause trouble." Turner's bushy face went serious. "Not after him eatin' dinner with that Booker T. Washington in the White House. That was just insultin' to ever' white man in the country."

In side-by-side voting booths, Mr. Woodrow Wilson picked up two votes from Tattnall Street, Savannah.

West Side, Savannah

Hannah Marie and Sherman Robinson walked home together from school Tuesday afternoon. They were polite enough on the sidewalk, but once inside their gate, it was a giggling race along the walk and up the porch steps to see who could tag the front door first. Hannah led, but Sherman covered the steps in one huge leap and tied her at the door.

"Okay, we'll call it even today," Hannah laughed as they tumbled inside a bit breathless. Beulah came from the kitchen to meet them in the parlor. Lucius had been napping on the couch there until the double hand slap on the front door.

"How was school today?" Beulah asked.

"Jes' fine, jes' fine," Hannah answered. "Geography mostly, and penmanship in cursive writing," she added proudly.

"And how 'bout you, junior carpenter?" Lucius asked, still blinking a bit and stretching.

Sherman said, "Spellin', 'rithmetic, and mo' spellin'. Them words are hard to learn."

"'Those words'," Beulah corrected.

"Yes, Mama. Those words are hard to learn. Who knew 'hoss' had a 'R' in it?"

"We also learned that today is Election Day for President," Hannah chimed in. "Mr. Wilson, Mr. Roosevelt, and President Taft are the candy-dates."

"Which one did you vote for, Grandpops?" Sherman asked eagerly. His eyes widened in sad surprise as a stricken look crossed Lucius' face.

"Now Sherman, we talked 'bout that," Beulah began, but Lucius held up his hand.

"No, no, it's all ratt, Beulah. Its time both chillun heard it from me." They settled at his feet while Beulah sat down beside him on the couch.

"I was cuttin' some leather straps for a harness at Hawkin's Livery Stables in November 1866. A Union major came by to pick up his hoss. When I brung out his black mare, he said to me, 'Have you voted yet?' I said, 'No sir. What's that?'

He said, "Part of bein' a free man is gettin' to choose your own leaders. Today is choosin' day for mayor and for Congress. Down at the courthouse there be men tellin' you which man stands for what and agin' what. You choose who you like. C'mon. I'll go with you. It's just a couple blocks."

"Old man Hawkins and his son Turner stepped up and said, "No you won't, boy." The major pulled out his pistol and said, 'Oh, yes he will. 'Bout time you secesh men learned who won the War.'

"So I went with the major, still wearin' my leather apron. The major was right about those men talkin' at the courthouse. They'd say how their man was a humble, church-goin' family man with a heart of gold, and that the other man was always a stone-hearted, swamp-runnin', no-count cracker or a dainty, snobby, soft-headed rich galoot. 'Course other fellas would say jes' the opposite."

Lucius chuckled in spite of himself and muttered, "Still say the same things fifty years later."

He sighed heavily. "For 'bout fifteen years, I went every election day to do my choosin'. But them white folk got together to make all sorts of laws to have only white men vote: ownin' property, readin', and explainin' the Georgia Constitution, havin' a grand-daddy who voted."

"But why?" Hannah cried. "Why did the Union men let them do that to colored folk? Why didn't they make Washington laws to stop the Georgia laws from doin' that?" Tears welled in her eyes and Lucius cupped her cheek in his hand.

"The Union men went back to their own homes after a time. They did put in a Washington law called the Fifteenth Amendment to let any man vote. But these Southern white men..." his voice choked in anger as his fist crashed down on the arm of the sofa "...these evil white *boys*.." he said with venom, "... they are from the Devil himself in findin' ways to keep colored men from votin'. They stole the governor's election and turned old Tom Watson from a good man for the poor and us coloreds into the skunk he is now. They tell ignorant colored men, 'White men vote on Tuesday. Black men vote on Wednesday' and then on Wednesday they laugh at all the dumb men who got fooled."

Beulah and the children swallowed hard. Lucius said with a forceful dignity as tears rolled down his cheeks, "Good will defeat evil. I believe that in my bones." His narrowed eyes made the children's eyes go wide as he said to them, "You two. With God as my witness don't you ever forget. Don't you ever let down. It may take fifty years and you may have gray hair, but both of you, never rest until you vote. You vote, like any man," he said to Sherman; then he turned from Hannah to Beulah and back. "Like any woman. Like any American who's free."

His face softened and he gave a small smile. "Now go study yo' books so you can out-think 'em."

"We will, Grampops, we will," they answered, first with hugs, and then by marching to the dining room table with their books.

Rutland

Calvin had been battling a cold the last few days. He came down for breakfast but felt miserable enough that Eleanor sent him back to bed for more sleep. When he awoke next it was early afternoon. He felt peaked but improved. He dressed and came down to find the house empty. On the kitchen table was a note:

Went out to the library and for an errand. Soup is simmering for tonight. Will be home before five. Hope you are better and if you are, don't forget to vote.

Love, Eleanor.

Well he was better, so he put on a light coat and left for the courthouse. The day was still with low, gloomy clouds, and the chill reminded everyone winter was on the way. He could see workmen with picks and spades digging on the sidewalk and street in front of the Rutland Free Library so he cut around north past the First Congregational churchyard and went in by the courthouse back door as he had for thirty-seven years. In the lobby were two voting booths, each sporting a burlap curtain. Men chatted while waiting for their turn to step in and mark their ballot. Clerk of Courts Tom Cockburn was there with his inevitable mug of hot tea checking off voters on the voter rolls.

"How are you, Calvin?" he asked after a sip. "Oh, sign on this line here," he added, pointing to a spot in the ledger.

"Well, better Tom, thank you," Calvin answered as he signed his name. "Eleanor's been keeping me in tea and toast the last few days and it's finally done the trick."

"Ah, it's the tea," Tom chuckled.

Calvin waggled his eyebrows at him and joshed with him as they had for years. "Coffee, Tom. Coffee is American. Tea is too British. That's what made it easier to dump the tea in Boston harbor. We didn't want it anymore."

"Ha! But this tea is not political or I couldn't work here today. Besides, like you just said, it's the tea that got you down here to vote."

"Touché, Tom," Calvin said with a chuckle.

As they exchanged smiles, a ruckus arose behind Calvin. Josiah Trimble had come to the head of the line of voters waiting for booth number one when the burlap curtain pulled back and Ashton Melo stepped out and held the curtain for Josiah. Trimble had been earnestly campaigning in line with GAR post commander John Franklin and a middle-aged grocer behind him and hadn't noticed Ashton come in.

Dumbstruck by Ashton's appearance, he stood still, debate written on his face whether to enter a booth that had just been used by a colored man.

"Oh, for heaven's sake," Commander Franklin growled, stepping forward. As he passed Josiah, he said to him, "Officers to the front as an example to the men." Franklin nodded to Ashton and said, "Thank you," and stepped inside. Ashton gave Trimble a sidelong look and moved on to the ballot box.

Calvin waited his turn and then carefully but reluctantly marked his ballot for Mr. Taft. In a nostalgic mood, he went up to the second floor and stopped by his old door. He could still faintly smell the aroma of the leather law books and the linseed oil on the wood panels. He meandered to the big second floor window in the hall that looked out over the small park across the street.

From here the Union soldier statue was almost eye level, slightly greenish. He let his eyes linger for a moment, remembering the statue's face, but a lump rose in his throat so he looked down. At the foot of the front steps was a double line of white-hatted, white dressed women walking back and forth with signs. As he looked one made the turn and he could make out the words on the sign: "Port Royal Woman for the Women's Vote." Startled, he hurried back down the stairs and out through the front doors.

"Eleanor!" he stammered, then stumbled a bit sideways as he realized she was not going to stop walking while he talked to her. "I ah, well, is this…um, I see. This must be the errand you had."

"Yes it is, Calvin," she nodded. "Did you vote already?"

"Ayup, I did."

"I would have liked to also. And these young ladies deserve that voice."

"You tell him, Mrs. Salisbury!" came several voices from the moving line.

"But Eleanor… Ellie. This is so, I mean, I didn't think it was so important to you."

Eleanor shouldered her sign with a new determination as she made the turn at the end of the line. Ashton Melo and Randolph the barber came down the steps from inside. Both colored men tipped their hats to the ladies. "Fifteenth Amendment for us," Ashton called to the marchers. "You deserve your own." The marchers waved handkerchiefs and called back their thanks.

"I've decided it is, Calvin," Eleanor said. "Port Royal was important to the free folk, and this is just as important for women everywhere. And…" She swallowed hard. "I'm doing this in honor of Amanda. It's just the sort of thing she'd do and expect us to do." Calvin stopped walking as Eleanor went on. He knew it was settled. He thought briefly, then called after her, "I'll be right back."

He went back inside and found Tom Cockburn's table was quiet for the moment. He took Tom aside and they went down to Tom's office. Calvin warmly shook Tom's hand, then took Tom's spare mug and a packet from

Tom's collection with him to the men's washroom. He ran the left faucet until it whistled and steam rose from the basin. Then he filled the mug and dropped in the packet. A minute later he realized he didn't have a spoon, so he used a pencil to fish out the tea bag. Back outside he came up to Eleanor shyly and held out the mug to her.

"It's chilly this afternoon. I think a capable woman like you can carry a picket sign in one hand and a mug of tea in the other while marching."

"Yes I can. Thank you, you dear man." Calvin blushed. "I'll see you at home."

Wednesdsay, January 1, 1913

Rutland

New Year's morning, Eleanor paced the floors, not from the cold seeping in, but from nerves. Calvin heard her quietly trying out passages from her notes, and he offered to be her audience. "No, but thank you, Calvin." She muttered things like "fifty years is such a milestone" and "why would they want to hear from me of all people? Don't their own preachers have enough to say?" Later as she fussed in the kitchen, she stopped once and exclaimed, "Oh, I wish I'd never said yes."

"I'm sure you'll do fine," Calvin answered for about the tenth time. "But I admit it's odd. Going to church midday on a Wednesday would throw off a lot of people, let alone this kind of church. It won't be Presbyterian, that's for sure."

"Read me something from the paper," Eleanor asked. "Maybe it will distract me." Calvin picked up the *Herald*. "All right. Here's '1912, A Year in Review.' In April the Titanic sank with loss of 1,500 lives."

Eleanor glared and Calvin gulped. "Ah, well, um. Here. Mr. Thomas Ince began competing with Mr. D.W. Griffith in filming the longest motion picture ever made, over an hour in length. Both are working on separate stories of American history."

Calvin read a few more as Eleanor got dinner on the table. What seemed to help Ellie the most was when he read her from the third page an Emancipation poem from James Weldon Johnson of Florida, which opened with the lines,

> *O BROTHERS mine, to-day we stand*
> *Where half a century sweeps our ken,*
> *Since God, through Lincoln's ready hand,*
> *Struck off our bonds and made us men.*
>
> *Just fifty years – a winter's day –*
> *As runs the history of a race;*
> *Yet, as we look back o'er the way,*
> *How distant seems our starting place!*

"Careful down the steps, Ellie," Calvin cautioned as they started off their porch about a quarter past twelve. "Thank you, Calvin," she answered, grateful for his arm. The temperature at Christmas had been twelve below, so sixteen above today felt almost comfortable. They made their way down the walk between hip-deep ridges of snow to the corner streetcar stop.

When the car pulled up and the conductor sold them their tickets, they could see the seats were packed; a steamy, huddled mass of people yearning for more heat from the coal stove in the middle of the car. The conductor's glare fell on an old colored woman and a younger man who could be her son. Calvin and Eleanor looked at each other quickly and Calvin said to the conductor, "No need for seats, sir. Eleanor and I prefer to stand."

The conductor peered at Eleanor, who nodded firmly. He looked again at the sitting pair and said to Calvin, "There is a court ruling…"

"…As a former judge I can tell you that ruling is wrong," Calvin snapped. The old lady beamed as the conductor looked puzzled. The colored man stood up and tipped his hat to the Salisburys, gestured to his seat and said, "That ruling was indeed wrong, but it's only proper for a gentleman to give a lady his seat." The conductor shook his head and walked away as Eleanor smiled her thanks and sat down.

It took several stops in town and across the valley until Calvin and Eleanor stepped off at Marble Street in West Rutland. Two blocks walking into the wind brought them to a bundled-up usher working as a doorman. "Come on in out of the cold," he said through his scarf.

Their glasses fogged up immediately, so they had to feel their way forward from the doors. From the mist a familiar voice said, "Calvin. Eleanor. Glad you made it. "

"Is that you, Sam?" Calvin answered.

"It is," Sam replied. "Here, Eleanor, try this on your glasses" he added, pressing a handkerchief into her hand.

"Thank you, Sam," she said, stopping and wiping them clear. "That's better." Calvin had wiped off his own foggy spectacles. He shook hands and said, "Happy New Year, Sam," while helping Eleanor out of her wraps.

"There's a couple empty hooks on the wall over here," Sam said, taking their coats. "Allow me." The Salisburys' coats hung down next to a white cardboard bucket holding coins and bills marked, "Gettysburg for our veterans."

"Thank you, Sam. That's very kind." Conversation around them took a happy bounce as folks noted Calvin's uniform. Sam came back, looking equally dapper in his sergeant's dress blues. Calvin saw several other members of the Stannard GAR post and nodded to them. Eleanor said, "You go ahead, Calvin. I need to find the other ladies. I'll see you inside."

"Good luck, Ellie. Remember, be ready for anything." She gave him a tight smile and fidgeted pulling on her white gloves.

Ashton Melo came over beaming and said, "Calvin, let's all meet ovah there with the rest of the men. We knew Commander Franklin was visiting family in Maine, but this note," and here Ashton's face hardened, "came from Josiah. As ranking officer, I guess you're on for some speaking."

Calvin opened the heavy linen paper embossed with a large "JT."

> *I feel I must decline the duty of speaking today. It is quite unlikely the church in question will offer the dignity and solemnity of a proper worship service of the Almighty. —Josiah Trimble*

Calvin looked at Ashton sideways as he and Sam joined the other GAR men. So Josiah Trimble had decided to stay away. Not unexpected, but it rankled, almost like dereliction of duty. Calvin only half-listened as Ashton ran down the order of service. He wrestled with his annoyance while he thought about his remarks and scratched down a word or two on an old envelope he found in his suit pocket. The organ inside the sanctuary swelled from a pianissimo that covered people's arrival to a stately prelude. Members and visitors surged through the inner doors to fill the pews. The Reverend Homer Stanton appeared in black ministerial robes, a gold velvet stole sewn into the front. The GAR men formed a double file and he led them in. The first three pews on the pulpit side had been reserved and as the GAR men filled them, the whispers around them turned into a low rumble.

Stanton stood at the head of the aisle and opened his arms to the congregation. "Who came today to get the Spirit? Who came today to catch the fire? Do you feel it? Do you?" He worked his way down the first pew pointing to members of his congregation. "Do you feel it?" he kept asking.

"Yes I do." "I feel it." "Amen." "Yes" came the responses. One woman stood staring at the floor and shaking visibly.

"Did you come to catch the fire, Mildred?"

"No, sir, I didn't come to catch the fire," shaking harder.

"You didn't?"

"No," lifting both hands and a face of pure joy, "because I brought the fire with me!" she shouted. The room erupted with "Amens" and "hallelujahs," applause, and random chords from the organ.

Stanton rang his voice off the rafters. "Hallelujah, hallelujah! There is no need to hold back. It is the fiftieth year since the Emancipation, the year of Jubilee. Glory to God!"

When the roar subsided by a third and everyone was seated, he called out again, "You can see in the flesh right over here," gesturing toward the veterans, "some of the men who helped make the Emancipation a liberation from Egypt. Gentlemen, won't you stand and turn around please so the people can see you and welcome you!"

They did, most looking down in Yankee modesty, hoping to sit back down as soon as possible. Most were expecting smiles and some polite nods from the congregation, the way such things were handled in their own churches. Calvin guessed Ashton's congregation might be a bit more forward and might even applaud.

They did applaud. They also stood, shouted, roared, and drummed thunder off the backs of the pews in front of them. The organist added glory from the pipes. Two or three in the choir behind the altar shook tambourines. Congregants sitting nearby offered backslaps. As Reverend Stanton moved toward them with his hand out, dozens of his flock exited from their pews and surged around the front three pews on the pulpit side. Shouts of "Glory," "Amen," "Thank you, thank you," "Praise the Lord," "Lincoln Soldiers," crossed over each other. Ashton Melo was a particular favorite. The Stannard Post men grinned like bridegrooms at their own reception.

"Great God Almighty," Sam yelled in Calvin's ear, catching their spirit. Wide-eyed at the raucous reception and startled by Sam, Calvin called back, "Amen!"

When the enthusiasm ebbed and people were drifing back toward their seats, Reverend Stanton held up his hand. "Hold on. We're not done yet! Not for a Year of Jubilee! Not only do we have the GAR men here today, but four other honored guests." He gestured to a short side pew facing the altar at a right angle. Typically Stanton, a deacon, and an acolyte or two perched here but not today. "We also have four lady veterans here," indicating Eleanor and three other well-aged women. "Not soldier men, and not in uniform, but veterans all the same. These are four ladies of the Port Royal Experiment who taught the freemen, the freewomen, the children of Israel how to read and write and figure."

A gasp ran over the congregation, followed by renewed applause and shouting. The choir was particularly enthusiastic and the organist pulled out all the stops. Calvin blinked back his pride as the GAR men joined the applause and were first out of their pews to shake hands with the women. The congregation followed with an odd, loud tenderness. Instead of backslaps, the ladies received two-handed handshakes and embraces from the women. But the quartet was most moved by the old men who simply shook hands and said a gentle, tear-streaked "thank you." When all had offered thanks and praise, the building shook with the revival hymn, "Blow, Trumpet, Blow."

A bit later, Calvin offered remarks for the GAR men. He was nervous at the mishmash of thoughts and half-remembered phrases. He read from his hasty notes until the room was almost verdict quiet and then said, "Ours was a generation called to duty and country. But the Almighty had a greater aim in mind, which was brought to flower by President Lincoln."

Reverend Stanton took a chance Calvin would not be thrown off stride and called out a soft but clear, "Brother, preach it." Startled, Calvin looked up at Stanton and pulled off his glasses. From the second pew Sam called out, "Preach, Calvin." "You can do it, Judge" someone said, and Calvin nodded.

"You're right," Calvin announced. "It's not my courtroom, it's a church. And a church needs preaching." Eleanor put her hand over mouth in shock as "amens" rocked the room. "Let's do this together," he shouted. Eleanor stared at him, wondering what had happened to her precise judge of a husband.

"Ours would be more than a struggle for Union. ("O yes!") Ours would be a fight for liberty, ("That's right!") for the promise of freedom. ("Say it, brotha.") We were touched by God's fire ("Amen!" Mildred hollered from the front pew) to win freedom for all Americans. ("Glory, he's got it now"). The challenge remains to make that freedom real for all Americans, regardless of color ("All right!") Can the rule of law prove stronger than the lynch rope? ("Yes it can.") Can life, liberty and the pursuit of happiness overcome prejudice and segregation? ("Yes, Lord, make it so!")

"The days are fading for the men of Lincoln's army. But the challenge does not fade. ("That's right.") Will you make Mr. Lincoln's Emancipation a full one? ("Preach it, brotha!") Will you make Mr. Jefferson's promise come true?"

It was not a speech Josiah Trimble would have made.

Eleanor had a sweet, light voice but between her age and nerves it lost power. People strained to listen, but her words faded past the fifth pew or so. Homer Stanton nodded to his wife Dahlia. She came up into the pulpit and said, "Mrs. Salisbury, I'm here to help you."

Eleanor blushed, feeling ashamed.

"Now, don't fret. It's just you've got the willies and your manners."

"I beg your pardon?"

"Mrs. Salisbury. would you take off your gloves?"

"My gloves?"

"Yes, your gloves. I'll hold 'em for you." As Eleanor pulled them off and gave them over, Dahlia continued. "You see, Mrs. Salisbury... Eleanor...these gloves and fancy manners are for tea with ladies and for lookin' glasses in theater boxes. But while you're here at our church I'll hold those gloves and manners for you."

Eleanor nodded rather numbly but gulped in relief. Dahlia nodded toward the back of the church. "Now, do you see that green hat on the lady in the last pew? That's Iris Young. That's her pew for at least forty years. Now you tell your story to Iris in a bold voice from here. Just her. The rest of us'll listen in. I'll hold your willies, your gloves, and your lady manners and give them all back to you when you go home. Oh, and by the way, Iris is a little hard of hearing."

"I am not," came Iris's sharp reply, igniting a round of laughter. Eleanor took a deep breath and began again. She was surprised how much Dahlia had helped.

"My friend Amanda Fairchild," Eleanor swallowed, "was our superintendress. She was a determined, even fearless, woman. In January 1865, General Sherman visited Port Royal from Savannah. Everyone was very excited and a little afraid. But when he came into our house and sat down, Amanda immediately said, 'General Sherman, how good of you to come. You are just the man we want to see.' We all saw he was a bit surprised."

A chuckle ran around the sanctuary at the image of the fearsome Sherman being nervous. Eleanor saw only soft and supporting eyes, and the laughter was with her, not at her. She relaxed a notch and Dahlia whispered, "Keep goin'. You're doin' good."

"The general said, 'What can I do for you?'"

"Amanda piped up, 'General, what will your men do after the War?'"

"Why, they'll go home to their families. Many of them will farm or work in their shops. Some may go west and homestead."

"Then Amanda said, 'General, here live thousands of newly freed people, eager to learn, and ready to work for themselves. But where? They have no farm, no shop, no land, no means to go west to homestead. Something practical needs to be done and right here, General.'"

Port Royal memories crowded Eleanor's mind. Dahlia whispered, "Now you got it."

"As the general ruminated, Miss Anna Louise took courage and added, 'All this plantation land lies fallow. The freed men could work it for themselves, feed their families.' When General Sherman got back to Savannah he instructed plantation land be broken up and given to the free folk to work and feed their families. He called it Special Field Order 15, but when we read it we thought he was quoting Amanda and Anna Louise."

"Amen!" Dahlia burst out, and the room echoed in reply, with "Order 15!" being repeated frequently. Eleanor saw Calvin's eyes shining. Understanding flared in her mind. This was not just her story but the congregation's story. Her voice flexed with confidence and an old spirit blew on the embers of her soul.

"Amanda was a very determined woman and her students knew it. We teachers knew it. The officers and men at Port Royal knew it too. To overcome ignorance and prejudice took Amanda's kind of determination."

"Take your time, sistah," Dahlia said. Eleanor looked around, her eyes sweeping the room in Vermont, her mind on the South Carolina coast fifty years ago. The organist began fingering chords very softly under Eleanor's voice and she unconsciously raised her volume.

"We taught the ABCs, numbers, writing, and reading. We taught in the mannings, afternoons, evenings. We taught in rooms, in a barn, under the trees. We taught by daylight, firelight, and lamplight. We taught until Amanda ordered us to sleep, so eager were the free people to learn." ("That's right" someone called.) She felt what had gripped Calvin.

"As the men of the Union army stood shoulder to shoulder facing the worst, so did Amanda, and," she turned and gestured to the bench behind her, "Anna Louise McCloud, Priscilla Martin, Katherine Stone and I." The glimpse of Anna Louise beaming carried Eleanor like a wave.

"We did not face bullets or shells or the sword. But we faced a people whom the slave owners had tried to destroy in spirit." The soft chords from the organ went into a minor key. "We faced some of the bitterness the lash had driven into their backs." Certain faces in the pews winced. "We faced despair because these gentle people had been taught with terrible force that they were of no account, inferior, worthless, and dangerous.

"Bit by bit we gained our battle. ("Now you're talkin'!") Little by little they began to believe they were safe in Port Royal and it was safe to learn, and not just book learning. People learned to look each other in the eye. They comforted one another as they told of plantation life. They rejoiced over their chance to be men and women and free." ("Speakin' truth now.")

The congregation saw this small woman with the carefully wound white hair and wrinkled cheeks take on a certain air. The flame rose in her heart and gleamed through her eyes. They could well believe this sweet but steely-eyed woman could teach with compassion, and teach dignity and respect by her very bearing.

"I remember one day an old, old woman so bent with age she could hardly walk came up to Anna Louise. With a shaky scrawl she wrote out the whole alphabet on the blackboard. Then she wrote P-E-R-L. She turned around with tears on her face and said, 'That's me. That's my name. I'm Pearl. I can write my name!' And then she fell down dead."

The congregation needed a moment to recover. Calvin's heart and eyes overflowed.

"I remember the young colored men at Port Royal who wanted to be soldiers. ("Hear the call.") Fifty years ago today, the men who wanted were sworn in. ("God's glory!") Sergeants drilled them by day with rifles, and we drilled them by night with books. Between the two, they drilled for war and for peace. Some of them were buried up the Carolina coast at Battery Wagner. The rebels took their rifles, but they buried them with their spelling books. ("Free in glory!")

"Now the War is long over. Except for parades the veterans no longer march. Yet ignorance and prejudice are still alive. I hope what the women of the Port Royal Experiment did is still marching across our land and among free people everywhere. Thank you, and congratulations on the year of Jubilee."

Dahlia threw her arms around a shocked Eleanor. Rejoicing rattled the windows as the organ swelled with jubilation. Eleanor even saw one old GAR vet standing in the aisle, wild with clapping and tears on his cheeks. She looked twice, but yes, it was Calvin. Applause crashed as Eleanor tried to retreat to her bench, but Reverend Stanton waved the four to the front so they could all be seen and honored. They nodded and smiled shyly and exchanged warm looks. As the applause finally dropped off, green-hatted Iris Young, clutching a handkerchief, came up to them, turned and waved for quiet. In a cracked voice she called out, "All together now," and began singing, "A-B-C-D-E-F-G." For perhaps its only time, the "Alphabet Song" of school children was sung in church harmony and with brimming eyes.

Friday, March 21, 1913

Montpelier

Both the anteroom and the gray-suited secretary himself gave off an air of hard, New England formality. The furniture was whitewashed or black, all right angles down to the matched, black-bound books on every shelf. Calvin flicked an imagined bit of lint. A fourth look at his pocket watch showed only two more minutes had passed. He uncrossed his legs, then crossed them the other way. The bench was first cousin to a church pew.

All those letters to legislators in the fall had been one thing, he thought to himself. Those three trips here to Montpelier to share whiskey with legislators who should have just passed that bill as they finally did in January – well, he felt queasy just looking back. But this afternoon, this was a march in the wilderness under Grant, thickets everywhere and dangerous.

Several blocks away, Eleanor and Anna Louise were reveling in the crisp sunshine that at least looked like spring even if the temperature was still near freezing. Unlike nearly all the scurrying ladies on the sidewalks, these two were talking, laughing, and simply wandering in town and in each other's company. They stopped at a corner newsstand, chuckling, and idly scanned the afternoon edition.

"Wait," Eleanor said. "Look at this."

She thrust the paper at Anna Louise while quickly producing a nickel for the shivering man in the booth. They both read through the story. Anna Louise spotted a church clock and then said, "If we hurry we can get there just in time." They went off for the office as fast as ground-length skirts and interior layers allowed.

Just beyond the secretary, one of the pairs of tall doors to Calvin's right opened and a portly gentleman in a brown suit carrying a gold-topped cane waddled through. He noticed Calvin briefly, then said to the secretary in a deep bass voice, "Good day to you." Calvin saw from his walk that the man's fancy cane was only for show. But he made well-practiced use of his chestnut cane as the secretary came out saying, "The governor will see you now."

Calvin walked deliberately through the door telling himself, "Treat it like a big case," trying to summon up his judicial dignity. As the secretary announced him, he was able to say in a fairly confident tone, "A pleasure to meet you, Governor." Allen Fletcher dismissed his secretary saying, "Thank you, Williams."

"Judge Salisbury, please sit down." The governor indicated a matching pair of leather chairs angled toward a low round table. Calvin sat as the governor went to a sideboard cabinet, opened a door and pulled out two cut-glass tumblers and a flask.

"I always need a drink after dealing with a man like Smathers," the governor said. "The whiskey gets the taste of him out of my mouth." Pouring himself about a quarter of a glass he asked, "Would you like to join me?"

Calvin thought sharing a drink might set a good tone, but he paused for his reputation. Guessing the reason, Fletcher smiled broadly and said, "'Sober as a judge', eh? But then, you're retired, and some things in this office really can remain a secret." Calvin smiled and nodded, and the governor poured.

Sitting down, the governor toasted, "To good government." He threw back his drink with a single gulp. Calvin returned the salute but only sipped.

"What can I do for you, Judge?" Fletcher asked in a down-to-business tone.

Calvin began as he had rehearsed. "Governor Fletcher, Vermont has about 1,400 living vet'rans of the Civil War. All of them have been invited to the Encampment at Gettysbaag this July. The State of Vermont voted to pay their way to Pennsylvania."

The governor nodded. "The bill passed unanimously in both houses. I was very proud to sign it. January eleventh was a great day for Vermont." He raised an eyebrow. "I understand a certain retired judge from Rutland was very effective lobbying the legislators over whiskey." The governor poured himself another drink and offered to freshen Calvin's, but he declined.

"The appropriation makes sure all of you will be going," Fletcher added, waiting.

Calvin picked up his cue. "All going, Governor, but not all welcome. Thousands are coming nationwide and I'm looking forward to it very much. But there are about 150 Vermont men who could go but can't."

"Judge, the U.S. Army is hard at work building a tent city at Gettysburg, complete with water fountains, kitchens, infirmary tents, and even electric lights. There will be entertainers, opera singers, and speeches from governors and old commanders. I just got a letter last week saying they are expecting over forty thousand veterans, maybe fifty thousand, and at least that many civilians every day. I expect most of them will be there to see something historic, to see if you veterans say it's all right to live in peace. If the army is getting ready to handle that many I'm sure 150 more won't be any trouble. I'm sure there'll be room for everyone."

"Room, yes, governor, but not welcome. The army is keeping us on tenterhooks but it's very doubtful any of the Union Colored troops – including

Vermont's 150 – will be accommodated at Tent City. Very likely only white veterans will be welcome. I would imagine colored civilians might only be tolerated if they are servants, cooks, wagon drivers, and such."

The governor's eyes narrowed. Fletcher was the son of abolitionists and was distantly related to William Lloyd Garrison himself. He took a thoughtful sip. "Thank you for telling me this." He looked off a minute and mused. "Last week I went to Auburn, New York, for Harriet Tubman's funeral. It was full military honors and she was buried in a Union uniform. This is the sort of thing she fought against her whole life, so…" he mused. Then he went on, "I guess it's time for us to pick up the torch and carry on. Do you think an appeal from a governor to the army might make a difference?"

"I doubt it, Governor," Calvin replied. "Quite a few Southern politicians and the UCV, the Confederate veterans group, have made it plain they won't attend unless colored troops are banned. Since the whole point of this Encampment is reunion between the sections, it's a serious issue." As Fletcher absorbed this, Calvin added, "Since Inauguration Day, the army has been taking orders from the new president, and Mr. Wilson is not going to disappoint his friends and relatives in Virginia."

"And points south," Fletcher added. "All true, Judge. How can I help?"

Calvin tossed off the rest of his drink with a flourish he'd learned in the Army of the Potomac, hoping his manly gesture might impress Fletcher. It did earn him a refill.

"There's a plan afoot, governor. When word came that the Encampment might be 'whites only' we held a meeting last fall. The GAR New England district commander, vice commander, and most of the post commanders all met in Boston at the post down the street from the Robert Gould Shaw Memorial."

"My wife and I saw St. Gaudan's statue last summer," Fletcher interjected. "Magnificent monument!" he mused. Calvin plowed on.

"We drew up two plans. First was a series of petitions and a letter-writing campaign, which has cut no ice with the army. So now we have a second plan. The U.S. Army's Tent City for the white veterans will be set up *southwest* of Gettysbaag on Seminary Ridge and along the Emmitsbaag Road. We are organizing a camp *east* of town near Culp's Hill for the colored men. Two farmers will rent us the land, but the army won't help us with supplies.

"This week we're asking the New England governors and you as commander of the Vermont National Guard, if you will issue an order allowing the GAR to borrow the militia's – I mean, the National Guard's – tents for the occasion?"

Governor Fletcher blinked. "Interesting idea, Judge." He smiled a moment. "All the New England governors in the same week? An excellent bit of military planning. If we all issue such orders, they would have a place and tents. But what about food? Water? Getting in and out of Gettysburg? Would there be someone to protect them from some of the fire eaters from down South?"

"The plans aren't finished yet, Governor, but so far 'Camp Lincoln' will have Rock Creek for water. GAR posts across the North have furnished funds for plank streets and at least a few electric lights. We think enough of the colored folks in and near Gettysbaag have wagons and buggies to help move men around. I admit the food and medical care still have us stumped. But what do you think about the tents, Governor?"

In the anteroom, Williams the secretary looked up to see two finely dressed women at his desk, both a bit breathless. He wondered what could leave such elderly women so winded. "May I help you?" he said in his official tone.

"Yes," one of them panted. "My husband, Judge Calvin Salisbury, is meeting with Governor Fletcher right now and I must speak to him this moment."

"The governor appointments are private and he cannot be disturbed."

"Sir, you don't understand," the other woman said crisply. "We have new information that bears directly on the governor's appointment with Judge Salisbury."

Williams was unimpressed as he stood up. "If the governor needs information of a political or any other character I'm quite sure a man can provide him with it. Now ladies, I bid you good day."

Both Eleanor and Anna Louise looked to the tall double doors straight ahead, Williams at his desk to their left. Williams blinked in surprise, then moved left to come around his desk to block them. Anna Louise stepped forward and turned to meet him in the little aisle between his desk and the bookcase. Her right hand came up to gesture at Williams as she began to say, "Now, Mr. Williams," but her left fluttered down to her hip and she gave Eleanor a discreet wave ahead. Eleanor strode to the door as Williams sputtered, "Now, see here. Just a moment. You can't go in there." He retreated and moved to circle his desk the opposite way. "Stop." Eleanor turned the handle and went in.

The governor and the judge started, then rose in surprise. Calvin stammered, "Ellie, um, I ah. Governor Fletcher, may I present my wife Eleanor?"

Still surprised, Fletcher said, "I'm delighted," and offered his hand.

Eleanor placed the newspaper in it and said, "Governor Fletcher, the Secretary of the Army has had decided officially, as you can see here in the afternoon edition."

Fletcher had just time to read "Secretary of the Army declares Gettysburg encampment to be for white veterans only," when the combined commotion of Anna Louise and Williams burst through the door.

"Now, you can't go in there, either. Please leave at once. I'm sorry, Governor,," panted an exasperated Mr. Williams. "They both got by me."

Meanwhile, Anna Louise was already making herself at home, and commented sweetly, "What a handsome office, Governor. Very manly, yet approachable."

Fletcher saw Eleanor's poise, Williams' embarrassment, and Anna Louise's confidence. He looked at Anna Louise closely and seemed to recognize her. He broke into a great laugh which stopped everyone. "I'll wager a twenty-dollar gold piece one of you women was at Port Royal."

"Better pay forty, Governor," Eleanor answered, laughing. "We both were."

Still laughing, Fletcher turned to Anna Louise and said, "You are delightfully attractive in person, madam. Your arrest picture in the paper from Election Day along with the other suffragettes did not do you justice." He bowed gallantly and Anna Louise beamed back while Eleanor and Calvin exchanged amazed glances.

Fletcher turned to Calvin. "I'll get on this right away." He began escorting them all toward the doors as he said, "Williams, you do a wonderful job fending off legislators and the press and I'm very grateful for your work. But against these women – you never had a chance! But don't feel bad. Neither did General Sherman, so you're in good company."

As Calvin, Eleanor, and Anna Louise went down the hall they heard Fletcher say, "Now Williams, send a messenger to the National Guard armory. I want to see the quartermaster still today, and have him bring along an equipment inventory. After that, go down to the telephone room and put through a call from me to Boston to Governor Foss. Let me know when the call is ready."

At Anna Louise's house that night they offered up two toasts with wine. One was in memory of Harriet Tubman, with a prayer that the flame of her cause would be picked up by someone else. Then they toasted the governor with hearty cheers followed by the full tale of the suffragettes and the police in Montpelier from last November.

Saturday, April 12, 1913

Savannah

"I'd like to thank Miz Gordon for her remarks tonight." Robert Bidwell's voice was drowned in Longstreet Post UCV applause. General Gordon's widow was definitely a feather in the cap of any United Confederate Veteran post. "While we're applaudin', let's pass on some o' that to the dear ladies of the UDC who arranged tonight's wonderful banquet."

Scraping chairs, hand claps, and whistles summoned Pauline, Emily, Juliette Low, and several others out from behind the dessert table. Usually, regimental events were clubby men's affairs with average food but heavy on whiskey and cigars. But this Fort Sumter Day, the UDC treated the men and families in Savannah's DeSoto Hotel ballroom. The hotel served supper and the UDC brought cobblers, puddings, and pies.

"Now I'd ask Miz Libby Pocklington to come forward," Bob said as everyone sat down. The heavyset wife of the electric company's president rose at the head table. She sported a pleated blouse, a heavy pearl necklace, and a medium blue hat with a long feather. Despite her impressive air tonight she was easily tongue-tied before a crowd. She couldn't read her writing until she pinned her note – and her hand – to the little podium.

"The UDC Savannah chaptah has worked hard fo' the last nine months with the aim of helpin' veterans attend the Encampment at Gettysburg." A round of applause encouraged her. "The Central of Georgia, the Atlantic Coast Line, and the Norfolk & Southern are giving reduced fares through states not paying vet'rans' fares. Virginia, Maryland, an' Pennsylvania are payin' fo' all vet'rans travelin' in their borders, so it was up to us to get our boys from here to Virginia."

More applause followed, and a couple wags raised the old Northern battle cry, "On to Richmond," with a friendlier intent than McClellan, Hooker, or McDowell had.

"We asked fo' donations at the Fourth of July parade and kissin' booth, and the Labor Day parade. At the New Year's gala ratt in this ballroom we had a Dime Dance. We held bake sales at our churches and tonight you've been tasting some of the recipes. Finally, some private donations and grants from some businesses make it possible for me to say: The UDC Savannah Chapter is pleased and proud to fund the rail fare to Gettysburg this summer for every Savannah veteran!"

Applause boomed and the men beat the tables so the glasses danced. The Rebel yell added to the din. Dooley Culpepper stood on his chair clapping while Turner Hawkins sat grinning in tears. Zachariah clapped toward Lee and then toward Emily. She beamed at him and he stood. Then very gallantly he put his right arm across his belly and bowed. As he came up and caught her eye, he blew her a kiss, carried over the applause by a chorus of female "aws" and "how sweets." For a moment Emily regretted she and Lee had decided not to vacation in Gettysburg that summer. When her father could be this noble... but then Zack turned back to the table and took a long pull from his "ZH" pewter flask. Emily's eyes and smile dimmed.

Zachariah looked around tight-throated at some of the impoverished men. No way could Jim Calhoun have attended. He'd probably have to ask the post treasury for meal money but at least he could go. Dooley too would have had to stay home, although Zachariah had a hunch Dooley might have tried sneaking rides in boxcars.

As the banquet broke up, men buzzed over the news that maybe forty thousand veterans would be coming to Gettysburg, matched by a like number of civilians every day. While it looked like the Union men would outnumber the Johnny Rebs by about two to one, the men jibed, "We whipped 'em down three to one in General Lee's army. Two to one for handshakin' ought to be easy." Indeed, the thought of so many men willing to come from across the country tightened many throats of all ages across the room.

Lee and Emily were about to set out for home with Zachariah when he stopped Robert Bidwell by the door and made an offer. The post treasury would make a gift to Jim Calhoun, but it would also receive a contribution from Zachariah Hampton. Fifty cents was in cash, and the other $6.50 was deducted from the UDC funds for Zachariah's travel. Bidwell thanked him and then asked, "Why $6.50 in rail fare?"

"From thirty-six years of conductin' fo' the Central of Georgia," Zachariah answered. "They don't pay pensions, but I've got a lifetime pass in the state, like from here to Augusta."

"Thanks, Zack," Bidwell answered warmly. "I'll keep it quiet from Jim."

"Much 'bliged," Zachariah answered. "Okay, let's head home," he said to Emily and. Both father and daughter were in a crosscurrent feelings that Lee noticed left them both unusually quiet.

Saturday, June 28, 1913

Rutland

Calvin and Sam grinned like boys on Christmas morning, shaking their heads in wonder. Sam looked positively dazed, staring woodenly out their train compartment window. The Governor's Special had chuffed out of Rutland over Otter Creek, and was pulling up the first ridge west toward Albany.

That morning, Rutland's churches held a combined worship service. Eleanor, Calvin, Sam, and Ashton weren't alone finding it odd worshipping on a Saturday, and odd again entering the hulking First Congregational Church behind the Rutland Free Library, but space was needed. The scale of the place awed Eleanor and she was equally amazed that Father Mason of St. John's Catholic was present. Next to the plain-suited Protestant clergy, his green-and-white chasuble struck her as gaudy, and yet its cheeriness seemed attractive. Then too, his easy smile and delightful prayer partway through the service had a joyful quality to them that...well, she had to admit a certain attraction despite his being utterly Catholic.

The end of the Service of Godspeed had marked the change from peculiar to fervent. Fifty-seven Union men, freshly barbered (free haircuts, Rutland's barbers had agreed), hats at their sides, massed themselves shoulder to shoulder between the chancel and the front pews. The chock-full congregation, jammed into the wrap-around balcony, sitting on spare chairs, and standing across the side aisles, looked on in solemn expectation.

It had been a formal New England service, done with smart precision. Rutland's clergy had parceled out speaking parts and been commendably brief. Now they spread across the chancel ready to raise their hands over the men. Reverend Homer Stanton would lead the closing blessing.

Homer looked out on the massed Vermonters, milky skinned except here and there with members of Free Baptist like Dahlia and Ashton. He saw their love for these men, their respect and pride at odds with New England decorum. He locked eyes briefly with Eleanor, and in that instant she remembered a much younger Calvin, wavy auburn hair and grizzly, patchy beard, blinking back tears as he and his brother Michael had boarded the train to the War. Love and determination passed across his face while his eyes showed that delight in life she had loved and married. She wished she could see Calvin's eyes now.

As arranged, Stanton intoned, "Let us bless these men on their journey." The ministers raised their hands over the men, palms prominent, to bestow the blessing on behalf of the people. Across the sanctuary, heads bowed and numerous women and men took the moment to wipe away a tear. Abigail Trimble sobbed openly and Eleanor almost joined in.

Homer began, "People of Rutland." Heads raised up in some surprise. "You are the ones who sent these men off over fifty years ago. You sent them to answer their country's call to save the Union. But God called them through President Lincoln and gave them a greater cause. Not only would the Union be saved, but liberty would be advanced. Not knowing it, but God knowing it, you sent these men to make freedom ring in places where freedom had not rung before.

"So first, men of the clergy, let us bless the people." Fifty-seven old hearts jumped into the veterans' throats as Stanton's blessing rose past them and broke over the congregation. "May God almighty grant you blessing for sending forth these men. May He comfort and console you who saw that some did not come back." Calvin bit his lower lip. "And may He grant honor to such a people who would send out these men in such a righteous cause. Men of the clergy, let the people be blessed."

They answered with dignity, "Let the people be blessed."

"And now," Homer went on, "let this blesséd people come forward and bless these men. You blesséd people in the front pew, reach forward now, and put your hand on these men in blue." Rutland's Mayor Howe and the other front pew dignitaries squirmed. After all, for New Englanders touching a stranger other than a handshake was crossing some sort of line. But they did it. Homer continued.

"And now, since rest of you cannot reach these men, just reach forward with your right hand and take hold of the shoulder ahead of you." A soft buzz arose and Eleanor looked around nervously. She caught sight of Dahlia and remembered New Year's Day.

"Go on, that's right." With a deep breath she handed off her nerves and put her right hand on the dark brown, suited shoulder ahead of her.

"Touch someone who up here is touching a man in blue." She felt a handkerchief and then fingers gently light on her own shoulder.

Homer wasn't finished. "Now go ahead, with your left hand, go on now, and put it on a shoulder to your left." As she reached left Eleanor smiled to her right, reassuring the bespectacled and blushing teenage girl in the emerald green dress. "It's all right," she whispered. A nervous obedience gripped the congregation. "That's right, go ahead."

"And now!" Homer roared, "Now that the blessed people are all in union with these men and in union with one another," he lifted his arms, "Great God almighty, let your blessing for safe travel, your blessing for reunion with comrades, your blessing for surprises from old friends, your blessing for surprises from old enemies, your blessing for good health, your blessing for the joyful return of these men to their homes, Lord almighty, let that blessing flow from your great white throne, through your blessed people, upon these veterans as they go to the Encampment in Gettysburg." After a lush, heart-pounding, throat-catching, tear-streaked pause, Homer asked, "Can I get an 'Amen' on that?" Even for a bunch of proper, stoic New Englanders, Homer was impressed.

A pumper truck and a hook-and-ladder led the way, the smoke eaters on board cranking the sirens about every half block. A color guard sporting the national standard, Vermont's ensign, three regimental flags and four GAR post flags came next. Several motorcars carried veteran's wives, including Eleanor in one marked "Port Royal Women." Finally came the block of Union veterans in good ranks. Behind them, the Rutland Fire Department band played them down the hill of Center Street from the huge steeple at First Congregational Church to the Rutland station.

Cheering Rutlanders packed sidewalks waving hands and hats. The police officers standing about every fifty feet kept busy brushing streamers and confetti from their uniforms. At the depot's main doors, wives and families were waiting to see the men off. Brass bands and pushcart vendors added to the excitement, but all the merrymaking could not fully overcome some of the worries among the crowd. Even with two years' work, was the U.S. Army up to the job of organizing, feeding, and tenting all the old vets? Could the Pennsylvania National Guard keep order among tens of thousands of spectators? Or even keep traffic moving? And where would those civilians sleep and eat?

The veterans' hearts were churning. They fairly ached to go to the Encampment, see old friends and make new friends while jawing over old battles and their old army days. The size of the army effort left them breathless but the army veto of any colored veterans made many wonder just who had won the War. Could the men from both sides live up to the official name of the gathering, the National Peace Jubilee? Could there be peace if the Johnny Rebs really believed they had never rebelled against the Constitution, never fought for slavery, and had lost to only overwhelming numbers rather than military skill? Could there be peace if the Yankees really believed they had shed their blood to save the nation, free the slaves, and destroy rebellion, if there had been no rebellion? If liberty and slavery were enemies, how could liberty and Jim Crow be friends? Such thoughts lingered at the edges of people's minds as they cheered on the boys in blue at the train station.

Caught in the excitement, several veterans publicly kissed their wives goodbye, but most of them settled for being pecked on the cheek.

Calvin and Sam were luckier than most, each getting a pair of kisses. Eleanor delivered one. Anna Louise McCloud, off the Governor's Special from

Montpelier to stay the week with Eleanor, delivered the other. Sam couldn't stop blushing, his fingers touching his cheek again and again where Anna Louise had bussed him. As the train pulled out, men waved from the windows until the last glimpse of the townsfolk disappeared around a bend.

The train was a rolling celebration. A stream of civilians poked their heads in at the compartment door offering Calvin and Sam good wishes. One was not such a stranger. Calvin looked up suddenly into the face of Allen Fletcher smiling at him.

"Judge Salisbury!" he boomed happily. "On the way at last!"

"Yes, sir, Governor," Calvin answered, a bit surprised Governor Fletcher remembered him.

Fletcher reached over from the door and shook hands with both men. He gave Calvin a knowing look and said, "From what I hear, *all* the veterans are going to be very comfortable camping around Gettysburg."

Calvin nodded, then broke into a grin as Ashton Melo's face popped up in the corridor behind Fletcher. Fletcher saw him too, turned on his politician's smile and stepped out into the swaying hallway. "Glad you're on board, Private," he said to Melo.

"Very happy to be here, sir," Ashton replied, not quite used to spontaneous greetings and handshakes from white men, even though today on board it was happening a lot.

"I'm Governor Fletcher, and I'm honored to make your acquaintance." Ashton gulped, dazed, as Fletcher added, "Why don't we head over to the club car for a drink? I'd like to hear about your service with the 54th Massachusetts." Others joined the flow and "54th Massachusetts" was repeated several times.

As Fletcher and Melo headed for the rolling saloon, Calvin heard Josiah Trimble's voice trailing after, saying "I don't know if I'll ever get used to seeing cuffie hair under a Union cap." Whoever he was talking to answered, "Well if you really can't stand it you can always get off at Albany like you did back in '64 until the Encampment's over." Trimble growled back something about grinning and bearing it. Calvin pointedly looked out the window and listened until Trimble's heavy tread passed the compartment door. The Governor's Special rolled on.

Savannah

Zachariah, Emily, and Lee sat waiting on the front porch. A packed satchel flanked Zachariah's rocker.

"How long have reunions and encampments been happenin'?" Lee asked.

"Better'n forty years," Zachariah said, decked out in his freshly pressed gray. The three gold stripes on the jacket sleeve almost glowed against the gray. "My first one was in Chawleston in 1872."

"Haven't some been with both Confederates and Yankees?" Emily asked.

"That's ratt darlin'," Zack nodded. "They's been a few at Gettysburg, Vicksburg and such, sometimes just fer gettin' together, an' sometimes fer somethin' mo'. When Ulysses Grant died, the Stonewall Jackson UCV post and the David Farragut GAR post in Norfolk held a wake together."

"What's the one you remembah most?" Lee asked.

"Atlanta, 1886," Zachariah answered immediately. "There was almost fifty thousand of us. John Gordon was campaignin' for governor an' Jeff Davis was with him. Davis was windin' up speakin' when Gen'rul Longstreet came ridin' in."

Of course, Emily thought. The old commander had to figure in somewhere. She kept herself from rolling her eyes.

"Longstreet hadn't been invited, some said, 'cause he'd been sulky at Gettysburg, some said 'cause he held coloreds should vote, but mostly 'cause he'd say we'd lost the War an' had t' live with that."

"President Davis didn't cotton to that thinking, did he?" Emily asked.

"Nope. Davis never did admit he was a beaten man so fo' years he was cool to Longstreet. Well, here he comes right up on the platform and we wondered what Davis would do. The President looked at him, looked at us, then said, 'Gen'rul Lee's old warhoss' an' threw his arms 'round him like Jacob 'n Esau. We cheered ourselves hoarse."

Hugo Ratzinger's top-down Thomas clattered around the corner and pulled up along the curb. Zachariah eyed the motorcar and wished he could take a quick drink. As all three stood and moved down the porch steps, Lee asked, "Think Gettysburg will be anything like Atlanta?"

"Don't know," Zachariah replied at the gate. "In Atlanta we were all Confederates. Don't know 'bout the Yankees." The thought made Zachariah wish for a second drink.

One more check of Zachariah's luggage showed the tickets safely stashed inside his satchel by his traveling flask. The four of them chatted amiably until Hugo turned the corner onto Broad Street near the station.

"My heavens!" Emily exclaimed. Nostalgia and sentiment she figured on, but the scene before them left her flabbergasted.

"Great horned toads!" Zachariah exclaimed.

"Whooowee!" and "My stars!" echoed from Lee and Hugo.

At first look, Broad Street in front of the station looked like a re-enactment of the Panic of 1861. On second look, they realized this multitude of Savannahians was turned out to see off the old veterans. Emily spoke for all four in the motorcar when she turned to Zachariah and said in an awed voice, "Daddy, this is for you. I can't believe it. All these Savannah folks…" She finally remembered to put a hand over her open mouth as she alternated between staring at her father and the crowd.

Lee was pie-eyed at the joyful, weeping throng packed a solid block in all directions. Hugo pointed between the two Italianate towers at the long flat station roof thick with onlookers and called, "I didn't know you could even go up there." The flags of the Longstreet, Gordon, and McLaws UCV posts waved from one of the third floor windows.

Banners proclaiming "Bon Voyage" and "The South Forever" waved atop long poles. Street vendors briskly sold food, drinks, and cut flowers. Men, boys and even the odd lady stood on the streetcar benches waving their hats or handkerchiefs. The Thomas crept past fire department bands that could hardly be heard over the incessant cheers. The Savannah police department, both mounted and on foot, could barely keep the streetcar tracks clear, let alone maintain order among the high-spirited merrymakers.

Hack cabs, carriages, and motor cars were directed to drop off passengers a good block away. Hugo said in a low shout, "Zack, I cain't get you any closer. It's shank's mare from here." Zachariah nodded, a lopsided smile on his face.

Lee opened his door, stepped out and swung his seat forward and said grinning, "Just remember, all these folks are friends!"

Zachariah nodded, then turned to Emily and said tenderly, "Honeybunch, I'm off to Gettysburg, and…" Emily surprised him by putting her arms around his neck. Through her tight throat she got out, "Daddy, I hope…" She was weeping but couldn't say why.

With shining eyes he said back, "I hope too."

"For what?" she managed.

"I don't know, but I think whatever it is…"

"Hope?" she asked.

"Could be, and I think somehow it's at Gettysburg."

Both Hugo and Lee looked away as father and daughter used handkerchiefs on each other.

"Wait for me to come back?"

She nodded. "Hoping every day."

Zachariah's eyes went wide in surprise. In a faraway voice he repeated, "Hoping every day? The very words your mother said to me when I left for the War…"

Emily stared.

"…and in every letter she wrote me during the War… and in every letter she sent when I had the overnight stay on the Atlanta run twice a month." He swallowed hard, "…and when I left for Gainesville in '04 when she… when you…I'm so sorry I wasn't there with you when she passed on. But that's what she always wrote… and lived. Hoping every day." His voice trailed off as he looked at her deeply. Something changed in Emily's face.

She whispered in his ear, "I never knew she did that. How she loved you, Daddy. And I do too, so much. And I am proud of you too. All right, if it was good enough for Mama, then it's good enough for me." She took him by both cheeks and said, "Daddy. I'm hoping every day of the Encampment is wonderful for you. I almost wish I were going too. But now I'll wait for you, hoping every day." Her kiss on his bearded cheek tickled her lips. "Better go now."

He hugged her once more and then said, "Yep." Grabbing his bag, he shook hands with Lee and Hugo and plunged in. Every uniformed old vet was serenaded by spontaneous choirs and cooled by endless ladies' handkerchiefs and hand fans. Offers to carry baggage touched off friendly calls of "Let me carry it a few feet!" In other stretches, bags passed from hand to hand, bucket-brigade style, keeping pace with their owners. The vets were patted on their backs by hundreds of hands in the Biblical manner, seeking to touch the hems of their garments. Several veterans who were unsteady on their feet due to wounds, arthritis, or artificial limbs were carried bodily through the crowd with shouts of "Comin' through!" and "Make way for a veteran!" A pair of men would make a fireman's seat by joining arms underneath and behind an old codger in a human bench. By this courtesy, they felt they were practically serving under Robert E. Lee himself.

There was a tingle in the air about this 1913 gathering, the largest of its kind ever attempted. The army had spent two years planning and arranging supplies and accommodations for this week. There would be speeches by old commanders, governors and cabinet members, perhaps even the President. There would be entertainers, orators, concerts, and displays on how much things had changed in fifty years. There would be formal ceremonies promoting reconciliation between both sides. Lots of handshaking around campfires would hopefully set the stage for a huge handshake along the stone wall on Cemetery Ridge, planned for Friday.

But anxieties lurked in the excitement. Even with the help of the U.S. Army, the Pennsylvania National Guard, and hundreds of constables, could a town of four thousand really host over fifty thousand veterans and handle as many as a hundred thousand spectators a day for an entire week? And if the logistics could be managed, how would the veterans get along? Was understanding, let alone reconciliation, even possible? Could Northern arrogance (as seen from Savannah) and Southern pride (justifiable and righteous) find a common ground on some of the country's bloodiest ground? How deep was the division, North and South? Or was there a still deeper unity that could bind up the veterans – and the country?

The veterans would find out, for themselves and for the nation.

The multitudes sensed this, making their hearts nostalgic, mournful, and yet hopeful. The well-wishers couldn't decide whether to cheer, smile, weep, embrace, tremble, or even dance, so among themselves they did them all.

In the station, the 9:50 train was jammed with passengers, revelers, decorations, relatives, travel bags, and presents of food and drink, both hard and soft. The noise was even louder, resounding off the hard surfaces. Ladies' handkerchiefs and men's hats waved furiously from the platform. Episcopal clergy in robes moved about blessing the men car by car. More bands played Civil War tunes, streamers festooned the cars and station, and confetti flew by the fistful.

With a steam whistle caterwaul, the engineer worked his levers and valves. Earnest cries of "goodbye" and "good luck" floated out as the last visitors stepped onto the platform. The conductors called "All aboard," waited a moment, then swung their two-step stools up the ladders and hopped on. The car couplings tightened and the cars of waving veterans crept past the hundreds of onlookers on the street beyond the end of the rail yard.

As the cars trundled across some of the west side crossings, good-sized crowds of black Savannahians also waved and cheered the "boys" heading out. A bit puzzled but still delighted, the UCV men waved back enthusiastically. Just ahead of the caboose in the Jim Crow cars, Lucius Robinson and several other GAR men grinned and waved back from their windows.

Their big celebration had been last night in the basement of the Second African Baptist Church. Elijah Porterfield had invited the Rufus Saxton GAR post veterans to a dinner and gala, and Savannah's west side had come out in force. Police had noted the turnout, but Wednesday evening services were a longstanding custom among the Baptists of both colors. Those arriving were chattering excitedly about "revival," which quieted police curiosity.

The veterans had disappeared into the choir room for a few moments as everyone else joined in singing the Johnson brothers' new marching hymn, "Lift Every Voice and Sing."

Then the reverend tapped on his glass at the head table until the general conversation subsided.

"I'd like to take this opportunity to thank y'all for comin'. In fact, there are several folks in need o' thankin'. First, I'd like to thank the ladies in the kitchen fo' gettin' all this food put together fo' y'all." Porterfield waved at the group of reluctant women clustered at the kitchen door. "C'mon out now and take a bow," he called over the rising applause.

"Next, we need to thank all the ladies in the room. Stand up now, ever' one of you." They stood, modest and mystified. "This night and this journey to the Gettysburg Encampment are due in large part to the ladies you see befo' you, an' I'll tell you how. Gennulmen, take a look at how purty the ladies look tonight." The men swiveled their heads.

"Do you see how purty their hair is? Well maybe you don't because of their hats. Ladies, fo' a moment I ask you to uncover." Hesitantly, the ladies took off their headgear. "Now, you see how nice their hair is? Did you men wonder at yo' wimmin when they spent all that time today doin' up their hair just to hide it all under a hat?" Chuckles ran around the room as both sexes recognized the exchange. Rufus slapped his knee in delight while Beulah gave him a wry grin.

"Thank you, ladies, fo' fussin' with yo' hair," Porterfield boomed out. "Thank you. You fussed, an' rinsed, an' curled, an' straightened, an' you used some of Sarah Breedlove's hair and beauty fixins, ratt? Been using her fixins for years haven't you? Well because you have, because you've spent your pennies that way, Sarah Breedlove, now Madame C.J. Walker of Indianapolis, has become the richest colored woman in America, a millionaire even. And Madame C.J. Walker's grant of $75,000 has paid the train fares of the USCI and the USCT, the United States Colored Infantry and Troops, to Gettysburg. Not just here in Savannah or Georgia or even the South; no sir and no ma'am, but every colored veteran in need in all forty-eight states is able to attend because of that $75,000 grant. So yes, ladies, you and yo' hair fussin' have been bread cast upon the waters, and it has come back, pressed down, shaken together and overflowin' to the USCI veterans. Gennulmen, join me in a risin' ovation to thank the ladies." The women beamed, self-conscious at being hatless, but enjoying the roaring applause. As the din dropped off Porterfield roared out, "Now let's get on with the revival!"

"Revival" tonight was something rather different from the usual preaching for conversions and rededications to righteous living. Tonight the planners aimed at a revival of the liberation spirit of the War. Tonight would remind the generations born free since 1865 that their old men in blue had not fought to save the Union, still less for states' rights. They had fought to ratify emancipation so it would not be just a gift bestowed, but a deed earned for their people, for their dignity as men, for their own honor.

Over the past week, the veterans had brought their uniforms to Jennings' dry cleaning establishment on West Bay Street. To keep prying white eyes fooled, a delivery wagon had brought the church's choir robes as usual from the store to the church, each robe stapled inside long brown paper. The old uniforms – cleaned, pressed, loose threads snipped away or carefully re-sewn, smudges worked out, blue dye here and there, buttons polished – were smuggled in covered with brown paper as well and delivered among the robes. The veterans used the choir room to change into their wartime gear. On this cue of "revival" from Porterfield they entered in close ranks, double file, into the big basement room under the sanctuary.

Their entrance brought the onlookers to near hysteria. Some veterans were put in mind of their march through Georgia and the Carolinas with Sherman. Just like then, here were cheers, embraces, kisses, tears, drumming, trumpet calls, screams of delight, and children scampering. People reached out to pat the men, touch their uniforms in blessing and wonder, to confirm with their fingers the reality of their eyes. Younger men like Rufus alternated between applause and holding both fists in the air like a boxing champion, all while cheering their hearts out. Hannah, Sherman, Ralphie, Abner, and other children dodged in and out between adults, at times jumping up and down furiously in sheer excitement. Like so many women in the room, Beulah and Alma cheered tears onto their cheeks, embraced each other and any veteran they could get near. Soprano and alto laughter and merrymaking made the air vibrate with its own excitement.

For the older, slave-born generation, here were their "boys" (in the affectionate use), black men under discipline, proud, strong, determined. In their very persons these men were the death of slavery and freedom incarnate. The veterans' shoulders and beards were wetted by the tears of their contemporaries, their hands wrung with gratitude.

For those freeborn, this was the first time they had seen the men in their uniforms massed together. Sure, dad, or granddad, or uncle modeled for them once in a while at home with shades down against passing white eyes. But it had been too dangerous to go about in a Southern city in black skin and Yankee blue. GAR post meetings were in their Sunday best, with maybe the post commander smuggling his old uniform to and from the church basement. So to see these vets, military proud, resolute, joyful, and in particular, massed together, was to glimpse the "sable arm" of the Union Army in the flesh. The men were the lions of the night. The *Savannah Colored Tribune* reporters had them pose like an athletic team for a page one photo.

Under the excitement also skulked a set of worries. Would the plans for Camp Lincoln be equal to caring for five thousand men for a week? Without Pennsylvania's aid or the U.S. Army's help, could the Negro communities in Baltimore, Philadelphia, and Harrisburg even feed everyone? Would the New England governors really provide equipment from their National Guards? Who knew if the Gettysburg farmer would really let out his land for a colored camp? And what if someone got sick, or simply passed out from heat stroke?

While the Encampment was on Northern soil, how safe would their men be from unreconstructed Southerners and northern racists? Would the policing be fair? Effective? Since they were officially not invited, how would the army patrols treat them? Was anyone ready for a mob of "White Liners" turned out with pistol, torch, and noose? Could they count on the GAR men, who had backed down from their initial position of an integrated Encampment? How would the white veterans and civilians treat them? There was real concern and real admiration in the room at what these old men were risking by attending.

After the excitement subsided to frantic, each veteran was asked to recount a war yarn. The congregation's attention was so riveted, Porterfield and the other preachers in the room were envious. Some of the young women studying office skills at the Georgia State Industrial College practiced their stenography taking down the stories.

Charlie Gilbert's tale took them up Missionary Ridge outside Chattanooga in a storybook charge that looked like mass suicide but became a thundering Union victory. Former United States Congressman Robert Smalls was there, skippering a hijacked Confederate ship out to the Union blockading force off the Carolina coast. Reuben Keyes awed them, serving as an impromptu bodyguard when Abraham Lincoln walked the streets of Richmond. Two days after Jefferson Davis had fled, Mr. Lincoln, flanked by members of the US Colored Infantry, walked from the James River landing to the Confederate White House and sat down in Jeff Davis' chair.

Far into the night, Porterfield finally sent them all home. The crowd and veterans and left almost en masse, seeking safety in numbers. The uniforms made it home in the dark, with pants rolled up in many a ladies' oversize purse, and tunics worn inside out to hide the gleaming brass buttons. The Savannah police noted a large number of colored folks out late, but all had been peaceful as befitting those whose faith had been revived by the Spirit of the Lord.

The train carrying both white and black, gray and secret blue, clattered past the edge of Telfair Hospital and headed out of town, rolling toward Port Wentworth and Augusta. It took better than two full days and nights and several changes of cars and lines before they arrived at Gettysburg.

Part Two

WEAVINGS

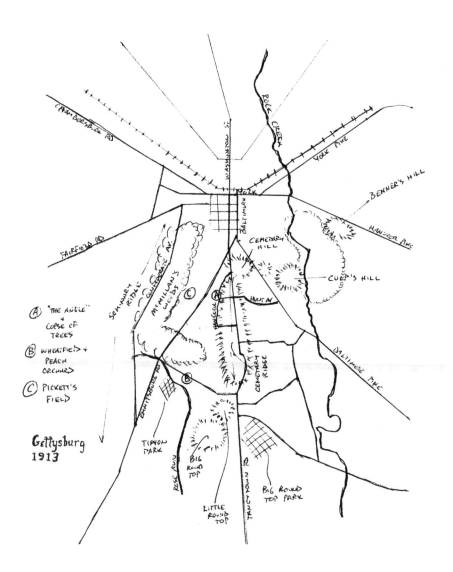

CHAMBERSBURG RD

ROCK CREEK

YORK PIKE

BENNER'S HILL

HANOVER PIKE

WASHINGTON ST

YORK

BALTIMORE

FAIRFIELD RD

CEMETERY HILL

CULP'S HILL

SEMINARY RIDGE

CONFEDERATE AV.

McMILLAN'S WOODS

HANCOCK AV.

HILL AV.

Ⓐ "THE ANGLE" + COPSE OF TREES

Ⓑ WHEATFIELD + PEACH ORCHARD

Ⓒ PICKETT'S FIELD

Gettysburg 1913

CEMETERY RIDGE

BALTIMORE PIKE

EMMITSBURG RD

TIPTON PARK

ROSE RUN

BIG ROUND TOP

LITTLE ROUND TOP

TANEYTOWN RD

BIG ROUND TOP PARK

Saturday, June 28, 1913

Gettysburg

Any other summer, Luke Benner's herd of Jerseys would be grazing and resting among the grass and trees of his west pasture. This summer Benner's meadow was a village of canvas welcoming an army.

Benner was a square-built man with the broad shoulders, bulging forearms and hard-scaled hands of a farmer. The Benners had been farming east of Gettysburg and downwind from Culp's Hill for over one hundred years. In 1863 the family had fled down Hanover Pike to hide with relatives. As abolitionist leaders in Adams County, the Benners were a marked clan in the presence of Southern arms.

On the second day of battle, Confederate General Jubal Early had ordered twenty-year-old Major Joseph Latimer and twenty-four guns up Benner's Hill in support of an infantry assault. Benner's was bald of any cover and fifty feet shorter than Culp's Hill. Within minutes of Latimer's opening fire, Union guns on both Culp and Cemetery Hills had blistered the Confederate gunners, cannons, and caissons with a metallic storm lasting nearly an hour.

After the battle, five-year-old Luke had enjoyed collecting bits of shell and minié balls from the family hill. He had learned farming in between daily two-mile walks to the Gettysburg school. True to his abolitionist creed after the War, Luke's father had organized county "ratification rallies" for the Fourteenth and Fifteenth Amendments to the Constitution.

By the summer of 1912, plans and work for the national Encampment had been underway at Gettysburg for nearly two years. A group of black businessmen and veterans from Baltimore and Philadelphia had doubted all along the army would welcome colored veterans, so they drew up plans for an alternative. When they approached Luke with the idea for Camp Lincoln they'd picked the right man. The entire Benner clan and neighbors like the Ladys, Rummels, Henders, Wolfs, Schallers, and Culps had all swung into the project.

The Baltimore group and the local men met several times with Colonel Lewis Beltier, the U.S. Army's Encampment planner and director, and peppered his staff with questions. They looked over the army effort underway for over fifty thousand veterans, refined their own plan with new and borrowed ideas, and added their own improvements.

Seed money came from Baltimore, the remnants of the old abolitionist societies, and the Walker Foundation of Indianapolis. Schaller & Rummel, professional surveyors, platted the site along the east bank of Rock Creek and produced contour maps. The surveyors, students from Penn College in Gettysburg, and several local men and boys had tramped the tract for days that fall, staking out camp streets and tent sites, talking over water, sewage, drainage and lighting issues.

One issue threatened early disaster. Hours of meetings led back to the same impasse: Hanover Pike would be one solid traffic jam for all seven days and their camp would strangle from lack of supplies and sheer immobility. It was late summer before the Wolf family came up with an answer. Could they build a temporary road south across their land from the camp to Baltimore Pike? But then Rock Creek, five feet deep and fifty wide, became a barrier. At last Professor Heinrich of the college suggested building a bridge as an engineering class project.

The election of Woodrow Wilson in November with heavy support of Southern white voters strengthened the resolve of the Lincoln Committee to build their camp. Over winter they precut lumber for three assembly platforms around the camp. Using dimensions mailed from the Connecticut governor's office, they precut floor platforms for the sleeping, infirmary, and mess tents, and for the mass-meeting assembly tent. They designed a wooden water tower which went up on a spur of Benner's Hill as soon as the frost went out of the ground.

The March 1913 army announcement of a "whites only" Encampment in Tent City gave the Camp Lincoln project members a curious sense of satisfaction that their work would now truly be needed, and they worked with a fresh sense of urgent pride. An early spring and a solid March week of showers and downpours answered fervent prayers. Neighboring farmer Bill Lady towed over an old road roller, a solid stone cylinder over twelve feet wide and nearly four feet in diameter, pulled by a team of six draft horses. The roller was from colonial times when settlers used it to compact snowy roads into solid, snow-paved highways for sleigh travel. The committee laid out camp streets with two-by-ten planks on the rain-soaked ground. Bill had led his team of Percherons along the roads and the roller squeezed the planks into the spring mud. When the weather dried, a set of wood-paved streets was good for foot, horse, wagon, and even motorcar traffic. Afterward, the fall rains and winter freezes would decay the planks and fertilize Benner's pastures.

Hardware store owner George Mattox and his sons spent weeks running several thousand feet of pipe for water and drainage. They copied an army idea and placed a dozen water fountains across camp. By running some pipe back and forth about five feet under each "bubbler," and encasing the resulting switchbacks in a heavy crate underground, they could dump chipped ice into the crate from a chute. The buried ice would last two or three days, cooling the pipe. In July's average ninety-four degree heat, the ice water bubblers would be wildly popular.

Some townsfolk wheedled several spare coils of wire out of the Army Signal Corps. A crew of Henders, Rummel, and Culp had strung two miles of wire from the power station on Washington Street out to camp using Western Union telegraph poles.

Early on Sunday, June 22, a brief worship service was held on Platform B to dedicate the camp. In the manner of a barn raising, the rest of the day saw hundreds at work, local folk as well as tradesmen from Philadelphia and Baltimore and even stage crews from New York's theaters. Dozens of people set up tents, wired up lights, checked pipes for leaks, and raked gravel into low spots. Wooden steps marked various changes in elevation and the plank roads added log curbs. Canvas flies between trees added shade over picnic tables. One long, open-topped tent had four dozen canvas stalls, each holding a bathtub and a long-handled scrub brush. At the north end, a crew hooked up an electrical water pump to an intake pipe from Rock Creek. They ran the water through a settling tank and then filled the tower.

At the south end where Rock Creek rounded the bulk of Culp's Hill, the college engineering students had built a sturdy bridge wide enough for two loaded wagons side by side. A packed gravel road across Wolf farmland fetched up to Baltimore Pike. By a series of turns on roads that fifty years ago had been the Federal rear, a wagon could roll south from Camp Lincoln to Round Top Park while avoiding both the town of Gettysburg and the Tent City main encampment.

Big Round Top Park was east of the big hill of the same name, a place of rides, midway games, entertainment, semi-permanent pavilions, and several dining and saloon halls. These halls had much practice in bringing in, cooking, and serving food to thousands of park customers a day. The Camp Lincoln committee had worked with the park owners over winter and spring for a bulked up food operation beyond the park's needs to bring supplies to Camp Lincoln. Extra delivery wagons and horse teams had been hired in early June and drivers had practiced the route from Big Round Top Park to Camp Lincoln both day and night until it became familiar.

The same Sunday when the Lincoln Committee and friends had turned out for the "camp raising," crews of extra hands from Round Top Park, Harrisburg, Baltimore, Frederick, and Philadelphia had swung into action to feed them dinner and then supper. Not only was the food top notch, all agreed a set of buried ice chests, like for the bubblers, had worked quite well for the ice cream – chocolate with walnuts. It was a good rehearsal for the kitchen and cleanup crews.

One incident refreshed everyone's hearts. The food crews sat at several picnic tables, having a breather between dinner and supper. Under a summer hat freckled with daisies, an owlish white woman, Wanda Wilhelm, led several women from St. James Lutheran Church to the tables, saying to the crews, "Sit still. Just stay seated." The women then passed around boxes of their home-baked treats. Men and women working on the camp stopped and pointed with some wonder at the obvious camaraderie. Then they wondered why this should be notable and not just ordinary hospitality. But there black folk sat, and white folk stood and waited on them, passed plates of cookies and peanut brittle – Wanda's specialty – and moved around refilling lemonade cups and beer mugs. These old stock German Lutherans were pouring cold beer on a hot Sunday whether the teetotaling Methodists liked it or not.

When evening came Jamie Benner had said, "Let's keep going!" and had thrown the switch on the trunk line. The yellow-white glow of over one hundred light bulbs attracted bugs but delighted everyone. Cots, canvas camp chairs, and wash basins went into the tents over the next days, and by Thursday the 26th, Camp Lincoln was ready for veterans.

Sunday, June 29, 1913

Washington

"Finally made it here," Bob Bidwell said softly.

"Yep," Zachariah breathed back.

The two stood at the west steps of the U.S. Capitol Building. They had swung off the train earlier at Washington's Union Station, checking their bags for a few hours at the luggage room. The white dome with Lady Justice holding her scales floated above them against a deep blue sky.

"Looks grand from up close," Zachariah observed.

"Had that look to it in 1864 too," Bob answered. That summer the 8th Georgia had marched on Washington as part of Jubal Early's 15,000. On a July morning they had gone into battle formation aiming to capture everyone that mattered. The Army of the Potomac's VI Corps arrived in the nick of time and although Early's men actually brought Abraham Lincoln himself under fire, the only look they got of the place was a far-off glimpse of this dome.

"I wonder iffin' we'd made it here in '64 how things'd be different," Zack mused. Bob didn't answer, but they both took the steps to get a view down the Mall. From the portico the view was grand but cluttered. Just below them was a jumble of construction scaffolding. The Smithsonian poked in from the left partway down to Washington's Monument. Farther beyond was a large construction site with cranes poking up from behind a board fence.

"Here's what it'll look like, gentlemen," came a high voice from their left. A shoeshine boy in cap and shorts waved them over to a table set back from the elements. He was vigorously polishing the right shoe of a colored man about fifty years old in a dark green suit, glasses, and a pearl pin in his silk tie. The shoeshine boy said, "Just a moment, sir" to his customer (who was intently reading a magazine) and pointed his caramel-colored finger over the scale model that filled the table. "Here we are. Just below's where General Grant's statue's gonna be. And out there's gonna be that Lincoln Memorial." A collection box held a sign reading, "Help finish the National Mall. Your coins here."

"Shine for you while you look it over?" the boy asked, eager for his next customer. Both men grinned. "Sure son," Zachariah drawled. "How much?"

"Just two cents, sir. A penny a shoe. Just as soon as I finish over here."

"I'll take a shine right now," Bob said.

"Yes, sir," the boy piped back. "Right away. Right after I finish."

Zachariah gave him a look. "He said 'Now' boy," as the journal reader looked up. The boy looked unhappily back and forth between Zachariah and his current customer. The green-suited man gazed steadily at the two rather travel-worn old-timers, showing no hint of "race etiquette" in his manner. He closed his magazine, which Zachariah noticed had the words "Journal" and "Medical" on the cover, and then said, "Go ahead, Alex. You were about done with me anyway."

Alex gulped in relief. The man bent over and picked up a small black bag that nearly matched the color of his hand and that the Georgians hadn't noticed. "I need to be getting on to the hospital anyway." As he walked off and Alex started on Bob's left shoe, Zachariah asked, "Boy, do the hospital orderlies in Washington City all dress that nice?"

"I wouldn't know, sir," came Alex's muffled answer from the floor. "But Dr. Francis always does. He's a surgeon you know."

As Alex worked. both men studied the model in silence, not really seeing it as they pondered a colored man as a doctor.

Baltimore

Lucius strolled through Baltimore's new Union Station to the lunchroom near the Western Maryland & Atlantic ticket windows. A band of black musicians played Sophie Tucker's "Reuben Rag" as he sat down at a small table chomping two frankfurters and sipping a paper cup of Georgia's own Coca-Cola. A group of well-dressed, middle-aged Negro men spread through the restaurant approaching all the older black travelers.

"Excuse me, suh," said a forty-ish black man in a sharp tan bowler hat, double-breasted suit and white spats. "Are you headin' fo' Gettysburg?"

"Yes, I am," Lucius replied.

"Would you be a civilian or a veteran?" the man asked.

"I'm a veteran."

"Ah," he said, shaking hands, "then we should talk. My name's Michael Judson. My father's a member of the O.O. Howard GAR post here in Baltimore."

"I'm Lucius Robinson from Savannah, Rufus Saxton Post. What can I do fo' you?"

"It's mo' a matter of what we can do fo' you. Jes' wanted to fill you in on Camp Lincoln."

"Good to hear." Although no white folk were nearby, Lucius bent close.

"East of Gettysburg, Hanover Pike runs by Culp's Hill. At Rock Creek there's Benner's farm. We been workin' all winter and spring and Camp Lincoln is a fine camp," Judson said proudly, and Lucius could tell he'd been working there in his spare time.

"Camp Lincoln," Lucius nodded back.

"In Gettysburg," Michael beamed, "ask any o' our people for Camp Lincoln and we'll get you a ride out there. It's not that far from town but you catch a ride, okay?"

Lucius wrung Judson's hand. "Thank you very much."

"Get yo' ticket here and have a good time," Judson finished, turning and resuming his queries to others. Lucius paid his fare, put the ticket stamped "Gettysburg" in his pocket and headed toward platform six.

Before he got close, angry shouting and porter's whistles came from a crowd of over a hundred mostly colored folk striding grimly back toward the center of the station from under the sign that read "Platform 6, Colored Left, White Right." As Lucius watched, the front of the group parted. Taking the lead were three or four ranks of men in matching, billed caps and dark blue jackets with glittering brass buttons. As the train porters marched past him in step, something old stirred in Lucius.

"C'mon, c'mon," some in the crowd urged him. "If you're on platform six you want to be part of this." Porters and passengers from other platforms kept swelling the crowd.

"What's it all about?" Lucius asked out loud as he reversed course. His feet instinctively matched the porters' tramping and his free hand took up a forgotten, familiar swing.

"Some nasty yard master decided this train should have passenger cars, a baggage car, and one boxcar," said a man dressed in a railroad platform guard uniform. "The boxcar is for colored passengers. When our people in the segregated line complained, word came back to the ticket sellers that we should be grateful it wasn't a cattle car."

Lucius trooped along, astounded at both the gall of the train assembler and at this reaction. Some near him wondered if the bewhiskered codger with the squared-up shoulders and faraway squint might have been a porter once himself. Michael Judson stared at the passing porters, Lucius on their right end looking at home, and felt his stomach recoil, first in fear, then in a rush of pride. White passengers seeing the familiar dark-blue uniforms were calling out "George" or "Here's my bag, George" in the usual fashion of addressing a colored railroad baggage man and getting no response at all from the porters. The porters led the crowd down a side hall to the offices behind the ticket counters and burst in.

The Western Maryland & Atlantic station agent was alarmed at the crush of upset colored faces in his usually cozy, always-white office area. Amid great shouting, the porters insisted they couldn't properly do their jobs on a train with a boxcar. The agent first claimed train assembly was not under his authority, but backed down fast when a wave of ticket clerks reported lines of customers, mostly colored but some white as well, demanding refunds so they could change to the rival Pennsylvania line.

When he announced the boxcar would be removed, there was a cheer. The yard master sent word no other regular passenger cars were available. Helpless in a room of hard stares, the agent ordered a first class car hooked on in the usual Jim Crow position. The porters had to go back to the way the old Pullman Railroad Company had taught Americans to treat them, using George Pullman's first name to address the porters. But seventy-six colored passengers who usually had to make do with second best thoroughly enjoyed their train trip this day to Gettysburg and points west.

Princeton

Calvin slipped his watch back into his vest pocket, glanced over the car's timetable, and frowned. He'd slept badly last night in New York City as a string of thunderstorms had banged and boomed until three in the morning. The train was definitely slowing but it was too early for Trenton. He craned his neck and pressed his cheek against the window but could only see more New Jersey countryside.

Sam stood at the corridor window also looking up the track. "I can see a water tower."

"Can you make out the name?" Calvin asked over the undercarriage clatter.

"Not yet. We need to come around this bend and get a bit closer." The engine chuffed in a slowing rhythm. The squeal of the wheels against the curve grew shriller. "I can see it now," Sam said. "We're almost to Princeton."

Calvin sat down, wondering about the unscheduled stop. But they crept past the platform and the fence boards of yards backing up to the tracks. The train banked slightly and began a long right curve. Calvin could see the intersecting beams of two railroad bridges rising ahead. A dirt road paralleled the tracks and ran up to a flat bridge. Some afterthought plank fencing on either side of this bridge pretended to discourage jumping or plunging. The train stopped just as a Pullman porter wedged his beefy frame into the corridor. Calvin's ears twitched to catch the man's words through his thick Southern accent.

"Ladies an' gennulmen," he said in a bass voice so deep Calvin imagined the floor boards vibrating, "da bridges here over Assumpink Creek lost a suppoat 'cause o' last night's gullywashin' storm. All passanjuhs are asked to take their hand luggage an' walk 'cross the road bridge and boad da other train waitin' to take y'all to Philadelphia. Yo' checked bags from the baggage car will be handled by the railroad. The Pennsylvania Central apologizes fo' the inconvenience."

The cars ahead of Calvin and Sam were discharging passengers. Porters and various gentlemen were helping passengers down the extra high steps to the ground. The porters' two-steps were good on raised station platforms, but were puny out here. Ladies were in an awkward spot with their full-length skirts, but with help they managed.

In the Victorian humanity streaming toward the road bridge, Calvin and Sam saw an odd sight for inland New Jersey. Among the bobbing ladies' hats of silk, flowers, and feathers were two dozen men in U.S. Navy dress uniforms. Officers to a man, they were carrying a menagerie of hand luggage and hat boxes for the ladies of the next car. But each of them also carried a small black leather satchel. A close look at their collars showed a badge depicting a pair of intertwining snakes around a T-shaped pole, signifying the wearers were doctors.

Governor Foss of Massachusetts was responsible. Back in March, he had gone down to the Boston Yard to lay out Camp Lincoln's medical needs. Foss had swung over Commodore Saltonsall when he pointed out the Navy's long history of integration. Foss won him completely when he suggested this opportunity for the navy to make a contribution, however small, to the otherwise all-army event at Gettysburg. The commodore had written to Washington and set telegraph wires humming. On his own hook, he had his staff draw up a roster and assemble a supply list from the Yard's own stores and the Massachusetts' Guard stocks. Assistant Naval Secretary Franklin Roosevelt had actually used a long-distance telephone call to give final orders. If the Camp Lincoln men were felled by heat stroke, accident, or any medical condition, they could get help, even surgery, at the two hospital tents, complete with "New Hampshire Nat. Guard" stenciled on the sides, on the north and south ends of Camp.

Three or four Princeton constables were handling traffic, both motor and foot, at the bridge. Adding to the crowd, a road crew was working along the eastern approach as Calvin and Sam came up.

"Look there, Calvin," Sam remarked. "See the marker on that post the men just set up?" Calvin peered between the men and grinned. An arrow pointing up topped the post. Underneath was a script letter "L" and a familiar bearded silhouette about eight inches high, done in bright blue.

"Talk about treading history, Sam." Calvin smiled as they began trooping the bridge boards. "George Washington crossed Assumpink Creek to fight the

British at Princeton. Here we are crossing it the other way to visit Gettysbaag. And that marker says we're walkin' on a piece of that Lincoln Highway the motorcar people are pressing for."

"'A stone road from coast to coast'" Sam quoted from some article. "Would you want to motor coast to coast, Calvin?"

"Don't think so," came the answer as they put floor boards behind them. "Not enough hotels. Don't know if there'd be enough hardware stores or Mr. Rockefeller's pumps for gasoline. A train can go thirty-five miles an hour and you can eat and sleep on board if you like."

Sam nodded as they turned toward the waiting train. "Me, too. But still there's the thought: a hard, weatherproof road, from Atlantic to Pacific." He stared off, remembering the trackless Nebraska prairies and the twisting trails called "roads" in the Wasatch range.

They climbed up, then helped various ladies aboard, and got settled. It all went fairly smoothly, but it cost them an hour. They would need a later train to Gettysburg, which would put them in about 2:35 instead of 1:05 that afternoon.

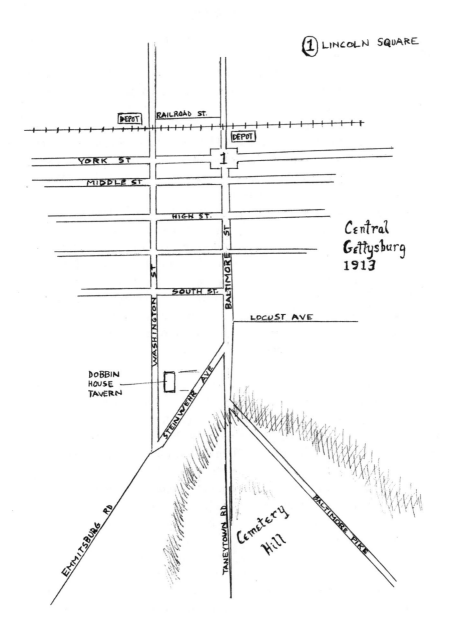

Gettysburg Depot

A steam whistle's howl cut through the train bell's clanging. Both sounds reflected off the underside of Gettysburg's depot roof and melded with the deep rumble of the creeping locomotive and the screech of steel on steel. With a dying trilling of wheels and a heavy thump of couplings, the 2:20 from Baltimore halted in a hiss of steam.

The opening carriage doors signaled the Gettysburg Fire Department Band to break into "You're a Grand Old Flag." Station sounds, conductors' cries, porters' calls and vendors' hawkings were covered by the bright strains of the George M. Cohan tune. A giant banner hung from the rafters: "Welcome Veterans, Blue and Gray, Encampment 1913."

Hundreds of aged, male faces wearing white or gray beards in various styles, lengths, and trims, began moving away from the train. Many shuffled with an old man's careful step. Many others limped favoring an artificial leg. Here and there medical attendants unloaded a wheelchair and guided or lifted their battered but determined men into its embrace. Canes were common, crutches less so. Empty sleeves pinned at the shoulder were frequent. A few dragged along small trunks, but most had luggage consisting of a valise or grip, either leather or heavy cloth – fairly called "carpetbags" – which looked like vastly overgrown snap purses.

Fortunately the veterans' walk with their domestic burdens was short. A swarm of olive-khaki-dressed boys appeared from everywhere, each wearing a round-brimmed hat with the crown pinched in on four sides, and sporting a neckerchief. The new Boy Scouts were at Gettysburg in force. Calls of "Carry your bag, mister?" "Can I help you with that, sir?" "Give you a hand, sir?" were everywhere, and many three-fingered, brim-touching salutes were thrown at the vets. The elderly wondered if they themselves had ever looked quite this fresh-faced as drummer boys and enlistees. The old men and young scouts oozed through the depot and spilled onto Railroad Street.

This pavement between Washington Street and Baltimore Street was a glomeration of farm wagons, hack cabs, pushcarts, buckboards, motor cars, delivery vans, and carriages from rough to genteel. Acne-tinged voices chanted, "Tent City, this way for the blue and gray." Drivers' shouts, horse whinnies, pushcart hawkings and bellows from dozens of constables and Pennsylvania Guardsmen compounded the unwieldy tangle of horseflesh. Flash powder smoke poofs made exclamation points over newspaper reporters. Thomas Ince, D.W. Griffith's rival, had camera crews shooting film from the depot tower, a second floor window at the Eagle Hotel, and in Lincoln Square. Pamphleteers pressed their handbills on passersby, and veterans later read pocketed sheets urging the women's vote, the fundamentals of Christianity (Protestants only welcome), or a national minimum wage and forty-hour workweek. Rival fire company bands struck up competing tunes, so once again "Dixie" was at war with "Battle Cry of Freedom." The Sunday afternoon heat and a fine film of dust covered everything.

Zachariah Hampton, 8th Georgia, had made it off the train nimbly enough but the combination of men, platform vendors, spectators, and Boy Scouts formed a mass that only seeped through the depot. He was well short of the three arched portals when another train whistle sounded on the second of Gettysburg's two tracks. Someone had blundered scheduling all these arriving "specials" in a minor station like Gettysburg. Zachariah put his old conductor skills to work and angled away from the depot to see if he could squeeze outside between the platform and the tracks. He made it, only to be swallowed up by the crowd on Railroad Street. The throng from the Baltimore 2:20 was still snail-paced on the platform when the Philadelphia 2:35 pulled in almost eight minutes early. Another trainload of alighting vets and civilian day-trippers gridlocked the platform. More than a few on the 2:35 looked at the teeming confusion and decided to do their waiting sitting on board.

Railroad Street ebbed and flowed in human eddies and crosscurrents. Zachariah was nearing the edge of the mass when another human current brought him elbow to elbow with Dooley Culpepper.

"We gonna git outta this mess, Zach'riah?" he asked impatiently. "I feel like a Yankee runnin' away at Manassas."

"Hah!" Zachariah snorted with a wry grin and hunted look as they were pinned against the brick wall of a warehouse. "C'mon. I think we can get away over here." They joined a single-file trickle of humanity leaking along the wall.

"Hoowee! At last," Zachariah exclaimed as they cleared the end of the wall and found themselves on Baltimore Street with merely a Fourth of July sort of crowd. The Hanover Fire Department band was playing Sterling and Titzer's "Under the Anheuser Busch" next to a small cart holding a barrel marked "Cold beer, five cents." Zachariah and Dooley dropped their bags and breathed freely, getting a first look at the town. Sidewalks ran up to mostly red brick walls, most often set off by cream painted trim. Sitting right here with his back to the bricks was a lean, cucumber-chinned Yankee veteran with a red-and-black plaid carpetbag. He was pale as his droopy moustache and could hardly fan himself. Zachariah bent over him, noting his "PA" badge. "Are you all right, Keystoner?"

"I'm so hot, so hot," the man gasped.

"Stay with him, Dooley," Zachariah said. He stepped over to the beer cart and planked a nickel and two pennies. "Let me have a beer and fill up my kerchief with some o' that ice from around the bottom of the barrel."

He handed the paper cup to Dooley. "Let him sip this a bit at a time." Zachariah began swabbing the man's face and hands with his ice compress. He also loosened the man's tie and collar, pulled off his suit coat and rolled up his sleeves so he could swab there too.

The man rallied strongly after a few minutes. "Oh, that's much better. Thank you," he said between sips. Dooley looked on with a mix of annoyance and thirst. Zachariah noticed and said winking, "That beer does look good."

The man sat up smiling, his color much improved. He said to Dooley, "Here, sir. I'm all right. Have the rest of it, please. It's the least I can do." Dooley wavered, then finished the cup in two gulps.

They helped him to his feet. "Thanks again. My name's Tate, Oliver Tate, from Titusville, Pennsylvania. I'm glad to be here and grateful to you both," shaking hands.

"You all right now?" Zachariah wondered aloud, and even Dooley looked concerned as Tate swayed slightly.

"As good as ever," Tate answered. He dug in his vest pocket for two nickels. "That's for the beer," he said to Zachariah handing him one. "That's for the help," handing the other to a surprised Dooley. "Thanks again." With a shaky but jaunty wave, he picked up his bag and was swallowed by the crowd.

The two Southerners shook their heads at each other. Each man took out a pocket flask and toasted the other before taking a belt. "Coupla Boy Scouts, ain't we?" Zachariah said. "Five cents ahead," Dooley grinned.

A buckboard wagon pulled up with four longwise benches, two outside facing in, two down the center, back to back facing out. The horse was pretty calm in the bedlam, gaily caparisoned with red, white, and blue ribbons braided into her mane. A schoolboy's chalkboard tied by the driver's bench read "Wagon to Camp" and one more word partially smudged and continuously hidden by passersby. The young black driver with a gold bandanna hopped down nimbly, tethered the horse to a handy lamppost, pulled a set of steps from under the center benches and clamped it to the tail end. Dooley snatched up his valise, scooted across the street, plunked up the steps and took a seat, leaving a look of surprise on the driver's face.

Zachariah decided to walk a spell, so he picked up his bag and ambled south a short block to York Street. Looking right, he could see streetcars lined up a block over. The crowd here was just Christmas shopping thick, so he made his way without undue trouble. Every car the Gettysburg Electric Railroad Company owned stood facing south on Washington Street. They were hung with various signs: "Welcome to Gettysburg," "Tent City Special," and "Veterans Only, Please." They looked full, but Zachariah called up at the open windows of a winter car pressed into off-season service, "Is there one mo' seat fo' a Georgia rebel?"

A Texan already festooned with souvenir buttons and ribbons all over both lapels called back, "Yew bet, you goober grabber," bringing laughter from his window-mates at the old term for a Georgian. "Git on at that end an' there's a spot here." Zachariah headed past a man selling Jack Daniel's whiskey from a large tub for ten cents a shot to board.

Calvin Salisbury, 14th Vermont, was still caught in the human turmoil at the station. His pocket watch was crowding 3:00 p.m. when he finally decided to swing off the Philadelphia 2:35 and join the molasses-speed mass on the platform. Sam had taken his chances earlier and would meet him in camp. Calvin last saw him from the window, about twenty feet wide of the unmistakable bulk of Josiah Trimble. Some vet was talking Sam's ear off while pointing repeatedly at Josiah.

The Boy Scouts had been swamped by both arriving trains so Calvin had to wrangle his own leather bag. He was amid a large tide of old colored men and felt odd being the only white face. "Must be how they often feel," he mused, shuffling nimbly, almost dancing, first left, then right. When the crowd loosened, he found himself in the middle of a street by a buckboard wagon with four longwise benches on the back. A sweat-faced constable was mediating a dispute between the driver and a solitary passenger in Confederate gray.

"I'm a veteran here fo' the Encampment," the old Reb was saying, "an' that's where this boy's gonna take me," jerking his chin at the driver.

"But officer…" the driver responded, but the constable cut him off.

"Just hold on, son," the Gettysburg chief of police grunted. "I'll fix his flint without your help." A bony man of average height, he had a gaunt face with a heavy jaw under bushy eyebrows. Turning to the passenger perched defiantly on the bench, Walter Krauss brandished his billy club and said, "So a secesh grayback on Northern soil is demanding free transportation to the Encampment."

The dark-eyed Johnny Reb with a "GA" state badge on his collar bristled at "grayback." Its double meaning referred to both a Confederate soldier and the endless lice both armies fought incessantly when they weren't fighting each other. This policeman apparently meant both.

Thrusting a gnarly finger at the driver, the Georgian growled, "This boy is takin' on riders, an' I'm ridin', an' I ain't gittin' off 'til camp." A helpless smile broke across the driver's face as the rebel snarled, "You gittin' uppity, boy? What you smirkin' at?"

"He's smirkin' at the horse's ass he's got on his buckboard," Krauss roared. Calvin started and the passenger's deep-set dark eyes flamed in anger. Krauss tapped the chalkboard. "You idiot rebel! This is a segregated buckboard, going to Camp Lincoln where all the U.S. Colored veterans are staying." Krauss grinned with relish as he tried a mock Southern accent, "Boy, yew are either gettin' off that thar buckboad or you'll be sleepin' with th' niggas."

Utterly deflated but looking snake venom at Chief Krauss, the livid man clomped off the buckboard and stomped off south, grinding his heels into the pavement. As Calvin gingerly followed the bowlegged Rebel, he heard Krauss say to the driver, "All right boy, load up some darks and get 'em out of town."

Lucius Robinson, 2nd South Carolina Union Volunteers, had been on the opposite side of the buckboard while Krauss had settled the Georgian's hash. His 2:06 train had been on time, but it had taken a good twenty minutes before everyone discovered that while Gettysburg had only two tracks, it unexpectedly had two depots to go with them a block apart on Railroad Street. Letters and written instructions advising how to get from "the station" to "the camp" had usually missed this, adding to the confusion and human gridlock.

Lucius watched the bandy-legged hothead storm off while several vets in gray and blue followed at a prudent distance. The driver came around the back of the wagon, smiling. "C'mon gentlemen, let's get you to Camp Lincoln." The men from northern and western states began moving, but Lucius and other Deep South men didn't react when he called them "gentlemen." For them it was not an ordinary address. The driver repeated to Lucius, a bit quizzically, "Gentlemen?"

A Michigan cavalryman from Sheridan's old command grinned and slapped Lucius on the back. "That's right. You's gentlemen here in town, and 'specially at Camp Lincoln. Better get used to it."

"I b'lieve I could learn to like it," Lucius rejoined, grabbing his satchel and heaving it onto the buckboard. Assuming his Sunday manners but still enjoying the word, he helped his mates up the steps before he was helped up. The word "gentlemen" was flung around like straws on a hayride. The driver put up his set of steps, unhitched his horse and led her around by the head across Lincoln Square until they were pointed east on York Street. Then he sprang up onto the driver's box and trotted his latest load of gentlemen veterans out to Camp Lincoln.

Gettysburg

The veterans' Sunday supper officially opened the Encampment, and Gettysburg was in a festive mood. On the north edge of town, the rail stations continued flowing. On the south edge at Philippoteaux's Cyclorama, an admission line formed that seemed to last all seven days. Everyone seemed to want to see the forty-two-foot-high, 360-foot-long battle painting that had toured around the country and been displayed at circus midways. Two miles south of town, Tipton Park and Big Round Top Park sold food, had carnival rides, and offered midway games. Dancing pavilions at both parks were packed, Sunday blue laws notwithstanding. Civilians and veterans danced gaily, and dance hall women did a brisk, respectable trade selling their services as partners at five cents a number. Some women also offered what the vets called "horizontal dancing" in tumbledown park buildings featuring beds, though mostly for younger clientele, for more than five cents. Constables from across Adams County were swamped keeping crowds orderly at the parks.

Major Charles Rhodes of the U.S. 15th Cavalry had his mounted men patrolling in pairs around the town. Lincoln Square rated two pairs, as did the Western Maryland & Atlantic station. Otherwise, cavalry patrolled east and west on York Street, and north and south on both Baltimore and Washington Streets, from the rail lines down to Steinwehr Avenue. The U.S. 5th Infantry and Pennsylvania Guardsmen worked on foot in pairs and squads along the cross streets of Middle, High, Breckenridge, South, and Lincoln.

The west end of Lincoln and the south end of Washington were closest to Tent City, and many veterans passed through the southwest quarter of Gettysburg. They crossed paths with the local poor folk of both colors, many of whom drew their household water from a well built into the wall of the Dobbin House Tavern down near where Steinwehr angled across Washington. Major Rhodes and Police Chief Krauss agreed this area could be a flash point and they arranged more frequent foot and mounted patrols through the area.

St. Paul's African Methodist Episcopal Church was here too, on Washington Street, the heart of Gettysburg's colored community. Encampment or no, Sunday was Sunday and evening worship was on. The church was chock-a-block full with an amalgamated crowd, the balcony crammed, and each open window had a cluster of folks outdoors catching the singing and the preaching. Thanks to a cousin of a cousin, the Reverend Obadiah Jones' voice carried strong tonight, boosted by a three amp microphone, an inside and an outside megaphone, and a "loud speaking" machine. Although it was Obadiah's first experience with a microphone he was a natural.

Lucius Robinson and several other USCI vets had wandered by, not planning on worship, for services at Camp Lincoln were almost continuous for the duration. But they had been brought bodily into the church and found themselves accidental heroes. Some vintage church women unabashedly wept over the "Lincoln soldiers" and broke into impromptu dancing, foot-stomping and hand clapping "in honor of the year of Jubilee."

Calvin and Sam were walking past the church when a Mississippi captain looked twice, stared hard at Calvin, and stopped him, pointing a gnarled finger. Sam lined up as an ally. "May twelfth, at the Mule Shoe," he rasped through a crooked nose and wide mouth, framed by an Amish beard running in a three-inch ruff from ear to ear without a moustache. Calvin stared hard at the man's face. Then it came to him, the same face, unlined, brown beard, all in a smoky, green-tinged shadow.

In a dawn attack at Spotsylvania Courthouse, Hancock had broken Lee's line at its center angle, shaped on the map like a mule shoe. Thrown back by a savage counterattack to the captured log breastworks, fifteen thousand Federals had fought nine thousand Rebels on either side of the wooden wall for sixteen mortal hours. Corpses had been piled six deep in places, riddled with bullets that had missed the living. About two o'clock, a twelve-pound shot had carried away a chunk of top log, leaving Calvin staring at this man, ten paces away. Both men had raised their pistols like duelists and then paused. Amid the roaring terror and screaming wounded, for an instant both men had seen not "the enemy" nor even a soldier, but a man, and their mutual humanity had stayed their pistols. Then with a huge crash, a two-foot-diameter oak tree, its trunk chipped and riddled by hours of .58 caliber Federal bullets that had missed flesh, had fallen toward the disputed breastwork. Calvin remembered as the man had turned to look behind and above him that his pistol muzzle had flamed toward Calvin's left and the man had disappeared under leaves and branches.

Calvin staggered back a step on the Gettysburg sidewalk, pale with remembrance. In that same pistol-and-tree instant fifty years ago, a scream had come from his left. Despite the endless uproar and despite the pitch and pain in the scream, Calvin thought he had known whose voice it was. He had ducked and run left. Michael lay atop another corpse, his eyes screwed shut, blood staining his tunic, his mouth open and soundless.

Calvin looked now at the Ole Miss man, his stomach churning, and said shakily, "Mule Shoe. A tree fell on you."

The man nodded and scowled with utter hate. "I should have shot you Yankee son of a bitch fifty years ago when I had the chance." Sam felt the loathing like a sharp icicle on bare skin. Calvin staggered backwards.

A mass of swaying Rebel revelers swept the Mississippian into their ranks. The men were away from home, drunk, and feeling whiskey-brave. They lined up outside the church and began hurling epithets at those clustered around the windows and calling in through the wide-open double doors. Derision at "nigger preaching" and "African jungle music" competed with Reverend Jones' amplified voice across the lawn. Sam noticed one bandy-legged Confederate sporting a "GA" state badge on his collar with deep set eyes gibbering out hate of all things black or Yankee. He was egging on the rest of the vets, who showed signs of a mob. Civilians were stepping away, sensing danger. Those clustered around the windows worried as the mood turned ugly.

Still pale, Calvin unconsciously gripped his cane tighter and looked around for help or escape. He sighed in relief seeing Privates Weston and O'Connor from the U.S. 15th Cavalry arrive mounted, carrying extended billy clubs. A bit farther away, several Guardsmen swung around the corner from South Street. Weston and O'Connor moved their thousand-pound mounts broadside between the "wallpapered" group of Southrons and the church. O'Connor's horse cocked his tail and made an earthy deposit on the curbstones.

"Careful where you step," one of the revelers called. "Now there be Yankee brains on the street." Bawdy, flask-fueled laughter rang out.

"Move along there," O'Connor growled.

"Out of the way, nigga lover," the bandy-legged leader snapped.

"Keep the peace or I'll run you in," Weston barked at several men. He backed it up by having his horse clatter back and forth in small steps that rang the hooves in loud clops and struck horseshoe sparks from the paving stones. Several belligerent ones stepped lively to get out the way and kept going into the gloom. The ringleader scooped up a piece of broken brick and cocked his arm.

"Drop that rock," bawled Chief Krauss from the head of the column of approaching guardsmen. The veteran looked over, seemed to recognize Krauss, dropped the piece, and ground his heels as he scurried off into the back alleys of Steinwehr. O'Connor was about to pursue, but Weston said, "Naw, it's over now. But let's head south an' make sure they don't circle back." As they moved off, the guardsmen showed a studied casualness as they looked over the various passersby once again flowing through the area. Calvin leaned pale and shaky on Sam's arm as he recovered in the church yard and found himself caught up in the cadence and fire of the liberated as Obadiah Jones rolled full tide.

"The people of Israel came out of Egypt – and they camped.

"From the Red Sea to Mt. Sinai – they camped.

"Around Mt. Sinai, when God gave the Word to Moses in thunder – they camped.

"Every day they packed up, struck the tents, and moved on until the Lord told them to stop – where they camped.

"The children of Israel camped forty years. Forty years of camp food. Forty years of finding water – and sometimes not findin'. Forty years camping in a jackal land, a poor land, two rocks to one dirt land. For God's purposes, for forty years – they camped.

"But campin' was better'n what they were leavin' behind them.

"They left slavery behind them. ("Amen!" came the answer.)

"They left slave driver's whip behind them. (More "amens")

"They left fear behind them." The congregation was alive now, answering, helping preach, making the story their own, the church as the Body answering her Lord.

"They left pain behind them. ("O yes!")

"They left despair behind them. ("That's right!")

"They even left death behind them. ("Glory!")

"God was leadin' them, leadin' them to a promised land – a land flowing with milk and honey – a land of fertile soil, a land they could call their own. ("That's right!")

"They moved on from Egypt. They moved on from the wilderness. They moved on to a place – a good place, a godly place, a resting place, a stayin' place. ("Make it so, Lord.")

Calvin was unconsciously swaying in rhythm with so many others around the yard. He had heard preaching like this before, most recently January first at Homer Stanton's church, and Homer's blessing from yesterday morning rang again in his head. But Obadiah Jones was taking him to a new level as his heart both wept for Michael and was healed in the weeping while the preaching washed over him.

"Now Gettysburg is a giant camp. The veterans who camped as comrades and as enemies now camp together. Men in blue camping with men in gray. One more time they live by camp time, by bugle call and drum tap. And these men who are camping around Gettysburg, south and east, they camped for God's purposes and camped as God was leading them to a promised land!

"They camped all over slavery land – and brought the slaves out with them. ("The year of Jubilee!") That was God's purpose for them.

"They camped all over wilderness land – and I believe they want to leave the jackals behind, leave the shadows behind, leave the snakes behind, leave the dry places behind, leave the bitterness behind.

"A camp ain't for stayin'. ("No, suh.")

"A camp is for movin' on. ("Yes, suh.")

"Movin' on *from* some place ("That's right!") and movin'' on *to* someplace. ("Say it now.")

"Brothers and sisters, the blue and gray camping together before our eyes, who fought on this battlefield and other battlefields, have moved on.

"The blue and gray, who fought and died over the issue of black and white, have moved on.

"From fighting for two causes to living as veterans of one country, they have moved on. ("Yes Lord!")

"In the words of President Lincoln, because so many men from both sides were willing to consecrate this ground with their own blood, this nation can move on to a new birth of freedom. ("Thank you, Jesus.")

"This nation, conceived in liberty and dedicated to the proposition that ALL men are created equal can move on to be a promised land. This nation can live down her shame and move on to live out God's dream for her. ("Praise God, praise God.")

"Let this nation break camp and move on... ("Yes, Lord!")

"...strike the tent and move on.

"Let this nation move on through the wilderness. ("Preach it, brother!")

"...move on past the shackles of slavery. ("Amen!")

"...move on past the jackals of discrimination. ("Praise Jesus!")

"Let this nation move on and be no more bitten by snakes of hatred...

"...move on from the poison of prejudice...

"...move on from a wilderness that dries up hope.

"Let this nation move on toward a greater opportunity, ("Praise the Lord!")

"...move on over Jordan...

"...move on and *be* the promised land." ("Hallelujah, hallelujah!")

The organist had actually been warming up at the keyboard for some little while and knew what hymn was called for now.

The organ swelled and the congregation rose in thunderous rendition, spilling through the open windows across the yards and streets in every direction.

> *Mine eyes have seen the glory of the coming of the Lord;*
> *He is trampling out the vintage where the grapes of wrath are stored;*
> *He hath loosed the fateful lightning of His terrible swift sword;*
> *His truth is marching on.*
>
> *Glory! Glory! Hallelujah! Glory! Glory! Hallelujah!*
> *Glory! Glory! Hallelujah! His truth is marching on.*

As the second verse unfurled, the sound sagged as the words about camping caught in many throats, but rallied again for the chorus. Sam was belting out the verse for all he was worth. He looked at Calvin and put his arm around him. Calvin's head was thrown back and his eyes were closed, but tears ran unabashed down his cheeks. His lips moved unbidden and his voice joined the verse in a fine tenor harmony, but with an extra wide quaver.

> *I have seen Him in the watch fires of a hundred circling camps*
> *They have builded Him an altar in the evening dews and damps;*
> *I can read His righteous sentence by the dim and flaring lamps;*
> *His day is marching on.*
>
> *Glory! Glory! Hallelujah! Glory! Glory! Hallelujah!*
> *Glory! Glory! Hallelujah! His day is marching on.*

Traffic on Washington Street halted and incidental noises died. Calvin opened his eyes and both he and Sam came to military attention as they saw scores, no, hundreds of vets and civilians massed about. Some took off their hats, others locked arms with strangers on either side. One of the endless fireman's bands drew up at the edge of the crowd and their conductor pulled out a small baton. He listened carefully and whispered, "It's B flat gentlemen, key of B flat." As the third verse came up, the drummers added their snare and bass thump. Three trumpets joined in, two playing melody while the third soared through the night on a high descant.

> *He has sounded forth the trumpet that shall never call retreat;*
> *He is sifting out the hearts of men before His judgment seat;*
> *Oh, be swift, my soul, to answer Him! be jubilant, my feet;*
> *Our God is marching on.*
>
> *Glory! Glory! Hallelujah! Glory! Glory! Hallelujah!*
> *Glory! Glory! Hallelujah! Our God is marching on.*

The fourth verse threw a hush went over the multitude. Spontaneous harmonies resounding from all points shook souls and made hearts and lower lips quiver.

> *In the beauty of the lilies Christ was born across the sea,*
> *With a glory in His bosom that transfigures you and me:*
> *As He died to make men holy, let us die to make men free;*
> *While God is marching on.*
>
> *Glory! Glory! Hallelujah! Glory! Glory! Hallelujah!*
> *Glory! Glory! Hallelujah! While God is marching on.*

Calvin had always been a man of faith, but his was a careful, New England kind of faith, the mind leading and conversing with the soul, both keeping heart in check. Occasionally he had had hints of what a heart-led faith might be like, but they had been fleeting. Now tonight the Faith burned in his heart and dazzled both soul and mind. The Faith of the saints, done in the key of black Baptist, a key forged in shame and agony, but now undergirding liberation and hope, tonight taught Calvin's faith a new song: all heart, all soul, taking mind and memory captive, transfiguring, transforming.

Monday, June 30, 1913

Camp Lincoln

A two-door, maroon Stanley Steamer with its top down took Colonel Nicholas Biddle from the Great Tent in Pickett's Field southeast of Gettysburg up through town to the Rock Creek bridge on Hanover Pike east of town. It was early Monday, with heavy dew on every leaf.

"Much obliged, sir," Biddle said as he climbed out. "You're very welcome, Colonel," the driver replied with a civilian's exaggerated salute.

Biddle saluted back, then turned and walked with an eighty-five-year-old's care down the plank road. The freckles around his eyes hinted he'd once been a redhead and his muscular manner pointed to his boxing years. Camp Lincoln stirred with men visiting latrines, washing, dressing, and shaving or trimming their beards. Pale smoke curling under the trees carried a mouthwatering scent of bacon and coffee.

Hearty male voices merged with mess kit clankery into eager chow lines. The lines led up to long half tents with serving tables running longwise and servers bustling to and from stoves set up along the back wall. At the far end, men spread out to tables under canvas flies. Cream and sugar, salt and pepper, and bottles of vinegar passed around in jerky rhythm.

Colonel Biddle angled toward a stack marked "visitor's plates." While a fair number of colored folk from emancipated to youngsters off school for summer were already in camp for a look at their liberators, so far white visitors were pretty scarce. Biddle's "chicken guts" of rank (gold braid and an eagle) brought many sidelong glances in a camp consisting almost entirely of privates and noncoms.

"Step right here, Colonel," Ashton Melo said to him. "Honored to have you with us today."

"Thank you, Private," Biddle replied as the man straightened with pride. "But you should eat first. Officers have no business cutting line on enlisted men."

Melo grinned and stepped back in line. "I'll take that as an order, sir." It was then Biddle noticed Melo's "MA" and "54" insignia. He stepped up alongside Ashton in line and said, "I see you were with the Mass 54th. I'm Colonel Nicholas Biddle of the Mass 55th," and he shook hands.

Conversation around fell off as men eyed Biddle with new respect. The 54th and 55th brother regiments were famous. The 54th under Colonel Shaw had won glory in a desperate assault on Battery Wagner, South Carolina. The blood of the 54th had buried the idea that colored men wouldn't, or couldn't, fight. The 55th had been part of the besiegers that had finally captured Charleston.

A small knot of men, all veterans except one civilian in his mid-forties, gathered as Biddle asked them, "Are there any other USCI officers here this morning?"

"No, sir. No other officers about right now," came several snatches.

"What about some of the noncoms or Ethiopian officers among you?" Biddle asked. "I'd like to meet with them..." he arched an eyebrow, "...to plan a maneuver for the camp."

Interest crackled like skin ice breaking on a pond. Exclamations of "Maneuvah, huh?" "The whole camp?" and "Yes, suh!" all overlapped.

Melo handed Biddle a cup of coffee and said, "Colonel, why don't you take this an' sit down over at the Assembly Tent?" pointing to the large canvas elephant further on. "We'll send you all kind of officers fo' the... the strategy meetin'."

"Very good," Biddle answered, taking the offered mug. "But tell them to have breakfast first...and after the enlisted men."

"Yes, suh!" said Melo and the squad of men, who, en bloc, stepped back into line for bacon, biscuits and gravy, oatmeal, grits, and cheese. Biddle walked to the back of the line carrying his plate and sipping coffee. The middle-aged civilian walked with him and pulled out a small pad and a pencil as he introduced himself. "Colonel Biddle? How do you do? I'm Joseph Blackburn."

"A pleasure, sir," Biddle answered, tucking the plate under his arm so he could shake hands. He noticed a slight twang in the man's voice as he asked him, "Where are you from, Mr. Blackburn? Why are you here?"

"I was born and raised in Topeka, sir, but I lived for a time in Montana as well. Right now I'm with the *California Eagle* newspaper in Los Angeles and I'm here writing about the Encampment."

"Is that right?" Biddle said in surprise. "California? You know, strictly speaking Camp Lincoln is not the Encampment proper. What will your editor think?"

"Well sir, Miss Charlotta Bass, the editor and owner of the *Eagle*, is just the kind of woman who would think the colored folk who read the *Eagle* need to know about their liberators of both colors."

"Indeed, they do. And a woman for an editor. Amazing." Biddle whistled softly. "Well, what can I do for you, Mr. Blackburn?"

"I wonder if you'll fill me in the meeting you're going to have. Sounds interesting."

Biddle thought for a moment and then said, "I will on one condition. For this idea to work will require surprise. Can you keep a secret Mr. Blackburn? At least until Friday evening?"

"On my honor, sir," Blackburn answered.

"All right. Here's the idea…" Biddle began as they reached the serving tables.

Tent City

On the south edge of Pickett's Field, old graybacks were washing up their souvenir mess kits from breakfast when a drum roll sounded. Men looked up, startled, then relaxed as they recognized the drum call from local music students for Assembly-Dress Parade, old army talk for announcements and inspection. Just like fifty years before, the shouts went up, "Fall in, fall in." The men began chanting their regimental numbers to attract each other: "10th Alabama", "3rd Florida."

Zachariah and Bob hollered, "8th Georgia, 8th Georgia!" and by old habit the men sorted themselves and fell in quickly. A Maryland colonel called them to attention, then called for parade rest.

"Some things you should know, gentlemen. Meal times are breakfast half past six to eight o'clock, dinner noon to half past one, and supper five-thirty to seven o'clock. You can eat at any of the 173 field kitchens." Impressed mutters ran through the ranks.

"Second, there's seven thousand tents" – the men buzzed – "yep, seven thousand tents, set up along forty-two miles of streets. The streets are named after states, so if you get lost while you're fraternizing, just keep asking for your state to get back to your tent." More mutters and whistles.

"Third, the lowest numbered regiment in a state will have an extra tent for that state's mail. Mail will arrive twice a day. The mail tent will also sell stamps and will hold and send telegrams.

"Fourth, next to the mail tent will be one or more sutler's tents selling necessities and luxuries." A voice called out, "I believe a breakfast see-gar is a necessity!" Over the chuckle, a neighboring voice provoked a louder chuckle, "With the rope you smoke a breakfast flask is my necessity!"

"All right, all right," called the colonel, "Listen up. On the flanks here, we already have lots of civilians and a whole bunch of Yankee boys visitin', so let's give 'em all a good Rebel yell for old time's sake. Brigade, atten-hut!"

The men snapped to. The colonel called, "The general has called for an attack in the next five minutes. Are you ready?" The ranks began yipping and hollering.

"I said, 'Are you ready?'" The noise grew and the drummers joined in, now beating the "long roll" for line of battle. Men stomped their feet, waved their hats, and roared in reply.

The colonel screamed like in the old days, "We're goin' in. On the double-quick. Now yell like furies!" and for a moment the old banshee screech rang out, stunning the civilians and setting off bluecoat memories.

"Dismissed!" the colonel called and the men fell out to the welcome of the onlookers.

To their right, Zachariah and Bob saw a gangly Yankee with an elaborate, almost a "Burnside"-style moustache and chop whiskers. He stood shaking with his eyes screwed shut.

"Hey now, hey now. It's okay, old fellow," Bob said gently.

Zachariah noted the man's collar and added, "Buck up, Corporal. You Connecticut men were strong fighters."

The man bowed his head onto Zachariah's shoulder, and Zack embraced him awkwardly by gripping his stripes.

The New Haven man quieted some and blubbered, "I'm sorry. Certain things bring back the War, but your yell just now…" He stepped back and wiped his cheek. "It's a good yell."

"Uh, thanks," Zachariah mumbled, letting go now that the man seemed more settled. The next moment, the Nutmegger grabbed Zachariah's hand and shook it with both of his.

"No, no. Thank you. Yes, even for the yell. And for coming for the Encampment. Where else in the world could I get scared to death and back by the Rebel yell? I tell you, it's a tonic!"

Bob and Zack eyed the man carefully and looked around casually for a medical attendant or family members, but he kept insisting, "It's all right. It's all better now." He frantically shook Bob's hand. "I'm glad to shake hands with both of you, you being Rebels. We are all *here*, you understand? All! Billy Yanks. Johnny Rebs. The Colored troops over at their camp. Civilians by the bushel, here to watch us shaking hands to let bygones be bygones. That's why I wanted to shake your hands, to show even a man from Andersonville prison doesn't hold a grudge."

Bob went pale at the word "Andersonville." Zachariah found the lump in his throat even harder to swallow since his mouth had gone dry at the word.

"You were at Andersonville?" Zachariah asked in a half-whisper.

The man nodded, then said with an unsettling grin, "It's all over now. Washed right over me and left me be. Been right as rain ever since…" A grating woman's voice from the crowd interrupted him. "Stanford Ridderbough, you wait right there for me. You promised you'd mind."

Ridderbough's eyes lit with a dancing glow as he smiled at them and said gleefully, "Now I get to hide again!" He ran off west chuckling and disappeared into the crowd as a determined-looking woman and a manservant emerged from the east.

"Come back here, Stanford," she called as Hampton and Bidwell side-stepped her charging presence. "Come back here so Mr. Jaspers can give you your medicine."

As she and a man who was presumably Mr. Jaspers passed into the crowd, Bob and Zachariah each took a new cup of coffee and sipped off half. Bob ventured, "Seems like one of those wounded cases, but not in the body." He carefully avoided "insane" or "mental" or even "unbalanced."

"Could be. He did seem a little…off."

Bob wondered, "Could the Rebel yell heal a man?"

Zachariah sipped. "He was powerful grateful for it. And you know, there is somethin' in what he said 'bout everybody bein' here."

"Well them Camp Lincoln boys ain't 'zackly here," Bob said. "And I'm not plannin' on bein' with them there, so he wasn't right 'bout everything."

They were both thoughtful until the bottoms of their cups, trying hard not to think about Andersonville or mental disturbances. Then they ambled to the Georgia mail tent.

Even though it was only Monday, a surprising number of men already had letters from home and several even had packages. The clerk in the middle calling out names and towns abruptly called, "Hampton, Savannah." Zachariah called, "Here," then, "Hampton, Savannah" as the paper came to him hand over hand. It was a telegram. Zachariah took a deep breath and opened it. Bob looked on worriedly. He saw Zachariah's lips tighten and tears welling. He asked carefully, "News?"

Zachariah nodded, then smiled. "Yep. Good news" and passed over the message. It read, *"Hoping every day in Gettysburg is rich and full for you. Love, Emily."*

"What a ratt sweet thing to do, Zack," Bob said. "Very sentimental."

"It sure is," Zachariah answered. He read the telegram twice more, then folded it carefully and was about to put it into his pants pocket. He changed his mind and slipped it into his breast pocket and gave it an extra pat. Bob wondered about that change of pocket and the pat but Zachariah was mum, keeping the extra meaning of the telegram's first three words to himself.

Camp Lincoln

Midmorning found Colonel Biddle studying a tall brown wagon marked "Mannheim's Grocery, Westminster, MD". The strategy meeting earlier had gone well and Biddle had volunteered for some on-the-ground reconnaissance. If he could do it sitting down, so much the better. A lanky black man in a blue-checked shirt was climbing onto the driver's bench.

"Morning, sir," Biddle began. The driver was startled by the white face and beard as Biddle went on. "The sign says this wagon's from Westminster. Did you drive here today from there?"

"No, suh," the driver replied. "Jes' from Round Top Park."

"I see. And did you come by the main road up here?" gesturing toward Hanover Pike.

"No, suh. I came by a track 'long Rock Creek."

"Aha!" Biddle's face lit up. "Are you heading to Round Top Park?"

"Yes, suh. Would you like a ride?"

"Thank you," Biddle answered and stiffly clambered up. Flicking the reins, the driver brought the wagon around. As they drove along, Biddle was all eyes, studying the ground, mentally measuring the distance between certain trees, sizing up the lay of the land among the saplings. They passed occasional veterans on foot, mostly from Camp Lincoln, but some from Tent City, and a steadily growing number of civilian pedestrians of both races. After about a half a mile, the trace curved to a rough-hewn, new-looking bridge. Horse hooves clopped loudly on the timbers as the grocery wagon crossed south. The woods thinned quickly as the graveled road now crossed through a break in a fence into a field.

"Could you stop here, please?" Biddle asked suddenly. The driver halted his team. "Thank you very much," Biddle said excitedly, scrambling off. "Much obliged."

The driver shrugged. "Yo' welcome, suh."

As the horse team started up again, the driver craned his neck to look back. The old colonel was unfolding a large paper and looking west toward Culp's Hill. He was tracing something with his finger and nodding with excitement.

Gettysburg

Lucius and a new friend from the 54th Mass strolled west over the Rock Creek bridge by Camp Lincoln. A long-chinned white Union man who was carrying a red-and-black plaid carpetbag stopped them and pointed.

"Is this part of Tent City?" he asked.

"No, suh," Lucius replied. "This is Camp Lincoln."

"The camp for the U.S. Colored Troops," Ashton added.

The man's eyes gleamed. "So this camp is not run by the U.S. Army?"

Lucius and Ashton glanced at each other. "No, it's not," Lucius said as the man muttered, "This could be just the bird." He grinned a gap-toothed smile and shook hands with both of them. "Thank you. Thank you very much." He swung across the bridge with a tuneless whistle.

"What was that about?" Ashton asked as the two resumed their walk into town past all the stopped traffic.

"You got me," Lucius answered. "It's kinda early for heatstroke and I didn't smell nothin' on his breath."

"Well, I hope it's nothing in the water here in Pennsylvania that makes a man go daft and grow a chin that long," Ashton said. "He looked like a white cucumber with a moustache."

The sidewalks grew thick with pedestrians where York Pike joined Hanover from the northeast. They were nearing Woolworth's, each finishing half a soft pretzel, when Lucius nudged Ashton. "Look up ahead," he said, nodding.

Two 15th U.S. Cavalrymen on police patrol were tying off their mounts. The sergeant was maybe forty, a few inches taller than them, a handsome, black-haired man with a curly moustache. But the corporal flabbergasted them. The two-striper was in his early twenties and a specimen to behold. He was bent over holding his horse's right forefoot and working something loose that had apparently jammed in the shoe, but even in this pose he was huge. The USCI men blinked in wonder when the corporal let go of the hoof and straightened up. He had them each by a foot and maybe eighty pounds.

"Well I'll be John Browned!" Ashton breathed. "By his build are there two horses or three?"

Lucius breathed back, "With shoulders that wide, he fits through doors by the slanticular." Ashton whistled agreement.

"Picture postcards right inside," a voice called from Woolworth's. "Penny postcards, or two cents for the hand-tinted. Get 'em right inside." A clerk stood by the open door holding several samples in each hand. "Come on in, folks. Postcards and stamps right inside."

Ashton and Lucius stepped past the window to the door and slid by the hawking clerk. The store was a series of three-sided bays of counters all facing a common aisle that ran to the back. Overlooking the sidewalk, the counter against the window held spools of thread, needles, Butterick and McCall patterns, and various sewing notions, all being shopped by several women. Behind the women stood a line of shoppers aimed at a tall brown register. To the left of the line, the third side of this first bay, a crowd of noisy vets and civilians made their picks of postcards and souvenirs and joined the clerk's line. On the right was a richly dressed couple, the two on either side of thirty. He was an elegant colored man in a soft gray suit with embellished sleeves, matching gloves and homburg hat, and a wing collar. His striking purple tie was held in place by a ruby stickpin that matched his ruby cufflinks. He was shopping with a richly adorned white woman in a Directoire black dress trimmed in gold embroidery, a high lace collar blouse under a Merry Widow hat, and a diamond necklace that positively shimmered among Woolworth's glass baubles. What set tongues wagging softly not only was the couple's apparent wealth and not only was he colored and she white – "Lucille" he was heard to call her a couple times – but that she wore a costly and unmistakeable wedding ring. Woolworth's in Gettysburg was an unlikely place for an amalgamated married couple, yet here they were.

Ashton and Lucius looked over battlefield maps, recovered minié balls, and stacks of Lincoln's Gettysburg Address. They picked out several postcards apiece, Lucius splurging for tinted ones for everyone. They were in the cashier's line when two well-dressed men in their twenties came up. One was in a white linen suit, the other in tan, and both wore a Southern-typical string tie. Their accents confirmed their Dixie origins.

"That clerk's goin' purty quick," the tan-suited one said as Simon clanged away winding the register crank.

"Yeah, but this line's still longer than it oughtta be for a watt man." A woman by the sewing notions turned and rapped on the window, the sound lost among the shopper's voices and the register. Two cavalrymen in khaki looked up and she waved them inside.

"Well, it ain't that long," the tan-jacketed man replied. "We can gain two spots ratt here." They shoved their way into line ahead of Lucius and Ashton.

The USCI men looked at each other, Ashton upset, Lucius resigned. Ashton frowned at him and growled, "C'mon," and Lucius did a double-take. Turning, Ashton said with crisp politeness, "Pardon us, sirs, but we were in line first."

"Once we're done you'll have your turn," the sandy-haired man in white said rather loudly over his shoulder.

"We were here first and we'll have our turn now," Ashton said firmly, an ominous quiet about him. The clerk at the register looked up worried. The women at the notions display stopped shopping. The rich young man in the gray suit took a muscular stance in front of his wife Lucille. Both Southern rascals turned around and Lucius quailed, knowing their look from long, unwanted practice. But he noticed the hard stares all around were not aimed at him or Ashton. His mind worked to catch up with his pounding heart and setting jaw.

Tan coat said to his pal, "Say, John, you know why these two could never play baseball?"

"Why's that?" came the reply.

"'Cause in baseball it's three strikes and you're out. Each of these darkies are Yankees."

"Yeah but that's only two strikes."

"But bein' a darkie is worth two strikes all by itself." Tan coat grinned evilly at them. Lucius stopped himself from dropping his eyes and instead gave the rascals a narrow-eyed glare.

Ashton said icily, "We were in line first and we will pay first."

"Don't talk to me in that tone," John growled.

"It's the proper tone for Southern-fried bastards," Ashton answered, deadly cold. Lucius took a deep breath. The two scoundrels recoiled, nodded at each other, then both swung right hands to slap the USCI men. Lucius had recognized their escalation and timed it perfectly. As tan coat swung, he jerked back so the slap missed and the man took an awkward step forward. Lucius' right caught the man's wrist in an iron grip.

Ashton lacked Lucius' experience and didn't move. He caught John's slap full on his left cheek. His eyes blazed.

The clerk, the women, other customers, and from the doorway, Sergeant McMasters, all looked on astounded as Ashton instantly returned the slap on John. For good measure, he made it a roundhouse that followed through with a stinging slap on Lucius' man. In the shocked silence came a woman's voice by the window, "Sergeant, those two Rebels are disturbing the peace by cutting in line."

"I can see that," McMasters answered, stepping forward, spurs jingling in the hush. Behind him, a corporal backdrop loomed. McMasters read the clerk's name badge and said, "Simon, would you mind losing two customers today?"

Simon squeaked, "No, sir."

McMasters glared at the two troublemakers. "If I see you two again I'm running you in. Now get out!" The corporal mountain curled his upper lip. Both civilians paled, gulped, and scurried past the sergeant and his olive-khaki cliff.

Peaceful commerce resumed. Wanda Wilhelm, who had rapped on the window, paid ten cents for a new McCall's pattern for a shirtwaist blouse. Lucius and Ashton bought their postcards and stamps. As the two vets turned to make their way out, the wealthy mixed couple came up to them and the lady curtseyed while the gentleman tipped his hat and removed his glove. In an awed voice, he held out his hand to Ashton saying, "I'd be honored if you would shake my hand, sir."

"Of course," Ashton said, giving a manly shake.

The gentleman said, "That was a perfect roundhouse right you threw, just what those scoundrels deserved. And you got them both. Marvelous. In my line, I only have to face them one at a time."

Mystified, Ashton spoke for both himself and Lucius. "Now what line of work has you striking white men?"

"Ah, beg your pardon, gentlemen. I'm Jack Johnson, from Galveston. I'm a boxer," he said with a soft smile and holding out his hand to Lucius. Ashton gulped in wonder.

Lucius went from stunned to delighted and pumped the man's hand with both of his. "Jack Johnson? The heavyweight champion?" He tipped his hat to

Jack and then to the lady. "And you must be his wife Lucille. Pleasure to meet you, to meet you both. Oh, my son Rufus will never get over this. Jack Johnson! In fact, you got Rufus out of the doghouse back in 1910."

The Johnsons looked puzzled. "How do you mean, sir?" Lucille asked.

"Well, Rufus came home one week with five dollars missing from his paycheck. When his wife Beulah asked him why, he said he'd bet it on you in your fatt 'gainst Jeffries. Oh, she was so mad at him for throwin' away hard earned money like that, he had to sleep on the couch in the parlor for two natts. Then you won the fatt and Rufus cashed his chit and brought home twenty dollars. Beulah couldn't believe it. But she took him back off the couch."

Johnson chuckled as they all stepped out of the store onto the sidewalk. "I'm glad I could help restore your domestic tranquility." After a few more pleasantries, Ashton and Lucius continued their jaunt uptown while the Johnsons headed for a round of handshaking at Camp Lincoln.

Great Tent

After some postcard writing, dinner, and a short nap, Ashton and Lucius caught a ride to the south edge of Culp's Hill. They came on foot along Hunt Avenue and climbed up onto Cemetery Ridge. Ahead and to their left, a huge arc of pyramid, conical, and wall tents swept down the gentle western slope across Emmitsburg Road and into McMillan's Woods on up to Seminary Ridge, three-quarters of a mile away.

"Look at that one," Ashton said, pointing. A tent, enormous even at this distance, sprawled in the south part of Pickett's Field.

"Let's go take a look," Lucius agreed. Downslope as they climbed over a low stone wall, they pointed out the small grove of trees further north and they walked along, recalling and imagining.

At 200 by 450 feet the Great Tent put over two acres under canvas. Twelve thousand or more could fit inside for the various speeches, ceremonies, and programs. By luck, they had arrived between programs so Ashton and Lucius could gawk around in a suitably tourist-like manner.

They came to the southeast corner inside under some bleacher seats and found several small mounds of hay. A half-dozen black men were sitting around on bales chatting as Lucius and Ashton came up, staring. They stared because the men were in well-worn Confederate gray. The surprise was mutual as the six eyed the USCI men.

"How do you do?" Lucius asked, stumped.

"Just fine," one man answered in a similar hollow tone. "I didn't know any colored Yankees were in camp."

"Well, in my borned days the idea of colored Confederates never crossed my mind," Ashton answered in shock. "Where are you from?"

"Tennessee, mostly," another one answered.

"And how were you in the War?" Lucius wanted to know.

"Oh we were all body servants to officers. Frank here was owned by Colonel Rhodes of the 6th Florida. Michael was owned by General McLaws of Georgia." Then the man asked, "But what about you boys? Freeborn?"

"I was," Ashton answered. "54th Massachusetts."

Heads turned and low whistles sounded in admiration.

"How 'bout you?"

"Runaway slave," Lucius answered, "2nd South Carolina Union Volunteers from Port Royal." More whistles. Lucius looked around and asked, "Are y'all sleepin' here?"

The men nodded. "Well, yeah. Nobody made no arrangements for us, 'tho some of the Tennessee vets were seein' about a spare tent. That's where about eight other fellas are now."

"And food?" Ashton asked.

"Well, whatever the vets can scrounge up for us after chow lines close."

Lucius and Ashton nodded to each other and Lucius thrust his jaw at them. "Men, like General Sherman said, it's time to sling the knapsack for new fields. There's a colored veterans camp over past Culp's Hill. Come with us and you'll get a tent, cots, meals, the whole habit." An unusual blue and gray column marched across the battlefield until a Round Top wagon saved them some walking.

The USCI vets were as much amazed by the black Confederates as they were in awe of Camp Lincoln. "Well I'll be John Browned," one of them later said to Lucius as they stood in line at the bathtub tent. Passersby hawked lemonades, gospel preachers held forth on stumps at the log-paved street corners, women chattered about recipes and giggled like admiring school girls at the "Lincoln soldiers." But above the Bible verses and soprano chuckles, the black Confederate reveled in more domestic delights. "This camp is top rail. Six men in a wall tent for eight!" they marveled to Lucius. "Wash bowls, lanterns, and wood floors! Food is bully too. No desecrated vegetables or coosh but the real bird. Even ice cream! Hoowee, you fellas sure know how to keep tavern." Lucius smiled. "It beats sleepin' in the Great Tent barn, don't it?"

Cemetery Ridge, Pennsylvania Memorial

Sam worried about Calvin all Monday. He'd been deeply shaken by last night's encounter both with the Mississippi captain, and, very differently, with

Obadiah Jones. Sam watched him chew listlessly through breakfast and dinner, ignore the bands, sleepwalk through Tent City, and tour around in a daze.

Visiting Little Round Top that afternoon, Sam heard him muttering, "On the left. The left side." The 20th Maine had made their gallant stand here on Union far left, but Sam doubted Calvin meant the battle. They meandered north to the hulking Pennsylvania Memorial and sat down in its shade. Sam bought two lemonades from a pushcart and fortified them from his flask. They sipped in silence for some time.

"I saw that man once, fifty years ago, for maybe five seconds," Calvin began. "For a moment we were just two men. But after fifty years...he still hates me." He shook his head.

"That kind of hate can twist a man forever," Sam offered.

"Ayup. You know, I'm pretty sure he shot Michael." Sam saw the tear despite a manly effort. "I've got a case for hating him." Another pause. "But I don't. I can't make myself do it."

Sam took a swallow. "Most folks who hate don't talk about making themselves do it. They just do."

"I know. But I don't." Calvin took another sip.

"Maybe it's because you saw him as a man," Sam said. Calvin looked puzzled. "When I was out West, I was on picket duty one night with a wagon train. All of a sudden from the high grass a Comanche runs right past me and slaps me on the shoulder. I drew on him and he stopped and put his hands up. I could've shot him right there like the trail boss wanted. I could've held him prisoner so the trail boss would shoot him. But I could see he was just a young man."

Calvin nodded. "Had his whole life ahead of him."

"That's what I thought, too. And that's what he was proving, getting close enough to an enemy to touch him by surprise."

"Don't they do that and then leave each other alive?"

"Yep. So I sent him off. He nodded and ran and I heard a horse soon after."

Both men sipped their high-proof lemonade. Calvin took a long squint at Little Round Top to the south and mused over the fighting there as he said, "Count coup on your enemy instead of killing him. And we call them savages and say we're civilized." He sipped again. "I can't make myself hate him. That preacher last night was right. I've moved on."

"And that Mississippi man is still dreaming he's an Egyptian owner."

Tent City

Sunset's last beams poked through the gaps of South Mountain Ridge. By day, the Tent City roads carried foot, hoofed, and wheeled traffic. Here on Monday night, traffic was almost all on foot. Campfires speckled the Encampment's 280 acres and endless fireside conversations mingled with music. Sometimes bands played "Home Sweet Home," sometimes choruses sang "Aura Lee." From the New York tents came a chorus of "Du, Du, Liegst mir im Herzen" from the German-speaking troops who had boasted, "I fights mit Sigel."

Sam thought Calvin was improved as they sat stretching their legs toward a good-sized campfire. The cloud over him had gone, and in leaving, had lifted something else. Sam couldn't put his finger on it but Calvin's face was now settled in a long-ago way.

Camp chairs and logs were filled with New Englanders and a Pennsylvania Irish brigade enjoying a post-supper jaw. There were introductions, recounts of battles and campaigns, sightings of famous people (commonly called "bigwigs" or even "big bugs"), mixed with games of brag, rounds of hearty chuckles, and expressions of sympathy. One Vermonter passed around a good-sized regimental photograph of some of the men, including Sam, Josiah, and Calvin, from fifty years before and there were plenty of jibes about how well – or not – the men had held up.

Calvin glanced over to New Hampshire Avenue during his chat with a retired Scranton tailor. An old soldier stood there, barrel-chested and round-faced, his eyebrows standing out like two white arches against his chocolaty skin. Calvin scrambled to his feet, walked over, and said, "Evenin'."

"Evenin', suh. I'm Private Rockingham Brown, 26th USCI from Louisiana. Some of the men an' I've come over from Camp Lincoln lookin' to serenade the Massachusetts and New England men." Brown gestured to a double rank of men behind him stepping off the road.

"Well, I'm Major Calvin Salisbury, 14th Vermont, and this is the New England section." He pointed with his cane. "The Massachusetts tents start just ahead on your left about twenty-five yards. At this fiyah we're mostly from Vermont and Pennsylvania."

Brown smiled from inside his white Grant beard. "That'll do nicely. Would you men like a song or two?" The men around the fire had caught the chat and were already scooting into audience formation.

Calvin glanced back, then turned and nodded. "With great pleasure, sir." That "sir" earned Calvin's back a couple dirty looks.

He held out his hand to Brown for a handshake – which earned his back some more looks and a Vermont voice saying, "Two things I'll never shake hands with: a colored hand…" and a Pennsylvania voice finished "…or a rebel hand. You got it."

But the private gave Calvin a look of amazement and said softly, "Down South a colored man holds out his hand to a watt man to see iffin' he'll shake it – or not."

Calvin blinked in surprise, then thrust his hand again toward Brown. "America, like in Vermont, should be a place where a handshake happens from respect or friendship." Both men shook hands and swallowed hard, then both assumed a more manly air.

Calvin sat back down as the USCI men formed an inward-curving double line, took a pitch from a mouth organ, and then broke into "Yankee Doodle," accompanied by a drummer in the second row. Vermont and Pennsylvania clapped along and joined in the chorus the second time through. The singers were good, moving from unison, to two-part, to three-part harmony as the verses unreeled. Next came a fine rendition of "Rock of Ages," followed by "Rock-a My Soul." Each song earned progressively louder clapping, whistling, and foot stomping.

Then came "The Girl I Left Behind Me," a soldiers' favorite, done in a haunting four-part harmony. The campfire men applauded absently, remembering old sweethearts and longings. "Thank you, thank you very much," the men called as the troupe bowed and moved off toward the Massachusetts section. "Stop back anytime."

"Wasn't that grand?" Sam exclaimed. Calvin agreed it was. Josiah Trimble's face wore an expression of deep satisfaction as he remarked, "What harmony!"

"Born to it, I warrant," added a Pennsylvania private, having taken a beat to decode Trimble's "haahminy" as "harmony." "They're good for singing."

"They're a singing people, from church to heavy labor," Trimble mused, rubbing his beard on the backhand.

Sam cocked his head, not quite sure what he was hearing. Calvin was sure. "You saying colored folks are only good for plantation work, Josiah? 'Lift that barge and tote that bale' while singing in haahminy?"

"I'm saying every person has certain talents, some acquired in life and others inborn. Each race has certain gifts and certain shortcomings."

"I see," Calvin replied evenly. "So birth is destiny?"

"Naw, not that," said the Pennsylvanian. "It's just there's limits for anyone and any race. Even Booker T. Washington said that in Atlanta. If colored folks' edjication makes 'em better hands on the farm or in a factory, they'll be satisfied."

"To be the best hewer of wood or drawer of water they can be," Josiah added.

"In the army, all of us hewed wood and drew water," Sam said, staring into the flames. "Did that mean we were outside our limits?"

"It was the army," returned Josiah. "We were men under discipline and obedient to authority, even if at times it seemed degrading."

"Degrading?" Calvin asked. "Robert E. Lee said, 'Nothing is so military as labor' and made those fine Southern cavaliers dig trenches. Those white men took such pride in their 'degrading labor' we ended up getting shot to pieces at Cold Harbor."

"It's still a matter of the proper relationship among the races," Josiah insisted.

"I've heard your kind of talk before," Pennsylvania put in, aiming at Josiah. "You sound like my father." The dry goods man took out a wrinkled, yellowing envelope and carefully pulled out two sheets. "Both these were his." The first one he passed down was on Western Union scratch paper. Since customers paid by the word they practiced for a cheap message. This read:

> *August 11, 1863*
> *From: John McMahon, Williamsport, Pennsylvania*
> *To: President Abraham Lincoln, White House, Washington City*
>
> *Equal rights & justice to all men in the United States forever. White men is in class number one & black men is in class number 2 & must be governed by white men forever.*

"Absolutely well put," Trimble announced. "Your father expressed the sentiment perfectly."

"Well here's what he got back," said John McMahon Jr., passing down the second sheet. The Vermonters saw this was fine stationery embossed, "The White House" and signed by John Nicolay, Lincoln's personal secretary. After greeting and thanking McMahon for his wire, and noting the President had several others like it, he wrote

> *As it is my business to assist him whenever I can, I will thank you to inform me, for his use, whether you are either a white man or a black one, because in either case you cannot be regarded as an entirely impartial judge. It may be that you belong to a third or fourth class of yellow or red men, in which case the impartiality of your judgment would be more apparent.*

"That is just wrong," Josiah pronounced.

"That is applying the Declaration of Independence to say 'All men are created equal'," Calvin answered firmly.

The two men exchanged hard looks, but unlike many other times, it was Josiah who backed down first by muttering, "Well at least you think it should be all *men*."

Calvin remembered Eleanor last November picketing on Election Day and said, "I'm not so sure about that either." Sam and McMahon turned the conversation to lighter subjects.

Tuesday, July 1, 1913

Tent City

After breakfast Tuesday morning, Zachariah emerged from door eighty-one of the giant 120-door latrine and joined a growing crowd near a shaded platform. Above conversations, he heard an occasional shout, "Archer's Brigade, assembly. Archer's Brigade, fall in." Over three hundred Tennessee, Alabama, and Maryland men were forming ranks facing north, with the platform on their right flank. Everyone else formed a gray-blue crescent, Zack and Bob near one horn, and a block of USCI men at the far point.

A Yankee column of four approached up Iowa Avenue, paced by drum and fife. The blue vets halted, marching in place. Twenty-five men back, a sergeant bawled out, "First company, left face. Forward, march!" The first hundred men marched forward and south. As the last rank, which had just been the far right file, passed the sergeant, he raised his arm. The column moved forward another twenty-five men. The first company closed to within eight feet of the front rank of Confederates when a Wisconsin lieutenant halted them. Behind them, similar companies of a hundred men each faced left and marched up behind until over five hundred Union men had deployed facing the Archer boys. The Stars and Stripes, several regimental banners, and state flags from Tennessee, Wisconsin, Maryland, Alabama, Michigan, and New York shamed the trees drab.

Colonel Simon Briscoe, 6th Alabama, stepped onto the platform as the drum and fife finished. "Men of Archer's Brigade: Attention!" The gray ranks and many old soldiers looking on automatically, pushed their heels together, and faced eyes at the Yankees. "Right face!" came the next command, pivoting the brigade toward the platform. "Dress the line!" and the old men turned chin-over-right-shoulder and each lifted his left arm to feel for his neighbor. There was an extra pause as men missing a left arm looked back and forth to achieve the commanded spacing.

Colonel Quinton Hawthorne, 28th Michigan, stepped up alongside Briscoe and called, "First Corps, Iron Brigade, attention!" "Left face!" and the blue mass turned ninety degrees toward the platform. A moment later, "Men in blue, dress the line."

With everyone in place, Briscoe saluted Hawthorne and said, "Archer's brigade assembled and ready, sir!"

Hawthorne saluted. "Thank you, Colonel Briscoe." He turned to the two groups, gray left and blue right. "Veterans, parade rest." As the men took a small right step back and crossed their left hands over right at the belt buckle Hawthorne pulled a couple sheets of paper and a pair of glasses from inside his jacket.

"Gentlemen, on July first, 1863, General James Archer led an unsuccessful attack against the First Corps. He was captured during the counterattack. He offered his sword in surrender to General Wadsworth, who touched it and told him, 'Keep it. I only need one sword on this field.'

"Let me now read you the following letter." He put on his glasses, unfolded the paper and read,

> *Dear Colonel Hawthorne,*
>
> *I am Catherine Morris, widow of Lieutenant Ronald Morris who was on the staff of General Wadsworth, First Corps, Army of the Potomac. On the first day of the Battle of Gettysburg, General Archer was captured. As he was led away, I am ashamed to say that my late husband demanded General Archer's sword. Vainly did General Archer protest that he had already offered his sword to General Wadsworth. My husband insisted, and, as a prisoner, the general was forced to yield.*
>
> *My husband always kept the sword in our attic. Over the years many called on him to return it: General Archer's family, his brigade, Southern governors, the national GAR, even the Secretary of War. My husband refused them all. He insisted it was a trophy of the war and his to keep. Indeed in his last days he expressed the wish to be buried with it in his coffin.*
>
> *Colonel Hawthorne, please understand, apart from this obsession my dear Ronald was a good, hardworking man and provided comfortably for our family. But in this matter of the sword he was completely obstinate.*
>
> *I am writing to tell you that he died November 14, 1912. Despite his wishes we did not bury him with General Archer's sword. Instead Colonel, as you are commanding officer of the Michigan GAR, I am sending you this letter and the sword. I ask that you take it with you to this summer's Encampment at Gettysburg. I ask you find members of General Archer's brigade, or even of his family, and return the sword to them with all due honors.*
>
> *Colonel, the war is over. Let my husband's memory be put right by this act, and let his hardheartedness be buried with him. I hope this might serve as a sign to the men of both sections to do likewise.*
>
> *Yours very respectfully,*
> *Catherine Morris, Grand Rapids, Michigan*

The lump-in-throat silence that followed was broken by a drum roll. The Grand Rapids GAR post commander, flanked by two other veterans, came onto the platform, stiffly carrying a handsome mahogany case. Colonel Briscoe stepped opposite him, also flanked by two UCV veterans. The GAR man swung up the lid. The colonel took Archer's sword out of its velvet-lined depression, a thick gold braid hanging from the pommel, and held it vertically in front of his face in salute.

The drum roll halted. Michigan's Hawthorne called out, "Men in blue, attention!" The blue side stiffened noticeably. "Right face!" The Union men swung to a view of the Archer Brigade's left profiles. "Color guard, salute!" All the Union flags except the Stars and Stripes bowed forward toward the assembled Confederates. The command "Uncover" brought old kepis and newer civilian hats off to show gray or white hair, thin down to bald. "Eyes down!"

Hawthorne held his hat over his heart. "We Union men of the Army of the Potomac, First Corps, return to you men of the South a sword that was foully taken and shamefully kept. As men of honor we regret this stain upon the reputation of the First Corps. We hope you will accept its return and ask this dishonor be effaced from our name." He dropped his eyes into the heavy silence.

Colonel Briscoe stepped to the edge of the platform. "Archer's Brigade, atten-shun!" The graybacks snapped to, many eying the sword. "Left face!" and now the butternuts looked at their old foes' bowed heads. "General Archer's sword is returned from captivity. Shame has been confessed. A noble apology has been offered. Shall we accept the sword and those who brought it to us?"

A voice from somewhere in the gray ranks called out, "Them Yankees show promise!" The Southern color guards bobbed their flags in salute to the bowed Union ones as a cheer rose from the gray ranks. This brought a head-lifting, answering cheer from the men in blue.

As the noise subsided, the two colonels smiled, said something to each other, and shook hands. Michigan's Hawthorne called out, "Men of the South, right oblique." The men in gray performed a forty-five degree pivot toward the Wolverine. Alabama's Briscoe called out, "Men of the North, left oblique" and the blue bloc veered forty-five degrees toward the Yellowhammer. Together the two officers said, "Dis-missed."

As the formations dissolved and civilians and other veterans stepped forward in congratulation, a cluster developed around the sword and the case the GAR had had custom-built for it. Another cluster formed around Private Patrick Maloney who had personally captured Archer fifty years ago today and exclaimed then, "God almighty! Caught me a general!" Even though it was early in the day, numerous flasks passed around in toast and salute. Zachariah handed around his "ZH" flask after giving it a strange look. Except for Sunday's toast with Dooley, he hadn't touched a drop since Savannah.

There was much mingling and many handshakes all around. Men alternated between loud rejoicing with each other and misty-eyed quiet over handshakes that even became double-handed. More than a few hoped this morning's round of restoration with honors and apologies would be a forerunner to the big handshake planned for Friday. A wartime chaplain wandering among the veterans caught the mood by repeating loudly from the Psalmist, "How good and pleasant it is when brothers live together in peace."

A narrow-eyed North Carolina lieutenant with a Van Dyke beard was shaking hands when he held out his hand right while talking left. Looking back right, his arm went wet-noodle shocked in the grasp of a USCI man.

"Congratulations on getting yo' sword back, butternut!" the black private exclaimed, pumping vigorously. "Hey, you're from North Carolina too. Where 'bouts? I'm from Wilmington."

"I'm from Wilmington," the white Tarheel answered, his mood sliding from stunned to mortified. "Um, ah, look I wanta say how sorry I am for that thar riot back in '98."

The pumping stopped. The USCI man wiped his right hand down the side of his pant leg like he was trying to scrape off tree sap. "I lost my wife, father, and a brother in that riot." The private jabbed his finger. "Shouldn't take fifteen years for somebody to say sorry."

The old grayback paled and some of the private's friends grabbed him to hold him back. "Shouldn'ta happened at all."

Other Confederates stepped in front of the lieutenant, looking hard-eyed at the USCI men, and these men did not drop their eyes in the accustomed manner but glared back just as hard-eyed. Cooler heads and peace-making men pushed the two sides apart and jollier words floated around. The Johnny Reb Tarheel took the next flask offered and promptly downed half, then muttered something about being careful who you shake hands with. The USCI man stamped off growling to his buddies his hand would probably stink for the rest of the day from that handshake. Guardsmen pushed through the crowd and made sure everyone's handshakes stayed friendly.

Rose Run

As the crowd broke up, Bob Bidwell said, "C'mon Zack. Let's go poke around the battlefield."

"Sounds good to me," Zachariah answered. They clumped east on Missouri Road. "How 'bout if we catch the streetcar? Save a lotta walkin'."

As they neared the Emmitsburg Road, they passed a line of excited men waiting at a small desk manned by the Signal Corps. Zack and Bob heard one side of a conversation as the vet at the desk laughed and then half-shouted into a boxy apparatus, "That's ratt Mabel. It's me, Henry. I'm callin' yew in Memphis from Pennsylvania!" He paused a moment before saying, "Yep! Ain't this amazin'!? We get two free minutes on these Army telly-phones." He listened once more and answered, "Say hello to ever'body there at Virgil's store…"

Zack and Bob got lucky as they got to the streetcar stop. There was almost no line just as an open-sided summer car pulled up. They hopped on board and rode southwest most of two miles to Tipton Park by the Rose farm.

The scene was both familiar and odd. Here were the fields, trees, and Rose Run twisting along pretty much as they recalled after fifty years. But here also were monuments, endless civilians, pavilions, Tipton's photo gallery, dining halls, saloons, and a dance hall. There were lots of men in blue and gray looking far too old, much older than they themselves felt. It was easy in the mind to be twenty-six again, sinewy, determined, a new nation's independence dancing just one victory ahead.

"Let's see if we can find where we were," Bidwell suggested. They worked their way through some trees and came out on a road marked Sickles Avenue. They followed this southeast, unconsciously falling into step. Their crunching steps mingled with bird calls. Buzzing grasshoppers and cicadas hummed from the fields and from the tall grass toward Rose Run on their right. Echoes of other sounds seemed near: crashing cannon fire, the angry hum of shell fragments splitting the air, the long ripping of volley fire, the smack of bullets hitting… Zachariah pulled up.

"Over here to the ratt I think. Where this crick makes the bend there," he said, pointing. The two tramped through the waist high grass to the bank. Zachariah looked around. "I'd know it bettah from the other side." Like old times on an easy march, both he and Bob took off their shoes and socks and rolled up their pant legs and waded across easily.

"Nice an' cool," Bob said as they sat on the opposite bank, lacing up.

In a faraway voice Zachariah answered, "Yes, it was." Something was filling his chest, clutching his throat, watering his eyes. He shook his head for a moment, stood, and moved off several yards from the bank, stopping every few yards to look across toward the wheat field. He stopped at a waist high bush, pulled back some of branches and studied the base.

"What is it, Zack?" Bob asked softly.

"Look here," Zachariah answered, pointing. "Look how thick them little shoots are by the ground, an' how they head off away from the bank."

"Yep, I see 'em. Like they was a lot mo' bush once. An' a lot thicka too."

Zachariah stood stock still a long moment, then whispered, "Then it was here." He fought for manly control, but then sobbed. A long howl burst from his chest, not a cry of physical pain but the wide wailing of loss that grief presses from the lungs and gut. Bob put his arms around him and they stood a long while. Zack's tears stopped, but not the wail. They stood a while longer.

When Zachariah got hold of himself, he shed his jacket and unbuttoned the cuff on his left sleeve. "It was 'bout five o'clock on the second day. Sickles' Third Corps had pushed out to here. Longstreet ordered a counterattack, startin' down by L'il Round Top an' Devil's Den. I was behind this bush with my tentmate, Clint Taylor, and we were out front as skirmishers. I was pointin' at sumpin, jes' gettin' my arm up. Bullet missed my knuckles an' sliced my sleeve longwise." He pulled back his sleeve and Bob saw a long, dark red streak about a half inch wide from Zachariah's wrist to elbow. "Hurt like the dickens ever' heartbeat. Bleedin' bad. I was cryin', wantin' to hold it, an' not wantin' to 'cause it hurt like it did. Clint an' I laid down right here an' he crawled up to the Run to fill his canteen fo' my wound and us to drink. Yankee bullets and canister was rippin' through this bush, nippin' off branches ever' volley. Clint crawled off again an' didn't come back. Then Barksdale's charge wrecked Sickles, an' I could get up. Found Clint's body bleedin' into the creek. I walked back to a surgeon's wagon." He sobbed again, his face a wide grimace. Then came a shoulder crushing sigh.

As he buttoned his cuff, he went stark pale at a thought. "Because I got wounded, Clint died. But the sawbones listed me as 'wounded, unfit for duty' so I wasn't in Pickett's charge the next day and didn't get shot up on the ratt flank." He stared around for a while, seemingly listening for the ground or the bush to speak. Bob heard him mumble once, "It really is over. And it really is fifty years," but kept still as Zachariah wandered. Another shudder and wail wracked him but then he was calm. He came over to Bob with a spent half-voice, "I've seen what I wanted to see. Where'd you like to go?"

Bob said, "Let's cross back over. That monument over there, the cannon along the road? Looks familiar to me." They waded back, playfully kicking water at each other. Re-shod, they approached the cannon, plaque, and two Union vets, talking and pointing beyond Bob and Zack. An open buggy pulled up alongside the monument as well, and a bright-eyed woman of about fifty said softly, "Driver, wait here a moment." She pulled out a small pad of paper and cocked her ear to listen to the men.

One of the Union men laid his head on the other's shoulder and copied Zachariah's wail from a quarter hour before. The Georgians approached shyly, biting their lower lips in sympathy. While the old soldier composed himself, his companion said to them, "I'm John Morris and my brother Abner, 1st Ohio Light Artillery, Columbus. We were remembering another brother of ours, Steven, who died right here the second day." Bob and Zack gulped hard. The woman in the buggy scribbled speedily. "We were unlimbering when some of

Longstreet's skirmishers opened up on us. Steven went down in the first volley. We picked out some of them hiding in a big bush over that creek there and let loose with some canister."

Zack only stared but Bob put out his hand solemnly and said, "Shake! I belonged to the brigade that charged yo' battery twice. I'm Robert Bidwell, 8th Georgia, Savannah."

"Glad to meet you. You and your men did some pretty good charging."

"Yep, an' we'all thought you did some pretty good shootin'. We tried to give y'all yo' money's worth."

"You surely did. Anybody in the battery will acknowledge the corn of that."

Bob paused, caught up in the sense of the place, the park-like peacefulness clashing with his bloody memories. His eyes were brim full as he said in a strangled voice, "You know, this here reunion fo' both the armies in the fight, is one of the greatest, grandest things that a nation on the face of the globe can boast of. Right here, fifty years ago, we were in one of the greatest battles of the Civil War. Today we're old neighbors, friends even!" Bidwell choked.

Morris answered, "I know just what you mean. Sir, this is a great country, and one worth living for." Morris and Bidwell wrung each other's hands as did Zachariah and Abner. The woman put down her pencil and daubed her eyes with a handkerchief. The four swapped stories for a time until the woman broke in during a pause.

"Pardon me, gentlemen," she said with a rolling drawl. "Might I trouble you for your names?"

They moved over to the buggy as Morris asked, "Are you a reporter, then?"

"Actually I'm writing a daily column for the *New York Times* of my impressions of the Encampment."

"Well, ma'am," Bob said, smiling, "I imagine you might be givin' those Northern readers a Southern view of things, if I'm judgin' yo' accent rightly."

The woman laughed merrily. "I suppose my Georgia drawl marks me as much as your Georgia badges do." She held out her hand to Bidwell. "How do you do, Captain? Sergeant?" She beamed toward Zachariah. "I'm Helen Longstreet. I was the general's second wife until he died back in 1904." Bob startled in wonder. Zachariah stared hard, then came to attention with his cheeks wet and held a salute until Mrs. Longstreet told him quietly, "At ease, Sergeant. Let's talk about the general, shall we?" And they all did for some time.

The Great Tent

Tuesday afternoon's Great Tent program was over and about eight thousand attendees were leaving. Calvin and Sam sat talking as the crowds thinned. Along the east wall nearby, they spotted a pair of wheelchair-bound vets parked right hand to right hand. One was in gray with "VA" on his lapel. The other was in blue, turned away from them, a pair of crutches strapped to the chairback.

"Say, Calvin," Sam half-whispered. "Do you suppose the old vet in the invalid chair is Sickles?"

Greeting the oldest surviving – if rather eccentric – Union general from the battle would be a plum. Sickles was present, but it was a big camp, so it was best to grab the chance. They both joined other veterans with the same hope and idea.

A string of "hoowees" and "how 'bout that's" were passing around. Calvin and Sam wedged in close, but it wasn't Sickles. Yet on second look, both men were remarkable. They were positively ancient, even by Encampment standards. A Virginia man in an unusual Confederate States Navy first mate's uniform was bent over his fellow Virginian and speaking slowly into his ear trumpet. "Just how old are you, suh?"

The wizened little man stirred and croaked in a shriveled voice, "Ninety and nine. I's born 1814 in Charlottesville." Amazement ran around the group of veterans.

The navy man said again into the ear trumpet, "Well, suh, you jes' might want to shake hands with this man here," indicating the Union man in the adjoining wheel chair. "His name is Paul Nottingham, and he's born in 1814 an' is ninety-nine years old too."

"Izzat right?" squeaked the old man. He reached over and took Nottingham's hand. "I'm Charles Palmer. Good ta meet ya suh. Good to meet ya." All around, vets jabbered like kids in their presence, delighted at being fifteen or twenty years younger than *somebody* for the first time in ages.

The two hoary vets got acquainted, exchanging hometowns and places of service. Palmer had marched with Early in 1864 – Monocacy, Cedar Creek, Fisher's Hill – when the Confederacy drafted fifty-year-old men into their shrinking ranks. Nottingham, from Braintree, Massachusetts, had been an engineer on the U.S. Military Railroad outside Petersburg and helped fight off Gordon at Fort Stedman.

Calvin and Sam were sharing the general merriment when Calvin remembered something. He tapped the first mate on the shoulder and posed his question. "I'll find out," he replied with excitement. He clapped his hands and waved for quiet. Palmer swung his ear trumpet to listen. The old sailor knelt down in front of Nottingham and asked carefully, "Suh, yo' from Braintree. Did you ever know any of the Adamses there?"

The quiet became total as everyone caught their breath. Paul knowingly smiled his two-toothed grin. "I lived about a mile from the Adamses. When I was nine years old on the Fourth of July, old man John and his wife Abigail were riding to a banquet. I was comin' from fishin' and they stopped their carriage. I said, 'Happy Fourth of July, Mr. Adams. Thank you for helping make our country.' He smiled, reached down, and shook my hand saying, 'You're welcome, Mastah Nottingham. Happy Fourth of July' and then they rolled off to town."

Half the listeners gasped at the living history in front of them. The other half burst into cheers and applause. Charles Palmer stared in wonder at his fellow antediluvian, then held up his hand.

"If that don't beat all," he crackled. "Then I'd like to shake a hand that shook John Adams' hand." Instantly, every man listening wanted to do the same as Palmer continued. "But fust, Nottingham, maybe you'd like to know who you'll be shakin' hands with."

"How so?" Nottingham asked.

"You were nine years old, ratt?" Palmer asked. "So 1823?"

"That's right."

"That same Septembah in Charlottesville at the University main hall, I was heppin' my father delivuh some barrels of flour. I sees an old man ridin' to a hitchin' post. He looked kinda stiff in the saddle, so I went and held his hoss while he dismounted. He tied off and said to me, 'Thank you, son.' I said, 'Twern't nuthin, suh. By the by, suh, do I know you? I think I've seen you in our store but I don't recall yo' name, suh.' Well he held out his hand an' I shook it. An' he said, 'Pleasure to meet you, young man. My name is Jefferson, Thomas Jefferson.'"

If the veterans had thought fainting was manly, a dozen would have swooned right there. As it was, there were gasps, then cheers filled the emptying tent. Calvin and Sam were in the eager and patient line of men who shook two hands that had once been held by the noble Adams and the great Jefferson.

Dobbin House Tavern

After Tuesday's supper, veterans and visitors flowed along the state streets of Tent City, but many others headed into town. On foot, by electric trolley and by countless wagons, carriages, and motorcars, a good crowd crept up Emmitsburg Road into Gettysburg.

Like most veterans, Zachariah didn't walk long because every civilian wanted to ride with a "real veteran." A man in a dark brown homburg driving an open gig invited Zack along. His wife, son, and daughter all squeezed to one side of the bench and stared at the gray-clad graybeard. Their rather awestruck mother stammered, "We're from Chambersburg and we're delighted to give you a lift, sir."

"Much obliged, ma'am," Zachariah replied, waggling his eyebrows at the children.

The little girl gave him a shy smile. Her brother fidgeted and then blurted out, "Are you a real rebel?"

"I'm a real Confed'rit, but the War's over."

"And where do you call home, sir?" father called over his shoulder.

"Savannah. Sergeant Zachariah Hampton, 8th Georgia, at yo' service." They talked for about twenty minutes until the carriages and flivvers jammed solid in south Gettysburg and only walkers made headway.

Zachariah said goodbye and stepped onto the sidewalk of Steinwehr Avenue. He drifted north past the stalled traffic with a bunch of Deep South veterans. Across a small square on their left, they joined a line outside a large tavern for the chance to liquor.

At the head of this line, Langston Dobbin, third generation proprietor, smiled at Lucius Robinson and three other U.S. Colored troops. Ignoring some southern-accented rumbles, he called, "Right this way, gentlemen." He led them beyond a Colonial fireplace that formed most of a wall and past the jammed bar to the far wall and seated them at a round table. A couple more tables holding civilians spanned the distance to the deep-set window. Other square and round tables littering the room held a majority of Union men in groups of four to eight.

As Langston hustled back across the roaring room, like everyone else, the four USCI men took long sideways glances at a table of veterans two over from them. Four New York "Zouaves" sat drinking and talking. Early in the War, before regulations came down specifying blue and gray uniforms, militia units joined their sides in their own uniforms. Regiments of New York Zouaves wore dark blue jackets only elbow-length long and cinched at the belly. The belly sported a sash holding up bright red pants that ballooned Arabic style to the ankle, tied off there in white gaiters. The whole getup was topped by a fez, sometimes adorned with a tassel. Even though the bright red had faded to worn brick and the white gaiters and fez showed fifty years of grime, men from both sides still gave the Zouaves a second look.

The USCI men were still looking when their view was blocked by the ample form of Priscilla Dobbin, who took her husband's place at the side of the table. The men looked up slightly startled as she said to them, "Evening, gentlemen. Welcome to the Dobbin House Tavern. Delighted you stopped by."

"Much obliged, ma'am." "Yes,'m" they answered, their eyes wandering, unfamiliar with ordinary courtesy from a white woman.

"Are you gentlemen hungry, thirsty, or both?" Priscilla asked.

"Uh, mostly thirsty ma'am," Lucius answered for them.

Still marveling at "gentlemen," he was equally amazed at the title being used publicly by a white woman.

"Well, the bartenders have been boning up for you veterans. Heinz, Carl, and Booker have been practicing flips, fixes, crustas, and Corpse Revivers. What sounds good to you?" The mixed-drink names were long-ago-familiar, but figured to be pricey. "How much does a beer cost?" Lucius asked, fingering some coins in his pocket.

"Well, I'll tell you," Priscilla answered. "Usually it's five cents, but for you fellows I'm only going to charge you three cents. Can you each pay that much?"

"Yes, ma'am," came four eager replies, spotting a bargain when they heard one.

"Well, then, you plank me twelve pennies between you when I get back."

The foursome quickly dug out the coins and began jawing. Sooner than they expected, Priscilla reappeared. "Here you are, fellows." She hefted four huge gray steins etched with gothic German letters, expertly landing the lager and passing out at least a gallon four ways. "And here you are, ma'am." They all passed along their pennies, rocked by the size of the ceramic towers in front of them.

Priscilla swept nine coppers of "emancipation money" and three Indian heads into an apron pocket. "The Germans who settled here not only made beer, they always said it should be drunk in goodly amounts." The old vets chuckled.

Lowering her voice, she went on. "Besides, you fellas deserve it. When I was a little girl living across the street, old man Dobbin and his wife – my in-laws before they passed away – were always begging a loaf of bread or some medicine for colored folk on the run. See, it's only eleven miles to Emmitsburg, Maryland, and the Dobbin House Tavern was the first Underground Railroad stop in a free state. They tell me Harriet Tubman herself stayed in the hideaway room here a couple of times." Heads nodded and eyes went wide around the table.

"But nowadays you should just drink out here in the open, not runaways dodgin' hunters, but just fellas. If you gentlemen need anything else, just give a call, okay?" She turned and was swallowed up in the swarming mass.

"Hoowee! What d'ya thinka that?" Isaiah Dade exclaimed softly.

"Well," said Joe Clovese, "I think a place like this, servin' beer like this," still unbelieving his foaming pillar, "deserves a toast."

"That's it, a toast!" Floyd Tillman chimed in, and they hefted their stout mugs.

"Gennulmen and comrades," Lucius intoned, dropping his voice while glancing at a few tables of hard-eyed Confederates glaring at him. "To the

Underground Railroad and the Dobbin House Station." The beer foam expanded all four mustaches.

Traffic was finally moving again. From Lincoln Square, down the west side of Baltimore Street, came a double column of the U.S. 15th Cavalry at a slow walk. Each man wore the regulation 1902 single-breasted olive-khaki uniform. On infantry, the tunic had an odd flare at the hips, but on mounted men, the effect was sharp. A captain and lieutenant led the way, with a sergeant and oversized corporal paired next, followed by eight pairs of privates. Bringing up the rear, Private Weston, atop a roan mare, said to his partner, "Well, I'm glad to be riding again. Untangling civilian traffic isn't for me."

"No common sense at all," O'Connor agreed. "Good to be back among the veterans."

"They do mind better," Weston acknowledged. "Used to orders I guess. But we're not back to Tent City yet."

"Nope, and curfew isn't for a while. Still might have some policing around here."

"Hey!" Sergeant McMasters called back. "No talking in ranks!"

Weston and O'Connor stared ahead woodenly. As the troop crossed Middle Street and moved into shadows between gas streetlamps, the sidewalk chatter and traffic noises rose enough so that O'Connor felt safe talking again. "What do hear about the captain? Came in last week for this Gettysburg detail, and I hear he's shipping out again next week."

As they passed the turreted Episcopal church, Weston answered. "Well, for one thing, see how easy he sits in the saddle?" Both men saw the captain shifting in perfect rhythm with his mount. "He learned how from John Mosby out in California."

"Mosby? The Gray Ghost?" O'Connor asked in awe, using the Confederate's old Shenandoah nickname.

"The very same. Mosby's in his retiracy out there and doesn't like reunions. Anyway," Weston continued, "the cap'n's a West Pointer from '09 I think. Last year, he was on the team that went to Sweden for those Olympic Games."

"Is that right?" O'Connor answered, ducking under a tree branch as they topped the aptly named High Street.

"Yep. Anyhow, he was in some event for military messengers. You have to ride a horse, shoot, sword fence, and some other things."

"I wondered why he's been toting around that cheese knife," O'Connor said. "Seems kinda showy for just a captain on police patrol in Gettysburg, Pennsylvania."

Settling his horse's tossing head after a motorist honked at them, Weston said, "Aw, that's 'cuz he figures it gives him an in with the old vets. Lieutenant says the captain really wishes he could've fought with Lee or Grant. I guess being here this week is the next best thing." They crossed Breckenridge Street and angled off Baltimore onto Steinwehr Avenue. "Besides, I hear he's good with it. After that Stockholm affair the Army had him take sword fighting courses at a French academy."

"Dang," O'Connor exclaimed. "Graduate from West Point and see the world."

Weston chuckled back, "Enlist like you and me and see Podunk Pennsylvania."

The upright piano sounded only occasionally above the hearty roar of a very full house. Langston Dobbin, Priscilla, and the staff were pushing through knots of old vets talking, singing, gesturing, and mostly having a well-liquored good time. But Langston didn't like the serious tone of the Southern-tanged voices in one section. They were too earnest, with little of the cheer flowing through the rest of the tavern.

"Heinz!" he yelled through the cigar smoke.

"Yah," Heinz answered, lumbering over and leaning across the bar.

"Keep an eye on things for a few minutes, 'specially those guys at the six-top tables under the banner," nodding to his right. Heinz sized up several tables of Confederates.

"Okay," Heinz nodded. "I know who you mean. Some of them French-talkin' Louisiana fellers look like trouble."

"That's who I'm worried about," Dobbin agreed in a low shout. "I'm going to get some help." Dobbin untied his apron, passed it over the bar, and began scrambling toward the door.

"You are not from Louisiana?" asked a paunchy little corporal with pink cheeks and watery gray eyes. His English tangled with a growing French accent as his whiskey disappeared. His question came out sounding like "yew air noh from Louee-zee-ang?"

"No, sir," the freckled balding man answered. "I'm Private Pleasant Crump, 10th Alabama, Wilcox's Brigade."

"I am Corporal Jean Gastieu. We here at theez tableaux," he waved at several nearby tables, just a few yards from a table of USCI vets sawing away at four massive beers, "are the men of Major Roberdeau Wheat. General Zhack-sohn led us through the Valley of Shenandoah."

"Really!" Crump exclaimed, his eyes shining. "Stonewall Jackson's foot cavalry! That was one Sam Hill of a campaign."

"Mercí," Gastieu replied, sighing heavily. "A winning campaign, yes, but in a losing war." He swung his shot glass toward Lucius' table. "There sits the result of our loss." Growls of agreement rose from the tables around Gastieu and Crump.

"'Tain't ratt," someone piped up. "A dang insult."

"Easy, boys," came another voice. "They's a lotta Yankee blue in this place."

A very slurred voice answered back from another table, "Don't mattah none. One rebel can still lick ten Yankees in a fatt."

"That's ratt," several voices came back, mixed with a couple "Ouí" s from Gastieu's left.

A burly Tennessee lieutenant banged down his glass and rose swaying to his feet. He bobbed just an arm's length away from the table of fez-topped New York Zouaves. The lieutenant's eyes enlisted the tables of gray-clad veterans, then turned to the Brooklyn boys. "This'd still be a ratt great country if it 'twern't for a certain long-armed gorilla of a Prezdint the goddamn Republicans jammed down our throats!" he snarled in a rising voice, glaring and daring the Yankees.

New York rose as a man while heads turned and tongues flagged across the room. The piano player missed several notes of "Rosie O'Grady" as he looked over in alarm. Behind the bar, Heinz reached stealthily until his fingers found a rather well-worn club, which he quietly pulled out and held by his right leg.

A woozy New Jersey major tottered up beside the New Yorkers, glared at Tennessee and growled, "This *is* a great country in spite of Lucifer Jeff Davis an' his slave-drivin' scum tryin' to wreck it!" Pleasant Crump, Zachariah Hampton, and assorted men from Missouri and Alabama swung up alongside Tennessee and Louisiana to form a line to the end of the bar. Zachariah stared dumbfounded as the table full of black vets went into line on New York's right flank. Looking them over, in his mind the usual 'uppity' was immediately thrashed by the idea of 'determined' and *that* thought dried his mouth and pursed his lips.

The noise in the room was dying, marked only by chairs sliding and shoes scuffling across the floor boards. Knobby-knuckled fingers held table knives and forks at the ready. Heinz tightened his grip and brought the club almost level with the bar. A pang struck him as he picked which eighty-year old man he would hit first.

Langston Dobbin swore later that his teeth vibrated as a shrill whistle exploded inches from his right ear. The blast froze everyone in the room except for a lieutenant, a sergeant, a corporal, and sixteen privates in olive khaki crowding through the door behind their quick-striding leader.

As the cavalry captain let a chrome whistle on a string fall out of his mouth he advanced steadily toward the Tennessee lieutenant and the New Jersey major. He shoved an old Georgia vet with dismissive ease into a chair.

Zachariah took a sudden seat and Confederate men felt their age. The captain strode on, fluidly drew his polished sword, and crashed it down by its flat onto a table surrounded by Iowa vets. The blow made several glasses dance and tinkle as Union men cringed getting out of the way.

"Gentlemen," the captain boomed. His tone said they weren't.

"Gentlemen," he repeated, a bit softer, standing between the two ringleaders. "Some of you fought at First, Second, and Third Winchester." His eyes swept the room. Authority dripped from every word. In a gentler tone he added, "My grandfather was killed at Third Winchester." The men's attention took on sympathy.

"Some of you fought at First and Second Bull Run." He nodded curtly toward the Union part of the room, calling the battles by their Northern names. "Some others of you," he nodded toward the gray-clad section, "fought at that same place both times and made First and Second Man-Asses out of the Yankees there." Whoops and chuckles arose from the room as men caught the captain's pun on the Southern name for the battles: First and Second Manassas. The tension in the room sagged like a hammock.

"There was only one Battle of Gettysburg. And I can assure you, gentlemen," he added, a half-smile on his face, and they could see he now considered them gentlemen, "there will be no Second Battle of Gettysburg tonight." Eyes dropped away and stared at tabletops or, a bit sheepishly, at each other.

"Besides," the captain rasped, "you wouldn't want the Second Battle of Gettysburg recorded as a saloon brawl, would you? There's no medal of valor for defending rot gut or charging red eye!" Rueful smiles popped up around the room. "As you were, gentlemen. Go about your business." He glanced at his pocket watch as men began sitting down all across the room. "Piano man?" he called toward the ashen-faced young man, "Let's have music." As the shaky strains of "A Bicycle Built for Two" floated up, conversations resumed.

The captain stepped in among his troopers. "Go around table to table, group to group. Smile hard. Don't say much. Keep the peace, but eye them like first day recruits."

Heinz slipped the club back under the bar, limp with relief as he watched the khaki troopers saunter around. The few civilians were leaving with dignified hurry, but the crisis was over. Heinz watched the young lieutenant scoop up a loose chair and swing a leg over the seat. He sat athwart the backward chair, rested his arms on the seat back, and introduced himself to a startled table of U.S. Colored Troops.

"Evening b..." Lieutenant Chambliss sputtered, just catching himself from saying "boys" to Lucius and his friends staked out behind their beer towers. "Evening, gentlemen," he began again. "I saw you in the front rank just now;

right end of the line, the place of honor. You were ready."

Heads nodded around the circle. Floyd tipped his head toward Gastieu and the other gray veterans. "Some o' them Southern boys..." he let "boys" linger "...like to go on 'n' on 'bout the 'Lost Cause.'" He thumped the table top. "We all was jes' gonna remind them 'bout the word 'Lost.'"

"Amens" and a "Say it, brotha" scooted around softly as the lieutenant grinned wryly. The four quaffed their beers, their eyes meeting in a silent toast. Chambliss eyed Lucius' sleeve and the decoration hanging on his tunic. "Where did you earn that medal, Sergeant? It's the Cross of Valor, isn't it?"

"I earned my medal and my stripes on the same day, fifty years ago this week, ratt here in Gettysburg," Lucius answered.

"Really?" exclaimed Isaiah. "I didn't think no colored troops fought here."

"Do tell," Clovese urged.

"After 'Mancipation, I joined up there in Port Royal. They swore us in, drilled us, and then brought us north on a steamer. Early on, the army gave us no-account duties." The men nodded knowingly. "I was a teamster with the Second Corps, Army of the Potomac here at Gettysburg. The third day was a quiet mawnin' consid'rin' all the fightin' of the fust two days. Long 'bout noon an officer ordered me to fill up some kegs down at Rock Creek and bring water to the men 'long Cemetery Ridge. I filled up the kegs an' drove my wagon up the backside. Jes' as I gets to the top an' can see the II Corps men by the wall, they's two cannon shots from the Confederates. After that, it was like every cannon in the world was shootin' at us."

"That's right," Dade broke in. "A friend o' mine had family in Pittsburgh an' they could hear thunder from the east. The wind took the sound thataway."

Clovese scoffed. "Pittsburgh? Must' be over a hunnert miles from here. No way they heard it."

"God as my witness, they said it was heard in Pittsburgh."

"Porter Alexander's bombardment!" Chambliss exclaimed, naming General Lee's artillery chief. "The greatest barrage in American history. You know, I believe I read about it being heard in Pittsburgh. Could be." Turning back to Lucius he said, "Go on."

"The men dove behind the stone wall or jes' flattened out best they could. But them shells started landing mo' and mo' on top and on the backside. My team was rearin', shells was fallin', and ever'body was runnin' every which way.

"Then a shell landed ratt in front an' both hosses reared up. I stood up sawin' at the reins and another shell took off the driver's bench ratt behind me. The wind from that shell pulled me off the wagon and conked me out."

Joe nodded somberly. "I knew men killed by a shell jes' missin' 'em. Not a mark on 'em, but as dead as a wagon tire. Well, go on," Clovese urged, a veteran in Thomas' command from Milliken's Bend to Nashville.

"Yeah, don't leave us hangin'," Jones agreed, a rare colored cannoneer serving in Wright's Corps from Wilderness to Appomattox.

"All right, all right," Lucius grinned and took a huge gulp. "When I came to – found out later I laid there 'bout two hours – I was covered with dirt from other shells. The rebel guns was still shootin', and our side was thunderin' back iron lightnin'. I heard rifle fire. The Rebels was at the wall shootin' an' fightin' hand to hand in Pickett's Charge. Some grayback officer had his hat on his sword, leadin' the way. I got up and went past some of our officers. They was all on foot 'cept fo' one on hossback. Most o' them were shootin' their pepperboxes at the Rebels an' one of them kept yellin', 'See 'em, see 'em' after 'bout every shot.

"Well, I seed 'em just fine an' I seed we had to stop 'em. I didn't have no rifle but I ran toward the line anyway, figurin' I could get me one off o' somebody's darlin'."

Chambliss broke in. "Somebody's darling?"

Tillman explained. "That's what we called a dead soldier."

"Okay, I get it," Chambliss nodded. "Sorry to interrupt. Go on, please."

A relaxing wave ran around the table. Hearing "sorry" and "please" from a white man was like ice cream on the tongue.

"Somethin' was slappin' my leg," Lucius resumed. "As I ran, I looked down and saw it was my hosswhip still hangin' from my side. So, until I found me a rifle, I went in lashin' with my hosswhip. Soon after, Pickett's line broke apart an' they went back 'cross to Seminary Ridge. Everybody alive on our side was whoopin' and hollerin', an' some was yellin', 'Fredricksburg, Fredricksburg.'

"I came back up lookin' fo' my wagon an' team. The officer on hossback was bein' hepped down. His men was lookin' at him close and pullin' out kerchiefs. He was wounded in the leg but he still looked a fine sight of a man with a short cigar in his teeth.

"All of a sudden, a major from his bunch comes runnin' up to me an' yells out, 'Private!' I saluted an' said, 'Yes, suh.'

"He said, 'General Hancock over there wants to see you.'

"My eyes bugged out an' I looked at the major, and the general, then back at the major. 'Me, suh?' still holdin' my salute.

"The major grinned, saluted, and said, 'Yes, you! Right now. Come along.'

"So I went up to this flock o' officers with all sortsa chickenguts flappin' on their shoulders and I saluted the general layin' there. He pulled the cigar outta his mouth to salute me back and said, 'Parade rest, soldier. Wait just a minute.'

"Then he turned to this 'fraidy-lookin' young fellah with spectacles wearin' lieutenant's pumpkin rinds on his shoulders." Lieutenant Chambliss rolled his eyes as the whole table looked him over. "In a book he wrote down ever' word as fast as the general talked – never seed nobody who could wratt so fast.

Message to General Meade: Sir, the assault on the Second Corps line has been repulsed with heavy enemy loss. I myself have been severely but I trust not seriously wounded but I did not leave my troops so long as a rebel was to be seen upright. The enemy must be short of ammunition, as I am shot with a ten penny nail. Time 3:20pm, General Hancock.

"After one fella run off with the message, General Hancock waved me over an' said, 'What's your name and unit, Private?'"

"I got out, 'Private Lucius Robinson, suh. 2nd South Carolina Union Volunteers. I'm a teamster fo' your Second Corps.'"

"He says, 'I've seen all sorts of bravery in this war, but I have never seen your kind of courage.' He turned to the fast writin' fella and said, 'Orderly, take this down:

I recommend Private Lucius Robinson of the 2nd South Carolina Union Volunteers receive the Cross of Valor for conspicuous bravery in that on July 3, 1863, at Gettysburg he helped repel the rebel attack on our line on Cemetery Ridge armed with only a horsewhip.

"Sign it in the usual way. Next, take this down:

I hereby confer upon Private Lucius Robinson of the 2nd South Carolina Union Volunteers the rank of First Sergeant, with all the privileges, responsibilities, and emoluments accorded to the rank. By order of General Hancock.

"Then he took the book, signed his name an' pulled off the commission."

"Emoluments?" Clovese asked. "Hoowee! They's a ten dollar word fo' ya!"

Tillman grinned and joshed, "Well now just what ee-mol-u-ments does a Second Corps wagoneer get?"

"Okay, okay," Lucius replied, "I acknowledge the corn. I had no idea what emoluments was neither. But I found out after March 3, 1864."

The veterans surprised Chambliss by abruptly lifting their steins and toasting, "March 3." As they all gulped he asked, "All right, I'm stumped. What happened then?"

Lucius answered. "On that day the United States Congress passed a law givin' colored soldiers in the Union Army equal pay with white soldiers, rank by rank. When we found out early on the white privates got $13 a month and we only got $10, we decided to take no pay at all 'til it was the same. Didn't need it too much, since the Army was feedin' us, clothin' us, tentin' us..."

"...freezin' us in the winter..." Floyd chipped in.

"...marchin' our feet off to the ankles..." Isaiah added.

"...body licin' us ever' wakin' minute..." Joe put in, bringing a chuckle.

"...an' the army was willin' to have us get shot," Lucius concluded. "So fo' the honor of all that, we wanted the same pay. An' after March 3, 1864, we got it, goin' back to enlistment day."

"An' you got your emolument too, Lucius?" Joe persisted.

"That's ratt," Lucius grinned back. "By order of Gen'rul Hancock, this ol' wagoneer was now receivin' the emolument of twenty dollars a month fo' pay as a fust sergeant." Admiring whistles circled the table. "Lawsy, if that emolument don't cap the climax." Isaiah breathed.

Chambliss blinked in his reverie. "You were decorated and promoted on the battlefield by Winfield Scott Hancock. God, to have been there!" he said with more awe in his voice than he intended.

Lucius smiled and reached inside his breast pocket. He pulled out an old envelope and very gently removed a dog-eared paper. Unfolding it delicately along creases that nearly cut through the limp sheet, he opened it toward the lieutenant so he could read the fine but hurried hand of a young orderly. Below was the bold and vigorous signature of Hancock, still stark and strong despite fifty years. The others crowded in for a look.

"Hot damn," breathed Clovese. "Hancock hisself." Dade rolled his eyes and Tillman whistled softly through his gapped and yellowed teeth.

As Lucius devotedly refolded his commission, Chambliss remembered his duties. He rose and nodded crisply toward Lucius. "I'm honored to have sat with you," and paused, "sir." He spoke as a lieutenant to a sergeant, and Lucius blinked in surprise. Casting his eyes in an arc, Chambliss added, "Indeed, honored to have sat with all of you fighting men." The last few words had a strangled tone as he swallowed hard and turned away.

While Lieutenant Chambliss visited Lucius' table, his captain squeezed himself onto a long wall bench with the Louisianans. He wore an iron smile as he quoted Napoleon in excellent French: "I love a brave soldier who has undergone the baptism of fire." Despite many cold shoulders, his genuine eagerness and charm paid off. He broke through when he asked, "Anyone here part of the Louisiana men that made Nathaniel P. Banks the South's favorite commissary officer?" He remembered that in 1862, Stonewall Jackson crushed a force commanded by Banks and captured enormous quantities of supplies. Thereafter Southerners derisively called him "Commissary Banks," punning off the supply officers' banks of goods. In fits and starts, the captain won several over. Long before he wanted to, Lieutenant Chambliss sidled up and whispered, "Curfew time, Captain."

"Thank you, Chambliss. Very well," came a sighed reply. The captain rose, his mind awash with tales of Stonewall's long-striding men and slashing tactics retold in a delightful mix of English and French. He stood up on the bench, cupped his hands and roared, "Curfew, gentlemen. Curfew!"

Around the room, men began rising from their seats, some pausing to toss back the last of a shot glass, others swaying more than they expected. The 15th U.S. Cavalrymen formed a rough line down the middle of the room so the noisy gray ranks mostly left along the bar while the more numerous and also noisy bluecoats used the rest of the room. Sergeant McMasters was at the far wall shooing the men along, starting at a table of USCI men. As these four rose, McMasters saw one was a sergeant like him. He did a double take on Lucius, who likewise flashed recognition from yesterday morning at Woolworth's.

Lucius came to attention and saluted McMasters saying, "Thank you for your help yestidy, Sergeant. Much 'bliged."

McMasters saluted back and said, "Glad to have been of service, sergeant. We sergeants gotta look out for each other."

Lucius nodded. "Yep. Against recruits with two left feet."

McMasters smiled back. "And shave tail lieutenants with peach-fuzz faces."

Lucius chuckled, then said warmly, "And certain civilians. Thanks again."

In a wobbling stream, the blue and gray headed out, separated by khaki, but it was tight quarters passing the massive fireplace. Calvin Salisbury was squeezing past an equally massive corporal stationed here when he jostled up against a short, scowling Confederate with piercing eyes.

"Pardon me," Calvin called in the din.

Dooley Culpepper elbowed him hard into the corporal and hissed, "I never make way fo' scoundrels!"

Calvin caught his balance by bumping his right shoulder against the corporal's chest pocket. He looked a bayonet glare at Dooley and retorted, "I always do!"

From far overhead, the corporal furrowed his brow and flared his nostrils. Dooley glanced upwards, gulped, gave Calvin a stare and was swept out into the night.

A bit later in the square, the captain and lieutenant met under a street lamp. "Lieutenant, make a report of tonight's activities."

"Yes, sir." Chambliss produced an order book as the captain dictated. He ended with "Note we untangled a traffic jam in Lincoln Square. Note we broke up a saloon fight involving forks among veterans trading insults over Lincoln and Davis. See Major Rhodes gets the report. Send copies to the National Guard adjutant and the Gettysburg police."

"All right to release a copy to the newspaper reporters?" Chambliss wanted to know.

The captain paused a beat, then shook his head. "No real need. They only seem to want upbeat stories anyway. Anyway, take charge and take the men back to the barracks. I'm taking my horse for a walk." A low-slung wagon stood nearby, sporting bales of hay, a driver and team, and several Confederate veterans from the Dobbin House Tavern loaded up – in both senses – for the trip back to Tent City.

"Riding with the veterans, Captain?" Chambliss asked, knowing the answer.

"I'll see you at reveille." He tied the reins to the wagon and climbed up on a hay bale. Chambliss heard the accented conversation start up again.

"Now, like I wuz sayin'," came one cotton-slurred voice, "even in our War, cavalry weren't much good fer fightin' with them sabers. But Mosby an' Morgan had the ratt idea: ride with speed to a battle, then dismount and fatt on foot with carbines."

"And get behind their lines," the captain answered, picking up an earlier thread.

"That's ratt. Cap'n, you're a West Point man like Lee or Stonewall. But you have that cold fire they had in their eyes when their blood was up." Chambliss saw his commander look down modestly but also smile delightedly. "But take a lesson from them two. If you evah get in a fatt with your Army and you punch through or git around a flank, put your men on motorcars and hosses and let 'em go like hell to tear up ever'thing in the enemy rear. That'll pull down their whole line like dynamite under a bridge trestle."

The captain nodded as one man said, "What ze new war needs eez a Gatling gun on a tract-air."

"That's it," another voice agreed. The driver whistled to his team and pulled their heads around toward Tent City. "An' make the tractor like an ironclad on land." The young officer mused how to combine Lee and Jackson's tactics with motorized troops in land ironclads. Steel maybe? Tractor engines could move them, but slowly. And what wheels could hold that weight?

"Gastieu's reedy voice broke into his thoughts. "Capitaine? …capitaine, forgive me." The young officer looked up. "I have forgotten your name?"

A chuckling voice answered. "Pardone. Je m'appèlle Patton. George Patton." The wagon rolled toward the electric lights of Tent City.

Wednesday, July 2, 1913

Tent City

After Wednesday breakfast, Tent City swarmed with veterans and visitors. Checker boards, horseshoe pitching, and poker games could be stepped on anywhere. Brass bands and strolling choirs provided music and took requests. Thousands walked the battlefield, rode the electric trolleys, visited town, the Cyclorama, or the parks. At Tipton, many paid their nickel to view fifty years of battlefield photographs. At Round Top, the new casino had opened early.

Amid all the reunioning there came a hum, from somewhere, from everywhere. Heads turned and ears cocked all around, but sound and source were not pinned down. On top of Cemetery Hill, Thomas Ince and an assistant looked around puzzled while hefting a twenty-five pound mahogany-and-brass Moy and Bastie camera onto a tripod. Colonel Nicholas Biddle of the 55th Massachusetts and several USCI sergeants on the south slope of Culp's Hill paused from studying his map, and nearby musicians took a break. The sound grew louder, adding a faint fluttering quality, reminding some of the plainsmen of their windmills purring in a thunderstorm. Underneath was something faintly mechanical, but identity, source, and location remained a mystery.

Suddenly came a multi-pitched throbbing several octaves lower than bees, but with an insistent buzzing quality. Heads turned south and eyes rose, igniting wonder.

Two hundred fifty feet above the ground, three pairs of short, horizontal lines broke clear of the haze. Just behind each set of lines was a pair of grayish, circling somethings that made the noise. Then a few on the ground made them out and the words called across the battlefield. People began pointing with tremendous excitement: "Flying machines!" "Three of them!" "Look at 'em fly like geese!"

Captain Charles Chandler had arrived at the College Park, Maryland field about half past six. The weather was good with little morning wind. He set the mechanics working, rolling out the two Wright B's and the Burgess-Wright. He sat down with maps and aviators to plan their route. Just before eight o'clock, Lieutenants Frederic Humphreys and Benjamin Foulois were first up and did a long circle of the field. As their thirty-one-horsepower engines roared just behind them, they watched past their feet (Foulois saw his bootlace flapping) as the mechanics pointed the Burgess-Wright carrying Lieutenant Frank Lahm and Navy Lieutenant George Sweet (the others all were Army) down the 2,376 feet of level grass. Their pusher propellers, ninety-seven inches apiece, hand-carved from New Hampshire spruce, lifted them up to join Humphrey's circle. Then both spindly biplanes were joined by Chandler and Lieutenant Henry Arnold. They banked off northwest, then more northerly as they made their landmarks. Averaging just over fifty miles per hour, they covered the sixty-some road miles in a bit over an hour.

As Big Round Top came into view, Chandler waved the other two planes into a flying V formation. They formed up as Arnold gently dropped to about 150 feet. Chandler and Arnold followed Hancock Avenue north toward Cemetery Hill. To port and aft, Humphreys and Foulois traversed where Pickett had charged fifty years ago this week. Lahm and Sweet trailing aft starboard saw Baltimore Pike pass under them on the diagonal as the ribbon of Rock Creek twisted outside their sunward wing.

Each man in the copilot seat was wearing a good-sized knapsack, but backward, on his chest. Foulois, Sweet, and Chandler undid the top flap, reached inside, and began tossing handfuls past their feet. On the ground people wondered at the tiny black flecks dropping from each plane. Small boys scattering everywhere in excitement brought the answer. They were white pinchback buttons, the size of silver dollars, bearing the words "Blue and Gray Encampment, 50 years, 1863-1913."

The planes passed over town, made a pretty banked left turn, and came back, still in formation. Chandler's lead plane passed over Pickett's Field while Humphreys covered Cemetery Ridge. Lahm and Sweet made the big outside turn and passed over McMillan's Woods and Seminary Ridge. They repeated their button drop with hand waves and calls to the ground of "God bless you," then formed into column for the return flight. Reporters from the *Louisville Courier-Journal*, the *San Francisco Examiner*, the *Columbus Citizen* and the *Baltimore Sun* scribbled furiously on their pads to describe the remarkable scene of three aeroplanes all at once. Hands, tossed hats, and handkerchiefs beyond numbering waved farewell to one quarter of America's air power, along with one third of her entire force of trained pilots.

Gettysburg

Zachariah and Jim Calhoun stepped out of a shop on South Baltimore Street holding a couple of just-bought postcards when the beat of drums and angry shouting made them look south. Up the opposite sidewalk marched Gettysburg Police Chief Krauss with two Boy Scout drummer boys, followed by two Pennsylvania Guardsmen. Between them was a Union vet carrying a suitcase and wearing a crude front-and-back placard over his shoulders, the paint on both chest and back plank still gleaming and dripping. Behind came six more guardsmen taking turns walking backward. A furious crowd of mostly Union veterans spilled into the street, blocking traffic, shouting, waving fists, and throwing wadded paper, apple cores, cigar butts, or anything handy at the chin-down, fast-walking target. Some civilian mothers covered the ears of small children against the veterans' language, while others wagged fierce fingers at teen boys saying, "Never repeat any of those! Do you hear? Never!"

Zachariah and Jim made out the chest plank: "Martin Feeny: Shame of the 14th Indiana," and caught some of the accusations flying from the crowd. Then they joined in booing and jeering, because the South had had its share of these types too.

"How many times you figure?" Jim called. "How many times?"

"Four that we know of," a fast-waddling, pug-nosed bluecoat with a VT badge called back. "Maybe two more."

Zack hissed and booed lustily and then called out, "How much did he collect, ya figure?"

"At least five thousand dollars," someone yelled back.

"Hoowee," Jim spouted, and tongues wagged all along the sidewalks.

Martin Feeny was being drummed out of the Encampment for debasing a soldier's honor. His back plank read: "bounty jumper." Union, state, and county governments paid bounties totaling $500 to $1,000 for men willing to enlist or re-enlist in '63 and '64. Some would enlist, collect, desert to the homefront and enlist again in a different town or state, amassing a dastard's bundle.

As the fuming rabble passed north, a loud, low buzzing came from Cemetery Hill. Zachariah had a perfect view of Arnold and Chandler's machine coming over the treetops up the line of Baltimore Street. Silhouetted on top of the hill, Zachariah saw the tiny figure of a man peering through a mounted box, turning a crank. Zack looked left as Lahm and Sweet came on a beam over the far side of Culp's Hill. A few white pinchback buttons plinked down onto the paving stones, setting off a scramble of swarming boys.

Jim stood pie-eyed and gape-jawed. "The times we live in! A wonder ever' day!"

"First time you've seen one?"

"Yep. I was visitin' kinfolk in Augusta last Fourth of July so I missed the Savannah solo show. But this just beats all, don't it?"

"It surely does," Zachariah said. "The future just flew over."

The tide of small, button-hunting boys ebbed away and adult movement was possible again. "Ready to head uptown?"

"Give me a few minutes, Jim. I'm gonna sit on that bench," he pointed up the sidewalk, "and ratt a postcard to Emily."

Jim blinked. Zack had never seemed the letter-writing type, and he usually called her "my daughter" rather than Emily. "Go ahead," Jim said. "I'll poke around them sutler's wagons for a cigar. Want one?" Zachariah handed him a nickel and said, "Yeah. Pick me out a good one."

Zachariah sat and stared off, planning his words. Then on the back of the hand-tinted two-center he printed certain words and used script on the rest:

> *Dear Emily,*
> Hoping *you and Lee are doing well.*
> Every-*thing here comfortable and satisfying.*
> To-Day *we had a 3 aeroplane flyover for*
> *excitement and it's not even 9:30 yet!*
> *See you soon,*
> *Daddy*

Jim came back with two cigars. "Ready?" he asked.

"Yep, and I see a post box two lampposts ahead."

The two men puffed up town.

Camp Lincoln

Excitement exploded across Camp Lincoln during the flyover. Men scurried up Benner's Hill for a better look or ran to where the trees let off by Rock Creek. Talk everywhere used "flying" and "progress" and vets in mid-write on postcards and letters wrote the home folks about their first-ever sighting.

Lucius remembered last July, but three at once amazed him. For several minutes, his conversation at a north end table with many men, including two of the colored Confederates, was all about the wonders of the age and "progress."

After a time, they drifted back to a far more earnest topic. When the table full had sat down, a USCI artilleryman with a KS badge had refused to shake hands with the one-time body servants of Confederate generals. There had been tense words over a lack of Yankee hospitality, but things had died down when the planes had flown over. But now the Witchita man shook his head at the Tennesseeans.

"I don't understand you fellas," he said intently, Lucius and a couple other Union men in support. "You're here wearin' the gray. Those men owned you."

"Yes, they did," the Nashville man agreed.

"But that's over now," Ashton Melo protested. "So why are you wearin' the gray?"

"Look," the Memphis man replied, "Mr. Hardee, then General Hardee, was a good man. I took care of him in the War, and he took care of me."

"Same with General Sibley," the Nashville man echoed.

Memphis added, "After the War, we was free, but broke. Didn't have anyplace to go and didn't know how to do nothin' else. Stayin' with massa's family was a way to live."

"But where's your pride, brother?" Lucius burst out.

"Your self-respect?" Ashton echoed.

"Oh, but the Bible speaks against pride," Nashville answered. "Pride got Cain banished. Pride brought down Goliath."

"The Lord rewards the humble heart," the Memphis man intoned. "Blessed are the meek."

A Kentucky man gagged. "Tarnation! Is that what they've been feedin' you all yo' lives?"

"Safest way to have roof over my head and bread on the table," Memphis answered with a maddening serenity.

"Out on the Plains, we sleep under our own roof even if it's only a sod house," the Kansan threw out.

The Nashville man looked disgusted. "My room has wainscotin', kickboard, movin' glass windows, and two kerosene lamps beside the ceiling one. You won't stick me in no sod block."

"Besides," the Memphis man added, "we're old men. We gonna strike out on our own now? Learn a trade? Start farmin'? What would we do?"

The men in blue conceded, but not gladly.

McMillan's Woods

Calvin was part of a ring of blues and grays in McMillan's Woods. A poker game had passed from penny ante to high stakes. A Rhode Island sailor from Farragut's command was betting nickels and even a dime against an Alabama cavalry captain who had ridden with both Van Dorn and Forrest. Their silver coins piling up had scared off the Wisconsin ordnance corporal, the USCT Iowa trooper, the South Carolina quartermaster, the Tennessee riverboat soldier-sailor, and the Kentucky "sawbones." Surprise, then laughter, rose over the table as the hands were laid down: Rhode Island's aces over queens with the king of spades matched up card for card with Alabama's aces and queens and the king of diamonds.

"Split pot!" went the word. "Really?" "See for yourself!" "Card for card" "Lookee thar!" "Well I'll be a riverboat gambler's son of a gun." "Hoowee!" The winners were just finishing counting out half each of one dollar and sixty four cents when the air squadron made its first pass. The buzzing shook the leaves and faces looked up, alarmed. Those not frozen in place looked around for cover.

"What was that?" "Did you git a look?" "Tarnation!" "What the blazes is goin' on?"

A Virginia gunnery sergeant had the answer. "That thar's one o' them flyin' machines. I live near Fort Myers where they've been testin' 'em. Back in '09 I even shook hands with Orville Wright."

The men scattered. Some went to clearings, some up toward the high edge of Seminary Ridge where the tree cover was more broken. Many took a short trace toward Pickett's open fields.

Calvin was with these men, clearing the edge of the woods as the buzzing approached again, this time from the north. He saw one plane coming in over Gettysburg's church steeples, then another over toward Cemetery Ridge. He got far enough in the clear to see a third plane coming along Seminary Ridge. With a rising clatter and a rush of wind rippling the grass, the center plane bore down on Calvin. He was mostly amazed, although as the contraption closed on him at an astounding fifty-one miles per hour – about twice railroad speed – fear did begin putting a few fingers on him. One man was obviously flying, while the other was tossing small objects from a bag on his front. He was also waving and smiling to all the earthbound, and Calvin waved back.

"Bully for you!" he shouted at the plane, grinning and shaking his cane.

Suddenly the plane passed over and the buzzing sound dipped in a "yeeeoooooow" to a sharply lower pitch. The backwash of air rippled over him. Turning about face, he saw the three planes converge into a column just to the right of Little Round Top and then climb until they disappeared in the haze.

Ground talk turned to flying, air shows, and then more generally to the progress the veterans had seen in the past fifty years. Mr. Edison's electrical lights and Dr. Roentgen's X-rays came up and so did Mr. Alexander Graham Bell's telephonic telegraphy, as he first called it. Many pointed to nearby samples of Mr. Ford's self-moving carriages, called "auto-mobile" by influential students of Greek and Latin. Lighter fare figured as well: the nickelodeon, and the ice cream cone from the St. Louis World's Fair back in '04, for a couple.

Calvin fell in with a new group of old vets. The half dozen strolled to a picnic table that was both empty and shaded by a good maple. "You fellas want to hear somethin' 'bout flying almost nobody's ever done?" the New York corporal was saying.

"Sure," Calvin answered as they dragged out the benches and roosted at the table. "Is your tale about you?" he asked shrewdly.

"As a matter of fact, it is," the corporal replied. "My name's Marcus Frey. I was born near Dayton, Ohio and live there now."

"Ain't them Wright brothers from Dayton?" interjected a Kansas private. He wore an unusual dark green Union uniform trimmed in emerald piping, marking him as a deadeye member of the U.S. Sharpshooters.

"That's right," Frey answered. "I've met 'em both. But in between being born there and living there now, I moved around some. When I was born, my father was teaching in Dayton. After a few years there, my father was asked teach at Princeton, so we moved to New Jersey. He taught logic and rhetoric, and also practical science, which I really liked. That was surveying, levers and pulleys, usin' a block and tackle and suchlike. About a year before the War, they added telegraph work, and I took to it like a duck to water. I finished up at the Western Union school in New York City. My friends were members of the New York 7th, so I joined up too. After Fort Sumter, President Lincoln called for troops."

"Yep," nodded the Arkansas man, "an' that was it fer Arkansas stayin' in the Union," referring to his state's secession in response to Lincoln's call.

"Yep," countered the West Virginia Yankee, "an' that was it fer Virginia stayin' in one piece," referring to the western counties' secession from Virginia.

"Well anyway, the 7th New York was one of the first regiments to muster and head off. We had a parade down Broadway, a boat ride to Annapolis and then a parade right past the White House. We camped between the Capitol and the White House.

"One morning just after breakfast, the sergeant says, 'Frey, Captain Alfred wants you on the double.' So I report to the captain on the quick. Captain says to me, 'Frey, you're a telegraph man?' I said, 'Yes sir.'

"'That's what I thought,' he said. 'You got a penknife with you?' 'Yes, sir.'

"He said, 'That's all you need. Fall in with the detail.'

"So I fell in with the other fellas who had rifles. We marched up to the White House around to the front lawn." Here Frey smiled.

"Now, gentlemen, can you guess what was on the front lawn of the White House on June 18, 1861? Any takers?"

"I know," guessed the one-time Oklahoma scout, "it was Ulysses Grant in pink ballerina tights on an elephant!" Hoots of laughter erupted.

"Lemme guess," whooped Jacobson, the Minnesota fencing master, "It was Jefferson Davis wearing a hoop skirt and a Cheyenne war bonnet." Another round of laughter rang off the table top, with the West Virginia man almost reduced to tears.

"Okay, Marcus," Calvin gasped, "You'd better tell us before someone dies laughing."

"All right," Marcus answered the ribsore revelers. "A windlass was staked to the ground with a rope anchoring one of Dr. T.S.C. Lowe's balloons over five hundred feet in the air."

The men studied Frey closely, but were convinced he wasn't joking.

"A balloon over the White House?" Calvin asked.

"That's right," Marcus said. "Before Professor Lowe could work for the Army, he had to prove the idea, and he thought he'd go to the top man."

The group took a long pause. "Well, go on then, Knickerbocker," Arkansas chipped in.

"Coming off the rope was a wire connected to a telegraph sitting on a fancy little desk. Captain Alfred told me to sharpen up some pencils laying there, so I had at 'em with my knife. Then he handed me a blank dispatch book and told me to sit in a chair as fancy as the desk. Then he ordered the detail, 'All right men, keep quiet now.' He waved over to the far side of the lawn at two Signal Corps men. One man whistled toward the balloon and the other fellow waved a long-handled semaphore flag. After three or four whistles, someone up in the balloon – I found out after it was Professor Lowe – looked down over the edge of the basket and waved his hat. Then the telegraph started clicking.

"I grabbed a pencil and took it down. Everyone was real quiet so I could get all the code. Captain Alfred came over along with a couple majors and a Signal Corps colonel. They were crowding in trying to read over my shoulder or upside down."

"Didn't the Signal Corps have their own telegraph men?" Oklahoma asked.

"Yep, but that mornin' one was sick, one was missing, and couple were in the stockade for visiting the Row there in Washington City." The men chuckled knowingly and someone said, "Practicing horizontal dancing, eh?"

Marcus resumed. "I was getting down to the signature when they all straightened up to attention. I signaled back, 'Message received. Stand by.' All the officers had their backs to me saluting toward the front porch. Then a voice said, 'At ease, gentlemen,' and they all relaxed and a major stepped aside. Plain as day stood President Lincoln."

"Go on," a couple of the vets said with a gesture of dismissal.

"God's own truth," Marcus said solemnly. With thirty-seven years in the courtroom, Calvin felt he knew a true witness.

"What happened next?" West Virginia asked.

"I was so surprised I almost forgot to stand, but Captain Alfred caught my eye. Then the colonel came up and tried to pull the dispatch book from me saying, 'Mr. President, may I present a message, a telegram, from the air?' Now I got it. All them officers were crowding around wanted to handle the telegram from a balloon. You know, touch a piece of history."

"Yeah, but you wrote it," the Kansas sharpshooter pointed out.

"You're right," Frey replied, "and Mr. Lincoln figured that out right away too. So he said, 'Colonel, I'd like to hear the message,' and the colonel smiled, 'from the man who took it down,' and his face fell like a wave on a shore." A chuckle circled the picnic table.

"Then President Lincoln says to me, 'Private, what's your name?'"

"I gulped and said, 'Private Marcus Frey, 7th New York, sir.'"

"'Would you please read me the message?'"

"'Yes, sir. The message reads, from

Balloon "Enterprise" in the Air
To His Excellency, Abraham Lincoln
President of the United States

Dear Sir:

From this point of observation we command an extent of our country nearly fifty miles in diameter. I have the pleasure of sending you this first telegram ever dispatched from an aerial station, and acknowledging indebtedness to your encouragement for the opportunity of demonstrating the availability of the science of aeronautics in the service of the country.

I am, Your Excellency's obedient servant,
T.S.C. Lowe

The vets looked at Frey riveted. Calvin gave a low whistle.

"The Signal Corps officers were all looking at me sidelong but being good and manly about it. The President was thinking hard, and I thought it was something about the telegram so I asked him. I guess I shouldn't have, just flat out like that, and the one major gave me a dirty look. 'Mr. President, sir, is the message all right? Or is there a reply, sir?'

"He said to me, 'Thank you, Private. The message is fine. I was just thinking about how balloons might help the army. People have been telling me balloons are all moonshine and gas bag toys. But I'm reminded of the story about a young girl who hung her stockings up to dry overnight by the fireplace. The next morning she was putting one on and stopped and said, 'It strikes me there's something in it.' That's the case with this balloon idea. Thank you for your help, Private.'

"Then he turned to the Signal Corps officers. 'Gentlemen, come inside with me. I think Professor Lowe's ideas bear discussion.' We spent the morning there in case Professor Lowe sent any more messages, or if someone needed to send a message to the professor. Captain paced around and I think he was hopin' the Rebs might ride into Alexandria or some such so the professor would send a message and he could take it in to the President, but no luck."

Several seconds of silence followed Frey's recital. Jacobson had a question. "How do you know the message word for word? You only read it once fifty-two years ago."

"That's true," Frey replied. "I took the next sheet out of the dispatch book. When I got back to camp for dinner, I used a pencil to make a rubbing, then I copied it out full twice. I kept one copy with me and sent the other to my father. I've been reading it over ever since."

As the men exchanged handshakes with Frey, thanking him for the story, and each other just on principle, one of the endless bands came by, this one from the Chambersburg fire department according to the lettered bass drum. As Marcus finished his tale they struck up "Come Josephine in my Flying Machine."

Camp Lincoln

As Sweet and Lahm cleared Culp's Hill through the leaves over Camp Lincoln, they could see upturned faces and many hands waving off their starboard wing. But at their speed they could not make out a navy doctor at the south infirmary tent. As the camp bubbled with "flying" excitement, an anxious group clustered around the surgeon.

"I'm sorry, gentlemen. Just sheer old age. I pronounce Cyrus Turnbull, age eighty-four, dead of natural causes." He eyed his pocket watch and added, "Wednesday, July 2, 1913, at 9:07 a.m."

A wail of lamentation broke from one of the Tennessee black Confederates. "Oh no, oh no," he kept saying, alternating with, "Not Massa Turnbull. Not him, Lord. Not now, Lord." A civilian pastor who some recognized as Obadiah Jones pushed through the crowd to sit with the man. Men reached over to pat the man's shoulder and offered "too bad," "done joined the majority," and "God bless you, suh." The doctor excused himself to make out a certificate of death.

One of Thomas Ince's camera crews had discovered Camp Lincoln. They had filmed some homey camp scenes that would later be spliced in with similar scenes from Tent City. Now they had something dramatic to film. They first showed the naval surgeon walking slowly up Frederick Douglass Avenue, solemnly holding a sheet of paper and passing a large oak tree. Under the oak, the scene showed Joseph Blackburn with his hat off, tucked under his arm in respect, but also writing the story for the far-off readers of the *California Eagle*, and a white man next to him similarly bent over his pad to tell the story for the *Memphis Appeal*. Next came an impromptu collection of musicians. The readers would have to imagine, but Ince's crew heard them playing a slow-walk hymn with blue notes and syncopation. Cajun-flavored dirges may have been common in New Orleans, but they were head-shaking marvelous to the three white men around the cranking camera.

"The boss is going to love this next part," one man said to the cranker. The operator stopped turning and popped out from his side eyepiece. "Jack, change it to the closer lens." In a flash Jack was unscrewing one lens while Ed flipped open the lens case at his feet and gently lifted out a cylinder. Jack screwed on the new lens and the camera man squinted at the upside-down image. He reached around focusing as Ed closed up the lens case, noted a film gauge on the camera, and said, "About forty left."

Audiences would later see USCI veterans crowding the street between log curbs, all with heads uncovered and mournful expressions. Master Sergeant Turnbull, 7th Tennessee, in full dress grays was being carried on a stretcher by two of his old Confederate comrades and two white Union men. The front two places showed a USCI man from Tupelo and a weeping black Confederate from Memphis. The camera caught the shock on this man's face between sobs as he mutely wondered about his life to come now that his master was dead. The film ran out as they passed so the audience did not see Turnbull loaded onto a hay wagon to start his last journey. His family buried him four days later.

Thursday, July 3, 1913

Platform A, Camp Lincoln

Among the tens of thousands of daily visitors, a few were specially invited. At the Great Tent in Pickett's Field, mornings were filled with entertainers and amusements. On a couple days, acrobats swung near the roof or walked the high wire. From two to four o'clock, the Great Tent featured dignitaries making speeches, and in between, lighter fare: a poetry reading, vocal music by soloists or ensembles, and bands or an orchestra playing martial or popular airs.

Camp Lincoln's Assembly Tent also featured dignity and official events. From after breakfast until dark, veterans and visitors to Platforms A, B, and C enjoyed vaudeville skits, sing-alongs, preaching, joke-telling, ragtime, and even stage productions. From Washington City to Harlem, professional and amateur speakers and performers came in a stream to Gettysburg.

Philadelphia cleaning woman Anna and her sixteen-year-old daughter Marian were invited for Thursday. The Union Baptist Church choir had held bake sales to raise rail fare for them. Last Sunday, their pastor had pressed two silver dollars into Anna's hand for "travelin' money." Both wore their Sunday best, with Anna sporting a round straw hat she had decorated with daisies and clover she'd picked that morning. She had on a pale yellow, high-collar, square-shouldered shirtwaist blouse, given to her by one of the ladies she cleaned for, and a brown skirt that flared more than fashion allowed but which made walking much easier. The same lady had given Anna one of her teenaged daughter's blouses with the words, "It's either give it to the help or throw it out. Take it if you want it, Anna." Marian had on this somewhat out-of-date "Gibson girl" blouse, high-collared in green with a striped yoke and sleeves only down to Marian's elbows. Her dark green skirt was a good match for her little chaplet of a hat pinned to her hair. Anna carried sandwiches in her handbag while Marian carried a flat bag of sheet music. Like everyone else off the midmorning Philadelphia train, the pair was packed like herrings in a barrel in the Gettysburg depot, creeping slowly toward the doors.

Also caught in the depot's crush were a pair of white Philadelphians, sixteen-year-old Laurel and her mother Vivienne. The Philadelphia Choral Society had winnowed dozens of white musicians for the honor of performing in the Great Tent. Laurel was one of eight finalists. Vivienne taught social studies, composition, French, and piano at an academy. They wore matching navy blue dirndl skirts with a wide waist sash. Mother was in one of her white, mutton-sleeved academy blouses with a chin-high collar. Her strawberry-blonde hair was gathered under a summer hat. Laurel's wavy hair was blonder and her hat simpler. She had on her prettiest powder-blue blouse with loose sleeves and a flat collar. A ring-shaped pewter brooch held the blouse slightly open at the notch of her collarbone, making for easier singing. She carried a flat leather folder of sheet music.

The depot's far arches leading onto Lincoln Square were only ten feet away, but each cramped step covered only a few inches. The two girls were squeezed side by side with their mothers jammed right behind. Suddenly came a squeal and a pushing. A boy of about seven reached the end of his patience, ducked into a crouch, and pushed his way through below the general hip level. Not concerned with manners, he made good progress. As he shoved between Marian and Laurel, he knocked Marian's flat bag, and sheet music cascaded to the floor.

"Oh, no," she cried, "my music." In the press she could hardly bend over to collect them.

"Here's a few," Laurel said, squeezing down and plucking a few stray sheets within reach to hand them to Marian.

"Can you get that one up there?" came Marian's muffled voice. Laurel could see a finger pointing. One piece standing on edge between two long skirts was about to be crushed under a hobnail boot. With a long stretch she snatched it just in time. "Here you go," she said glancing at the title, a duet.

"You sing this?" she asked in surprise.

Marian nodded. "When I get a partner. It's hard." Then Marian did a double take. "Wait a minute. You know it?"

"Yes," Laurel answered. "I've just started working on it." The girls gained a few feet while chatting about music, their vocal teachers, and each other.

"Looks like you two are hitting it off," Vivienne said politely. Anna added, "Sure looks like it to me."

"Mama," Laurel said over her shoulder, "this is Marian. She sings."

"Mama," Marian echoed, matching intonation perfectly, "this is Laurel. She sings." Both girls giggled, and went on chatting. The doorframe was just ahead.

"Are you in town to…to tour the battlefield?" Vivienne stammered. Anna stuttered, "Uh, why yes, if we have time. Actually, Marian's goin' to be singin' today at Camp Lincoln for some of the vet'rans."

"Really?" Vivienne remarked. "Laurel will be singing in the Great Tent this afternoon. But what is Camp Lincoln? Is it part of Tent City?"

"Mama," Laurel answered. "Camp Lincoln is the USCI encampment," having just learned this from Marian. "Could we go hear Marian sing?"

"Laurel, I'm not sure we have time or if, if, umm…" Vivienne's voice petered into a blush as polite tangled with 'welcome' and 'appropriate.' At this moment, a final squeeze passed them through and into the loosening crowd spilling onto Lincoln Square. The flow swept them to a lamppost where they stopped to recover, exclaiming, "at last!" and "Finally!"

Laurel piped up, "So Mama, Marian's singing this morning and we don't have to be at the Great Tent until half past two. Couldn't we go hear her?"

The answer came roundabout in the odd form of two grand dames, both off the Washington train that had swamped the Philadelphia arrivals. The women were finely dressed but each was losing the battle against weight and age. They stopped at the same lamppost for adjusting their finery and straightening their massive flowered and feathered hats. Spotting the two girls, two mothers and two races amiably together, the taller one in yellow said in a trifle-loud voice, "It's completely scandalous."

The one in slate-blue sporting a weighty pearl necklace replied, "Well, remember Gettysburg's a one-horse Northern town. There are no proper facilities for segregation, but amalgamation certainly doesn't need to be encouraged."

This was aimed at Vivienne. Anna's cringe sank into resignation. Vivienne stiffened and took advantage of a convenient pause. In her classroom tone she aimed her words at a right angle.

"Anna, do you know that George Washington Carver of the South and Gregor Mendel of Hungary have taught learned people that amalgams and hybrids are of higher quality and usefulness than common strains?" Laurel swallowed, alarmed. Marian's face was sober but her eyes were dancing. Anna missed the bit about Mendel and hybrids, but her eyebrows saluted Vivienne's spirit.

The taller woman tossed her head, "Oh!" but the pearl-rigged battleship was not silenced. She retorted to Vivienne, "You know, if you were educated I would have to regard that remark as a *studied* insult."

Green eyes flashing behind her wire-rimmed glasses, Vivienne smiled dangerously. "Tell me. At your finishing school did you major in boorishness, or did you arrive there as an ass?"

While slack-jawed astonishment echoed beneath feathers and flowers, Vivienne tossed her head, turned her back, offered her arm to Anna and ordered, "Come along Laurel. Marian's singing at Camp Lincoln." The stunned Victorian steamers couldn't see Laurel's face giggling or Anna's face smiling. But they heard Marian's laughter ring like silver dollars falling on marble.

From the edge of Platform A in Camp Lincoln, Reverend Obadiah Jones called like a ringmaster, "And now, gentlemen…." At that instant he spotted

Anna, Vivienne, their daughters and several colored women, one very nicely dressed, at the edge of the crowd and quickly added, "...and ladies...glad to have the fairer sex visiting Camp Lincoln." The women smiled to the smattering of applause from the massed veterans.

Jones continued from a small card. "For your pleasure and amazement from several circuses, I'm pleased to present Benny, Ralph, Adrienne, Scotty, and Esmeralda!" After each name a colored performer bounded onto the platform dressed in full body tights and took a bow. Then a smiling black giant of a man, also in tights, thumped his tree-trunk legs onto the stage. Jones deadpanned, "Oh yes. I forgot. This here is 'Tiny'." There were whoops and applause. The troupe began a show of floor exercises as Jones scooted off and spoke a moment with Marian.

"Okay," Marian said to Laurel. They were several yards wide of the platform. Vivienne and Anna were nearby, finding mothers can talk about daughters. "I'm on in twenty minutes. Warm me up."

Laurel looked at her. "You want me to warm up your voice?"

"Yes," Marian grinned. "You know what singers need to get ready better than anyone here."

"Well, all right," Laurel said, thinking how to do some of her exercises without an instrument. "Let's see. Sing these back to me." She sang a five-note scale, up and down. Marian repeated the sequence. Then Laurel said, "Good. Now work your way up by half-steps." Marian sang. "Now back down in reverse." Marian frowned but managed.

"Now I sing a note and you match me as quick as you can," Laurel said. The two girls chased each other in musical tag, complete with giggles, and in rising volume. Their wonderful voices and good spirits attracted a small crowd from passersby and the other ladies Jones had spotted.

"Okay," Laurel said. "I'll sing a song. You weave harmony and descant both above and below the melody line."

"What song?" Marian asked. Laurel felt a bead of sweat on her neck, grinned and launched into "In the Good Old Summertime." They worked sweetly through the piece and received a nice round of applause. Calls came: "Let's have another" and "Something down home." Reverend Jones looked at his pocket watch and said, "You've got about seven minutes."

"Okay?" Laurel asked.

"Why not?" Marian answered. "Same way. You do melody, and I'll weave."

"All right. Let's see. Hmm. 'Down home'." Laurel said half-aloud. Then she launched right into Stephen Foster's opening words, and Marian chimed in after the first notes:

> *"O the sun shines bright on my old Kentucky home,*
> *'Tis summer, the darkies...."*

As soon as the word came out Laurel's face fell. She covered her mouth and burst into tears. "Oh no! How could I? Oh no..." She turned and ran sobbing toward Vivienne. Their crowd had frozen, but then a few tongues thawed: "Insultin'" and "Got her nerve," and "Down deep they're all the same..." Vivienne held her shaking daughter and looked alarmed. Over to her right, a black finger pointed imperiously at Laurel as Obadiah Jones walked quickly to the front of the crowd. Still pointing he said, "I defy any one of you to say that girl has hate in her heart. If she did, would she be so shaken?" The crowd paused.

He eyed them like his namesake Obadiah the prophet. "Now if you want to see hate...self-righteous, arrogant, haughty, revoltin', treat-you-like-mudsill, kick-you-when-you're-down, walk-all-over-you repugnance just 'cause you're you!" ...he pointed his finger southwest like it would unleash a lightning bolt... "those Pharisees at the Great Tent won't let Marian sing. Not because she can't, but because of color. Now if you look at this white girl, hurtin', humiliated, and repentant, and you don't forgive her, well then you're no better than them." His audience flinched. He added more mildly, "As a pastor, I am not going to let you get down on all fours and look them Pharisees in the eye like that." Hearty, relieving, forgiving laughter burst out, along with several "Amen"s and some "preach it"s. One vet elbowed his companion and said, "Ain't that a purty way to call them a bunch of cur dawgs?" Somewhere farther back a voice called, "Lie down with dawgs and git up with fleas!"

Vivienne relaxed, and Laurel looked up to see many sympathetic and forgiving looks. Marian stood there too, reaching out her hand. "You didn't mean anything by it. It's just the way he wrote it, and it is a good tune." Laurel shook hands, nodded and dried her eyes. "I'm sorry," she whispered.

Marian smiled back. "I'm all warmed up and it's my time. Come over and listen." Vivienne looked in Laurel's eyes. "We'd be honored."

Jones led the applause at Platform A under the trees along Rock Creek. The group of circus acrobats were somersaulting and hand-springing off the far side. "Well, wasn't that a lot of fun?" he asked the assembled hundreds who roared their appreciation. Their acclaim attracted more passersby and the crowd picked up a ring of younger folks and showed a fair to middling number of white faces among the civilians.

"Now I'd like to introduce a singer from the Union Baptist Church of Philadelphia, known as the 'Baby Contralto.' Marian?" Marian stepped away from the piano where she had set up her sheet music for Jordan, who could read music, although Roscoe was just as talented playing by ear. Vivienne and Laurel were delighted as she sang first "Boot Black Rag" and then "Memphis Blues."

The veterans had braced for church music and were tickled by well-sung popular music. Roscoe took over as Marian swung into Foster's "Jeanie with the Light Brown Hair." Marian's effortless runs and intervals pulled out every lick of the song's sweetness. This applause was peppered with cries of "More, more."

Marian began the old soldiers' song, "Tenting Tonight." Here and there, a mouth organ joined in. On the second refrain, she motioned them all to sing. The men carried the melody and some fair harmony while Marian improvised a soprano descant that transformed all their singing like water into wine. More than a few veterans found the going hard as memories tightened their throats.

During the applause for "Tenting," Obadiah stage whispered to Marian. She nodded and turned to the men. "Reverend Jones says I have time for one more on this platform and then I'll move on to Platform B later today." She asked Roscoe for a pitch and then began a soul-turning gospel piece unknown to Vivienne and Laurel. Mother and daughter were utterly transported, taken down into the depths of Good Friday. Everyone was astounded by Marian's enormous range. Each verse opened with an awe-struck, "Were you there when they…" Then she would soar on a lonesome, aching "Ohh," then level out to a wistful, heartbroken, Jesus-crucified "sometimes it causes me." The three-time "tremble" wrenched souls and made knees ask for kneeling. The final verse carried them all into lilac-scented, raised-from-the-dead, hallelujah Easter morning, now trembling and limp-kneed for joy everlasting.

Obadiah finally dared applaud in the long-after silence. The men joined in, then thundered until they felt like their hands would fall off. The surrounding civilians redoubled the efforts of the veterans, all except for one fair-haired white man in a light summer suit and clipped moustache, hands limp at his sides holding a writing pad. His eyes were shut and he stood with the hymn still echoing in his soul while the ovation rang around him. Marian curtsied and they applauded. She bowed to the reverend and to the piano men and still the applause rang. She curtsied again, yet the applause continued. She made to move off the platform but men swarmed the steps and blocked her, continuing the ovation.

Her poise had carried her through the hymn, but now it sagged under the acclaim and she almost broke down. At last she locked eyes with her mother in the first row, regained her composure, and began singing. Roscoe cocked his ear and picked out the key. Jordan swung in next to him on the right side with some high note work. Four drummers from the Fisk Jubilee Singers – next for Platform A, they were waiting back right – came to attention and began softly beating rhythm. Marian's voice gathered power like a spring river carrying the winter melt: "at the twilight's last gleaming." On she went, through "the perilous fight" and "gallantly streaming" until, as rockets were "red glaring" the Fisk Jubilee ensemble had moved up on stage and were harmonizing in six parts behind her.

Platform A practically glowed as Reverend Jones called, "Let's have one more round of applause," he waved insistently until Anna at last stood, turned and bowed, "for Mrs. Anna Anderson and her daughter Marian!"

For special guests, the Camp Lincoln committee had set up an open-sided tent: a pavilion with picnic tables dressed with checkered tablecloths and cut flowers in unused coffee pots. Marian and Anna were escorted here by a grateful assembly. The Andersons insisted over Vivienne's protests that all four of them take dinner here. Having filled their plates and finding both coffee and pitchers of lemonade on the long, decorated table, the four Philadelphians sized up the others sharing the shade. There seemed to be an invisible line about fifteen feet out around the pavilion, beyond which veterans whispered vigorously and pointed to their tablemates. Joseph Blackburn was there too with his reporter's pad for the Los Angeles colored readers. He stood along side the blond-haired man with the clipped moustache, who turned out to be Mr. Percy Sutcliffe of the *London Times*. As sometimes happens, the opposites had instantly hit it off as fellow reporters and stood throwing hushed phrases back and forth and almost daring each other to keep up both throwing and writing while the singers and their mothers took dinner.

Vivienne sat down opposite a middle-aged colored woman who had a square face, firm jaw, and prominent nose. Her rich, brown eyes knew hard work and success. She wore a high-waist apricot silk dress with black brocade and pearls. She had on a medium-brimmed hat with a high-arching plume. A handsome young man stood behind her almost at military attention and on one side was a well-dressed woman in her twenties, also very attentive to the lady.

Vivenne held out her hand and asked, "How do you do? I'm Vivienne Deveraux of Philadelphia."

"Delighted," the lady replied, shaking Vivienne's hand. She turned to the man seated next to her, a stocky, square-built white man in black suspenders, a dark green shirt with rolled up sleeves, and a straw basket hat. "May I present Mrs. Vivienne Deveraux of Philadelphia?" The man scrambled to his feet, pulled off his hat and offered his hard-scaled hand. "Welcome to Gettysburg, Mrs. Deveraux. I'm Luke Benner."

Vivienne blinked and Anna, seated next to her, stared. Vivienne had picked up enough about Camp Lincoln she was able to say, "Are you related to the water tower behind you there on Benner's Hill?"

Benner, his plain-dressed wife, and three teenaged children all laughed heartily. "No one's put it quite like that, but yes ma'am, this land is our farm."

Marian whispered to Laurel, "No wonder everybody's gawkin' at him."

Luke said in a courtly way, "Mrs. Deveraux, may I present Mrs. C.J. Walker of Indianapolis?" None of the four from Philadelphia could hide their surprise.

Mrs. Walker gallantly put them at ease by saying, "Please call me Sarah. How do you like camp food? I'm sure you didn't expect roast beef, but here you are." Now Laurel and Marian knew a second reason the veterans were in awe, grateful for two people who had made Camp Lincoln possible. Easy, delighted conversation rose among the adults, and between the Benner teens and the singers. As everyone was starting in on Pennsylvania Dutch cottage cheese pie with raspberries for dessert, the suddenly familiar racket of a flying machine passed over camp and was gone. In the co-pilot's seat, with a camera mounted between his feet, an eyes-shut Thomas Ince cranked the handle with a white-knuckled grip while the Harrisburg pilot buzzed over Gettysburg.

Gettysburg

Around six o'clock, both camps served up supper under ominous skies. Thunderstorms arriving over South Mountain blocked the setting sun and got many of the veterans into tents earlier than any other night of the Encampment.

Calvin and Sam let supper settle, half-listening to a buzz of conversation. Toward the back of their tent was an earnest but friendly conversation going on between two Vermonters and two Alabama men about the causes of the War.

In the front of the tent, a sketch artist was drawing pencil sketches of Calvin and Sam from their War days using the old regimental photograph borrowed from the Burlington man from Monday night's campfire jaw session. They each paid ten cents for a full sheet drawing. Sam admired the man's talent and paid another dime for a set of four matching sketches on a sheet. As the artist worked in the cozy glow of extra lanterns, Sam read a copy of the *Baltimore Sun*. A special section covered the Encampment from Great Tent speeches to an estimate that sutlers were selling five thousand cigars a day. Industrious reporters noted only six deaths had occurred, that F.W. Woolworth's had sold enough postcards to fill a hay wagon, that the Thomas Ince Company had used eighteen cans of film, and that crowds for tomorrow could cap the climax, maybe reaching 150,000. Sam looked up from time to time and saw Calvin at a camp desk. He was writing his evening letter to Eleanor and also speedily filling pages in a half-sized, soft leather journal.

Over on Seminary Ridge, some Georgia men had borrowed a canvas fly, a pole, and some rope from the army. They used these to stake out an inverted V on the nose and front pole of a wall tent, giving it somewhat of a porch. When the rains came, the tent flaps could be left open for better air inside. A couple poker games were near the front, matched by a couple checkerboards near the back. Zachariah was waiting to play the winner between Indiana and Texas. While it was a Gray tent, the men inside were from both sides and regardless of who lost at cards or won at checkers, there was always a handshake at the end, sometimes reinforced by a backslap or two. Through the tent and porch, tall tales and remembering went on. An Ohio artilleryman named Dilger bragged that his battery had liked to work so close to the front line, one of Sherman's generals had proposed fitting the guns with bayonets.

When the rain came, the beating on the canvas made men drowsy. At Camp Lincoln, Lucius snuggled down under the patter, his mind full of musical snatches, still excited from meeting Madame Walker and Luke Benner. He took a childlike delight at being warm and dry while, inches away, the damp and chill flailed away harmlessly. He was soon asleep, with rain and running water in his dreams all night.

Later that night, a lightning bolt struck the north slope of Big Round Top and the thunder crash woke Sam. He looked over toward the tent door, the single top flap propped open to give some circulation. By a banked lantern light, he could see Calvin lying on his cot by the door. Calvin was awake but didn't notice Sam's rousing. He was looking up and out through the triangular opening, his fingers laced behind his head. By the glare of another flash, Sam could see Calvin was smiling, just watching the storm.

Friday, July 4, 1913

The Great Tent

Gettysburg Chief of Police Walter Krauss rose early on Friday and dressed carefully. His jacket, starched shirt, and pressed pants over shined shoes, and bowl-shaped, brimless cap with a star, all looked more composed than he felt.

Lincoln Square was its incessant, crowded self even as the depot clock struck eight, but this morning the police presence was more noticeable. Gradually, Krauss and other constables, aided by members of the Pennsylvania National Guard, reduced the motorcar and wagon traffic through the area. Sometime after nine o'clock, the various pushcart vendors were ordered one by one over toward the eastern side of the square and the pedestrians mostly went with them. When a train arrived, passengers could alight quickly and move through the western side of the square with little delay. Newspaper reporters from the *Chicago Tribune* and the *Washington Post* sauntered around, only partially hiding their interest, their instincts telling them that certain rumors they had heard over drinks last night among their rivals at the Gettysburg Hotel might be true.

Finally, a little after ten, a private train with a special passenger pulled into Lincoln Station. Constables and guardsmen tried to look casual, their eyes darting for danger. Unlike every other visitor to Gettysburg, this man passed effortlessly through the station to a waiting motorcar.

As eleven approached, the Great Tent on Pickett's Field filled to capacity. Helen Longstreet for the *New York Times* had a bit of time being admitted to the press section because a pair of obstreperous guardsmen was enforcing a rule of "No Women, No Colored." But led by Mr. Percy Sutcliffe of the *London Times*, the power of the press prevailed as men from New Orleans to Boston and from Minneapolis to Phoenix rained down requests until the guardsmen relented. The arguments from *Atlanta Constitution* and *Savannah Tribune* men were particularly pointed when they found out it was Helen Longstreet being stopped by Yankees, but all ended before any accounts were transmitted about "ill-mannered country rubes" and "block-headed Northern martinets." Twelve thousand veterans, civilians, press, locals, and tourists chatted excitedly ahead of a Fourth of July speech by President Woodrow Wilson.

Wilson agreed late to attend, interrupting the beginning of a family vacation to stop at the Encampment on the way to New Hampshire. He made his speech brief, knowing his words would fail miserably when compared to those of the last President to speak in Gettysburg. He spoke of the past valor of the men of this reunion, nimbly ignored both the causes and results of the War, and called on his listeners to look to the future. The press thought he did well, and the crowd strongly applauded him for his nostalgia and brevity.

During Wilson's short visit, tens of thousands of people were on the move in and around town. Police Chief Krauss left things under control in Lincoln Square and moved on to his other assignment for the day. Just reaching his assigned sector north of the Pennsylvania Memorial – and Krauss knew all the back ways – left him a half hour late. He, several guardsmen, and a couple of U.S. Cavalry troopers strained under the awesome crush of veterans, civilians, and wheeled traffic.

Calvin, Sam, and other members of the 14th Vermont moved north along Cemetery Ridge mid-morning. They were scouting out their location for the afternoon ceremonies and found that the organizers had indeed staked out their place along the wall where they had been posted fifty years ago. Calvin could look across to the west as the crowds swelled in a vast ring around the Great Tent. The President's slow progress could be marked as his motorcar, invisible among the crowds, touched off a moving wave of hats being waved and small children being hoisted onto fathers' shoulders. Overwhelmingly Republican, the Vermonters were content to watch the Democratic president's progress from this distance. Whatever his speech was, they would be able to read it in tomorrow's papers. Calvin sat on the stone wall resting both hands on his cane when an agitated, well-dressed man in a brown derby of maybe twenty-five came up to him.

"Beg your pardon, sir, but is this you here in this picture?" Calvin looked at the man's copy of the *Gettysburg Star*. A caption read, "All Gathered at Pennsylvania. Several vets gather at the Pennsylvania Memorial. From left, R. Simmons of Ark., C. Salisbury of Vt., L. Miller and S. McCormick of Ind., O. Tate of Titusville, Pa. and G. Woodhull of Fl."

Surprised, Calvin said, "Yes, I'm Calvin Salisbury of Vermont."

"Sir, this man here," he said, pointing, "Oliver Tate, is my grandfather. Our family has been looking for him here at Gettysburg all week. He is not a well man and all of us are quite concerned about his condition. Can you say where we might find him?"

Calvin studied the picture of the old gent with a small white moustache riding above an endless cucumber chin. "I'm sorry. I don't know. I only stood for the picture because the photographer asked. I didn't actually speak with Mr. Tate."

The man sighed. "I understand. Thank you anyway," and moved off.

As Calvin wondered about Tate, another veteran sauntered along the wall and said, "How do you do, Vermont?" apparently noting Calvin's VT designation on his slouch hat.

"Just fine," Calvin answered, shaking hands. "I'm Major Calvin Salisbury, 14th Vermont, Stannard's Brigade."

The man looked at Calvin with respect. "I'm Private Albert Woolson, 1st Minnesota."

Despite the heat, Calvin paled. "1st Minnesota you say? We're you in the charge?"

"Yes I was," Woolson answered. Calvin gulped and turned to Sam and several others. "Fellows? Fellows this here is Albert Woolson of the 1st Minnesota." The men stared. Turning back Calvin asked, "Can you tell us about the 1st Minnesota's fight?"

"All right," Woolson said, "but only if you tell me about Stannard's 'swinging gate' afterwards."

"Ayup. It's a deal," Calvin said.

Woolson, Calvin, Sam, Josiah Trimble, and several more detached themselves from the western side of the stone wall and walked Dixie-ward, eventually passing the looming Pennsylvania Memorial. This side of Cemetery Ridge was dotted with small knots of men in old dark blue and butternut or gray, talking, pointing, and gesturing. A batch of civilians added themselves in among the veterans. For at least a few minutes, these civilians could listen first hand to deeds of courage and loss that had made this sod Lincoln's hallowed ground.

Woolson led them to a vantage point on Cemetery Ridge where everyone could see clearly to the south. Just ahead and to the left, the ridge petered out to a flat spot prior to Little Round Top just beyond. Straight west were Rose Run, the Wheat Field, and Peach Orchard. Off to the southwest were the tumbled boulders of Devil's Den. A handful of Confederate veterans stood nearby wearing Alabama insignia and they joined the veteran and civilian mix of maybe forty listening to Woolson. "It was about over here," he began, pointing toward the sinking part of Cemetery Ridge. "Sickles had taken his Third Corps off here, forward into the Wheat Field and Peach Orchard into a salient."

"Sticking out like a sore thumb," Josiah Trimble remarked, and others nodded grimly. Dan Sickles had lost a leg in the fight but even that sacrifice hadn't earned him much respect. The veterans' view of the general's incompetence had been cemented by his postwar obsession with his amputated leg. Sickles had had his leg saved and mounted on display in a museum, where he visited it regularly for hours at a time over the next fifty years.

Woolson continued. "About 4:30, the Rebs attacked. Even though they were posted badly, the Third Corps men fought like hell for a couple hours."

An Alabama veteran nodded vigorously. "I'll acknowledge the corn of that. That fatt in the Wheat Field and Peach Orchard was as hard as any Longstreet's men were in."

Woolson tipped his hat to Alabama and then went on. "Still, 'long about 6:30, they were all gone up. Hancock rode his horse up there from the valley. He could see the Johnnies coming hard at the low spot over there and it was empty, not a single Union man."

"Yew got that ratt," one of the Alabamians exclaimed. "We pushed past Devil's Den on this side and could see the fightin' to the south and bluecoats dug in up here on the ridge to the north. But straight ahead east, it was wide open, straight to your rear."

The civilians looked at the park-like fields dotted with similar clusters like the one here around Woolson. They struggled to imagine the shell-swept, bullet-riddled scene from late afternoon fifty years ago. The veterans didn't need to imagine, but rather struggled inwardly as old, painful scenes forced their way front and center in their minds. A few in the group were old Third Corps men. They remembered running back, the Rebel yell ringing from behind them, the sagged end of Cemetery Ridge lit by the yellowing sun riding down toward Devil's Den, and the smell of black powder rose acrid in their noses. Again in their minds rode Hancock, a lone horseman among shell bursts gouging craters, picking his way among smashed cannons, dead horses, dead men, whimpering wounded. Trying to salvage Sickles' mess, Hancock later wrote, "Gibbon and Hays had been sent for and were coming on the double, but the Rebels were coming and in five minutes the cause would be lost."

Woolson pointed to the end of Cemetery Ridge. "We came out over there in a column of four, Colonel Colvill in the lead. Hancock came up and reined in as the colonel called halt. Hancock looked down there in the valley" – here Woolson pointed between the ridge and Devil's Den – "and saw maybe two brigades coming. Hancock says, 'Colonel, what regiment is this?'"

"'1st Minnesota, sir!'"

"Then Hancock looks at our ground-down regiment, sets his face, and says to Colvill while pointin' at the Rebels, 'Colonel, do you see those colors?'"

"The colonel looked. We all looked. The Rebel battle flag and the Alabama flag were in the middle of the brigades. Colonel said, 'Yes, sir.'

"'Well, take them.'

"And the colonel saluted, turned to us and called, 'Right face. Extend the line to the left. Fix bayonets.' We stretched the line out toward Little Round Top and clamped on. Then the colonel drew his sword, pointed to the Alabama flag and said, '1st Minnesota, forward!'"

Although the day's heat was scorching, many of the old vets shivered involuntarily at Woolson's plain description of "seeing the elephant," the old term for combat. They understood, and yet understanding, still they cringed at the desperation of sending 262 men – all the bled-down strength that was left of the 1st Minnesota – against Wofford's four thousand, over this open ground, without cover, and only long-range artillery support.

"Every man could see what was being asked, and none of us figured to survive. I stayed next to the Colonel and the Major and started beatin' the quick step and off we went. The Rebs couldn't believe it. You could see surprise as their whole line kinda stutter-stepped. Some stray shots dropped a few of our men. We were wantin' to shoot back, but instead the Colonel called out, '1st Minnesota, on the double-quick.' So Tommy and I took it to 180 beats a minute and we were practically runnin'. The Rebels almost halted and we started shouting." Woolson's arm swept in a slow arc toward the floor of the valley.

"Over all the noise we heard the colonel yell, '1st Minnesota, halt. Aim. Fire.'

"We were so close nobody could miss. We gave them a good fire and they dropped like cut wheat. Then the colonel yelled, 'With the bayonet, charge!' Since we didn't have time to reload, that made the most sense to us, so in we went."

A Birmingham man broke into Woolson's account. "It was the dangdest thing I saw in the whole War. You men were like wildcats, or tetched in your haids crazy, and it made at least a few of us wonder what was wrong with y'all."

Woolson looked surprisingly modest as he continued. "The rebs were tryin' to shoot, but we were in so close their own men was in the way. We fought with bayonets, rifle butts, and hand t' hand. I was with the Colonel when he got wounded. He said to me, 'Stay with the major for orders.'"

One of the graybacks from Alabama pushed his way forward to stand almost nose-to-nose with Woolson. After a long stare, he went white and said in a half-whisper, "I drew a bead on you, drummin' next to yo' major. Had you ready to blow to kingdom come when you turned your haid my way. You looked jes' like my boy back home" – his face scrunched up – "and I couldn't shoot a boy." Tears ran down his cheeks as he choked out, "I'm sorry boys had to go to war and see what you saw." He held his hand out to Woolson. The two men were so moved they shared a long, double-handed handshake. The other vets looked on or looked away, swallowed hard, or in church-like silence exchanged handshakes with each other regardless of whether a cuff was blue or gray. Several civilian men took off their hats and two or three women wept and clung to their men's arms.

It took Woolson a long nose blow and two tries to get his voice back. "After forever the major called, '1st Minnesota, fall back to the ridge.' So I beat the retreat and we did, walkin'. When we got back, Gibbon's and Hays' men opened ranks and let us through, then volley-fired on the 'Bama boys, and they never did come any closer. When we counted noses later we had forty-seven men not hit. But…" Woolson pulled himself up as his listeners swallowed hard at the old drummer boy's story, "…General Hancock had said he needed five minutes. When we got back on the ridge, it was ten minutes later."

After a time, Woolson regained his composure and ambled back north. Several of the veterans also welcomed the chance to walk while they thought, felt, or just blew their noses very loudly and long. The knot of veterans, blue and gray, and a thoughtful group of civilians made their way back toward the Vermont regiments' spot along the wall. On the downslope western side were other clusters of veterans mostly in gray telling stories and pointing. Woolson broke up the silence with a sigh and then asked, "Well, that was my fightin' on the second day. You Vermont men had a time of it on the third day. How'd it go?"

Calvin, Sam, and Josiah exchanged glances while the civilians pressed in, eager to hear a second tale. Calvin said, "Okay, I'll start. You fill in." Sam and Josiah nodded. Calvin pointed west and somewhat south about three quarters of a mile where the woods south of Lee's monument bulged east toward the Emmitsburg Road. "About the last of the men in Pickett's charge started from there. They were all aiming for the angle an' the copse of trees in Zeigler's Grove," here he pointed straight north along the wall about two hundred yards ahead, "so they came forward, but on their oblique."

"Pilin' up to break our line," Josiah added helpfully, putting himself in charge of explaining for the civilians.

Calvin continued. "Our artillery on Little Round Top and Cemetery Hill hammered them and the batteries here on the ridge loaded canister and opened up when they got in range. At about three hundred yaads, our brigade started giving them a good fiyah. But you have to admire them: under all that lead they kept coming, moving on the oblique. Colonel Stannard saw the end of their line passing across our front."

The civilians looked west and saw a gentle slope falling away into a swale a couple hundred yards ahead. Waist-high grass barely stirred. A fine trail of dust hung in the air each time a motorcar clattered over the dirt of Emmitsburg Road. The Union men looking west saw this too, yet the mind kept playing tricks, as though in the distance was the twinkle of massed bayonets carried above the shoulder. Heat mirages and memories combined at the corner of the eye to perhaps see rows of gray and brown caps and hats, and also sudden dirt towers leaping up and collapsing as shot and shell pounded the approaching infantry.

Josiah picked it up. "The colonel ordered 'cease fire' and 'stand up'."

Calvin pointed south along the wall and put in, "The colonel told me what he wanted and sent me and a drummer boy way down to the left end of the line."

"All the sergeants were yelling, 'Over the wall and form ranks'," former sergeant Sam Wentworth added.

"Ayup, me too," Calvin said. "While I was running, I was calling 'Form ranks. Reload. Form over the wall. Reload.'"

Sam said, "We were almost formed when General Hancock rode up with his staff. The Colonel stood up on the wall and called out, 'The eyes of General Hancock are upon Vermont!'"

Calvin jumped in. "I heard him shout that just as I reached the end of the Vermont line. The whole brigade roared a cheer. Then Stannard ordered, 'Brigade, right. Grand right wheel.'"

"We all cheered again and moved on the pivot," Josiah said. He held his arm out due south, then slowly swung it ninety degrees until he pointed west. "You could see the Rebels pointing and looking scared as the far end swung out."

Calvin resumed. "Hancock called it a big, swinging gate, nine hundred men in formation, square on the end of Pickett's right flank. We couldn't help in the middle, but from the side we could cut down the number of men Pickett could bring to the wall. The colonel called, 'Aim. Fiyah.' The Rebels dropped by the dozens. The colonel ordered a slow walk forward, halting every twenty paces to fiyah again. We had to step over scores of dead and wounded Rebels."

Sam noted, "Hancock was so impressed he galloped off to the other end of the line to order some regiments there to do the same gate swing and form a three-sided box on Pickett's men."

Calvin's eyes were hard as marble as he announced the verdict. "Stepping over those dead or screaming men, seeing arms an' hands an' legs laying around from the artillery fiyah like pieces of dolls thrown under a train" – he gulped hard – "it still makes my stomach turn. But hundreds of men were kept from the center of Pickett's attack, and he couldn't break through. General Lee failed and Gettysbaag became the turning point in the East."

The civilians and veterans gazed over the slightly rolling field waist-high in dry grass, trying to picture Pickett's twelve thousand butternuts. The civilians saw heat waves shimmering, tents in the distance, other civilians and aged veterans tramping the fields randomly, traffic moving up and down Emmitsburg Road, the electric trolley clanging by. But many of the veterans saw the fields and heard again the roar of muzzleloader-massed volleys, rank upon rank of men in gray looming ever closer, wounded men crying. In their minds sounded the screams of shells, the ugly plop of severed limbs, cannon blasts shaking the earth. For an instant, the septic smell of blown-open intestines rose in their noses. Then they looked and saw what the civilians saw, and they were grateful. "Glad you stopped 'em," Albert said.

"Glad it's over," Sam answered.

"Amen," said Calvin and Josiah together.

Gettysburg Depot

President Wilson had wound up his speech at the Great Tent. Like any good politician, he worked the front row of the stands, shaking hands and smiling broadly. When he came to the press section, he was delighted to meet *New York Times* special correspondent Helen Longstreet. In a gallant gesture, he invited her to interview him on the motorcar ride back into Gettysburg where he could resume his train ride.

They arrived at Lincoln Square just before noon and Wilson was every part the gentleman as he handed the widow Longstreet out of the back seat and bade her farewell. But as he began walking to the depot, he stopped short. By a popcorn stand, a lively, cheerful conversation was bouncing along and what drew Wilson was the mix of those in the group: several veterans, North, South, and USCI; two white women who might be from town; and an elegantly dressed black woman. They were sipping lemonades, pewter flasks, and at least one paper cup of beer.

Wilson walked over, curious, trailed by a young man with his appointment book and two hard-eyed Treasury Department men, who looked around anxiously and felt for the pistols on their hips. Helen Longstreet circled back as well, thinking something more interesting than Wilson's careful answers from the car ride might come up here. One of Ince's camera crews caught Wilson's wondering look and later amazement in their lenses.

Wilson turned on his political smile and said, "Morning folks. Good to see you here."

Recognition, then nervousness, ran across the group. "Hello, Mr. President." "How do you do, sir?"

One Union man stammered, "Would you like a beer, Mr. President?" offering his.

"No, thank you," Wilson answered. He said to the white veterans, "Can I ask what such a diverse group of you find in common to talk about?" and was thrown off stride by the female voice to his left.

"All of us are Americans," Sarah Breedlove Walker said, "and it's the Fourth of July. We talk about liberty, freedom, emancipation, and about living in the greatest country in the world and how to make it even better for every American. Isn't that enough?"

As Wilson was left tongue-tied, Walker tossed out some campaign phrases. "Isn't that what you mean by 'reform'? By 'progressive'? Perhaps we should progress on civil rights?"

One of the townswomen nerved herself to throw in, "Or the women's vote?" A USCI man and a white Confederate took some delight in Wilson's discomfort and happened to say together, "How 'bout it?"

"Um, ah …thank you for your thoughts," giving them all a sweeping, deep nod, starting with Madame C.J. Walker. "I'll have to consider them closely," he said, turning to go.

"We'll be watching," a Union man remarked.

"Safe travel, Mr. President," an old grayback tacked on, and the whole group hoisted flasks and cups. Back on board the Presidential train, Wilson's secretary noticed that he was unusually quiet. Helen Longstreet followed Mr. Wilson into the depot, but then turned to the Western Union office. She took several sheets of practice paper and turned her hasty notes into two crisply lettered stories. Then she stepped over to the window and had the operator wire off both the motor car interview and the human interest companion story in time to make the afternoon edition of the *New York Times*.

Zeigler's Grove

As Gettysburg's church clocks struck noon, the men of the Vermont brigade were pleased to discover a field kitchen had been set up not far north of their position. Under the trees of Zeigler's Grove, the men ate under shade that was delightful yet just a touch unsettling. Fifty years ago yesterday in front of Seminary Ridge, General Lee had pointed to these very trees and told General Pickett to have his troops converge here to try to crack the Union line in half

The long tables held both blue and gray and there was a fair bit of chatter about "finally getting here" and "good to have you on the right side at last." Calvin and Sam had just found a spot to land their plates and deploy tableware when the conversation across from them turned serious.

"This is going to be some handshake across this wall later today," a Maine man said to a couple Mississippians across the table. "We vets have been practicing all week across Tent City and around campfires, so I think the civilians will believe we mean it when we shake."

The lanky master sergeant from Biloxi swallowed abruptly and stared hard across the table. "My brother wouldn't give any of you Yankees the time of day, let alone a handshake or a good word."

After a hush, the Maine man answered, "Sounds like he's got his reasons."

"He's got four hundred an' twelve of 'em," the Biloxi man retorted. "That's how many days he was at Elmira's Prison in New York. When they let him out at the end of the War, he weighed ninety-seven pounds and was a walking bag of bones."

The Maine man went white at the mention of Elmira, bitterly nicknamed "Hellmira" by those who had survived its brutal winters and rotten food. Conversation died and like others, Calvin and Sam stared at their plates of food, suddenly nauseated by what had been a tasty midday meal served up under shade.

Calvin looked up sadly at the Mississippi man and said slowly, "I'm so sorry at what happened to your brother. No excuse for it, none. But tell me. I understand why he wouldn't come to a reunion like this. But why are you here? Were you at Elmira too?"

"I wasn't captured," the man answered. "I got wounded in the foot about an hour earlier and was in the rear waiting at the surgeon's wagon. But I'm here to see iffin' the Yankees are still them inhuman devils who set up Elmira, or iffin' y'all might be remorseful and even repentant sinners."

"What do you think?" Calvin wondered.

"I don't know yet," came the reply.

"Fair enough," Calvin said. "I hope you get a good answer." He tried a bite of turkey, but it just sat in his mouth. Sam was chasing peas around his plate for amusement but not nourishment. The glanced at each other and nodded. They rose and Calvin said, "Good day, gentlemen. I think I might find a place for a nap before the ceremonies this afternoon." They dully turned in their plates at the dishwashing station, appetites gone even after a vigorous morning. Like Andersonville, Elmira did that to a man.

Cemetery Ridge

Last night's thunderstorms had soaked Gettysburg's fields, ridges, and hills. The heat topped ninety degrees by noon and baked the moisture out of the ground, turning it into sweltering humidity. Cicadas chanted their buzzing love songs. Carriage and wagon wheels roused flights of grasshoppers. The grass and ground launched dust in a fine sheen into the air.

The grass was stirred, not by wind, but by thousands of shoes and boots of every description. Civilians came for the day from a vast triangle bounded by Pittsburgh, New York City, and Richmond. They endured hours on foot, by wagon, in motorcars jouncing over poor roads, or in the swaying clatter of dozens of railroad Specials and Extras put on the tracks for this day. Others had come days before from Michigan or Georgia, Ohio or Colorado, the well-to-do and some of the middle class, choosing to spend their precious days of vacation not in the mountains or on the seashore, but here in rural Pennsylvania.

They came to see the veterans, the Civil War embodied in the aging flesh of men from nearly every state but all from a different time. These men of

America had fought and hurt and killed each other for four mortal years from Pennsylvania to New Mexico, from Kansas to Florida. Would they make peace? Could they accept each other and publicly welcome one another as friends and fellow countrymen? After all the speeches were delivered and songs were played and sung, after all the prayers were prayed, the veterans were asked to step to the front under their old flags and perform a simple act on behalf of the country.

The plan called for the veterans to cap today's solemnities on either side of the wall atop Cemetery Ridge. For several hundred yards of wall, the Southerners facing east, the Northerners facing west, reporters writing endlessly and even photographers at the ready, the old soldiers were asked to do a mass handshake. Could they shake hands with each other and shake the off the scars of the past? If they could, the country could move forward as one nation under one flag, healed in some way of its deepest hurts. If not, then maybe the only way to meet the future would be to wait for these old men to die off and take their hurts and hates with them to the grave.

Despite the sultry heat, women wore high-necked, long-sleeved dresses or blouses under colorful, shoulder-wide flat hats. Northern men mostly wore dark suits with high-collared shirts. Some Southern men stood out in white linen suits. Small boys wore jackets soft caps and short pants. The girls were mostly in lighter colored versions of the women's dresses, as though age meant dark clothes.

The veterans in Tent City were fifty-four thousand strong, yet civilians flowed everywhere, outnumbering the veterans by three to one or better. The 15th Cavalry, the Pennsylvania National Guardsmen, area constables, and even the Boy Scouts struggled mightily moving people along. The general idea was to form an enormous ring around the veterans, centered on the west slope of Cemetery Ridge. The civilian circle began at the south edge of Gettysburg itself, running clockwise in a flattened way along Hancock Avenue atop Cemetery Ridge behind the Union ranks. Then massed spectators curved southwest off Cemetery Ridge to the Emmitsburg Road. They carried past Trostle farm to the edge of the woods toward Seminary Ridge, then fringed the woods where Pickett's men had begun their charge, and finished at town's edge.

Inside this ring, the veterans assembled in their own ring, mostly blue to the north, east, and south, and a long gray arc along the west. The middle of the circle would be kept clear for the upcoming ceremony. Along the border between civilian and veteran rings, buckboard wagons were spotted at regular intervals. Each wagon sported a well-dressed man, chosen for his clear diction and powerful voice.

These hours of coping with the rising tide of civilians that never ceased wore Police Chief Krauss to near desperation. He was working on Cemetery Ridge north of the Pennsylvania Memorial with several constables from surrounding towns, about eight Pennsylvania National Guardsmen and Privates Weston and O'Connor from the US 15th Cavalry. The growing heat and growing crowds eroded most of Krauss' veneer of humanity and consideration, leaving his self-importance and prejudices prominent. He stamped around blowing his whistle and waving his billy club, but already by eleven o'clock his eyebrows were leaking sweat into his eyes. He could feel moisture and smell his stink. He remembered with an odd clarity reading the tag on the one-piece, four-limbed red long johns that morning, "Cotton Summer Weight for Comfort." He wiped his brow and vowed to himself, "Next salesman from that Interior Wear Company is getting locked up in Summer Weight Comfort for three days!"

Crowd movement slacked off after noon as veterans took their dinners at field kitchens and civilians picnicked everywhere and often stretched out for a nap. Weston and O'Connor found handling both their mounts and the crowds easier the more they ignored Krauss. The vendors kept up a steady chant selling their wares, and Krauss vented his spleen by ejecting several who could not produce an Encampment Commission license.

Afternoon shimmered with heat as speechmaking in the Great Tent wore to a close. North of the angle under the trees of Ziegler's Grove, a swarm of newspapermen wrote of bands, flags, dignitaries, and veterans. Photographers fussed with their accordion-ribbed boxes on spindly tripods. Some trained long lenses on the Confederates forming on the Emmitsburg Road. Others pre-focused their Kodak thirty-eight-pounders on the Union veterans assembling at the angle and in the grove, waiting to shake hands across the wall with their old foes. Thomas Ince set up one of his moving picture cameras to the south, using Gettysburg town as a backdrop.

Thousands of Union men gathered in their old units at the wall stretching along Cemetery Ridge toward Little Round Top. Behind the Gettysburg veterans – those who had actually been in the fight here – were regiments and brigades of other Union men. Civilians filled in behind these up onto Hancock Avenue. Here they thinned out because the natural amphitheater effect disappeared along with a good view of the proceedings. But the civilians were a long-circling, multicolored mass so large that those in it were awed by themselves. A *Baltimore Sun* reporter thought yesterday's estimate of 150,000 looked low today.

The Emmitsburg Road, about a quarter mile west of the wall on Cemetery Ridge, was closed to all vehicles starting at one o'clock for today's ceremony. Likewise, the electric trolley that plied the track just next to the road also stopped running for the afternoon. In the field along the west side of this stretch of road, large pavilions had been set up to provide shade and seating on folding chairs for several thousand Confederate veterans. The men filtered out of the woods on Seminary Ridge after dining among tents. Their passage from the woods and through the civilians was slow, accompanied by a long series of whispers and pointed children's fingers, handshakes, backslaps, and awkward civilian salutes. Women waved handkerchiefs and said "Thank you," tourist men offered congratulations and hat wavings, children screwed up their courage to ask for a handshake or clung shyly to their mother's skirts. Under the pavilions, the oldsters could assemble in the shade until it was their time to move out. Here Boy Scouts provided pitchers of ice water and paper cups; the men of Lee and Jackson, Johnston and Bragg, Longstreet and Beaureguard, often fortified the position from their pocket flasks.

After Gettysburg's church clocks struck three, the gathered humanity watched a large troop of musicians march in column from town. Not just a band, this collection of one thousand bandsmen at full regimental strength was eastern Pennsylvania's finest. In their wake walked a larger block of well-dressed civilian men, mostly clean-shaven except for frequent mustaches, each carrying a black folder under his left arm. The sparse number of programs circulating hand to hand among the crowds – no one had thought to print in such numbers as today – said the band would be doubled by a two-thousand-voice choir, providing an impressive set of patriotic airs.

As this column of musicians wound toward a staked out area midway between Cemetery Ridge and the Emmitsburg Road, bands across the fields and slopes fell silent. But some spectators up on Hancock Avenue heard the sound of other drums, out of rhythm with the column of bandsmen coming from town. At first, some thought it was an acoustic trick or an odd echo. Looking around, they heard a crisp, growing drumbeat from behind them. Turning to the eastern slope of what had been the Union rear stretching toward Culp's Hill, they began pointing. Police Chief Krauss, having finally caught a breather as the milling mob settled in for the ceremonies, groaned almost audibly. "Now what?" he wondered, and pushed his way along Hancock Avenue to see what was coming.

What was coming were two columns of Union blue. Curling west around Culp's Hill, a heavy column split in two, one coming up Hunt Avenue, the other in the adjoining field. The Hunt Avenue column was mincing with the twenty-two-inch step of the old Army of the Potomac. The field column was springing along at the twenty-four-inch stride of the Western veterans of Sherman and Thomas. Like at the Grand Review in Washington after Appomattox in 1865, spectators today were hard pressed to decide which they admired more: the careful precision and tighter ranks of the Easterners, or the springy bounce of the Westerners that made them "march like lords of the earth."

The men marched with as much resilience as old bones and stiff joints allowed, but every man marched with high pride. Each column had teenage drummers spaced at intervals, faces solemn as pallbearers and hands lively as hummingbird wings. Led by a few uneasily mounted white officers, and cadenced by sergeants two steps wide right, there came the United States Colored Infantry and Troopers of Camp Lincoln.

The Stars and Stripes rippled in the lead while regimental flags waved along each column. GAR post flags wigwagged over the approaching columns, and spectators could make out "Robert Gould Shaw GAR Post, Boston, MA" and "Abraham Lincoln Post, GAR, Springfield IL" near the column heads. Further along were post flags named in honor of Grant, Sherman, and Frederick Douglass, and the lesser known O.O. Howard, Rufus Saxton, and Thomas Higginson. Wide of each column came a cloud of civilians walking along, mostly colored, but sprinkled with white faces as well. These throngs waved handkerchiefs and hats, hoisted small children on their shoulders, or watched their older ones scamper along with high-pitched squeals. Camp Lincoln cooks and dishwashers waved towels and clanged pots with ladles in time with the drummers. Reporters like Joseph Blackburn and Percy Sutcliffe, as well as the newsmen and newswomen from Memphis and Mobile, Chicago and Boston, nearby Philadelphia and far off San Francisco, bobbed alongside the marchers, doing their best to write, walk, and cheer all at once.

O'Connor and Weston spotted them early and came up Hancock Avenue at a fast walk. Mounted, they moved faster than Krauss or the other foot-bound guardsmen. They neared the head of the field column led by an old mounted officer. The reverse slope of Cemetery Ridge slowed the men as they passed Meade's old headquarters.

Despite his years, Colonel Nicholas Biddle, 55th Mass, easily handled the light gray gelding he had hired today. He snapped off a crisp salute to Weston and O'Connor, who automatically returned it.

"Uh, Colonel?" Weston asked. "Who are these men and where are they going?"

Biddle drew rein alongside both troopers, keeping himself between them and the marchers. He made no move to halt the column closing behind him, using the column's momentum for strength. He paused, pulled himself to monument pose in the saddle, and mustered an extra loud voice so the spectators would overhear him.

"Privates, these War veterans are part of the 180,000 volunteers who took up arms for their freedom. The official Encampment ignored them and the U.S. Army banned them from Tent City." He paused to let this sink in. The column heads were only a hundred feet from Hancock Avenue. "They had to arrange their own camp, but on this day, a formal day of reunion and reconciliation, on

America's day of the Fourth of July, they have as much right to be here as any veteran. They want no part in the ceremonies, but these men, my men, have earned the right to be present."

Weston and O'Connor looked at each other uncertainly. Chief Krauss had come close enough to hear. "No, sir," he snapped. "There's no space for them." His voice rose and he also played to the crowd. "These spectators have come from miles away. They can't be moved in time and they won't give up their viewing spots." He began sputtering, "A bunch o' no-account, boot-shinin' garrison troops, thinking wearing the blue makes them any kind of men worthy of..."

He was interrupted by a middle-aged, well-dressed Massachusetts woman who had spent some of her girlhood at Port Royal while her father was commander there. She said with most unladylike force, "Oh, rubbish, officer." Turning to the onlookers, Sarah Higginson called out, "Make way for the veterans. The freedmen are here! The freedmen!"

The crowd was instantly converted. As the first ranks of the columns crunched the gravel of Hancock Avenue, the cry ran ahead of them: "Make way. The veterans, the freedmen are coming." The sweating ranks of USCI troops grinned at their acceptance and at a few of the obviously white voices intoning an "amen" or "glory hallelu."

"Now just a minute," Krauss bawled out, but O'Connor and Weston mutinied. They turned their horses past him and trotted up to the head of the column as escorts to Biddle. Krauss' police whistle ironically added to the pot-clanging noise-making of the escorting colored folk. "Close ranks!" called the sergeants. The drummers drowned out Krauss. The columns rolled past the odd New York Tammany monument that was shaped like a Plains Indian tepee. Biddle and the planners had worked it just right as the marchers came up to their old abolitionist allies from New England. The civilians melted back to form a convenient space behind Stannard's Vermont brigade and among several Massachusetts regiments.

On the gentle west slope of Cemetery Ridge, the thousand-piece band formed ranks. The two thousand singers massed around them, facing outwards in four directions. A director and three sub-directors led several dignified patriotic airs for the surrounding myriads, finishing with all four verses of "The Star-Spangled Banner." As the musicians retreated, all eyes and ears turned to the hundreds of buckboard wagons spotted between the civilian and military rings.

The chosen men, well-rehearsed and strong voiced, climbed onto the wagons and began speaking. Like distinguished battlefield guides they delivered the same memorized speech to all within earshot, outlining the battle events of all three days and ending with Lee's army poised for Pickett's desperate charge on the third day.

Two cannons flanked the Confederate brigades formed on Emmitsburg Road. The buckboard speakers finished and sat down. On this cue, the south-facing gunners touched a slow match to the vent. A tremendous report crashed out in a bluish-white cloud of smoke. As the boom of the blank round echoed back from the rocks of Devil's Den, the northern gun fired in reply, reverberating off the houses of Gettysburg.

Thousands of old men in gray – including Bidwell, Calhoun, Dooley, and Zachariah – waved their hats. They screeched and howled and did their level best to summon up once more the banshee yowl, fox hunt yip, sphincter-tightening Rebel yell. Stiffened lungs, false teeth, and fifty years had all taken their toll, but enough came through via heart and memory that most spectators felt a chill and swallowed hard. Enough came through that Union vets unconsciously clenched teeth and whitened their knuckles as a decades-old tightening coiled their intestines.

As the yell died down, an endless applause and cheer rose from the civilians. The drum corps from the U.S. Army band beat the old regulation direct step, ninety beats per minute. Brogans and boots took up the pace, supplemented by cane tips and crutches' feet. Dooley Culpepper had been working among the assembling gray coats, and he was not the only one. In among the veterans and out of earshot from the civilians or any newspapermen, he kept saying, "Don't do it. They're Yankees, fer cryin' out loud. They shot down your brothers, invaded our land, burned our houses, ran off our niggers. Don't go shakin' hands with them. Don't do it. Stay here. Don't do it."

Dooley and other bitter-enders had had some success, and a trickle of men fell out of the forming brigades into the crowd who would stay put on the Emmitsburg Road. He picked up more for his efforts when he began invoking the prison camps. "Remember Elmira. Remember Camp Douglas. They had the food but they let our boys starve. They had the blankets but they let our men freeze. Don't do it. Stay here. Ain't anybody over there you want to shake hands with. Stay here. Stay here."

He made his plea to the 8th Georgia men and a few did retreat. He tugged the sleeves of Jim Calhoun and Turner Hawkins, and Turner actually took a few steps out of line. Then he looked at Zachariah and Jim and Bob Bidwell holding their places and turned back to join them, saying in a troubled voice to Dooley, "I cain't stay here with you, Dooley. I'm sorry. I know what you're sayin', but I cain't do it, I cain't stay here. I gotta go with the regiment."

Dooley drifted back to the mass of yelling graybacks who were going to stay put along the road. At the last minute, a Mississippi man from Biloxi stepped up from them and moved to join the brigades. Dooley stepped in front of him. "Don't do it. Stay here. Let the damn Yankees stand there empty-handed. Remember Johnson's Island. Remember Elmira."

In a husky, heavy voice the man answered, "I remember Elmira ever' day. I cain't forget. My brother was there and he won't let me forget." Dooley nodded encouragement. "He ain't never been to a reunion where the bluebellies were invited too, so he ain't here neither. If he'd a come, he'd be standin' ratt here goin' nowhere." Dooley almost smiled.

"But that's him," the man choked out. "That's how he remembers the War. But it was my War too, and I ain't my brother. Step aside, suh. I'm joinin' up."

Dooley started to say something, but then saw a look in the man's face that struck him mute. He gulped hard, hung his head, and stepped over. The Mississippi man limped up to the fourth rank and squeezed into line.

An old North Carolina brigadier squinted through his thick round spectacles and saw the front rank – among them Bidwell and Calhoun – marching in place in good rhythm. He raised his sword and screamed over the drumming, "Brigade! Forward!" The Charge of 1913 began.

Zachariah felt a surge, a very old surge, as he and the second rank stepped off and joined the advance. Memory splinters swirled through his mind like a photo album tumbling off a table. It had been this hot crossing Bull Run Creek on a July Sunday. Three times they'd crossed it, then crossed it back, without seeing anything or using their newly issued rifles. The fourth time, he had seen a squad of blue-kepied young men and thrilled at spotting the enemy.

He had looked down the line and another fragment had sailed by, an enormous line of screaming men advancing under supporting artillery fire. Porter's Union Corps had dissolved into dead men and writhing wounded as Longstreet had wrecked John Pope on the fields of Manassas.

Zachariah's left arm began throbbing, his fast pulse pressing the nerves along the old scar. He instinctively gave it a rub, but it still hurt. All along the line, men were breaking step as they lost rhythm among the uneven parts of the ground and their own tired feet. There was a sudden thud as a seventy-seven-year-old South Carolina corporal fell. That sounded too much like… Three or four others stopped to help him up.

To Zachariah's right, an eighty-two-year-old Arkansas private went down in a clatter of crutches and a pitiful "Ow, ow," just like that same whimpering by Antietam Creek.

Zack caught a toe and stumbled. He just caught himself, but it had been a close call. The Florida private next to him asked if he was all right, and Zachariah nodded. Then Florida stumbled in turn, lurching left and banging into Zachariah. Zack remembered the undergrowth along Chickamauga Creek when another man had sagged into him like this, dead at his feet. The two old men swayed for a minute, then both found their balance and went on. Zachariah's right shin smarted from where the Floridian's cane had accidentally smacked it.

It was only a quarter mile of grass from the Emmitsburg Road, rising maybe ninety feet. At twenty-four inches to the stride, a quarter mile was about six hundred sixty steps. Six hundred sixty steps surrounded by roaring and sympathetic civilians beyond numbering. A quarter mile to old foes willing to be old friends, waiting at the low wall for the planned handgrips and welcome.

It was a quarter mile of dead calm, summer-hot air catching in stiff and shriveled lungs. A quarter mile walking while a leg stump chafed raw, blood leaking into the end grain of a wooden leg. A quarter mile of crutch work and cane work by weak hands and swollen joints. A quarter mile of sweat drops rolling to mouth corners in salty deposits. A quarter mile of saliva gathering into a gummy mouth cotton. A quarter mile of frantic heartbeats. A quarter mile of exhaustion-threatening heat stroke.

Age began winning over pride. Men in gray bent over with heaving chests. Others continued to stumble and some to fall. One of Ince's cameras on Emmitsburg Road filmed as one vet lost a crutch from under one arm, caught his balance with the other, and then, being in the last rank, turned very slowly toward the dropped crutch. Hundreds, no thousands, in the spectator's circle saw him and hearts broke at the silvered, bent eighty-two-year-old hopping pathetically on one leg. Many rose, ready to go to his aid, but the oldster managed to scoop up the crutch, do an about face, and resume his deliberate charge up the slope. Eyes brimmed over at the sight of the small but determined man slowly crutching his way after the ranks of his comrades.

Chief Krauss was south of the charge, just west of the stone wall in front of a mass of Union men. He could see the elderly Gray charge breaking down and it annoyed him. Being a strapping man himself, he had that strong man's contempt sometimes seen for those weaker. "Damn it," he thought to himself, "the Rebels are going to mess it up." For Krauss and the planners, the Encampment's high point was this handshake along the wall. True, handgrips like this had been done before, but this was fifty years, this was fifty thousand veterans and uncounted civilians. If stretcher bearers had to carry off some of the old butternuts or an ambulance wagon had to drive down the slope, people would remember that more than the handshake at the wall.

"Damn it, the whole thing is falling apart," Krauss thought to himself. "Damn Rebels can't do anything right." Across the wall, he could hear arguments going on even now, with the charge underway. "Step back," bitter, hard-shell men were saying to other men. "Step back. Don't shake hands with

Rebels. Rebels, I tell you! Traitors. They brought on the War. Traitors to the nation, I tell you! They shot down your cousins and brothers, made widows of women you know. Don't do it. Don't shake hands with the likes of them." Krauss could see a small but steady trickle of men retreating from the wall to ranks several yards upslope.

The imploring voices from his right went on as Krauss walked north. "Remember Andersonville. Andersonville! Look how they treated your comrades in arms. Starved them to death. Shot them down like dogs, like runaway slaves. They had the food. All those stories about hungry civilians digging wild turnips are just stories. Lies! They had the food. They had the medicine. They just didn't *want* to give any to our men. That's how traitors are. If they would try to wreck the country, of course they would kill our men in prison. Don't do it, step back. Don't shake hands. Don't do it." Confusion churned in Krauss' mind. He understood, even agreed with, those not wanting to shake hands with Rebels, but all the work of the last two years was aimed at this moment. If the Rebels didn't make it to the wall, the big handshake would be a failure. But if they did and hardly any Union men were there waiting for them; that would be disastrous. He didn't know what to think or what to hope for.

Zachariah caught his toe in the tall grass and went down. He put out both arms to catch himself, but his left gave way as his old wound flared. White cotton saliva leaked out the corner of his mouth, and the dry smell of grass mixed with the dust in his nose and made him sneeze. The explosion shot through his heaving lungs and made his ribs ache. Someone else thudded down, and Zachariah saw a Mississippi man with an artillery redleg stripe roll onto his back, holding his knee up toward his chest whimpering. He sounded just like that artilleryman at Winchester in '64.

A rolling Southern voice called from close behind Calvin Salisbury's ear: "We gotta hepp 'em. C'mon, men!" A colored sergeant nudged past Calvin, put his butt on the stone wall, and swung his legs over. Calvin followed suit instantly as did several of the 14th Vermont and a couple dozen USCI troops. Behind him, Calvin heard Josiah Trimble yell savagely, "Stay where you are." Calvin looked back and saw men frozen in the act of going over the wall. He kept going but saw Trimble standing with arms akimbo, shaking his head in a deep frown.

Krauss came up in a hurry, waving his billy club and calling, "No, no. Don't ruin it. Hold your ranks. Stay here on your side of the wall. That's the plan. Stay here. They'll get here… Maybe," he added under his breath. "Eventually," he said to himself. The command tone in Krauss's voice halted many others who had not been stopped by Trimble's order. Beyond Krauss's voice though, many members of the Philadelphia Brigade, holding the post of honor to the north at the Angle were also over the wall. Drum rolls erupted from the bands across the fields and hills and the civilians stepped up their cheers as these old men, bent and hobbled by age, went down the slope at a walking trot. They were nearly running, in the stiff, shaky stride of old men who should never be required to move faster than a comfortable walk.

Zachariah's eyes were closed and his ragged breath tore at his throat and ached in his lungs. He heard thumping footsteps and soon the swish of grass stirred by shoe and pant leg. Then came a voice, a Southern voice, accompanied by a touch on his arm, fortunately above his throbbing old wound. "C'mon, sawjint," the voice said gently, puffing a little. "Yew can make it. Just a few mo' feet an' you'll be there."

A second set of footfalls came close and he felt another touch under his right armpit. A tangy nasal voice sounded to him like, "Let me hip ya, sahjant. Can ya stand? You see the wall coming? It's just a few steps more." To Zack, his "more" sounded like a calf mewling "maah."

Zachariah opened his eyes right and squinted upwards. A small-boned man with a shock-white moustache connected to a wedge chin beard, surprisingly smooth cheeks and brow was looking down at him with a mix of concern and encouragement. His old blue shoulder straps bore the facing gold leaves of a major and a lapel pin read "VT." He was on one knee next to Zachariah while his right hand braced himself on a sturdy cane, ready to pull both its owner and Zachariah upright.

"I think ah can git up," Zachariah panted. "Been catchin' my wind fer a minute," he added with a thick tongue. With two helping hands, he pulled himself up to all fours. He now looked left. Another blue sleeve met his eyes, and traveling up, he took in the stripes of a noncom, a sergeant like himself. On the left breast hung a cross-shaped medal, its ribbon partly hidden by the straggly white fringe ends of a full beard. Above the beard were the full, smiling lips, dark-chocolate-colored skin, and deep, brown eyes of a black Yankee. The lips parted and an unmistakably Southern voice rolled out, "C'mon, suh. Yew kin make it. Sergeant Lucius Robinson at yo' suhvice, suh."

Zachariah gulped away some of his saliva and felt a drop of sweat roll into his left eye. The salty drop made his eye water as he said to Robinson, "Much 'blijed."

With Calvin and Lucius giving support, Zachariah regained his feet, swaying slightly. His eyes swam as he blinked away the salt. His spirit willed his flapping flesh, and Zachariah resumed his charge, walking slowly but steadily between the two in blue. Still somewhat groggy as cheers beat his ears, he saw a swirl of gray and blue, black and white, shaking hands, bald heads, gray beards, all a swaying, misty-eyed mass of old soldiers.

All along the Confederate line, old boys in blue were holding out arms and hands to old boys in gray. Something snapped in the veterans and handshakes were suddenly inadequate. To be sure, there were all manner of handshakes, but manners were hanged, dignity and airs were forgotten. There were embraces, arms locking arms, hand grips, backslappings, arms over shoulders, even hands cupping cheeks and, in the biblical manner of Jacob and Esau, men fell upon each others' necks and wept. Their tenderness caressed the hearts and throats of the watching multitudes.

A sound rose from the spectators that could hardly be described. It was one part crying, sorrow at the suffering of these old men, echoing the suffering of their youth.

The sound was one part pity, seeing old men staggering under heat and slope that were a cruelty on loose flesh, brittle bones, and worn joints.

The sound was one part wonder, seeing those who had struggled with all human strength against one another now using their age-shriveled strength helping one another.

The sound was a cry, a keening, an eruption from somewhere in the human spirit where hope, brotherhood, and peace live together.

The sound was a sigh, a gasp, a cheer, a noise that pushed past the lump in the throat. The sound ricocheted around the chest cavity, vibrated the intestines, jiggled the stomach, and squeezed tears from the eyes. The sound brought up fingers to cover the mouth and transfixed the eyes. The sound made the heart beat harder, snagged breath in the chest and rushed blood through the ears so hard that eardrums quivered. The sound took larynx, throat, tongue, and teeth captive, forced itself past these and tingled electricity through goose-fleshed skin and hair-standing scalp.

Who can describe the sound of brothers meeting for the first time as brothers, knowing for the first time they *are* brothers? Who can describe forgiveness, acceptance, and welcome galvanized in human flesh? The overwhelming thousands who saw the embrace saw the Civil War end before their eyes. In the same heartbeat they also felt and knew in themselves what Lincoln had called "the better angels of our nature" here on Gettysburg's ground.

Krauss was not happy as mingled blue and gray came up to the wall from his left. He had kept more from running down and joining the rebels, but it was a mottled line that came up to the wall. The Union men were starting to climb back over to pose for the official photographs that would go into the history books, but Krauss couldn't accept it. Perhaps the heat had shrunk his focus too much, or perhaps a lack of water had brought on the opening symptoms of heat exhaustion. For Krauss, somehow the embrace downslope seemed less real than the original plan for handgrips along the wall. Maybe these factors, maybe the strain of the past week, maybe being short of sleep for days on end was the final reason. But something snapped inside him and he came along the western side of wall waving his nightstick and roaring, "Blast it! It's all wrong. Dang rebels couldn't get here fifty years ago and they still can't. As useless as niggas wearin' blue. Just ruination. Just being rebels, bringing ruin and wreckage." Red-faced, he was screaming at the Rebels and their Union friends.

Zachariah, Lucius, and Calvin heard him from just a few yards away. A courage rose in Calvin, overlaid with an outraged righteousness he had never felt before. Decades of personal prudence and judicial equanimity fell aside. He barked, "Stay with him," with such force that Lucius almost felt he'd been hit in the face. Zachariah had the queer sense that Calvin's words went by him with the vacuum of a closely passing train.

Calvin stepped out toward Krauss not knowing what he was going to do. His hands did it for him. His right thumb worked a tiny, well-oiled hasp under the top of his cane. His left hand grasped the cane's shaft and pulled.

Krauss' tirade stopped dead mid-rant. Calvin had come toward him and at about six feet had pulled a sword out from what a moment before had been a cane. The old major swung the sword at his stomach and the glint off the blade matched the glint in the major's eye. Krauss knew this sword was not for show and this man knew how to use it. Worse, he might be willing to use it. Krauss stood stock still as the major said, "Hands up." For a second, he toyed with making a move with his nightstick, but then raised his hands.

Troopers Weston and O'Connor had considered Krauss more a hindrance than help for a couple of hours. When the Camp Lincoln men had arrived, they had been ready to escort him from the field, but the chief had more or less behaved himself. But as the charge had drawn near and Krauss had headed toward the rebel line, they had swung into action. They had come up on their horses at a fast walk behind Krauss and had almost reached him when Calvin drew his sword.

Krauss had been so fixed on Calvin he hadn't heard them. As he kindly raised his arms at Calvin's order, Weston and O'Connor obligingly each grabbed one and picked him up, much to his surprise. Krauss' short constable's jacket rode up and his pant cuffs exposed his ankles. Before Weston, O'Connor, or Krauss could react, the major gave Krauss a full chisel look of utter fury and said, "At Appomattox Court House, General Grant said, 'The rebels are our countrymen again.'" With a deft turn of his wrist, Calvin flicked his sword – honed sharp faithfully twice a year – first left, then right. The blade easily sliced the upside-down Y's just above the waistline. Freed from their waist buttons, the front straps of Krauss' suspenders slid up his chest and his pants drooped to half mast. Krauss' bright red underwear went on public display.

Onlookers burst out in relief and laughter. Relief, because many had been seriously worried Calvin was going to run Krauss through. Laughter, because nether-garments, let alone fire-engine red ones, were just not seen in public.

Weston and O'Connor turned a half-circle toward the Pennsylvania Memorial with Krauss still suspended between them, and moved south. Their own laughter became so strong it took the strength from their hands. First Weston, then O'Connor, let Krauss drop and each bent over his saddle horn, guffawing to tears. Krauss's blush very nearly matched his union inexpressibles as he yanked up his pants and headed off for someplace private. Given the huge attendance, privacy was far away from here, and Krauss walked for a long time.

Mueller's Restaurant

Three veterans presented themselves at the sharp-looking restaurant on York Street near Woolworth's. The headwaiter eyed them, not quite sure what to make of two white men in opposite uniforms and a black man in Union blue.

"Table for three this evening," Calvin said.

"Three, sir?" the waiter asked, his eyes shifting back and forth among them.

"That's ratt, three," Zachariah added with a hard stare.

"Um, well…uh, just a minute. Let me see… let me set up something. Just a moment, please."

It was more than a moment before he returned and led them down the side of the room. He seated them at a table hard by the double doors of the kitchen, where both noise and smells seeped out. Zachariah started to say something, but Calvin stopped him.

"This will do nicely, I'm sure," he said to both Zachariah and the waiter. They sat down and studied menus for a few minutes. Waiters bustled in and out of the kitchen, all woodenly ignoring the three old men at the bad table. Looking up, the veterans watched as a lanky man with a white bib apron tied at his waist brought a tureen of soup to an older couple seated two tables away. He was about to turn away from the three in the corner when Zachariah snapped his fingers at the man. Zachariah's fingers and palm allowed for a loud snap, and this was an up-close human pistol shot.

Startled, the two diners and the waiter instinctively turned and stared. Calvin took his cue and announced through the momentary silence, "We're ready to order, sir. Here's what I'd like to start with." There was nothing for the waiter to do but pull out his little pad and step over. He scribbled fast keeping up with Calvin's staccato list. Calvin turned and said, "Now gentlemen, feel free to order as you please. This is my treat. What do think of a beefsteak?" Both

Southerners glanced at the right edge of their menus and their eyes widened a bit in recognition of Calvin's bounty.

Lucius swallowed once and said softly, "Well, all right, I'm obliged fo' yo' gen'rosity. I'll have the porterhouse steak, cooked medium rayah," he said to the surly waiter.

Zachariah chimed in, "Make mine the same, uh…" he glanced at the waiter's name tag, "Burrows."

"Then three, all the way 'round, Burrows," Calvin finished. The waiter collected the menus, turned curtly, and strode away, punching open the right kitchen door with unnecessary force.

"I'm grateful fo' yo' kindness in treatin' us-all," Zachariah said to Calvin.

"My pleasure," Calvin grinned.

"Ya know, Judge…" Zachariah began, but Calvin broke in, also looking at Lucius. "Zachariah? Lucius? Let's leave titles aside for tonight. Call me Calvin, would you both?"

"Fine by me," Zachariah smiled.

"Me too…gennulmen," Lucius said with a sly grin, and they all laughed easily.

"Now, Lucius," Calvin said with mock seriousness, smiling broadly, and Zachariah gave Lucius a genuinely playful push on the shoulder. "C'mon, Lucius, lighten up. No titles. Calvin ain't no gennulman tonight."

Lucius took a deep breath, gave Zachariah an answering push back and said, "Okay, Zachariah, Calvin. We's just three ol' soljahs." Suddenly his eyes filled and he said in a tight voice, "Just bein' three ol' soljahs havin' suppah an' swappin' yarns is all colored folks ever wanted."

Calvin nodded, his throat also tight. He read the pinkish ribbon on Zachariah's lapel, one the souvenir veteran's ribbons, "Only a few left". He pointed to it and managed to say, "That's us. Three old soldiers. And as the Good Book says, 'Behold how good and pleasant it is when brothers dwell together in peace.'" All were silent as the moment washed over them, and each fought with himself to maintain a manly demeanor and not give way to his surging heart in front of the other two.

Zachariah began again. "Ya know, Calvin, just now you said it was yo' pleasure to treat us to suppah. Now we ain't known each other but a few hours, but I b'lieve it does give you pleasure to treat us. Almost as much pleasure as it gave you tellin' off that constable this afternoon. I think you enjoyed yo' sword play on his suspenders."

Calvin blushed slightly. "I shouldn't have lost my temper that way. First time I've ever actually drawn it in public."

"It was fo' a good cause, Calvin," Lucius said softly. Zachariah looked up sharply at the word "cause," his mind suddenly racing with word, sifting years of views and values. "The best cause," Lucius finished.

Zachariah nodded to Calvin, "I like how you told him off usin' Grant's words."

"It's what came to mind," Calvin said. He was uncomfortable in the hero's role, and he turned the chat in another direction. "If we are indeed three old soldiers having supper, or eating bait as we used to say, shouldn't we swap tales about when we were young soldiers? How did each of you join up? Who's command were you with?"

Zachariah and Lucius looked at each other. Through Zachariah's mind flashed images of black folk holding doors, curtseying, standing aside on a streetcar. He nodded and said, "Why don't you go fust? Whenja join up?" Lucius gave him a double look, silently mouthed the words "go fust," then stammered ahead.

As the tales flowed, Burrows the waiter plunked three glasses of red wine onto the table, then plopped down a basket of dinner biscuits with an unnecessary snap. He left quietly enough and as he entered the kitchen Zachariah murmured to the other two, "He's gonna give Yankee hospitality a black eye." He suddenly stared at Lucius, afraid he might have offended the Ethiopian at the table.

"Zachariah," Lucius said easily, "we-all git black eyes too," and Zachariah relaxed. "But yo' ratt, this waiter is bein' a bad egg." Looking over at Calvin he said, "Hey, pass over them rolls an' let's see if they're better 'n the army's worm castles."

"Worm castles? Do what?" Zachariah asked, stumped.

Calvin smiled, buttered up a biscuit, and said, "Yeah, you know. We called 'em teeth dullers." Zachariah was still lost as Lucius took one and said giggling, "Sheet iron crackers. Yeah, crackers. Hardtack."

Zachariah chuckled. "Ain't I the coot? It's fitten' you blue bellies came up with names fo' them crackers. You had to eat 'em all the time."

"If we could!" Calvin replied. "When we boiled water for coffee, if we put the hardtack in the pot maybe in an hour you could start gnawing."

"Waitin' for coffee water to boll! Pshaw!" Lucius jibed. "No wonder you Army of the Potomac boys took so much time fightin' Robert E. Lee. In Sherman's army we'd jes' get out a cracker an' go up to a tree or a fence post an' get a pry on it to break it ratt up." Calvin horse laughed and Zachariah guffawed as Lucius went on.

"Of course it went fastah when them flyslicers in the cavalry would hook up a couple hosses on each side of a tree an' let 'em pull on a crackah till it broke." Zachariah and Calvin dissolved in tears as Lucius deadpanned, "Some hosses were so strong we could break three crackers at once."

In the kitchen, Burrows loaded his tray: three steak dinners, medium rare, green beans, and a baked potato dripping butter. O'Reilly the cook raised a finger until he locked eyes with Burrows. He pointed and said, "This one," indicating the only steak wearing a sprig of parsley, "is for the darkest part of the corner table."

"Gotcha," Burrows said. He hoisted the heavy tray into carrying position and headed out the right side kitchen door. As he pushed it open, another waiter came in. Burrows' eyes flicked toward the in-swinging door and the incoming waiter. He didn't notice that the swinging doors stirred enough air to lift a parsley sprig for a moment. His walking speed carried his tray about eight inches until the floating sprig dropped back onto a different steak.

"Here you are, gentlemen," Burrows said, his voice as oily as his hair. He expertly lifted down three plates, making sure the darkie got the parsley sprig marker. "Enjoy your dinners," he said, bowing himself away. He got to the kitchen before permitting himself a vengeful grin.

Calvin beamed. "I'm delighted we can all share a supper like this," he said sawing his meat. "In fact, I'm trying to remember the last time I had a steak like this. How about you two?"

Lucius inhaled the delicious scent. "Last time fo' me was the end o' the War. One of Gen'rul Saxton's milk cows broke a leg so he shot her. The gen'rul put ever' company's name in a hat an' drew one out. Our company won, so fo' two days we had beef fo' dinnah, beef fo' suppah, even beef fo' breakfust. Then we mustered out." Calvin shifted uneasily at Lucius' offhand poverty.

While Lucius talked, Zachariah fussed with his potato and cut a bite of steak. He lifted it to his mouth and bit down. Instantly his eyes watered and he gagged. Manners be damned, he spit out the piece. Salt, mineral spirits, more salt, a retching, gummy collection of burnt grease, and still more salt all raged in his mouth. He reached for his water glass, took a mouthful and swished the water around. Opening one teary eye he saw a large potted fern only a few feet away. Grabbing his glass he lurched over to the fern, emptying his mouth into it.

Calvin and Lucius were alarmed as Zachariah took another mouthful, then doubled over for another spurt into the floor pot. Lucius moved over quickly, producing a small flask of whiskey. Zachariah took the flask with a toasting gesture to Lucius and then drew a swig. He swilled his mouth with the whiskey and then swallowed.

Meanwhile, Calvin reached over and deftly cut a bit of meat from Zachariah's plate. Holding it at close range he gave a wary sniff. This near, he could see a shiny, black gummy something on the meat. He grazed the tip of his tongue against it and felt the salt tang, even from this lick, run strong through his mouth.

A jowly gentleman, nearly as wide as he was tall, had noticed the commotion. He came rolling up to their table as quickly as bulk and dignity would allow and said politely, "Gentlemen, is there some problem? I am Eric Mueller, the owner of this establishment."

Zachariah's voice had not yet recovered. It was just dawning on Lucius that this had been aimed at him, and his anger was rising. But Calvin seized the chance to present the case. Rising to his feet, he quickly sliced off another piece of Zachariah's steak and held it inches from Mueller's nose. "Mr. Mueller, lick this." Mueller was so surprised he did, then winced hard. Swallowing with difficulty, he looked around and sized up the situation. In a low voice that leaked gall, he said to them, "Gentlemen, would you follow me, please?" A bit surprised, the trio fell in behind Mueller's 250-pound barging mass.

Kiefer was over by the big stove stirring the twenty-gallon pots. O'Reilly was just putting another couple of plates together. Burrows and two or three other waiters were lined up, trays ready for another pickup. Two young busboys were lugging a big waste can toward the back door.

Everyone knew the right door rule but now both doors swung open together, surprising everyone in the kitchen. Mr. Mueller lumbered in at a fast walk. A few steps behind him came three old men. The white man in Union blue said briefly, "The string bean one."

Mueller dropped his armful of menus on a table without breaking stride and closed on Burrows. He grabbed Burrows' shirt chest high and used his momentum to force him against a wall. Mueller leaned his bulk against Burrows' ribs and asked with a glare, "Did you serve these three men steak dinners?" When he got excited, Mueller's German upbringing came through. "Including ze black one?"

"Yes, I did," Burrows gasped out.

"You wanted to give him the bad one, ya?" Burrows nodded, writhing under Mueller's pressure. "Still trying to make yourself a man by making another man look bad." Burrows groaned through clenched teeth. "In mein restaurant a customer is a customer. I have told you before, if their money is green or silver you will serve them if they are white, black, red, brown, or yellow. You are fired," Mueller said. "Give me your apron."

Before Burrows could move, Mueller took a half step back and swung a short right jab into Burrows' midsection. Burrows doubled over, whimpering for air. Mueller reached to the now-convenient bow knot in front of him and pulled it free. At the same time his other hand slipped the apron's neck loop over Burrows' head.

Mueller stepped over to the pickup counter and snapped the apron on it like a horsewhip, eying O'Reilly. "Burrows vas only serving zat beefsteak, but it did not end up soaked in salt und grease by itself, did it?" O'Reilly gulped, wide-eyed, and retreated along the pickup table as Mueller scorned, "You vould only have them cook und clean for you? Hah! For this one" – he gestured toward Lucius – "you are not good enough to shine his shoes. Out!" Mueller barked. O'Reilly nimbly undid his apron and headed toward the swinging doors.

"Halt!" Mueller ordered. "You and Burrows should not offend my customers. They are good people, not like you. Leave through the back."

The busboys had been amazed, but now they left their waste can and held open the back door for O'Reilly and the still-unsteady Burrows. "Bobby. Jimmy. Take the rest of the waste out now and come back right away," Mueller called.

He turned to the three veterans. "Gentlemen, if you will give us another chance, you will be my personal guests this evening." The three swapped glances and Zachariah said beaming, "That sounds like a huckleberry above a persimmon to me!" Lucius reached over and shook his hand in agreement as Calvin and Eric shifted their eyes, stumped. "Tell ya later, Calvin," Lucius said confidentially, "but it's a good thing."

"Good!" Mueller said. Turning to the staff he commanded, "Robert, take these gentlemen to my table by the window and bring them each a beer. Kiefer," he said to the cook's assistant, "you are cooking for the rest of the evening. Jimmy," he said to the lad who was just returning as Robert led the trio out of the kitchen, "take these," producing three silver dollars from his vest pocket, "go over to the Gettysburg Businessman's Club and bring back three, no four, cigars and a bottle of their best brandy."

Folks passing on York Street saw three old veterans in a window table, dining heartily on steak dinners, a waiter at their every beckon. Later, passersby saw the three sitting with a chunky civilian, sipping brandy, wreathed in cigar smoke, and obviously enjoying each other. Veteran or civilian, northerner or southerner, white or black, no division made any headway against the camaraderie or bonhomie at the table.

Saturday, July 5, 1913

Camp Lincoln

Dawn lit the treetops along Rock Creek while among the trunks, tents sagged with the morning's dew. Peter Judson, fifteen, pursed his lips while his father Michael put away his pocket watch, raised his choirmaster's baton, and beat a quick tempo. Peter pointed his bugle down Fredrick Douglass Avenue and blew "Reveille." In Peter's head, the irreverent words from his friend Lamont threatened to pull his lips out of the bugle into a full smile:

> *"I can't get 'em up,*
> *"I can't get 'em up,*
> *"I can't get 'em up this morning*
>
> *"I can't get 'em up,*
> *"I can't get 'em up,*
> *"I can't get 'em up at all.*
>
> *"The sergeant's worse than the corporal,*
> *"The captain's worse than the sergeant,*
> *"The major's worse than the captain,*
> *"And the colonel's worst of 'em all!"*

Lucius woke up taking in the slanting tent roof. Looking over, bleary and bloodshot, he saw a tuft of Zachariah's beard rise every couple seconds. Calvin painfully pried one eye open. He saw his spectacles resting on an upright crate.

Lucius groaned, "I hates bugles in the mawnin'. They wake snakes."

"I'm feeling about snake high," Calvin moaned.

Zachariah grunted and rolled onto his side. "Mawnin' up No'th comes way too early."

Calvin managed to sit up, took a deep breath, then closed his eyes against the spinning. He sniffed and said, "There's hope. I smell coffee."

Lucius said, "Okay. Make mine black an' then just fetch my breakfust here, my good man."

"Thats ratt, Calvin," Zachariah chimed in. "Lucius an' me decided last natt Georgia outvotes Vermont. Serve my breakfust with a fresh rosebud in a silvah vase iffn' you would."

Calvin served them each a hat swat in bed.

The trio was about to clear the end wall of a mess tent. Calvin and Zachariah were both surprised waking up in Camp Lincoln and trying to remember how last night's supper had ended. They had been swaying on York Street, then…then swaying in a hay wagon. They had slept on the ground a while and been awakened by… shellfire? Ah, not cannons but… firework shells. They were on Culp's Hill and the army put on a grand show from Little Round Top. The three had "oohed" and "aahed" like boys. "Thirty-two pounder!" or "Columbiad!" other old vets had called out. The loud bangers only made them laugh. Then all three had come down the Hill asking for Camp. Calvin thought he remembered water running, but it wasn't clear past the throb in his temple. Zack was pretty sure he'd heard feet tramping on wood boards, but it was rather hazy.

"Take one o' these here," Lucius said, tucking his mess kit under his arm and handing over a large plate apiece to the pair. The clatter and chatter of the mess line rang in their heads like forks falling from a drawer. "They be extry spoons an' such on the tables."

"Will there be enough food?" Zachariah asked, feeling suddenly anxious in Confederate gray and white skin. "I don't want someone here goin' hungry 'cause I'm eatin' bait."

A Missouri corporal next in line deliberately bumped him from behind. As Zachariah turned, the abrupt movement made his stomach quaver. The man said, "They'll be plenty fo' yo' kind 'round back by th' kitchen door…boy." Zachariah's stomach turned over and he blanched.

"There'll be plenty fo' ever'body, corporal," Lucius answered with a steady gaze. Zachariah let out a deep sigh of relief but his face was paler than before while they waited.

"What are they likely to be serving?" Calvin wondered.

"It'll be good, whatever it its," Lucius drawled. "Yesterday fo' peas in the trencher we had…"

Calvin interrupted, "'Peas in the trencher?'"

"You know, breakfast," Lucius answered.

"I know now," Calvin said with a slight smile, rolling "peas in the trencher" around his head as Lucius resumed. "Yestidy we had fat back, flapjacks, enough o' yo' Vermont maple syrup to stick down every plate in camp, fruit fixins, an' lots o' coffee."

"The real Rio," Zachariah chimed in, recovering somewhat from his earlier scare and licking his lips. "You Yankees sure could make coffee."

"Well, the coffee here is a real bird," Lucius bragged.

"Step lively, gennulmen," called Julia, a young, athletically built, oval-faced cook from Charlottesville. She ran a students' boarding house and was used to noisy, major meals. Armed with a ladle and a take-charge voice, Julia oversaw a crew of servers, cooks, and cook's helpers who were mostly teenaged boys. "Get yo' grits here. Eggs is jes' ahaid. Move along now."

As Calvin cleared the end canvas wall, Julia beamed at his Union officer's uniform, even allowing for its rumpled, slept-in look.

"V-T?" she asked, eying the small brass letters gleaming from his hat. "You from Vermont, suh?"

"He shore is, ma'am," came Lucius' voice, poking his head around the tent wall. "He's a major, a volunteer veteran," he pointed out Calvin's chevron on his sleeve, "a retarred judge, an' a gennulman to boot."

Calvin's eyes fluttered down at the praise but her voice clanged in his head and shook his delicate condition.

"Well, you are very welcome here, Major. Care fo' some grits?"

"Uh, well," stammered Calvin, "I guess so, ma'am. I've never had grits in my life."

"Well then it's 'bout time you did," Julia answered, pouring a ladle-full onto his plate. She turned to the middle-aged woman next to her who was her second-in-command. Gail had taken Julia under her wing in the boarding house and although Julia had moved up to be in charge here at Camp Lincoln and back in Charlottesville, they were still close. "Now Gail, you fix up the major here with some dat hen-fruit scramble. He's tryin' grits fo' th' fust time in his life but he'd bettah get th' whole shebang."

Gail beamed as Calvin stepped over. "Have some eggs, suh. An' next we got some o' yo' Vermont cheese."

Peter Judson stood by an enormous cheddar wheel holding a serious knife. With a gleaming smile he asked, "How large a slice would you like, suh?" pivoting the blade like a clock hand. As Calvin collected his cheese, conversation died to his left. Lucius was getting eggs when Zachariah stepped up to the grits pan. Julia froze at the Confederate sergeant in full gray.

Lucius said, "Ma'am? Miz Superintendriss? Ma'am? This is Sergeant Zachariah Hampton from my hometown of Savannah." Julia swallowed as Lucius continued softly, "He fought on the losin' side here at Gettysburg an' was kind enough to share my supper last natt." When Julia made no move Lucius said, "Don't treat him like mudsill. I'm shore he's hungry, an' he knows 'bout grits."

Julia still made no move and Gail could see the confident young lady had had a shock of some kind. She moved to rescue her. "Peter, come here a minute. C'mere, Julia honey." She led a pie-eyed Julia back to the stove wall as Peter whistled for his friend Lamont to leave off stirring a pot at the stove and come help on the serving line. Gail took her friend by the shoulders until Julia looked her square on. "Julia, what is it? You've seen Confedrits eatin' here befo'."

"I... uh, well, he's from Georgia, but he's the spittin' image of a Johnny Reb I knew in Charlottesville. That man was the meanest man on earth to colored children goin' to and from school and we had to go by his house ever' day. He'd yell at us, try to knock school books outta our hands, spit tobacco juice at us, throw leftover Fourth of July firecrackers at us in the fall. Dead ringer fo' him."

"But it's not him."

"No, ma'am. But it's like all that hurt comes back when I look at him."

"Now, Julia, you remembah yo' Bible?"

"Yes'm?"

"I know servin' a man like that is a hard thing, but the Bible says, 'Iffin yo' enemy is hungry feed him, an' iffin' he's thirsty, give him somethin' to drink.' Remembah the next line?"

Julia blinked and then smiled. "'For by doing so you heap hot coals upon his head.' Yes. Thank you. I'm all right now."

Zachariah overheard bits of this as he got his eggs and cheese. He watched very closely as Julia wielded the big cheddar knife and cut him his slice. "Welcome to Camp Lincoln, suh," she managed, just giving him a glance. "Much obliged, miss," he said carefully, then added, "Bein' an old buzzard don't excuse scarin' children...of any color." Julia let slip a small smile of gratitude as Zack walked off.

As Calvin got his coffee and waited for Lucius and Zachariah, he overheard snatches among the Camp Lincoln veterans mighty similar to Tent City chats. Two vets at one table were saying, "It's like Cunnul Chamberlain wrote down. The fight on Lil' Round Top with th' bay'net charge was th' turnin' point."

"You's right fo' the second day but I'm talkin' 'bout th' third day. I was a hoss holdah fo' the Michigan 6th Cavalry. Jeb Stuart an' his troopers was out there at East Cavalry Field. Just when Lee's artillery ceased fire, Stuart's cavalry tried to pass 'round our ratt. He wouldda come up on the rear o' the ridge the same time Pickett wouldda come up on the front."

"But that didn't happen."

"The reason it didn't happen was Custer and the Michigan 6th. Custer charged 'em an' made 'em go from travellin' line to fightin' line. They couldn't get to the ridge so Pickett didn't have no hepp an' got cut to pieces."

"Naw, that ain't it."

"I was there, an' that's what happened."

The trio sat down at a picnic table across from three vets. Before any pleasantries could be said, all three black vets stopped, frowned at Lucius, gave Calvin a disgusted look, gave Zachariah bayonet glares and rose together. They collected their breakfasts, walked off to the next table and pointedly sat with their backs to the mixed three. As Lucius had promised, the food was the bird, but Zachariah chewed mechanically, not tasting his breakfast, thinking hard.

Calvin finished breakfast first. The grits had been an adventure. The Vermont cheese had been, "of course, magnificent," and he'd taken double-barreled Georgia joshing in return. He dropped off his dishes at the dishwashing tent with a walk fairly steady now and refilled his coffee. He was headed back when a table of veterans flagged him down.

"Beg pardon," one of them called. "Could you join us fo' a moment, suh?" Calvin looked over to his Savannah men. He recognized Ashton Melo just taking a seat next to Lucius and the three of them getting acquainted. They looked over to Calvin, who waved him toward the table, then resumed their chat.

"Of course," Calvin answered and sat down on the table's long side among seven or eight USCI veterans.

"Yo' hat says Vermont, is that ratt, major?" asked a nasal-twanged short man sporting an AL on his collar.

"Yes, sah. Major Calvin Salisbury, 14th Vermont. I'm from Rutland." He tapped his hat brim in civilian salute. The Deep South men cocked their heads slightly while deciphering the tangy vowels and staccato rhythm of his New England speech.

"I'm Sawjint Major John McCauley, 26th USCI, from Mobile, Al'bama." Calvin unconsciously cocked his head in return, working through the broad Southern vowels and winding tempo. "We'all at Camp Lincoln is grateful to you steady habit men" – old-time slang for New Englanders – "fo' the tents, cots, and gear." The men all chimed in and offered tin cup coffee toasts. Calvin toasted back modestly.

McCauley continued. "But I gotta ax you. I cain't undastan' why all you good Union men are lettin' the old Confedrits put in all this Jim Crow. I'm tellin' you, it's jes' one step up from bein' slaves an' 'bout six steps back from Reconstruction." As McCauley went on, Calvin struggled between three corners: a judicial mindset, as though he were hearing opposing counsel in his courtroom; a certain defensiveness, which whispered "we freed the slaves, now it's up to them"; and an old righteousness.

New Orleans Private Stephen Plessy piped up. "We could vote. We 'lected colored men or white men, just as we liked, to city an' to governah an' to Congress." Calvin nodded.

"Our cartridge box led to the votin' box," McCauley mused.

"We could own land an' farm," South Carolina Private Mitchell Cosgrove added. "I was there when Gin'rul Sherman announced we'd all get forty acres an' a mule, an' we did, an' we went to work."

Plessy made the case. "My cousin's boy was the one who sat down on the streetcar an' ended up suin' the New Awlins streetcar comp'ny prezdint Ferguson. In 1896, the Supreme Cote said 'separate but equal' would be the law o' the land."

"I remember," Judge Calvin answered, righteousness gaining ground. "I read that decision. It was a tragedy and disgrace."

"How 'bout some hepp when we'all is in the front line 'gainst Jim Crow?" McCauley challenged. "'Bout ten years back did you do anythin' 'bout the Mobile boycott?"

Calvin frowned. "I try to keep up on news, but I don't remember any from Mobile. Could you help bring it to mind?"

"Goes like this," McCauley answered. "The Mobile Streetcah comp'ny would carry ever'body sittin' as you pleased. In '02 the city council voted segregation, settin' up Jim Crow streetcahs and Jim Crow seats on some o' them. Well, suh, we colored folk started a boycott."

Seeing a couple mates frown at the unfamiliar word, he said in aside, "We wouldn't ride at all lessen' we could sit where we pleased."

"We walked ever'where and only rode in a brotha's cart or wagon. We walked all fall an' into the winter. The streetcar comp'ny went broke 'cause not enough folks was ridin'. But we nevah heard from nobody with no hepp so finally in the spring we gave it up."

Calvin shifted uncomfortably and his hangover made a bit of a comeback. "With God as my witness," he swore, "this is the first time I've ever heard a whisper of this. I don't recall a single line in a newspaper, nor an article in *Harper's Weekly.* I'm sorry."

"You know why," Plessy chimed in. "White newspapers won't print nuthin' good 'bout coloreds. And," he gave Calvin a suspicious look, "white folk mostly don't read black newspapers."

Calvin blushed. "I'll air up to that. I doubt I've read a black paper more than a dozen times in my life."

"Major," Cosgrove said, "don't feel too bad. It ain't yo' fault yo' news has been watt-washed."

Calvin glanced over and caught the small smile of forgiveness, and smiled back as he caught the double meaning. "Still," he answered, "even if Northerners had known I don't know what we could have done."

"Well," Cosgrove drawled, which struck Calvin's ear as "whale," "'magine iffin' ever' day a white reporter wired in a story, 'The boycott goes on. The Mobile colored folk keep mawchin fo' justice.'"

Plessey jumped in. "Yeah, an' then supposin' some, say, Ohio Congressman would come investigatin' Mobile. Then mo' papers would write 'bout the investigations."

McCauley said with a sigh, "Folks could write us lettahs and telegrams, maybe even send shoes fo' the ones we wore out."

Calvin muttered, "If the white folks would know... in a continuous way... telegraph stories every day." Pulling himself up from his thoughts, "You know, something like that could work. But white folks would have to look in the mirror and make some changes. Certainly a President could help set a mood, and not one like Mr. Wilson."

Calvin jumped as he found himself receiving a "You got that ratt!" from Plessy and two or three "amens." Recovering, he went on. "The boycott idea is a good one, with the right support, and the right reporting. I believe a time will come." He received another "amen" and a "let it come soon." Stumbling a bit, he finished, "Keep the idea and pass it along."

Nods went around the table. Cosgrove said, "Let's start in camp. Veterans could take the idee back home. Keep the flame until the time comes. Iffin' not in Mobile, then maybe somewhere else." He stared off for a moment remembering something. "You know, back in March, Miz Harriet Tubman died. She brought me to freedom on the Underground Railroad."

"Izzat right?" the men said, impressed.

"She'd always say, 'Keep goin', whether it was dogs, or cold, or five mo' miles walkin', or dem hunters afta you. But I 'membah her also sayin', 'O Lord, you been wid me in six troubles, don't desert me in da seventh.' All dis Jim Crow and bad mouthin' Reconstruction? Dats been our six troubles. Six troubles, but we keep goin'. Six troubles, but we still fought for our flag."

"Dat's right," McCauley chimed in.

"Say it, brother," Calvin erupted, startling the tableful as Cosgrove resumed.

"Six troubles but we keep goin'. Conductor Tubman kept goin'. We kept goin'. Sharecroppin' for not much but we keep goin'. Sweepin' floors, makin' beds on Pullman cars, cuttin' hair, and all six troubles of dese last fifty years but we keep goin'." He raised his finger with intensity. "Harriet Tubman is at rest but we gotta keep goin'. We gotta tell this boycott idee to ever'body. Dat way we pick up her torch. Dat way we carry on her cause. Hell, maybe we become six trouble for dem white liners!"

"You got it," McCauley exclaimed.

Plessy chimed in, "Tell our chillun' an' granchillun. They'd listen."

"Dats right," McCauley answered, with something catching in his throat. "And I know one who's gonna pick up Miz Tubman's torch and keep goin.'" He dug out a pocket photo and passed it around saying, "Here's a carte de visite o' my new grand niece. I'll tell her..." Suddenly his face fell. "I don't have any my own chillun no mo'." His tears rolled. "My son, his wife, and their baby girl died when their house burned down durin' the boycott. Sheriff said it was accident, a bad stove." Head shakes ran around the table and several hands reached out for shoulder pats. McCauley sniffed bitterly, "Bad stove my ass. When the undertaker fixed em' he found three bullets in my boy's body."

"Dang shame" and "Lawd have mercy" rumbled from the men as Calvin stared, tasting the terror.

Calming down some, McCauley went on. "That there picture is my new grand niece, born in February, jes' befo' Miz Tubman passed on." His wet face added unusual emphasis as he vowed, "When she gets old enough, I'll tell her... 'bout her uncle, an' auntie, an' cousin an' how they died. An' yeah," he finished, "I'll tell her 'bout the streetcah boycott. The time may come in her time, an' she'll be ready."

The men squinted at the head and shoulders image of the baby girl. "What's her name?" someone asked.

"They're callin' her Rosa, like the flowah. Rosa Louise McCauley."

Lucius, Calvin, and Zachariah enjoyed Florida poet James Johnson at Platform B. The author of the lyrics to "Lift Every Voice and Sing" charmed the crowd with the beauty and cadence in his words. Calvin remembered Johnson's Emancipation poem from New Year's Day, but he chewed a long time on the opening line of "Creation":

And God stepped out on space.

The two Georgians cottoned to Johnson's ode to "Sister Caroline" set in Savannah's Yamacraw district, just up river from the city.

And God said: Go down, Death, go down,
Go down to Savannah, Georgia,
Down in Yamacraw,
And find Sister Caroline.
She's borne the burden and heat of the day.

As Johnson finished, the trio watched, both amused and amazed, as word of a Chicago visitor's last-minute coming galvanized the camp. The Assembly Tent side walls were furled up and overflow benches and chairs added. Sunday night's loud-speaking machine from St. Paul's church was set up and tested (with some loud squeals). Several boys went shinnying up trees adjoining the tent, tying on extra canvas flies which broadened the shade into a great arc. Kitchen crews turned a vast pile of lemons into gallons of lemonade, complete with ice from the buried lockers.

Yesterday in the Great Tent over in Pickett's Field, a crowd of twelve thousand had noised excitedly before and after the President's speech. This morning in Camp Lincoln, a smaller but overflowing crowd, sipping lemonade and shaded by the Assembly Tent, trees, and canvas flies, also jawed in anticipation. In town the 10:15 was met by a delegation of the Camp Lincoln Committee. The Chicago man, editor of *Crisis Magazine*, mainspring of the "Niagara Movement" and its 1909 successor, the National Association for the Advancement of Colored People, was in camp for a speech. His carriage rolled slowly down the planks of Frederick Douglass Avenue, his passage marked by tossing hats, hands pressing on him endlessly, screams of excitement from young women, and every musical instrument in earshot making sound. He was William Edward Burghardt DuBois.

DuBois was in his mid-forties, balding noticeably but wearing a moustache and pointed beard in compensation. He spoke as he wrote, with the added advantage today of gestures and fiercely piercing eyes. He was passionate with conviction, meticulous in argument, and utterly dedicated to the cause of racial equality. His manner did not lend itself to a preaching cadence, and church-type calls of "amen" or "preach it" seemed out of place in his presence. But the veterans seated in front were riveted, taking in every word. The wide arc of standees behind, around the sides, standing on picnic tables, even leaning in from the trees, were more civilian than veteran, but virtually fifty-fifty between black and white, and they were likewise swept up by DuBois' vision.

He became so animated that at one point, the crowd, which had alternated between hard applause and concentrated silence, gasped in amazement. DuBois stepped back from the microphone and actually shed his suit coat. To cap the climax in that over-clothed age he then stepped forward again and, while still speaking, worked off his left cufflink and rolled up his shirt sleeve to make his point especially to the veterans. The crowd roared and shrieked and Julia, Gail, and other women in camp who were listening hid their eyes and blushed at DuBois' "nakedness" as they called it, but it was a memorable moment.

After his speech Dubois was applauded with thundering hands, whistling, hat-waving and foot-stompings. He shook hands for a time with a scholar's reserve, and was slowly led to the special guest pavilion for noonday dinner. He was completely unable to eat there, because unlike Thursday with the amazed circle that had formed at a distance from Madame C.J. Walker, he was incessantly interrupted. It wasn't until Julia came out from the serving line, used her sturdy ladle on several sets of knuckles, and stood sentry duty, that finally he and Johnson the poet could eat in peace.

At some tables along Rock Creek, the press was both comparing notes and eating. Percy Sutcliffe of the *London Times* sat apart for a bit, not from prejudice, but from the need to study Philip Yancey's notes from DuBois' speech, which Sutcliffe had missed. In exchange, Yancey of the *Savannah Colored Tribune* had been picked by his comrades to read President Wilson's speech to them because none of them had been admitted to the Great Tent yesterday. Yancey used Sutcliffe's notes and read the elegant, hurried words a bit at a time so men – and a few women – could get them down. The *Chicago Defender*, *Cleveland Gazette*, and *Pittsburgh Courier* had all ridden in on the train with DuBois. But as Yancey read, the rest of the country's colored citizens would soon read Wilson's words too: in the South in the *Richmond Planet*, in the Mississippi

River valley via the *Kansas City Rising Sun* and the *St. Paul Appeal,* and on the coasts in Los Angeles' *California Eagle,* and the *New York Amsterdam Times.*

As Yancey finished, Sutcliffe came over with a wondering look on his face. "You know, this is quite extraordinary," he said in a clipped and crisp British accent. "Both DuBois and Wilson are quite visionary, and yet..."

"...they might as well be talkin' to each other from opposite walls of the Grand Canyon," Joseph Blackburn of Los Angeles' *Eagle* finished for him. Sutcliffe chuckled while nodding. "A very American way to put it, but precisely the point."

"It's like they're talkin' to each other and past each other both at the same time," said the fiery little woman from Baltimore's *Afro-American.* Everyone studied the two speeches now side by side. Murmurs arose as the reporters' writing instincts kicked in.

"Could go to here from this one," *Chicago Defender* said softly.

"And then put these lines right after," the *Oakland Sunshine* replied.

"Back and forth in a double-wide column," said the *Nashville Globe,* and a chorus of "that's a good idea" erupted across the tables.

Sutcliffe looked puzzled at two or three sets of notes at the same point in DuBois speech. "I say," he nudged Yancey, "I can't make this out here or in anyone else's either. What happened?"

Yancey squinted at his own scribbling, then grinned broadly.

"Oh, well ratt here, just before Dr. DuBois started talkin' to the vet'rans, 'specially about "the sable arm," he took off his coat."

"Surely you're joking," Percy said with a half-grin.

"No suh, I'm not. And for a topper," he read from his notes, "he then worked loose his cufflink and rolled up his sleeve, exposing his nakedness to all present."

Sutcliffe blushed modestly and dropped his eyes. "I suppose that part will never be forgotten." Then he paused, looked up, and said, "But now let's get the rest of it balanced between him and Wilson's speech.". We've got to get his words and Wilson's down just right." Heads nodded and then bent and pencils flew between bites of lunch as the journalists cranked out words for a lead-in and a finish.

The reporters working dailies went off to Gettysburg depot first to wire in their stories while the others stayed to cover any other news and share it with the dailies. When they got back, the weeklies went off to Western Union while the dailies took their turn to cover. Sutcliffe could wait until evening to put his story on the trans-Atlantic cable.

So it was, starting the next day and through the coming week, readers from Los Angeles to London – and beyond London to far parts of the globe reached by the cables of the *Times* – could ponder the unintended debate and competing visions of Woodrow Wilson and W.E.B. DuBois.

Wilson: *"I need not tell you what the Battle of Gettysburg meant…In [the veterans'] presence it were an impertinence to discourse upon how the battle went, how it ended, what it signified."*

DuBois: *"We cannot ignore the War's significance to the nation. Abraham Lincoln believed America had become a house divided – and he expected it to become un-divided – either all-slave, or all-free. "We are still trying to believe that the President of the United States is the President of ten million as well of ninety million, and that though the ten million are black and poor, he is too honest and cultured a gentleman to yield to the clamors of ignorance and prejudice and hatred. We are still hoping all this, Mr. Wilson, but hope deferred maketh the heart sick."*

"What have [fifty years since the battle] meant? They have meant peace and union and vigor, and the maturity and might of a great nation. How wholesome and healing the peace has been!

"The Presidency, the Senate, the House of Representatives…on March 4th [passed] into the hands of the party which half a century ago fought desperately to keep black men as real estate in the eyes of the law…We did not vote for you and your party because you represented our best judgment. It was not because we loved Democrats more, but Republicans less and Roosevelt least, that led to our action."

"We have found one another again as brothers and comrades in arms, enemies no longer, generous friends rather, our battles long past, the quarrel forgotten – except that we shall not forget the splendid valor, the manly devotion of the men then arrayed against one another, now grasping hands and smiling into each other's eyes."

"In the struggle to un-divide the house of America, we were the slaves – for us the struggle was being fought. Should we stand aside while men bled and died over our fate? Should we let others decide the outcome of our destiny? Or should we join in the

American call of freedom and of equality? Should the black man's arm add its strength to the white man's arm in grappling with the monster of slavery and striving for liberty? It is no idle regret with which the white South mourns the loss of the old-time Negro — the frank, honest simple old servant who stood for the earlier religious age of submission and humility...To-day he is gone."

"How complete the union has become and how dear to all of us, how unquestioned, how benign and majestic, as State after State has been added to this our great family of free men."

"Sir, you have now been President of the United States [since March] and what is the result? It is no exaggeration to say that every enemy of the Negro race is greatly encouraged; that every man who dreams of making the Negro race a group of menials and pariahs is alert and hopeful."

"We have harder things to do than were done in the heroic days of war, because harder to see clearly, requiring more vision, more calm balance of judgment, a more candid searching of the very springs of right."

"We want to be treated as men. We want to vote. We want our children educated. We want lynching stopped. We want no longer to be herded as cattle on streetcars and railroads. We want the right to earn a living, to own our own property and to spend our income unhindered and uncursed."

"I have in mind another host, whom these veterans set free of civil strife in order that they might work out in days of peace and settled order the life of a great nation. That host is the people themselves, the great and the small, without class or difference of kind or race or origin; and undivided in interest, if we have but the vision to guide and direct them and order their lives aright in what we do."

"In the words of Frederick Douglass, 'Once let the black man get upon his person the brass letters, U.S., let him get an eagle on his button, and a musket on his shoulder and bullets in his pocket, there is no power on earth that can deny that he has earned the right to citizenship. Mr. Wilson, you face no insoluble problem. The only time the Negro problem is insoluble is when men insist on settling it wrong by asking absolutely contradictory things. You cannot make ten million people at one and the same time servile and dignified, docile and self-reliant, servants and independent leaders, segregated and yet part of the industrial organism, disenfranchised and citizens of a democracy, ignorant and intelligent."

"What we strive for is their freedom, their right to lift themselves from day to day and behold the things they have hoped for, and so make way for still better days for those whom they love who are to come after them."

"The education of colored children, the opening of the gates of industrial opportunity to colored workers, absolute equality of all citizens before the law, the civil rights of all decently behaving citizens in places of public accommodation and entertainment, absolute impartiality in the granting of the right of suffrage – these things are the bedrock of a just solution to the rights of man in the American Republic."

"Who stands ready to act again and always in the spirit of this day of reunion and hope and patriotic fervor?"

"The forces of hell in this country are fighting a terrific and momentarily successful battle. You may not realize this, Mr. Wilson. To the quiet walls of Princeton where no Negro student is admitted the noise of the fight and the reek of its blood may have penetrated but vaguely and dimly."

"Lift your eyes to the great tracts of life yet to be conquered in the interest of righteous peace."

"On the other hand a determination on the part of intelligent and decent Americans to see that no man is denied a reasonable chance for life, liberty, and happiness simply because of the color of his skin *is a simple, sane, and practical solution to the race problem of this land."*

"This is what you veterans fought and bled and died for, that life, liberty, and the pursuit of happiness be the lot of every American regardless of color. Yours is the sable arm that would no longer endure the lash. Yours is the sable arm that carried a rifle in one hand and a spelling book in the other. Yours is the sable arm that refused any pay at all from the Union paymasters until the sable armed received the same pay as the milky armed. Yours is the sable arm of American citizens that dug bullets out of a cartridge box, and now is noble enough for the ballot box, is wise enough for the jury box."

"Come, let us be comrades and soldiers yet to serve our fellow men in quiet counsel."

"Mr. Wilson, your power is limited? We know that, but the power of the American people is unlimited. Today you embody that power, you typify its ideals. In the name then of that common country for which your fathers and ours have bled and toiled, be not untrue, Mr. President, to the highest ideals of American Democracy."

Camp Lincoln

The lunch lines in Camp Lincoln were especially noisy, fired by DuBois' speech for the ear and an aroma for the nose most of the men recognized as a special treat. While Calvin's ears rang with the rest, he did not know the scent and as he neared the serving line he couldn't make out the golden brown lumps being served up with tongs.

"This should be great," Lucius boomed, clapping hands together.

"My mouth is so ready," Zachariah echoed. Calvin looked from one to the other and asked innocently, "What is it?"

The Georgians' eyes widened and they exchanged quizzical glances. Zack handed Calvin his plate mumbling, "Hold this a minute, would you?" As Calvin held his own and Zack's plates, Zack stepped behind him and clamped both hands rather roughly on his shoulder and armpit and intoned, "Cote is now in session. The Honorable Judge First Sergeant Lucius Robinson presidin'." Lucius caught on, moved wide of the line a few steps and struck a magisterial pose.

"Bring forward the prisoner," he said, throwing back his head to look down his nose. Men in line whooped it up at the impromptu theatrics.

Zachariah continued. "Your honor, the prisoner has been found guilty of New England pot-roast lovin'…"

"The villain! How awful!" came the feigned calls from the crowd.

"…and Mason-Dixon line ignorance…"

"Ignorant? So he's an officer?" someone shouted, which touched off bawdy laughter.

"…in that he does not know Southern fried chicken by sight or smell."

"The fiend!"

"For shame!"

"Ignorance is no excuse!"

"A cooked up crime for sure!"

Calvin laughed until his tears rolled.

Lucius fought back a couple horse-laughs of his own before he put on a judicial air. "In view of the serious, narrow-nosed character of this crime, I have no choice but to sentence you to an entire plateful of fried chicken…"

"That's it judge!" hollered Ashton Melo, and Calvin's laughter redoubled as he recognized him. Zachariah offered a sham "no mercy!"

"…the plateful to be eaten without use of knife, fork, or spoon. Bailiff, make him use his fingers." A ribald crowd led Calvin, rib sore and wobble kneed, to a table, tied a napkin on him, and set the plate before him.

"Elbows on the table, you dainty Yankee."

"Don't bite your fingers," and other bits of friendly advice rained down. Lucius and Zachariah arrived with their own plates and cups.

Lucius banged the table with the butt of his knife like it was a gavel. "The court dismisses you to your own dinners," he commanded. "The bailiff and this judge will personally oversee the punishment of the prisoner."

Most of an hour later, the three ambled down Camp Lincoln's Frederick Douglass Avenue, still licking Calvin's sentence from their lips and fingers. At the corner of Lincoln Street was the usual cluster of stump preachers, vendors selling popcorn or lemonade, and earnest folk passing out fliers in favor of or against certain causes. A picnic table conversation here had two white veterans from each side jawing while several USCI men sat or stood around them and a further ring of civilians of both colors leaned in to catch the talk. Whatever had passed before suddenly turned into serious debate between blue and gray. As it did, several faces hardened or saddened and a certain tension gripped the crowd.

"I beg you pardon," came a refined British accent from behind Zachariah. As he turned to see who it was, Percy Sutcliffe tipped his light bowler to him and said, "Dreadfully sorry," as he strode quickly between Zack and Calvin on his way over to the scene.

Lucius thought he recognized one of the USCI men in profile and drifted closer to be sure. Calvin and Zack rather gingerly trailed after him. Lucius watched carefully and searched his memory. It looked like Floyd Tillman from Tuesday night at the Dobbin House Tavern, but he couldn't be sure. Tillman's expression was distorted by shock and rage.

As the three got closer they could make out that the two white vets were locking horns over prisoners of war. "Andersonville," "Elmira," "atrocity," "Camp Douglas," "torture," and "Libby Prison" flew back and forth in accelerating fury. Various men kept trying unsuccessfully to interrupt, either to make peace, or to add something else as Floyd was trying to do, but the two stubborn soldiers were not letting anyone else in to their fight. Percy Sutcliffe's pencil raced across his pad capturing the drama.

Finally, Tillman could take no more. He crashed his fist down on the table between the two and yelled, "Hold it!" In mutual wrath they turned on him.

"Hey!" the Fort Wayne Yankee shouted. "Men are talking here!"

The Charleston Confederate jumped right in. "Shut yo' mouth, boy!"

The word hung in the air as the colored faces in earshot recoiled and hardened. Both Tent City men turned deathly pale as they looked around in terror. They suddenly cringed as Floyd had his say at last.

"Andersonville?" he screamed at the Indiana Yankee. "It was horrible! Men died like flies. But there was worse." Taking a cue from DuBois that morning, Floyd pulled off his jacket as he turned on the South Carolina corporal.

"Elmira?" he screamed again, this time at the Palmetto man. "It was inhuman! Men starvin' and freezin' with food and blankets to hand. But there was worse." Tillman did DuBois one better while saying this. He swiftly undid his cuffs and first few buttons, then pulled his shirt off over his head, exposing a gaunt, almost sunken chest with a fuzz of white hair and showing every rib.

"This was worse," he snarled at them and turned his back to them. Everyone who could see it flinched or grimaced. Percy Sutcliffe shuddered and screwed his eyes shut. The two debaters from inches away could see dozens upon dozen of welts cross-hatched on Tillman's back. Some were thick as thumbs, others like pencils up to two feet long. There were short, lumpy ones that looked like cigar butts under the skin and long, skinny ones like a heavy wire. Years after the skin had grown back over the lash marks, the pain still throbbed beneath.

Up along the inside of the right shoulder blade was a dark, crusted wound that was slightly shiny. Tillman reached a finger over to point to this and said to the shocked silence behind him, "The Klan gave me this in 1873. After forty years, it still leaks." He turned around to the pair and rested both hands on the table. Zachariah and Calvin caught a horrible glimpse of the back through the crowd on this side, who were now flinching and turning their eyes away. Tillman said to the two recoiling men, "Andersonville? Elmira? They both ended. Slavery was worse." Both the Indiana and South Carolina man nodded tearfully, fingers pressed up hard against his lips, then each in rapid succession turned away and leaned over, vomiting up their feelings and their lunch.

Percy Sutcliffe wrote it all down. He was oddly grateful he needn't cable in his report of the day until later that night. He could use the time to debate within himself whether or not to include Floyd Tillman's account to the refined and genteel editors and readers of the *London Times*.

Calvin, Lucius, and Zachariah drifted away in silence, each man heavy in thought and wrenched in heart, meandering vaguely southward with the movement of the crowd. After some time of aimless plodding, one by one they pulled themselves out of their thoughts. As they neared Platform C, they could see a singing troupe was setting up and veterans were calling, "Sing it now, Mississippi!" and "Bring it on, Mississippi!" The name figured often enough that Calvin asked, "Lucius, what's with all the calling for Mississippi? I'm guessing it's not state pride."

Lucius led them toward some benches. "When we was slaves, the grapevine was Mississippi plantation men were the baddest. A slave who was too uppity, runaway or not workin' enough, well, their owner'd sell 'em down the rivah to the Mississippi plantations. To this day colored folk say 'sold down the rivah' to mean goin' to somethin' bad." All three minds flashed back to Floyd Tillman for a moment.

Zachariah carefully ventured, "Jeff Davis was a Mississippi planter but a fair owner."

"I won't fight you there," Lucius replied. Zachariah blinked and Calvin looked at him twice. "By all accounts iffn' you was Mr. Davis' slave it was purty good."

Calvin blurted out, "Jeff Davis? Never heard such a thing as a good slave owner."

"S'truth Calvin," Lucius answered. "Ever'body wanted to be free, but waitin' fo' freedom could be hard or not so hard. An' Jeff Davis was mo' than decent thata way. By accounts a fair man for an owner." He added with a smile, "But freedom's better."

On Platform C, Roscoe ran silken fingers across the piano keyboard. Another man sat among several different sized drums. A third man stood with a string double bass. Calvin's brow was still furrowed about Jefferson Davis and Tillman when he looked at the platform and recognized one of the singers. "I've met that fella before."

Zachariah did a double take while Lucius jumped and stammered out, "You funnin' me Calvin? Dat's Rockingham Brown, the Mississippi Bluesman. Where'd you hear him sing the blues?"

"I don't know 'blue' singing but Corporal Brown and several men came through Tent City one evening and give us a campfiyah serenade."

"Serenade!?" Lucius exclaimed, stopping his walk. "Rockingham Brown? Serenade? Are you sure? Calvin, I'd a paid cash money to hear that."

"Why?" Calvin asked, and Zachariah seconded.

The answer came from Platform C as music started up. Roscoe swung into a rhythmic piano line, backed up by the man plucking the bass strings, and bumped underneath by the man handling drums. A harmonica quavered out on top, overmatched by Rockingham's voice.

> Down Mississippi in da sharecroppin' fields
> Bossman walks a dainty walk an' look down his nose
> Workin' wid yo' hands, he thinks, is down at the heels
> Choppin' cotton, redneck, black folk, got da same woes
>
> Sharecropper blues, sharecropper blues
> Rich man's store, company store, give you da blues...

Harmony and handclaps surrounded the trio as they sat down. Calvin was fascinated how these men invented music as they went along, each player in turn freely improvising a solo, backed by the others. As it went on and on, one song melting into another, he felt, rather than heard, the sighing, the wailing, the lamentation oozing through the words, the music, the beat.

Zachariah too was moved, but differently. This Mississippi intensity reminded him of certain plantation songs, not the cheerful blackface of a Fourth of July float. He'd heard darker, sadder strains rising from fields, overseer's huts or from the basement windows of the slave auction house. He heard something and missed something. He heard the ache and sigh in Rockingham's words, yes, and expected whites to be the villains, but they weren't, not as a race. Indeed, rednecks, crackers, hillbillies, hard-luck bums, cast-off factory workers, dispossessed shop owners all found places alongside black farmers, house servants, menial laborers, and the debt-laden of both races.

Calvin and Zachariah swayed along, hummed along, clapped along, nodded along, with the blues, with Lucius, with Camp Lincoln, in touch with an ancient human lament. For serfs, vassals, apprentices, untouchables, plebes, and helots, all the way back to Pharaoh's slaves, the words had always flowed one way, in the same tone, "Make bricks without straw."

It wasn't race, except accidentally. It was rank. Caste. Hierarchy. Class. Position. Birthright. Bloodline. Breed. Group. And always, always, those who discovered, described, and enforced the ranks, classes, and bloodlines, were the ones who found themselves superior, elite, higher, better, richer, more at ease. They found themselves among the entitled; entitled to the finer, better, tastier, softer, sweeter things that were to be produced by those of the other, and always lower, class. Those on the short end were left with the labors, their cry for justice, their hope for equality, and with the blues.

Calvin felt the blues shaming him and consoling him. He felt guilty about his advantages but proud of his life in court. He felt sinful over the crowing triumph of North over South, and forgiven by the words and deeds of General Grant whom he'd quoted just yesterday, "The rebels are our countrymen again."

Zachariah felt the blues shaming him and consoling him. He felt guilty over his attitudes, yet faintly proud by sticking with Longstreet against the old Klan and the new White Liners. His heart wailed the blues at the loss of the War, and wept at the death of friends. But looking around he did not see color. He saw people, wrong-end-of-the-stick people, raw-deal people, left-out-in-the-cold people, but people. He saw men, men featured and foibled, men saints-in-the-making and sinners needing redemption. These men had reasons to love, hate, live, laugh, wonder, weep, strive, fail, achieve, lose, rest, remember, console, celebrate, die. Like any man. Like himself.

Lucius, Calvin, and Zachariah stood at the north end of the students' bridge. Since Rockingham Brown had begun the blues, the sun had swung noticeably toward Seminary Ridge, although supper would come first.

"Lucius, Zachariah and I should be heading back to Tent City. We both have lots of goodbyes to say and packing to do. You too I figyaah." Calvin's voice made it pretty steady so far, but now it choked tight. "I'm grateful for the chance to meet you, and… to visit Camp Lincoln. Thank you."

Zachariah had a husky voice. "Lucius, it's been an honor. The tent, food, well, just keepin' tavern, and, well… the m-m-men. It's been good talkin' to 'em, listenin' to 'em, a real edjication fo' this old Confed'rit."

Lucius' cheek showed the tear the other two were fighting to hold back. There was an opulent silence, filled with handshakes. Zachariah exchanged looks with Calvin and moved alongside him so they both faced Lucius. He looked right and reached left, finding Calvin's shoulder and spacing himself an arm's length away. Calvin caught on instantly, but Lucius snagged between bewildered and amazed.

"Line dressed, suh," Zachariah called.

"Line, atten-hut," Calvin answered.

Together the two said, "Present arms!" Confederate sergeant and Union major, Blue and Gray, South and North saluted the runaway slave, wagoneer, horse whipping sergeant of the 2nd South Carolina Union Volunteers. Lucius' hand shook just a little as he returned the honor.

"Request permission to retiyah to Tent City, sir."

"Pumission granted. Comp'ny, dismissed."

"Good luck to you Lucius."

"And to you, Calvin."

"Pleasure to meet you, Lucius."

"Delighted to make yo' acquaintance." So said the two Georgians, full eye to brimming eye.

Lucius watched them from the bridge until they rounded Culp's Hill.

They walked in silence, unknowingly retracing yesterday's USCI march. As they passed Meade's headquarters and headed up the east slope, they came across two other veterans, blue and gray. Near the crest of the ridge they had dug a hole. A photographer stood ready under his camera hood. One man reached over to a paper bag and pulled out a brand new hatchet. The two of them held the handle with all four of their hands over the hole as their cameraman clicked. With grins they dropped the hatchet in the hole, grasped each other in a wet-faced embrace, and then filled in the hole and tamped down the dirt. Calvin and Zachariah watched silently, then walked over the ridge together and down the west slope to Tent City.

Sunday, July 6, 1913

Gettysburg

On Sunday, Gettysburg was not a town but a parade. The majority of the veterans were leaving. Nine had left earlier in the week by dying. Hundreds had left on Friday, skipping President Wilson and the great handshake ceremonies. Thousands had gone yesterday. But today the rest of the men of the National Peace Jubilee, still better than forty thousand strong, packed their bags, complete with their souvenir mess kits, and exchanged addresses. Manly handshakes were everywhere, and often the men blessed each other with their tears.

Once more, Pickett's Field around the Great Tent saw massing regiments, flags, officers on horseback. Unlike 1863 when it had been all gray and butternut, today the field was a swirl of gray and blue, military and civilian, old-fashioned and modern dress, as all of the white veterans who had spent this remarkable week together prepared for their journeys home. When several regiments from the same state formed up to catch a certain train, organizers massed them into brigades. Often, men were catching a train to a different state. Some of the 14th Virginia, for example, had come four days from California.

Led by bands and trailed by baggage-toting Boy Scouts, the aged infantry marched in an endless double column on Emmitsburg Road. Once more the 10th Alabama or the 7th Virginia regimental flag waved over the old ranks and files. But unlike fifty years ago, this time the Southern banners on the road alternated with the 91st New York or the 17th Connecticut ensign floating over ancient Knickerbockers or aged Nutmeggers. At the town line, the eight-wide column split, one column of four moving up Washington Street to the Western Maryland depot, the other swinging onto Baltimore Street for Lincoln Station. Railroad Street between stations was restricted to vets only, so sorting out departures was easier than arrival had been. Lincoln Square in front of that station, where Baltimore Street from the south met York Street coming from the east, was foot traffic only, so civilians, Boy Scouts and departing veterans formed a human rowdydow.

The twenty- and thirty-year-old Pennsylvania Guardsmen and the career men of the US 5th Infantrymen lined the road and streets. Captain Patton, Lieutenant Chambliss, and other members of the U.S. 15th Cavalry backed them up trotting back and forth on their mounts. They watched for problems, but the crowds were friendly and the vintage vets marched well. Sergeant McMasters and privates like Weston and O'Connor could not keep the smiles off their faces as they caught old-time cracks and jibes from the marchers, the eternal grousing marching men always had for those who could sit in their saddles.

All Gettysburg, masses of reporters, and thousands of spectators were attending; waving hats, flags, and canes. Southern tourists and gray-bearded Graybacks who had come for the week carrying doubts or worries about their reception had had them washed away more each day, but this screaming, tearful farewell amazed them. Virginia reporter John C. Hill of the *Roanoke Times* assured his Southern readers that "every porch, every window, was filled with women from all parts of the country, waving flags and handkerchiefs, throwing kisses to the gallant old Confederates, and bidding them God's speed on the homeward journey." And it wasn't just the Dixie men who were swept up by the parting reception they were getting. Two veterans at Lincoln Station were so overwhelmed that, then and there, they stripped down and exchanged uniforms, the Northerner traveling home in Confederate gray, and the Southron surprising many on the rails and at home blazoned in Yankee blue.

Tent City was not the only place at Gettysburg wrestling with the logistics of moving out thousands of old men. On a smaller scale, Camp Lincoln was also teeming with a last breakfast together, packing, address swaps, and old men's tears. While their numbers were smaller, among the trees and tents along Rock Creek, the Colored Infantry and Troops didn't have a large staging area like Pickett's Field for organizing. The Camp Lincoln committee and some of their old officers pulled the men together into formation, thinking these men deserved one more chance to march as veterans. They also considered, with the crowd control power of police constables, regular U.S. Army, Cavalry, and Pennsylvania Guardsmen virtually all deployed on the south side of town and out into Tent City, there might be some safety in numbers facing the overwhelmingly white throngs in Gettysburg that morning. And finally, the committee, Colonel Biddle, and the other leaders, had planned one more maneuver for the USCI for anyone who cared to watch or listen.

Around half past nine, two brigades' worth of marching men were serenaded up Frederick Douglass Avenue by various Camp Lincoln performers and entertainers left from yesterday, clanged along by the food crews beating ladles and cooking spoons on pots and pans, hugged and even kissed by perfect strangers among the women. The formations wound out of Camp Lincoln onto Hanover Pike, crossed the Rock Creek bridge and moved into Gettysburg from the east. About halfway to Lincoln Square, the USCI men came up to where York Pike angled in from the northeast at the edge of town and the march went into slow motion.

Like the rest of Gettysburg, here were swarms of civilians clogging the sidewalks and spilling onto the street, looking west toward Lincoln Square, frustrated by their own numbers. Confederate or Union, veterans were all the rage and thousands yearned for one last chance to see a white beard riding above a blue or gray jacket so they could cheer and shout. Tens of thousands rose before the roosters crowed to try to get to Gettysburg this morning to see the veterans off. These on the east side simply could not get close to the south side, thwarted by human gridlock in every possible direction. Even the enterprising ones who tried getting through to the west and south by alleys and backyards were stymied by the multitudes already standing and spilling back from every vantage point.

Now suddenly, unexpected by any white organizers of the official Encampment, and unattended by any police presence except a few constables, here on the east side were genuine marching Civil War veterans. Overwhelmingly in blue, here were veterans under Grant from Missionary Ridge to Appomattox, and veterans under Sherman who had marched through Georgia and across the Carolinas. Here were veterans who had beat off an attack at Milliken's Bend, pursued Price from Arkansas to mid-Missouri to Texas, and battered Fort Fisher into submission.

When the Grand Review was held in Washington City in May 1865, Grant's men took eight solid hours to pass in review before dignitaries and the populace, and Sherman's men took all the next day. Yet these men in blue, the emancipated and victorious, doing their duty, volunteers to a man, had been turned away that May, barred from that honor and farewell. No black troops had marched in the Grand Review. But they had served, and endured, and now had reunioned at Gettysburg with all the nostalgia and honor they could wrest from a reluctant nation. All week a growing stream of white visitors to Camp Lincoln had seen, heard from, and mingled with these veterans, and they had been increasingly impressed. The parade denied these men in 1865, Gettysburg and her endless visitors now spontaneously tried to give them.

"Veterans! Veterans!" came the electrifying cry. Instant jubilation and impromptu celebrations erupted along York Street. By the thousands, people turned and lined the street, or hurried back to the fork of York and Hanover Pike, finally getting a parade they had come for. Small children were hoisted onto fathers' shoulders and boys climbed trees. Caps tossed and flags and handkerchiefs waved furiously from crammed sidewalks. Woolworth's front window was jammed. Strangers were invited into houses and businesses up to second-floor windows, to balconies, to attic windows.

The USCI men struggled to keep formation as they were swamped by well-wishers patting them on the back. With crowd controllers fully deployed on the south side to shepherd the white vets, this march of the colored men on the east side was more open, more casual, like a small-town parade. But the back slapping and yelling were definitely big city. "Hurrah" and "Thank you" and "God bless you" ricocheted everywhere with a fierceness that was one part frustration released but two parts vibrant patriotism.

Drummers leading showed off their talents with irresistible cadency. The men's progress was a creep, in tempo, but barely half even the old twenty-two-inch stride, such was the crush. Streamers flew and small firecrackers snapped on the pavement. Amid the screaming, under showers of confetti, one vet yelled something to Lucius Robinson that sounded like, "This is more like it," but Lucius couldn't be sure. After all, the man had only one voice and he was nearly eighteen inches away.

About the time the march of the Camp Lincoln troops went into low gear on the east side of Gettysburg, the 8th Georgia from Longstreet's old command came up Baltimore Street on the south side of town, passing the Presbyterian church where Lincoln had prayed the day of his Address. Boy Scout baggage boys – instantly labeled "baggage smashers" by the vets in honor of the railroads' talent for losing and abusing luggage – trailed each regiment, trying to match the veterans' marching and formation-keeping and finding it harder than it looked. Sergeant Zachariah Hampton was two steps wide calling cadence, close enough to the curb that many civilians patted him on the shoulder. Crowd controllers were hard at work keeping back the crush of civilians and the pavement was clear for the marchers so they could keep step to the strains of "The Bonnie Blue Flag" playing from a band.

The regiment was one of six, part of a Georgia brigade of Confederates. As this unit gained the south edge of Lincoln Square, their old officers, having conspired beforehand, showed off the men. In a series of commands they split the regiments, turning each out ninety degrees from the center line so they spanned the south width of the square. The following regiments likewise maneuvered in behind so the multitudes jamming the square saw the "evolution of the line" from column to massed ranks, facing north, ready for action. Applause rang, then faded, taking down some of the general roar.

An elderly one-armed mounted colonel bawled down from his saddle, "Dress the line!" and the ranks dressed. Then he ran them through the manual of arms. Surprised, the men caught on quickly and pantomimed the multistep instructions to ready a muzzleloader. To the crowd's delight, he even ordered, "First rank, aim, fire!" – and the front-rank men all aimed imaginary rifles and yelled "Bang" – followed by "Drop back, reload. Second rank, forward two steps. Take aim. Fire." The first rank men each took a step to their left and began walking backward between the files of men behind them, pantomiming reloading, while the second rank stepped up. With ranks eight deep – rare during the War – and about twenty seconds for reloading, the brigade ably demonstrated almost continuous firing.

Zachariah, Bob Bidwell, Jim Calhoun and the other first rank men cycled back up to the front. The "firing" had grown louder because each time a rank called "bang," more and more vets added their voices. The Augusta colonel called "Cease fire," then waited for the applause to die down. He solemnly took off his hat, which fixed every eye upon him, and held a letter trembling in his hand. In a subdued shout he began,

"People of Gettysburg, thank you. Thank you for this week. You have given to all the veterans what my cousin Berry Benson wrote in his memoirs about our dreams:

> *Who knows but it may be given to us, after this life, to meet again in the old quarters, to play chess and draughts, to get up soon to answer the morning roll call, to fall in at the tap of the drum for drill and dress parade, and again to hastily don our war gear while the monotonous patter of the long roll summons to battle? Who knows but again the old flags, ragged and torn, snapping in the wind, may face each other and flutter, pursuing and pursued, while the cries of victory fill a summer day? And after the battle, then the slain and wounded will arise, and all will be talking and laughter and cheers, and all will say: Did it not seem real? Was it not as in the old days?*

"On behalf of the men of this Georgia brigade, we thank the citizens of Gettysburg fo' their hospitality and goodwill and their foretaste of heaven."

He turned back and shouted, "Brigade! At-ten-SHUN. Sa-lute!" A smiling hush fell over the civilians, tinged with tears at those men who could only salute left-handed. The colonel's "Georgia Brigade, Dis-missed!" was answered by sustained applause and cheering. A band struck up "Dixie" to float over the merrymaking as south side spectators overwhelmed the crowd controllers and swarmed forward to shake hands with the boys in gray. The rest of the packed square could only hear the band and see the Georgia regimental banners and old Stars and Bars Southern battle flag waving over the endless heads and hats.

This handshaking was in full swing on the square's south side when a growing roar turned everyone's head east where York Street fed into the square. The York Street parade watchers who had cheered the Camp Lincoln marchers and backslapped the USCI men practically flat were not going to fit into the square, so they were sending off the colored veterans with a tumult that made shop windows tingle and left ears ringing.

Spectators in the square first saw a street-wide banner stretched between two twenty-foot poles reading, "Courage and Duty Then. Peace and Freedom Now." The crowd fell back as best they could to make way for these marching colored men, and in the newly opened space they saw better than two thousand men in column evolve south to the left, and at least two thousand more turn north to the right. The Camp Lincoln men formed a solid mass several ranks deep, a living rectangle with one end covering the eastern quarter of the square.

As the south-turning brigade of the USCI neared the southeast corner of the square, many on the Georgian right flank and their handshaking civilian fans fell back. Some of the Georgians spat out various curses at the Yankees, rather undercutting their salute from a few minutes ago. Other vets and civilians pointedly turned their backs or studiously ignored the black faces massing on the square's east sidewalk, curbs, and pavement, offering nasty comments about "ruination" and "amalgamation." A few young hotheads yelled something about it being "time to teach those boys a lesson," but a fair number of others worried out loud at what damage and destruction a riot of black men might cause.

With the USCI men all in place, a single horseman rode in from York Street, posting himself between the two halves of the USCI. Colonel Biddle's cry of "Camp Lincoln Brigades, atten-shun!" echoed off the buildings and overtopped the crowd noise. As they saw the colored vets snap to, rigid like any military men, the quiet in the square grew and the hotheads lost their audience.

"Present arms!" Nearly five thousand hands saluted as the colonel followed immediately with, "Present the colors." Both brigades unfurled the Stars and Stripes, then their regimental flags, and lastly their GAR post flags. Across an empty line formed between the Georgians and the black troops in the southeast corner, Zachariah Hampton was surprised to read "Savannah" as a GAR post flag opened on its staff. Looking more closely he saw, "Rufus Saxton Post, GAR, Savannah, GA."

Biddle next called, "Parade rest." Salutes came down, both hands met over belt buckles and the whole formation took a half step back in unison. The civilians relaxed a bit more at this demonstration of discipline and veterans around the square were duly impressed at the precision. A color guard came to the front of the two brigades. They carried flags and a large banner hoisted on a T-shaped pole. Each banner carried several names.

As had been arranged over the last several days of meetings, Biddle turned to the northern half and called, "Grant's troops, ready?" They all answered in unison, "Yes, sir!" He turned the other way and asked at the top of his voice, "Men of Sherman and Thomas, ready?" "Yes, sir!" rang the reply and the crowd suddenly passed from anxiety to curiosity.

The Grant half of the USCI men began chanting. Drums and percussion stationed between both sections near Biddle kept time. The southeastern group of Sherman and Thomas answered with a different singsong chant and people cocked their ears, trying to catch the words. One group was saying,

"Lookout Mountain" and the other "Missionary Ridge." The northeast group shouted "Wilderness, Wilderness" the top word on their banner, followed by "Spotsylvania Court House". The southeastern men replied, "Dalton, Resaca, Dalton, Resaca."

The chanting and shouting of battles in call-and-response style went on.

"North Anna, North Anna"

"New Hope Church"

"North Anna, North Anna"

"New Hope Church"

"Cold Harbor, Cold Harbor"

...and the southeast men bowed their heads and the drummers paused. White veterans from the Army of the Potomac around the square also bowed their heads and felt a catch in their throats. After a hush, the drummers took up the beat again and the southeast men shouted back,

"Kennesaw Mountain, Kennesaw Mountain"

"Petersburg, Petersburg"

...began the northeast square men and the rumble of the name went on and on as a smaller group fired off,

"Monocacy, Fort Stevens"

"Monocacy, Fort Stevens"

"Chatahoochee, Chatahoochee"

"Petersburg, Petersburg"

Ezra Church"

...answered the second chorus and then stopped.

The "Petersburg" chant also stopped. The drummers stopped. Silence threw itself across the square. The snare drummers turned to the cymbal carriers and started a long rising sizzle. The bass drum men joined in one by one until thunder filled the air. On a signal, the throbbing suddenly stopped, and in the shocked quiet all the Camp Lincoln men roared "Crater!"

As the northeast group resumed the "Petersburg" chant, understanding swept the square. "Fort Gaines, Fort Gaines, Mobile Bay" overlaid inner "Aha"'s. These men were naming off their battles similar to the way white regiments sewed the names of their battles onto their regimental flags. But the USCI vets not just letting the curious read the names, they were proclaiming to the world that the Republic's sable arm had been in the fight.

"Petersburg, Petersburg"

"Petersburg, Petersburg"

"Atlanta! Atlanta! Ours and fairly won!"

"Atlanta! Atlanta! Ours and fairly won!"

...the veterans quoting Sherman's telegram to Lincoln.

"Petersburg, Fisher Hill"

"Petersburg, Cedar Creek"

History books, monument makers and Jim Crow oppressors were laboring to shove the colored soldiers out of America's memories of the War, but these veterans refused to go. They insisted on their War and their battles as much as anyone camping at Gettysburg.

"Petersburg, Petersburg"

"Marching through Georgia"

"Marching through Georgia"

"Petersburg, Petersburg"

"Petersburg, Petersburg"

"Franklin, Nashville"

"Franklin, Nashville"

"Petersburg, Petersburg"

"Savannah for Christmas"

"Savannah for Christmas"

"Petersburg, Petersburg"

"Columbia, Charleston"

"Columbia, Charleston"

"Petersburg, Petersburg"

"Bentonville, Bentonville"

"FIVE Forks! FIVE Forks!"

...intoned the "Petersburg" contingent, signaling the end of the siege. All the black troops joined together in triumph:

"Richmond, Richmond,

RICHMOND, RICHMOND!"

...for the fall of the Confederate capital after an eight month siege in nearby Petersburg rated four mentions, and they all finished with:

"Sayler Creek,

Appomattox Court House!"

All week the National Encampment had been filled with tent talks and campfire chats, Great Tent speechmaking and spontaneous oratory at every turn, most of it focused on reconciliation between North and South. Lincoln was hailed and recalled as "The Savior of the Union."

A bargain was being struck among white Americans past and present. As fellow soldiers, North and South, the veterans stood apart from this unheroic and complicated present age. Both Blue and Gray were accepting that the other side had fought manfully and suffered as heroically as they had for a cause they believed in. As long as the causes and outcomes of the War were both mutually forgotten, a terrible national wound could be scabbed over.

But not everyone was buying the bargain. Not all were looking for healing. Bitter-enders on both sides, military and civilian, were willing, even eager, to go on hating. Former prisoners of war and their families and comrades often carried scars beyond healing.

This morning in Lincoln Square the USCI men were also challenging the bargain, picking at the scab. Not from bitterness or hate, they were challenging the bargain as inadequate and flawed. Their chant of battles had reminded hearers that Northern determination and Southern resistance dressed in white skin was American history incomplete. Their own empty sleeves and missing legs were mute testimony to a deeper meaning.

Their band broke into song and the USCI began serenading the crowd.

> *My country, 'tis of thee, sweet land of liberty,*
> *Of thee I sing.*
> *Land where my fathers died, land of the pilgrims' pride,*
> *from ev'ry mountainside,*
> *let freedom ring.*

The serenade was an offer of a balm to soothe and soften the nation's scab. It was an invitation to heal further, to move on to another stage of liberty.

The fifty-four thousand veterans of Tent City who had visited, shaken hands, recounted tales, consoled each other, embraced one another, had fulfilled Lincoln's call for Union. The tens of thousands of civilians who had visited Gettysburg daily had heard reunion, seen reunion, almost smelled reunion. The great embrace on Pickett's Field had wrenched, and healed, the hearts of all who saw it.

> *My native country, thee, Land of the noble free,*
> *Thy name I love.*
> *I love thy rocks and rills, thy woods and templed hills*
> *My heart with rapture thrills,*
> *like that above.*

Now the five thousand USCI men were hoisting Lincoln's other legacy – not only Savior of the Union, but also the Great Emancipator. The sixteenth president, calling for Union, had come haltingly to liberty. He had begun with limitation of slavery, then moved through ideas of slave resettlement, compensated emancipation, emancipation itself, and then to liberty, even equality. By their very presence the USCI veterans dared the crowds at Gettysburg and beyond them, the nation, to follow Lincoln's path.

The White Liners were all about limitation, badgering, harassment, threats. They were about resettlement, if not in Africa, then in heaven (or hell as they preferred) by lynch rope and arson torch.

Many Northern men of business were about compensation and money. They saw Southern poverty, but also smelled a market. They toured Southern cities, financed Southern recovery, built Southern factories and turned a blind eye to Jim Crow.

Many Northern citizens were grudging about emancipation, allowing black citizens a place in their towns, sometimes even talking about emancipation, especially every February 12 when schoolchildren brought home papers and stories on Abraham Lincoln's birthday.

> *Let music swell the breeze, and ring from all the trees,*
> *Sweet freedom's song.*
> *Let mortal tongues awake, Let all that breathe partake*
> *Let rocks their silence break,*
> *the sound prolong.*

So with reluctance, many second thoughts, and wildly unevenly, white Americans had inched down the path blazed by Lincoln. Would they now take heart from the national encampment of Lincoln's veterans? If North and South could meet eye to eye, turn away from all the hurt and live side by side and shake hands with honor, could now white and black do the same? If the war between sections could finally be healed, could the war between races also find a good end?

By the fourth verse the Camp Lincoln men were not singing alone. A solid week of reminders of both reunion and liberation had turned heads, softened hearts, and lifted souls. Civilians, Union vets, and not to be outdone, many hundreds of Confederate men joined in song.

> *Our fathers' God to thee, Author of Liberty,*
> *To Thee we sing.*
> *Long may our land be bright, With freedom's holy light*
> *Protect us by Thy might,*
> *great God, our King.*

A tight-throated hush fell over the throngs as the last chord faded, and many handkerchiefs were doing cheek work. In the quiet, Colonel Biddle's horse's hooves clopped loudly. He faced his horse west and saluted the multitudes. Although his voice fought against his own feeling rising in his throat, his old discipline served him well one more time and his spirit took captive his lungs. His shout and Jefferson's words ricocheted around the quadrangle and sank into many hearts. "'To this we pledge our lives, our fortunes, and our sacred honor,' so help us God." Almost five thousand affirmed this with salutes and a robust "Amen." They got an answering "Amen" from the many.

The crowd turned back into a crowd, photographers flashed their powder, Ince's motion picture men cranked their cameras, and the veterans got back to their leave taking. But not just a few of the Tent City boys were seen shaking hands with the Camp Lincoln men. Alabama gray and blue were over here, Tennessee blue and Florida gray were over there. A white Indiana cavalryman, a Georgia gunnery corporal, and a black Missouri sharpshooter were having a three way, six-handed handshake for a photographer.

In the northeast corner, men of the 14th Vermont were all shaking hands with their old USCI mates from the Army of the Potomac. Well, nearly all. One eager colored artilleryman thrust his hand toward Josiah Trimble, who was just turning from saying to a neighbor how unseemly it all was. Seeing the black hand and smiling face abruptly so close Trimble startled and stepped back. Unfortunately he was standing on the square's pavement just in front of the sidewalk. As he recoiled, his heel crashed into the curb and he sat down suddenly, hard on his tailbone. Calvin could not help smiling as he reached across to shake the cannoneer's hand while Trimble yelped in pain. Then he turned and together with Sam and Ashton Melo they managed to pull Josiah to his feet.

And over in the southeast corner, where before there had been a hollow line of hate, two Savannah sergeants, one blue, one gray, one white, one black, and both with matching gray hair, were shaking hands, no, forearms like the old Romans, and clapping each other on the shoulder.

CARL EEMAN

Part Three

TAPESTRY

Tuesday, July 8, 1913

Savannah

Lucius and Rufus came up Savannah's Broad Street from the station a couple hours before sunset. Rufus carried Lucius' big leather grip as his father bubbled like a mountain stream with Encampment news all the way to 305 Fahm Street. There Lucius frowned at the drawn drapes and general quiet.

"Didn't you say Beulah and the chillun were fixin' to put on the dog?"

Rufus had a puzzled look on his face. "That's what I left 'em doin'. I don't know." He pulled out his key as they came up to the front door and stepped on a squeaky porch board. Rufus unlocked the door, swung it in and said, "Go ahead, Pop."

Mystified, Lucius stepped in and punched the in-out double button of the light switch. The hall light came on. "Surprise!" "Welcome home!"

Shouts continued as friendly hands pulled open the drapes and let up the shades.

Rufus had worried all week about how Lucius would take a house teeming with family and neighbors. Sudden loud noises could reduce him to tears. Rufus relaxed as his father startled ordinarily, then waded into embraces.

"We gotcha, Grampa," Hannah bragged.

"Hi, Gramps!" Sherman said, running to tackle him with a hug.

Red, white, and blue streamers arched from the ceilings. New Year's noisemakers clattered, rang, and jingled. Ten hand-tinted Gettysburg postcards were passed around along with the food and drink. Men slapped him on the back and all the women lined up to kiss him. Lucius didn't know whether to laugh or cry, so he did both, exclaiming, "Well I'll be John Browned!"

Alma was last in the smooch line and led him to the parlor. Lucius saw a homemade banner of white butcher's paper hung across the wall proclaiming, "Welcome Home, Soldier!" Hannah and Sherman had gone through two boxes of expensive crayons decorating it in all manner of stars and stripes. As the night wore on, the decoration increased as everyone wrote messages.

Lucius was the hero and center of the party. Every tale of the Encampment or from fifty years ago had a willing audience of one to forty at any moment. About an hour along, he was telling of the comforts of Camp Lincoln while Sherman, Ralphie, and Abner stood near. He finished by saying, "That camp put our shebangs in the shade."

"Put your what in the shade?" Sherman asked. "Your shebangs?"

Lucius grinned. "Yep. After General Sherman marched north from Savannah he left men here on garrison duty. In our camp we built huts out of all kinda scrap wood and called 'em shebangs."

"I just thought it was a way of sayin' 'everything,'" Sherman replied, his friends nodding.

"Well, a shebang was ever'thin' we owned," Lucius agreed, "so maybe that's how it got to mean that."

"What all didya do here in Savannah on garrison?" Reverend Porterfield's wife Fancy wanted to know.

"Well, we policed the town in place of constables, enforced orders from the commandin' general Rufus Saxton," Fancy glanced over at Beulah and Rufus with a flash of understanding, "and carried out Special Field Order 15 so colored folk could start livin' their own lives. Did that 'til the War ended and I was mustered out."

The party had one of those sudden lulls just then so most everyone heard Lucius say in a husky voice, "I got mustered out but there was no home fo' me an' no one waitin' fo' me to come home." A sob broke his voice in the full quiet. He lifted his face, "Until now."

Beulah rushed over to him with arms wide and face wet and said, "Papa, welcome home from the War!" The cheering made the window panes tingle and the jollification went on deep into the night.

Lee and Hugo found Zachariah in Savannah's station. A big crowd of noisy relatives had a fair-sized block of veterans surrounded. The old Confederates were happy to be home, but they didn't want to leave each other quite yet. Even though they knew each other from around town, the Encampment had bonded them anew. Today's goodbye almost felt like their old muster out and echoed the great farewell in Gettysburg on Sunday, still fresh and bittersweet. But at last, little by little they broke up, calling "So long" and "See you soon" at longer distances until finally each was swallowed by family and friends.

Hugo drove with the top down, Zachariah chattering next to him, with Lee in the back seat leaning in to catch every word. Before Zachariah felt like he had hardly started telling about just the first day in Gettysburg, Hugo pulled to a stop on Tattnall Street. He reached his left hand to the large black rubber ball attached to the brass horn and began honking. The Thomas sounded like a demented goose with a giant head cold.

"What are you doin'?" Zachariah asked.

Lee and Hugo grinned back like boys on the last day of school. Windows opened up and down the street and front doors swung in. Neighbors along the block whistled, clapped their hands, and stomped their porches for the noise.

Women fluttered handkerchiefs and men waved hats. Maids and cooks leaned out of windows and banged pots and pans or gonged a spoon on a baking sheet.

Zachariah stepped onto the curb and did a slack-jawed slow circle as the street filled with neighbors. Shouts of welcome crisscrossed each other as the Thompson's door swung open. Lee held the fence gate and Emily hurried through, her face joyful.

Zachariah beamed and held his arms open to her. He remembered another walk, another yard, and another brown-haired, beautiful belle of his life throwing away all propriety and running hatless to meet him. He wrapped his arms around Emily just as if she were Matilda in 1865 and swung her off her feet. "Welcome home, welcome home," Emily kept saying in his ear. "I've been hoping every day. Welcome home."

Neighbor Ray Younger had brought a fiddle. As father and daughter finally unclenched – although Lee noticed they still held hands – Younger struck a few chords and called, "All together now!" The Tattnall Street singers gave a heartfelt serenade of "When Johnny Comes Marching Home." As though they had practiced – Zack never did hear if they had or not – the women dropped out to allow the males a hearty, "the men will cheer and the boys will shout." Then the men paused as the ladies all sang "they will all turn out."

Zachariah held forth from his front porch rocker, lively-eyed and laughing heartily, receiving kisses, handshakes, sips from various flasks, and endless food. At one point Emily came through the front door with a plate of gingersnaps she'd made that afternoon. She saw her father delighting in the festivities and the phrase "hoping every day" ran through her mind again like it often had lately. Tonight her heart leapt as though in answer to the phrase. This daddy, hearty, robust, and even playful; this was her daddy, the one she'd grown up with, the one she'd greeted every other night when he came home from conducting on the Central of Georgia. Her eyes were a bit damp as the block party rolled across the porch and front yard. Passersby were welcomed into the gala that went on long after the gaslights of street and house came up.

"Tattnall Street was one of many Savannah neighborhoods that held such events," next morning's *Tribune* reported. "Even the West Side had a gleeful air in honor of the returning Confederates." (The *Savannah Colored Tribune* reported it rather differently.)

Rutland

Eleanor and Anna Louise were on the front porch swing after getting supper ready. Anna saw Eleanor remembering.

"In 1865 I was swinging on this porch when he came," she said softly. "I wept from my soul, and I think I might have stroked his cheek raw."

"He must have looked wonderful," Anna answered.

"He did, but his eyes were changed. There was pain in them, and they were harder. They've carried a cloud many days since."

From down the long hill at Center and Evelyn streets came the long whistle of an arriving train. When the breeze was right, they heard the locomotive's bell. But the whistle went on and on. Then a locomotive at another platform joined in. A couple more down at the switchyard added their shrieks. Then the Nickwackett Firehouse cranked its street siren, soon joined by the other stations across town. The blare carried over Rutland's fourteen thousand and brought people to their doors and windows. Anna and Eleanor exchanged bright eyes and nods. "Won't be long now," Anna said.

And it wasn't, really; it only seemed so to Eleanor. Then the streetcar came rattling to a clanging stop down at the corner four doors down. As it pulled away, the bell kept ringing and they could see people hanging out of every window, waving fists, cheering, and blowing kisses toward two old men in dark blue who were rounding the corner onto East Washington. One codger had a full shovel beard and Ben Franklin locks, and the other had a moustache and chin beard of pure white.

Anna looked back and forth between Eleanor and Calvin as the men came up the walk. When Calvin reached the porch, Eleanor sprang off the swing, leaving Anna oscillating wildly, and rushed into his arms. She took him by his cheeks and gave him a huge kiss square on, then burst into tears while endlessly stroking his left cheek. Their words went back and forth between the present and 1865. Eleanor kept looking into Calvin's eyes. Something was missing there, but something old was back. Anna had known Calvin a long time but she'd never seen him so gallant, like a cavalier of old. Sam thought Eleanor was practically the bride he'd met before the War.

Then the Salisburys broke apart and looked at Anna and Sam as though seeing them for the first time in a month.

"Sam! You old rapscallion, you," Eleanor burst out. She came up to him so quickly he took an involuntary step back. She caught him by his lapels and gave him a big kiss on the nose. They both burst out laughing and Eleanor said, "Thank you for bringing Calvin back." They were both still chuckling when they turned to watch Calvin and Anna's meeting.

As Calvin approached, Anna held out her hand to be kissed saying, "Nothing more from a married man." Calvin changed strategy in mid-stride and said, "Au contraire." He took her hand in his left hand, put his right arm around her and pulled her into dance position. He led her in several turns around the porch as Sam and Eleanor clapped. He ended by pinning her to the front wall and giving her a lingering, noisy buss on the cheek, then breaking away laughing. Eleanor covered her mouth and said amazed, "Anna, you're blushing." Both men looked as the cheeks reddened on the most self-assured woman they'd ever known. Recovering immediately, Anna said, "For you Calvin, once every fifty years, I'll blush."

They moved inside and ate ravenously. Though the food was excellent, no one much remembered what they ate. It was as though they feasted more upon each other's presence. Anna and Sam shook their heads, amazed, as both Calvin and Eleanor brought out the cards and letters each had written the other twice daily while Calvin had been away. They were humbled as they handed these private thoughts around, read them aloud, exchanged warm looks, and let giggles erupt.

"So Calvin, Sam, tell us everything," the women asked when the dishes had been cleared. Calvin put his letters to Eleanor at his side to consult and pulled out a half-size leather journal and began, "Pulled out of Rutland on time on the Governor's Special…" The men recounted and regaled endlessly. When Calvin said, "So ended Tuesday," they all startled as the grandfather clock in the front hall began chiming ten. They all moved protesting muscles that had sat too long in one pose. "Sam, can you stay the night? We'll pick it up in the morning." And the recounting began again with sunrise.

Wednesday, July 16, 1913

Rutland

"How's it coming, Calvin?" Ellie asked, sitting down with him at the kitchen table.

His letter was stuck. "It's harder than I thought. Those two, Lucius and Zachariah, we talked so easily. We felt like... such..." his voice faded.

"Well, put that in the letter, what you felt," Ellie urged.

"Oh, I couldn't. I mean, I don't think...I mean, how would it look?"

"Calvin," Ellie's voice was as warm as her cup of tea, "there's no need to put on manly airs. For the last week you've talked like they're brothers come back from exile, even though you three had never met. Wasn't that one of the aims of the Encampment?"

"Ayup. It was." Michael's image rose in his mind. "Grant and Longstreet were friends before the War. Longstreet was in Grant's wedding. When the War was over, they went back to being friends. Longstreet said, 'Why do men fight who should be brothers?'"

Ellie squeezed his hand. "Tell them that. Quote Longstreet to 'em. You already gave 'em Grant when you sliced that martinet's suspendahs."

Calvin grinned wryly, then warmed his smile in gratitude. "Thank you. I'll tell 'em."

She saw under some of Calvin's papers a larger, heavier sheet poking out. "What's this?" she asked, pulling it free. There were four pencil sketches of Calvin from his war days and she recognized the style. "This is the same artist who did the full size one I just put up in our bedroom."

Calvin gulped sheepishly. "I, ah, that is, Sam, uh, really liked the man's work. So after he did that one from the old photograph in camp, I had these done too. I guess I thought, um, Lucius and Zachariah might uh..."

She smiled at him and scooted into the parlor to her sewing kit. She came back with her scissors and said, "No, it's not showing off. Yes, they should each have one. You write, and I'll measure and cut."

Mid-afternoon made a nice bit of shade on the east side porch. The men's Gettysburg tales flowed until Calvin remembered his manners. "Ellie, we must be boring you with all this old soldier's talk. But life didn't stop in Rutland while we were gone. Tell us the news."

"Yes, do," Sam added, his mouth dry from jawing.

"Well, it's sweet of you to ask, Calvin. The mayor's wife invited the wives of veterans to a tea that was delightful. The rule was we could only talk about you men from our courting days, so there was endless laughter." Calvin chuckled and blushed at the same time.

"Whose stories did you hear?" Sam asked.

"Well, Abigail Trimble's for one."

"Josiah courted her during the War, didn't he?" Sam asked, searching his memory.

"That's right," Ellie said. "Josiah served his enlistment, then proposed to her at her parents' home in Albany."

"Well then, I've had it wrong," Calvin admitted. "I always thought Abigail's family was from Connecticut."

"Could be you're mixing it up a bit," Ellie nodded. "Abigail is from Albany, but after Josiah asked for her hand, he couldn't afford to marry her. So he went looking for work, first there in Albany, then in, um, I believe it was Worcester, Massachusetts, and finally in Norwich and Hartford. Hartford was where he worked at the Colt factory making pistols. His talent made him a master metalworker so he was able to amass enough to marry Abigail and move back here to start his jewelry shop."

"I always wondered how Josiah got into that line of work," Sam mused. He and Calvin exchanged a glance as Eleanor rose and scooped up the empty lemonade pitcher. "I'll be right back," she said as she went inside.

The men dropped their voices to each other. "I thought he went to Albany in uniform," Calvin said carefully.

"That New York man from the Gettysburg depot when we arrived said the same," Sam agreed. He stroked his beard. "Let me write a few letters and see what turns up."

"Okay," Calvin agreed. "But make sure. The proof has to be strong."

They were choosing among Gettysburg yarns when Eleanor swung through the screen door. Sam thought he'd stopped in time but Ellie had caught the start of a story. She filled their glasses and her own and resumed her seat. "So go on, Sam. You were saying about the woman's mother from Cashtown."

"Uh, well, uh, that is…" Sam stammered, flushing slightly.

"Now, Sam," Ellie coaxed. "There's been so much talk about men and the battle and the War that I'd enjoy a tale about a woman."

Calvin tried, "Um, Ellie, it's maybe not just a story that, um…"

"Calvin. Sam," came Eleanor's "Port Royal" tone. "Is this a story of violence against the lady?" They both shook their heads.

"Some sickness or such?" Again a negative.

"Well then I'm ready to hear it, Sam."

Sam sighed. "All right." He tapped Calvin playfully. "But you've got to help me."

"Okay," Calvin grinned sheepishly, "if it's the tale I think you're going to tell."

"Well, a woman visiting the Encampment told a story about the last week of June, 1863. A couple days before the battle at Gettysburg, the Rebs were marchin' near Cashtown, Pennsylvania. Lots of civilians turned out to see 'em, just because it was an army on the march. She said her mother, a young woman at the time, turned out too, but she decided to let the Rebels know her politics. Her mother brought out three or four of those little flags on a stick children wave at Fourth of July parades."

"I know the ones," Ellie answered as Sam blushed.

Calvin cleared his throat uneasily. "It, ah, seems she wasn't content just to wave those little flags."

"Is that right?" Ellie asked sweetly while the men shifted uncomfortably. "What did she do with them?"

Calvin and Sam exchanged long looks. Finally Calvin stammered, "She, ah, that is, decided to, ah, wear the flags."

"Wear them? How so? In her hair? Her apron?

A man-squirming pause hung in the air. Sam stumbled, "She apparently was wearing, um, an informal, that is, not Sunday best, um, blouse."

"That's right," Calvin chimed in. "A, uh, country sort of, farm woman's blouse."

Ellie smiled at the men's modesty and tried to ease their discomfort. "I see. Something that would be cooler in the summer."

"Yes, exactly," Calvin agreed. "One that, yes, um, allowed a woman to be a bit cooler, in the, ah, summah."

Ellie sipped her lemonade. "Are you two rascals trying to say this farm woman put those little flags in the bosom of her blouse?"

"That's exactly correct, Ellie," Sam nodded. "She put 'em... just like that."

"Now see, that wasn't so hard to explain, was it you two?" Eleanor asked with a lilt in her voice and chuckling at the image. "A delightful little tale." When she found she was laughing alone she put down her lemonade and tilted her head. "So is there more to the story?"

Calvin blushed. "Uh...yes. She was standing by a fence, displaying her flags like... like that, as the Confederates matched by. Several marchers made comments about her flags and their, uh, position. The men had a lot of fun about it and the lady laughed along with them. Then came an officer on hossback, a Maryland colonel. He drew rein beside her on the road, pointed over his shoulder and said, 'Ma'am, comin' up jes' behind us are General Hood's men of the Texas brigade.'" Calvin laughed heartily and couldn't stop.

Giggling, Sam managed to add, "The woman said something like, 'How nice. They're pretty far from home aren't they?' And the colonel said, 'Yes, ma'am, but there's something you need to know about them as fightin' men.' "

"'What would that be?' she asked the colonel." Sam burst out laughing in anticipation and couldn't continue. Calvin was chortling, and even Ellie, not knowing, smiled broadly, caught up in the merriment.

"What did he say? Sam? Calvin?" Ellie asked, turning from one to the other.

Calvin leaned forward and gasped out between bellows, "He said to her, 'You best be careful, ma'am. Hood's men have never failed to capture those colors you're wearing...' " he roared until the tears rolled.

Sam finished out, "...those colors when they've been mounted on b-b-breastworks." He almost fell off his chair. Ellie slapped her hands down on her lap and added her mezzo soprano tinkling laugh to the tenor pitched guffaws echoing off the porch.

Late that night from the bedroom upstairs, Ellie's voice laughed again as she teased, "My, my, Calvin. You've learned something about carrying flag positions."

Friday, July 18, 1913

Savannah

Alma put away her hat and purse in a little cupboard in the Thompsons' kitchen. She checked the stove, saw her banked coals were still hot, and added some kindling to get the heat up. Then she worked the pump by the sink and filled the coffee pot all the way full. She found Emily's note in its box, and quietly began making breakfast for three.

A bit later she stood for a moment sipping her own coffee. She could hear the sounds of the Thompsons and Mr. Hampton stirring. Her nose crinkled, and she smelled her sleeve. Alma shook her head, dismayed that the smell of cigars from last night was still clinging there. As she looked around the kitchen for something that might cover the smell, she also wore a half-smile, remembering.

Her grandfather Lucius, about four or five members of the Rufus Saxton GAR post, her father, and another three men he worked with, had all packed the Robinsons' parlor and spilled back toward the dining room. Beulah and Alma had put Hannah and Sherman to bed, and then had been sworn to secrecy by the veterans, who were throwing ideas back and forth. Some of these had started back at Camp Lincoln or on the train ride back home. The first Saxton Post meeting since Gettysburg had featured a reading of W.E.B. DuBois' speech from Saturday and more idea swapping.

Alma and Beulah had pitched in the odd thought too while keeping the men in lemonade and iced tea. After much discussion they had agreed: they would target the streetcar benches over in Greene Square on the east side. If it went well, they would think about Bull Street near where it met Forsyth Park. The younger men would bring various tools from their work sites. The oldsters would "go on scout" as they put it, and provide reconnaissance, time the interval between streetcars, and otherwise act as both lookouts – "picket duty" was their term – and as distractions. They would start about ten o'clock this Sunday night.

After breakfast at the Thompson house, Lee left for work and Zachariah was bumping around in his room. Alma was drying dishes in the kitchen as Emily came in for something. "You seem rather perky today, Alma. Anything to account for the liveliness?"

Before Alma could answer, Emily cocked her head. She heard humming, very musical, coming from somewhere, followed by a knock at the back door. Emily was right by it and said, "I'll get it." She looked through the window at an old, bearded black man with crinkly humor lines at his eyes. She wondered, because he was nicely dressed rather than in work clothes. She pulled the door open a few inches and said, "Is there something I can do for you?" The humming stopped.

The man looked down, fidgeted with his hat and said softly, "Uh, yes, ma'am. I'm here to see Mistah Zachariah Hampton, iffin' he's at home."

Surprised, Emily stuttered, "Wait here. I'll see." Shaking her head, she closed the door, rounded the high cupboard, and knocked on Zachariah's door.

"Daddy?" she called. Zachariah pulled his door open. "There's someone at the back door, asking for you special," Emily said. "Did you hire a darkie for some odd job?"

Zachariah came out, pulling his suspenders over his shoulders. "No, I didn't." Emily stood aside as he swung around to the back door and pulled it ajar. With a breaking smile, he pulled it open and said, "Lucius! Well, bless your heart! Come in, come in. Don't jes' stand there."

Alma's eyes danced, and she fought to suppress a grin as she looked back and forth between Emily and her grandfather. It was hard telling which of the two was more surprised by Zachariah's obvious enthusiasm. Emily took the lead as Zachariah said, "Emily, this is Lucius Robinson. He's the Savannah man I told you 'bout from the Encampment."

"From, from the Encampment?" she stammered, her mind reeling. "But you never mentioned he was a c...I mean, he was a Camp Lincoln man."

Zachariah blinked and thought a moment. "No, I don't s'pose I did. I guess lookin' back on it, that didn't matta none."

Now Emily blinked as Zachariah fumbled about saying, "My manners, my manners." With fair pride he said, "Lucius, this is my daughter, Miz Emily Thompson. She is the wife o' Lee Thompson, who is the assistant city engineer for Savannah."

Lucius clutched his hat and nodded, viewing the toe of Emily's left shoe just peeping out from under the skirt hem. "Pleased to meet you, ma'am." Something about Lucius' toe-look on Emily bothered Zack, though he couldn't say why.

Emily managed to sputter, "Likewise, I'm sure." She sat down gratefully at the table while looking puzzlement at her father. Puzzled blossomed to stunned as Zachariah put his hand out and said, "Say, I'm pleased as punch you came bah today, Lucius." She looked on woodenly as a black man took and shook her father's hand, the one he'd held out first. This just wasn't done between the races, not like that. Behind Emily, the grin broke full strength across Alma's face as the two gents pumped hands.

The two old vets were nearly photographic copies of each other, one a print and one a negative: opposite colors, but within an inch of the same height, paunch, beard trim, and thinning on the head top. The contrast came in the faces: wavy eyebrows vs. curly, hawk beak nose vs. flat equilateral triangle.

Zachariah said, "Alma, do we have any coffee left from breakfast?" She answered with an inner satisfaction, "Yes, Mistah Hampton."

"Well, Lucius an' me'll both take a cup in mah room." He gestured toward his door. "C'mon in here, Lucius. Let's swap some more stories and have a game o' brag, jes' like at Gettysburg." The two old men passed into Zachariah's quarters. Emily hadn't moved. Alma asked, "Miz Emily, are you feelin' all ratt?"

She nodded and said in a pale voice, "I'm fine. Never better." Alma shrugged and carried in two mugs of steaming coffee on a small tray.

"Thank you, Alma," Zachariah said, then asked Lucius, "I like it black, but would you want cream or sugah?"

"No, black's fine by me." He winked. "Hepps me keep my color."

Zachariah stared at him, then they both burst out laughing. Zack said to Alma, "That'll hold us fo' now."

Alma did a little bob of a curtsey saying, "Yes, suh, Mistah Hampton." Then she bent a servant rule by patting Lucius on the shoulder and adding, "Grampa." She closed the door behind her as she went back into the kitchen.

Zachariah took a beat to register Alma's words. "That's ratt. Alma's yo' granddaughter ain't she?"

"Yep, she is."

"Well now, fill me in on yo' family, like Alma an' such."

Emily was still sitting like a statue at the kitchen table and could hear muffled conversation, even laughter, coming from the back room. As Alma put down her tray, Emily looked up at her. "What cups did you use for their coffee?"

"Why, two of those matching ones we use for house guests, Miz Emily."

Emily said with annoyance, "The matching ones? For Daddy, of course, but we've got some of those enameled tin ones good enough for tradesmen."

"Mr. Robinson," Alma said evenly, using the title deliberately, "is not here as a tradesman, but as a guest. I served him with guest china."

"Well now, just..." Emily began, but then broke off, searching Alma's face and finding a certain determination there, mixed with...what? Oddly enough it seemed mixed with sympathy as Alma said, "He's a guest under our roof, talkin' man to man with Mistah Hampton. Color don't make no difference; he's our guest."

"But color does matter," Emily said defensively, her annoyance back.

"Why should it, Miz Emily? Iffin' you been done ratt or been done wrong in yo' life I 'magine it's been done by both colors. People are people, good 'n bad."

Emily raised a finger to interrupt but Alma went on. "Cain't say all the good is in one color and all the bad is in another color. Otherwise why would white folk need to go to church? If all the good was in them, they wouldn't need it now would they?"

Emily found swallowing difficult. Her mind flitted across her memories as she felt the weight of Alma's words. Under those words, she could feel other ideas and assumptions cracking. Much of what she had been taught about life as a Southern lady was suddenly ringing false.

Still pondering, she stood up, moved over to a cupboard and pulled out a mug that matched the two in the back room. She paused a moment, then pulled out another one and set them both on the table. A thoughtful half-smile crossed her face as she said, "Alma, would you pour me a cup; black, please? And then, if you'd like to pour one for yourself and take a break, go ahead."

Alma gave a perfect curtsey, poured and said very humbly, "Thank you, ma'am. I'll have mine on the back porch."

"And I'll have mine on the front porch." She raised her mug toward Alma. "And it really is good coffee. Thinking coffee."

Lucius left around midmorning. He went out the back door and across the yard to the alley as was his habit from walking Alma to work. But today he paused, mulling over something. This first block of his usual back alley route toward Fahm Street had several colored faces moving here just now, but no white ones. Indeed, white faces in the alleys were rare, usually seen bringing garbage cans out on pickup days at servantless homes. Lucius shook his head and an old determination settled on his face as he turned the other way in the alley to come around onto Tattnall Street.

Zachariah found Emily on the front porch glider. She had her eyes closed, enjoying a cool northern wind. An empty coffee mug perched on the little table beside her.

"Yankee breeze feels nice today, don't it?" he said as he dropped into his rocker, a few sheets of paper in his hand. She opened her eyes and smiled.

"Yes it does, Daddy. Say, did you and that Lucius..." she almost said 'boy' but something left from Alma stopped her, "... have a good visit?"

"Well, fo' as long as it went, we sure did."

"Seems like it went about two hours, Daddy."

Zachariah reached out his railroad pocket watch. "Dad gum yo' ratt. It *was* two hours. Seemed like 'bout ten minutes."

Emily then saw something rare in the Tattnall Street neighborhood. A colored man was walking up the sidewalk. Not only was he colored – and nicely dressed for a workman – but he noticeably didn't shuffle with his head hung down. He walked like Lee or the neighbor men walked to and from work. Indeed, as he passed their gate, he looked over to the porch, tipped his hat and smiled. Emily saw these were directed to…to her father, who nodded and gave a half wave back.

Emily's mind snapped from seeing "just another black man" to recognizing Lucius and some of her earlier fluster from Lucius' arrival returned. She worked the idea of a colored man in her home as a guest, her father's guest. She looked at Zachariah closely and wondered. Whatever energy he'd acquired at Gettysburg was still running strong two weeks later. He hadn't looked this lively in years. She was surprised to find herself actually hoping Lucius' visit today would be a first visit, the beginning of others. "You know, Daddy, that Encampment at Gettysburg has done you good. Vitalized you."

Zachariah stared off after Lucius' retreating form. "Yes, it has. I haven't felt this young in a coon's age. Meetin' all the old boys in both camps, gabbin' with the blue bellies." He looked at her. "I was hopin' every day would go on forever." Emily was surprised by a tear on her cheek. "I haven't felt the need for mah flask the way I did and I'm sleepin' bettah too. My dreamin's mo' peaceful." He drifted off for a moment, then recovered. "Say honeybunch, remember I told you 'bout that Calvin Salisbury from Vermont?"

"Oh, about ten times a day," she smiled back.

He looked up sharply at her and saw the teasing dancing in her eyes. He guffawed and then said, "Well, Lucius had a letter here from him to us both an' left it with me, along with a pencil sketch of him from fifty years back. We put together an answer, but neither Lucius or me can write worth a dang. Could I ask you to copy over our lettah in yo' nice handwritin'? That way Calvin an' Eleanor could leastwise read it."

Emily sat up. "I'd be delighted to Daddy. I'll do it right now. No wait. Let's do it together. I'll need you to explain some of your hen-scratches," and Zack grinned at her. She rose and passed through the front door as Zachariah trailed behind.

Friday, July 25, 1913

Rutland

"He did it!" Calvin exclaimed, slapping down the *Rutland Herald* and throwing back his head laughing.

"Who did what?" Ellie asked, sipping her coffee and enjoying this free-spirited Calvin.

"Oliver Tate, that's who." He turned the paper around and showed Ellie the picture of an old Union veteran with a droopy white moustache and a very long chin.

"Oliver Tate's a Pennsylvania vet supposedly bedridden. He wanted to go to the Encampment, but both his family and his doctor said no. He secretly packed his bag and at midnight climbed out his window in his nightshirt, went down to the railyard, and hopped a boxcar. In the morning he got dressed, walked into the depot, and rode the rest of the way on his veteran's pass." He laughed again. "The whole family came after him, about a dozen – and his doctor. Tate dodged them all week, apparently living at Camp Lincoln. There were wanted posters around town, guardsmen and constables searched tents, and the family bought an ad in the *Gettysburg Star* begging him to give up. On Sunday he marched right past them and caught the train home. He was waiting for them on the front porch when they came later." He positively giggled. "He had to wait there because he'd forgotten his key."

"What a determined man," Ellie said, chuckling and shaking her head in wonder.

Calvin scanned the article and quoted, "...so strongly did the bugles of Gettysburg call."

"Did he say why he risked it given his health?"

"He said, 'If I'm going to die, then at Gettysburg among my comrades is where I want to die. And if I hadn't gone I would certainly have died; died of a broken heart for having missed it.'" His eyes went misty and Eleanor squeezed his hand. He pulled himself together and saw another article.

"Say, Ellie, here's something we really should take in," he said as Eleanor spread orange marmalade on a slice of her toast.

Mr. Thomas Boyle, manager of the Paramount Theater, invites the public to a performance of popular and classical selections as sung by

Marian Anderson of Philadelphia. Miss Anderson's voice has been called a wonder of the age by her teacher, the great Guiseppe Boghetti. Sunday, August 24th at 2:00 p.m. and 7:00 p.m. Tickets between 25 cents for the top balcony to $2.00 for the dress circle.

"That sounds wonderful, Calvin. Let's go." Ellie swallowed a corner of her toast. "You know, you usually aren't excited about concerts."

Calvin stopped short, embarrassed. Ellie guessed the reason and smiled. "It's all right Calvin, I like it. I'm just wondering."

"Well, you'd be surprised. At Camp Lincoln you could hear men saying, 'Marian this' or 'Marian Anderson that' about every minute. Seems she sang there earlier in the week. Ellie, some of those men really knew music, but when they talked about Marian they looked like they'd seen" – his eye twinkled – "a real huckleberry above a persimmon!"

Ellie stared. "'A huckleberry above a persimmon?' That phrase might stump Mark Twain. What on earth does it mean?"

Calvin grinned. "Those Southerners can really turn a phrase now and again. 'Huckleberry above a persimmon' is saying something is very good, or improving."

Ellie sipped her coffee. "What else did those men teach you?"

Calvin reached over to Ellie's plate with some of his toast and wiped up a few drops of marmalade. "Thanks for lettin' me wallop my dodger, cher bebè." Ellie giggled as he went on. "You should get out a spider and cook up some pone and chicken bosom so we can grab a root. Don't forget Lot's wife and a horn on the table."

"All right, Mr. Bigwig, what in the world did you just say?"

"If I learned it right, I just thanked you for letting me wipe up some jam or gravy with my piece of bread. 'Cher bebè' is your sweetheart." Ellie blushed. "Then I said you should use a frying pan to make cornbread and white meat chicken for our meal. The table should have salt and a glass of ale or liquor."

"My stars and garters!" Eleanor exclaimed, laughing all the while. "Or as Sam might put it from his Western days, 'well, slap my chaps and call me cowboy.'" Calvin laughed until his ribs ached. "Wallop your dodger," she giggled to him. "Grab a root," he chuckled back. Finally the laughter played itself out and Calvin finished his last swig of coffee. He stood and began clearing his dishes. He bent his legs into a half-hoop like he'd been three days in the saddle and walked in a stiff bowleg toward the kitchen. He growled at Eleanor over his shoulder, "Thankee ma'am for my vittles. Got any ropin' that needs doin'?"

Eleanor burst out all over again, then collected herself, sprang up and caught up to him at the sink, wrapped her arms around him from behind, and gave him a big squeeze. Then she turned him around in her arms and said playfully, "I'm glad I roped you, mister, back in '59!" and gave him a big kiss.

He gave her a long kiss back and held her. Finally she put her hand on his cheek and whispered in his ear, "Thank you for loving me. I'll look forward to tonight all day." Calvin blushed and inhaled sharply. Then he whispered back, "Now I will too."

He gave her one more long squeeze and she let him go. Calvin collected his hat and cane and Ellie gave him a goodbye peck on the cheek. "Greet Sam for me."

"Ayup," Calvin promised. "If Tom Boyle's there this morning I'll see if he has some tickets with him. Otherwise, I'll swing by the Paramount box office. Do we need anything else from Merchant's Row?"

"Not really," Ellie returned. "See you, and smell you, Mr. Bay Rum, when you get back." Her eyes twinkled. "Going shank's mare is good for your circulation."

Calvin grinned back and said, "Yes, I'll be walking." He started his Saturday stroll to the barbershop.

Ellie sat down with another cup of coffee and idly scanned the paper. Next to Marian Anderson's concert announcement and various local stories, her eye fell on a short story that left her thinking.

> *Mr. Thomas Ince of California announced his film*, A New Birth of Freedom, *is on schedule. Financing the longest motion picture ever created had proved difficult but Mr. Ince has found backers. Mr. D.W. Griffith's effort*, Birth of a Nation, *based on a Southern book*, The Klansman, *has been suspended yet again while he searches for moneyed men. In the race to be first between these two "picture makers" Mr. Ince has overcome Mr. Griffith's early lead.*

Down at Randolph's barbershop, Sam and Tom were at the checkerboard, but they were more listening than playing. The door was propped open for extra air, so when Calvin arrived, he walked into a conversation. Mr. Tom Boyle, manager of the Paramount Theater, and Josiah Trimble stood opposite the barber's chair by the wall with the coat hooks. Josiah was reaching into his breast pocket for his wallet. Tom was doing the same, only his jacket was on a wall hook and the barber's sheet was still draped from his neck and his hair was half cut. Randolph looked a bit miffed; he wasn't used to his customers getting out of the chair partway through a job.

"I've got sayveral with me," Boyle said with his Irish brogue, "both in the balcony and on the main floor," which sounded like "flahr" to Calvin's Vermont ear.

"Now, tell me again who took some blocks of tickets?" Josiah asked.

"Well, it was the Reverend Homer Stanton from West Rootland, who took maybe a thard of the balcony for both shows. And Father Mason from St. John's took a few fistfuls for the Knights of Coloombus."

"Hmph," Josiah grumped. "Well, with Stanton's emancipated crowd and all those mabble workers from Italy and Ireland counting their rosary beads with Fathah Mason, the balcony just won't do. Oh, hello Calvin," Josiah nodded politely, the sheen and scent of Brilliantine rolling toward where hat, coat, and cane were going up onto the usual third wall hook. Trimble studied the tickets Boyle was holding and scratched his beard on the backhand.

"Mannin' Josiah," Calvin answered back. "Sounds like a show at the Paramount."

"Ay sorr," Boyle nodded, sensing another possible sale. Randolph sighed while Tom and Sam grinned. "Miss Marian Anderson is coming to sing on August 24th."

"Ayup, I saw the story in the *Herald*."

Josiah cleared his throat. "All right, I'll take these two here. Main floor in this row." He handed over some bills and coins.

"Of course, sorr, Thank you. I'm shore you'll like the seats and the music."

"Hmph," Josiah nodded. He topped himself with his bowler and left. Randolph pivoted the big chair invitingly toward Boyle, but then Calvin said, "Can I see what you might have in the balcony?" Randolph rolled his eyes, propped an elbow on the top of the chair, put his chin in his hand, and sighed.

Calvin really liked some seats in the second row of the balcony, center section, but they were part of a block of four, and Boyle didn't want to break up the block. While they were in this snag, Sam left the checkerboard. He moved up next to Calvin and said, "Listen. If it will help, Mr. Boyle, sell Calvin the two tickets he wants and I'll take the other two in that block." He dug into his pocket for the money. Calvin looked at him sidelong. His look turned to amazement as Sam said, "I've written to Anna Louise McCloud already, asking her to visit that weekend from Montpelier. I haven't heard back yet, but if she agrees, could she stay with you and Eleanor? I know it's imposing and I hadn't said anything to you yet, but…"

"Not at all," Calvin exclaimed, as both he and Sam paid Boyle and got the tickets. "If she comes, of course, she can stay with us. Eleanor will be delighted." He stared at Sam and added, "And so will you. Well! I never thought I'd see the day."

Randolph rolled his eyes toward the three of them and then said to Tom at the checkerboard, "I'm never going to see the day when I finish these haircuts, am I?"

Back at the Salisburys' house on East Washington, a pair of tickets to the Paramount Theater lay unnoticed on the little table in the front hall. Calvin and Sam sat glumly on the parlor settee, the excitement from Sam's news gone like a popped balloon. Eleanor finished a second reading through the crabbed handwriting of a letter. She had tried several phrases out loud for their meaning, and the men had agreed with her understanding. She sat staring a long moment, then looked at the envelope.

"How do you know this man, Sam?"

"When we arrived at Gettysburg, I got off the train just behind Josiah into a huge crowd on the platform. That Lieutenant Kelly saw us get off together and buttonholed me as soon as he could. I asked him to investigate when he got back home and gave him my address. That's his answer."

"It makes no sense," Eleanor protested. "Josiah left the army so he could marry Abigail. Why would Lieutenant Kelly claim he re-enlisted? And in Albany, not here in Rutland?"

Calvin shook his head. "The best possible way to look at it is that Josiah was willing to serve but he didn't want to with our regiment. Men did that sometimes, thinking some other regiment was harder fighting..."

"...harder drinking..." Sam said ruefully, and Eleanor gave a quick smile.

"...more glamorous or had better officers. Sometimes the bounties were better in another state or town. Or sometimes a man had made enemies with his mates – cheating at cards, running away from battle, stealing."

"Sometimes men wouldn't want someone around because a man would always find ways to shirk picket duty, stretcher carrying, or grave digging," Sam added. "No one liked those orders, but everyone else did their manly duty when their turn came up."

Eleanor looked back and forth between them and heard their heavy sighing. "It must be awful for you to find Josiah joining another regiment. Do you think he did it for glory in..." she glanced at the letter's first page, "...the 91st New York? Or the bounty? Were there hard feelings among the Rutland men?"

The men shook their heads. Lunch was mostly a dull affair except when talk turned to Anna Louise's visit and Marian Anderson's concert.

Monday, July 28, 1913

Rutland

"Judge Salisbury. I haven't seen you down here since Election Day." Calvin smiled at Tom Cockburn's greeting. It was Monday morning in the public records room at the courthouse.

"No real need, Tom, since I stopped sending you case rulings and filings."

"So what brings you here on this steamy morning?"

"Well, I need to verify something in my brother Michael's property and our mother's property while I was in the army. Can I have the property tax rolls for 1864?"

Tom put down his mug of tea and lugged a large, black leather-bound ledger from its shelf over to a tall, slant-topped desk where patrons could read standing up. "Here you go, Calvin. This is the whole decade, 1860-1869."

"Thank you, Tom."

"Take your time," Tom said with a wave as Calvin took out a pencil and a couple sheets of paper. Court clerks and lawyers came and went, dropping off and picking up various papers, keeping Tom busy. Calvin wrote industriously and flipped certain pages containing the name "Trimble" back and forth for the next half hour.

Savannah

Not long after Lee had left for work Monday morning, Zachariah and Emily were in the kitchen with the *Savannah Tribune* on the table. Zack stretched and mentioned, "Won't be long now before Lucius gets here."

"You mean he's coming by for another chat?" Emily exclaimed. "I declare this will be his fourth visit in less than three weeks. What on earth do you two still have left to talk about?"

"Oh, still lots of old soldier stories left to go. And if we run out of those, we can always start jawin' 'bout the news here in Savannah," he said, gesturing toward the paper. "Mebbe try and figure out what's all the fuss about the streetcar benches."

"Now that's worth talking about, more so than Lookout Mountain or Sharpsburg. This is the fourth time folks have woken up to find the white benches and colored benches switched at a stop." Emily broke off as her father burst out laughing and slapped the counter. She finished gamely, "Whoever is doing it has to have some special tools to unbolt them from the pavement. Somebody is...is...what is it?"

He was still giggling as he said, "You jes' said folks have woken up to find the benches switched. Bob Bidwell told me the other day Dooley Culpepper was coming home real late one night from tying one on and sat down on a bench to wait for the streetcar. He laid down and went to sleep. He woke up to find hisself on a bench that had been carried right into the bushes near Forsyth Park." He chuckled once more. "He woke up at dawn and didn't know where he was. When he sat up, since it was one of the colored benches, a big old splinter went right up into his, um, well, his sittin' part!"

Emily smiled despite her effort to remain ladylike. She said in a low, almost conspiratorial voice, "Couldn't have happened to a better fellow."

Zack threw back his head gleefully and slapped the counter again. "That's what makes it so funny," and Emily agreed by joining in his laugh. They were just recovering when a knock came from the kitchen door. Zack ambled over and pulled open the door. "Hiya Lucius, come in. Come in."

"Yes, suh, Zach'riah. You're in a hearty mood today. Mawnin' Miz Emily," he said with a nod, but his eyes only went partway down to her toe. "You sound like you've caught the giggle bug from Zack here."

"Good mawnin', Lucius," Emily returned. "Daddy and I were just chuckling over some of the silliness going on with the streetcar benches being switched around between white and colored."

"Izzat ratt?" Lucius said, putting on his own smile. "Makin' folks talk about it, that's fo' sure."

"Anything like it happening on the west side that you heard tell of?" Zachariah wondered.

"Oh, I heard a couple of 'em being switched on Bay Street and somethin' 'bout it ovah by Telfair Hospital. But mostly seems like it's in a lot of the old squares."

"Why do you think someone's doing it?" Emily asked. "Is it some sort of game? A prank?"

Lucius looked like he was thinking a moment, then said, "I s'pose it's a way of turnin' the Supreme Cote's separate but equal rule upside down. Like maybe iffin' white folk thought 'bout it fo' a minute they'd see it wasn't equal, or iffin' they'd sit on 'em they'd *feel* how they ain't equal."

Emily and Zachariah passed a look between them, their eyes giggling at the thought of Dooley, but thoughtful, too, at Lucius' words. Then Zack said, "Well now enough o' this standin' around. C'mon in my room. Let's sit and be comfortable."

Lucius moved toward Zachariah's door and Emily turned to go up the hall. She stopped short when Zachariah said, "You too, honeybunch. C'mon in and sit a spell."

Both Lucius and Emily looked at him in surprise, but he was so earnest that they both passed into Zack's quarters. Zachariah carried in a kitchen chair.

Zachariah perched on his bed, Lucius sat in the ladderback kitchen chair, and Emily shifted uneasily in the horsehair armchair.

"Well, uh, Lucius, talking with Daddy must give you a different view on the War," Emily stammered. Social conversation with a black man was still a challenge to her.

"Uh, why, yes, ma'am," Lucius returned. "You hear a lot 'bout the War in all the speech-makin', but a soldier's side counts too. We figured out officers is officers in any army, an' iffn' somebody was a civilian skunk they'd probably be an army skunk too."

"Mostly," Zachariah put in, "but not ever' time. Some fellas actually improved, but others jes' got skunkier than ever."

"Once a bully, always a bully," Lucius said.

"Like that Gettysburg constable 'til Calvin fixed his flint."

"Oh, I loved that story!" Emily said, clapping her hands. "It's wonderful hearing about a bully put in his place. Goes to show even Yankees can do the ratt thing now and again."

Zachariah smiled at her. "That Calvin is a good man."

"Oh, come now, Daddy. You goin' soft on those northern boys? 'Specially a genuine New England Yankee?"

"I ain't goin' soft, but Calvin's of the fust water."

"Salt of the earth," Lucius echoed.

"Gracious! He must be quite a man if a Confederate and, ah, an Ethiopian both vouch for him." Emily said this lightheartedly, but was impressed. "What did he do after the War?"

"He was a judge thar in Rutland fo' over thirty years," Zachariah answered. "I think he'd run a coteroom evenhanded, but with no nonsense."

"That's it 'zackly," Lucius added. "You could tell he wouldn't let no slicked-down lawyer or high-nosed bully cut shines in his cote."

Emily was torn, enjoying the conversation, yet feeling awkward. "Well, Daddy, you two are probably hoping every day" – father and daughter passed a warm look – "will be like Gettysburg, talking man to man and" – giving Lucius an odd look – "soldier to soldier and I'm just feeling in the way. I'll go write some letters." She rose and both men rose in reply. "And you two just chat away."

Lucius winked at Zachariah and said to Emily, "Yes, ma'am. Slinging the knapsack for a new field are you?"

She couldn't help but smile at him from the doorway and then showed she'd been listening. "I'll leave you two in high feather, then."

She wasn't quite out of earshot when Lucius said, "She's quite a daughter, Zachariah. I like her fire. She puts me in mind o' one of them Pote Royal women settlin' a bully's hash."

Emily just caught this and curiosity gripped her. She saw Alma through the front door window sweeping the front porch. Although it wasn't polite, she tiptoed back across the kitchen.

"There was a hard-case corp'ral, Fletcher by name, who musta spent his life pushin' folks 'round."

"I know the kind," Zachariah nodded.

"He was a tall, fleshy fella with a big mouth an' a big fist. One evenin' he and three privates got corned on some high-proof applejack. They wandered over to the colored part o' the settlement and decided beatin' a colored man would be fun."

In the kitchen Emily cringed at the soldiers' idea of "fun."

"They cornered Ezekiel Adams in a barn stall. One man with a pistol held us off. The other three took turns cussin' and beatin' Ezekiel. One o' the chillun ran to get hepp at the house where the lady teachers all lived. It was 'bout sundown an' the ladies was jes' arrivin' from a ride."

"They'd been out in a carriage?" asked Zachariah.

"Nope," Lucius came back. "Them abolitionist ladies was each a hosswoman. No side saddle neither. They had them ridin' skirts, boots, gloves, the whole habit, an' they could fork a hoss better'n a lotta men."

"Hoowee!" Zachariah exclaimed. Emily was taken aback at the alarming feminism.

"Anyhow, jes' after Miz Annleez tied off her hoss, Lilly comes runnin' up callin', 'Hepp, hepp. Soldiers in the barn are hurtin' Ezekiel.' Miz Amanda called down from her saddle, 'Confederate soldiers?' An' Lilly says, 'No, no. It's some blue soldiers hurtin' Ezekiel.' Then Miz Amanda said, 'I'll ride and get Colonel Higginson. Eleanor, go find the captain of the provost guard. Anna Louise, you go with Lilly and see if you can get them to stop. Tell them the officers are coming.'

"So Miz Eleanor an' Miz Amanda rode off at a canter an' Miz Annleez footed it after Lilly. On the way, she poked her head in the doctor's tent but he wasn't there so she borrowed the major's sword. When she got in the barn, ratt off the reel she marched up to the soljah holdin' the pistol, looked ratt in the muzzle an' said, 'Either shoot me right now, or stand aside.' His eyes bugged out an' she jes' slapped the pistol outta her face. He stumbled left an' Hosea the blacksmith grabbed him, an' I pried the pistol outta his hand."

"He weren't gonna shoot a woman, I reckon," Zachariah remarked.

"I reckon," Lucius reflected, "her bein' a watt woman." Emily marveled at "Miz AnnLeeze's" pluck, but caught the fear too. If the white teacher had been a black woman...

"I finally gots the pistol loose an' was gonna stop the corp'ral, but there was no need. Miz Annleez saw how bad off Ezekiel was an' she looked sick fo' a minute. Then she bit the bullet an' looked real steel-eyed, like Miz Emily does now and again."

"I know that look." Zack nodded while Emily blushed. "Emily gets it from her mother."

"An' her father too, I think," Lucius returned. Zachariah gave an eyebrow salute.

"Well, in the stall, all three men had their backs to her, a private each holdin' Ezekiel's arms an' the corp'ral in the middle jes' givin' him licks. She swung the sword by the flat and whacked the left man in the pants like he was a rug on the line fo' spring cleanin'. He gave out a 'yeow' an' let go with both hands up. Two friends, Davey an' Joshua, had worked their way into the next stall hopin' to hepp. They grabbed that fella's arms and dragged him over the stall wall.

"The private on the ratt heard the yell and seed the sword, so he let go an' tried runnin' away befo' Miz Annleez could reload. He got outta the stall, but I tripped him flat. 'Bout three women, includin' Mary, jes' sat down on him."

Zachariah was puzzled. "Who's Mary?"

Lucius grinned. "Mary was 'bout five foot four tall... an' same wide."

Emily winced a smile while Zachariah hooted. "Oo, that'd smart. An' smell too, down on a stable floor."

"Well, corp'ral Fletcha turned roun' an' was lookin' at the business end o' Miz Annleez's sword. But he was so shot in the neck an' such a mean cuss he didn't want his 'fun' with Ezekiel to end.

"'You leave him be, corporal,' said Miz Annleez, with real pepper. We all admired her cheek, but we were 'fraid fo' her too, sayin', 'Careful, Miz Annleez' an' 'Watch out, Miz Annleez.'

"He made to grab the sword from the side or maybe even grab her, but she was quick as a squirrel in a tree. She hopped back a few steps an' he grabbed air. Then he gave her a bad-eye an' snarled, 'Ain't no nigga-lovin' schoolmarm gonna teach me nuthin.' He made like he was gonna turn an' start beatin' on Ezekiel again.

"Then Miz Annleez turned sideways, put her one hand on her hip, pointed the sword and said, 'If I can't teach you a lesson, then this sword will.' Then she stepped toward him and flicked her wrist like lightnin'. The sword done whacked his left arm on his corporal stripes. Then she stepped back with the point back in front o' him."

"Did she cut him?" Zachariah asked.

"Naw," Lucius drawled, "she twisted her wrist some way so she only hit him with the flat or the back edge."

"Hmm. Corp'rul got lucky. Did that whack stop him?"

"Well, it musta hurt 'cause he said 'ouch' real loud. Then he made fists and danced back an' forth, tryin' to get past the sword point. Then he swung at Miz Annleez like he was throwin' a rock."

Emily swallowed hard at the thought of a drunken, burly soldier attacking a woman.

"I think he was tryin' to knock the sword from her or maybe tryin' to knock her down, but she was too quick. She put the sword straight up in the air so the sword bell by her hand went ratt up to Fletcha's fist cummin' down so he crashed his knuckles. Then she said, 'Hah!' and lickety-split turned her wrist. The blade came down over his fist and gave him a snappin' whack on his ratt shoulder.

"Ever'body in the barn gives off a hoot an' a cheer. Somebody called out with sugar, 'Watch out there, corp'ral.' Lilly an' the chillun was clappin'. Hosea says to the pistol man he was holdin', 'Ain't you glad you stepped aside fo' the lady?'"

"Still didn't cut him?"

"Zachariah, iffin' she'd wanted to, I think the corp'ral woulda been missin' both arms by now." Zachariah gulped. Emily felt the hairs stand up on the back of her neck.

"He yelped like a dog hit by a rock an' turned away, rubbin' an' shakin' his fist. Miz Annleez stood her ground. 'Bout then, Miz Amanda an' Colonel Higginson came in the barn, an' so did Miz Eleanor an' the provost cap'n an' some guard troops. They'd all been down at the stockade settlin' the hash of some other men that'd been hittin' the joy juice.

"Ezekiel, layin' there in the straw, groaned an' Fletcha shuffled his feet like he's was fixin' to give a kick. Miz Annleez minced forward again an' gave him two licks, one ratt on his rear an' then circled the sword an' pinked him jes' over the knee. Then she skittered back like a frisky filly."

Zachariah slapped his knee exclaiming, "Jes' like the Bible says! She 'smote him hip and thigh.'"

Lucius blinked.

"Yo' ratt. Never thought of it like that, but yo' ratt. That's it 'zackly!"

"So then the colonel lowered the boom on ever'body?"

"Not quite yet."

"Do tell!"

"Well, I think the colonel was 'bout to when Fletcha jes' lost his head, put up his dukes, an' gave out a wildcat screech. He comes chargin' through the stall, fists flyin' an' all that fleshy body was gonna' run over ever'body. But

Miz Annleez did a dainty little two step left, swung the sword point past her feet, an' turned. As Fletcha went by, the sword came up an' round in a big circle an' walloped him on the back of the neck. Knocked the spots off him and he went down in a heap in fronta the colonel."

"Met his Waterloo," Zachariah snorted.

Lucius chuckled. "The colonel toed him over an' he looked up to see the colonel lookin' down an' the point o' the sword floatin' over his chin, 'cause Miz Annleez was still on picket duty."

Zachariah roared at the image, and fortunately this covered Emily's giggling from the kitchen or she would have been caught. She fled on tiptoe to the parlor where she could laugh unrestrained.

"Well, the colonel ordered the camp doctor to take care o' Ezekiel. Then he put the fo' soljahs under arrest.

"Miz Eleanor says, 'Anna Louise, are you all right? You could have been hurt.' Miz Annleez was fine. Then with her eyes smilin', real careful-like she gives the sword to the doctor sayin', "Major, I borrowed your sword. It's so unladylike for a woman to touch one, don't you agree?' We all had a big hee-haw at that, an' then Miz Amanda asked, 'Anna Louise, where in the world did you learn how?'

She said, 'My grandfather is from Tartwo in Russia. He was a master of sword for the czar's army before he migrated. He and my grandmother lived with us. When my brothers wanted to learn swords, I did too. My grandmother would try to scold my grandfather sayin', 'Gunnar, a girl doesn't need to know swords.' And he would always say, 'Vera, she wants to learn, she's a natural, and a girl might need to know as much as a man.'"

Zachariah pondered. "Sounds like she learned ratt well."

Lucius guffawed. "Corp'ral Fletcha sure thought so."

Zachariah toasted his iced tea. "To bullies gettin' their comeuppance." Lucius clinked his glass in salute.

"Amen!"

Saturday, August 2, 1913

Savannah

Saturday was always busy at the farmer's market on Franklin Square. The square's city benches, marked "Whites Only" or "Colored Only," were in full use as people posted family members, reworked their bundles and packages, waited for streetcars, or just took a breather.

Beulah bought fruits, eggs, vegetables, and the like at various stalls. Hannah or Sherman carried the goods to Lucius, watching over a growing pile of brown paper bags. He was perched on a whitewashed pew square in front of the Second African Baptist Church. The pew was the only sitting spot without a segregation sign.

When Savannah began segregating public facilities, the church put this old pew out on the sidewalk with a sign "Sinners Welcome." All Savannah had followed the court case before Judge Crawford. Colored attorney Mr. James Napier of Nashville had argued the congregation's original deed and survey from 1802 included the land that became a sidewalk. Next, the congregation built a brick sidewalk on its property long before the city even regulated wooden sidewalks connecting shop porches. When the city started paying for sidewalks and benches, the church declined both. For the city to tell a church what to do with its property on its property would be unconstitutional, Napier concluded. After a couple days, Crawford ignored the constitutional issue but found for the church based on property rights.

Lucius was humming a hymn in honor of the pew, reading today's *Savannah Colored Tribune.* A fiery editorial attacked D.W. Griffith for making a film based on Dixon's outrageous book, *The Klansman.* Editor Johnson saw the hand of the Almighty in Griffith's money problems and Thomas Ince's progress with *A New Birth of Freedom.*

Lucius looked up idly and thought he saw a familiar face over by the peach bin. Yes, it *was* Alma was carefully pressing peaches for ripeness. But if Alma were here, instead of at the Thompsons'....

"Why, hello, Lucius," came a voice from his right. He came to his feet smiling, holding out his hand. "Mawnin', Mistah Hampton," he said, observing the public black-white conventions: stand in the presence, eyes mostly down, title, never a first name, offer the hand first and wait to see if it would be taken.

Zachariah shook hands and plopped down saying, "Oh, sit down, sit down." He stretched out and crossed his legs. "You know, I think this pew sits bettah than the city benches."

"Yes, suh," Lucius ventured. "Ain't mass produced. Seat was spoke-shaved so it cups a… a body."

"Sits powerful comfortable," Zachariah agreed. They both watched the scene and the scene watched them. Despite the pew's welcome to both races, usually only colored folks sat here, and mixing was rare.

Zachariah offered, "Leastwise the benches on this square have stayed white and colored. Might be too busy for whoever's doin' the switchin' to try it here."

"Reckon' you're right," Lucius came back, "but they keep gettin' switched ever'where else."

"Got that ratt. Po-leese are stumped and the mayor is gettin' an earful from white folk, both 'cause you don't know what bench to use and 'cause the city has to spend money for city workers to switch 'em back."

"Might cost a lot less in tax money and in aggravation jes' to take down the white and colored signs." Zachariah blinked, then stared as Lucius added softly, "In Gettysburg town and Camp Lincoln ever'body stood wherevah they pleased, sat with whomevah they pleased, ate and drank with old friends or new acquaintances."

"But that was up North," Zachariah began, but then stopped, thinking.

Lucius went on. "Only white and colored signs were in Tent City and even there only when some of the U.S. Army soljahs or some o' the hard case Confederates made a big deal 'bout it." He looked Zachariah in the eye. "Did you feel like you needed a bunch of Jim Crow white and colored signs so you could mingle with a 'inferior race'?" Zachariah swallowed hard. Lucius finished, "Or did you mean what you said at the bridge, that it had 'been a real edjication for an old Confed'rit'?"

Both men were quiet in their thoughts a while. Then they looked at each other awkwardly, straining for a safe public topic. "This square's seen some history," Zachariah remarked.

"Sure has," Lucius agreed. "I was here fo' a bit of it."

"Izzat ratt?" Zachariah piped up with interest. "How so?"

"Well, in January 1865, I was ratt over there where them peaches are. Gen'rul Sherman stood ratt behind us on the steps," gesturing with his thumb over his shoulder, "makin' a speech."

"I'll bet there's a tale to that," Zachariah nodded.

"Yep. I was sittin' in camp with friends when this baby-faced Lieutenant Bingham from New Yawk yelled out, 'Sergeant Robinson. Cap'n wants to see all of you right away. Special duty.'"

"Sounds like fun," Zachariah drawled.

"Special duty usually was," Lucius answered and both men chuckled knowingly.

"Well, I gave him a nod," Lucius continued, "an' he got a twisty look on his face. He was one o' them paper-collar Easterners an' a nod wern't a salute. But all he said was, 'Right away, Sergeant.' Since he called me sergeant, I said to him, 'Yes, suh, Lieutenant.' I think he kinda liked that."

Zachariah squinted, remembering. "Lieutenants liked it mo' than most in Lee's army."

Lucius thought out loud, "An' in Meade's and Sherman's army too. What is it 'bout lieutenants?"

"Don't know," Zachariah pondered. "Well, go on."

"Okay. Half the regiment drew twenty rounds and marched in along Bay Street to here. They was no market that day. Lieutenant gave us orders to keep peace around the square, be polite to civilians of both colors, and take no guff off nobody. He even pulled out a piece of paper and said iffin' we needed to we could arrest any man causin' trouble and tell off any woman usin' General Butler's order from the occupation of New Awlins in 1862."

Zachariah stared, remembering the shock that had spread across the South at Butler's infamous directive. "That one aftah Admiral Farragut got ponked by a chamberpot on the street?" he asked.

"The very same," Lucius said with a half-grin, then recited like an old school lesson: "'Any woman who shall show disrespect to the United States' flag or any soldier serving under that flag shall be held liable to be treated as a woman of the town plying her trade.'"

Zachariah whistled in awe as Lucius resumed after a pause. "We spread out 'round the square an' watt and colored folks started commin'. The watt folks didn't like seein' so many coloreds an' the 2nd South Carolina Union was not their favorite reg'mint."

"Quite true. The 8th Georgia would be their favorite." Zachariah preened himself by adjusting his shirt cuffs in a dandy manner. Lucius chuckled.

"Well, there grew a space 'tween watt folk on the south side and black folk on the no'th side."

Zachariah cracked, "Got the directions ratt," and both men grinned.

"But ever' now an' agin' some watt man or woman would see an old house servant or field hand an' they'd meet in the middle."

"What'd they say?"

"Mostly the watt folk would say, 'Come back an' work for me an' I'll pay ya bettah an' treat ya bettah.' Or they'd raise a lamentation, 'I cain't b'lieve you deserted me after all I did fo' ya when you was a slave.'"

"Then the church clock struck ten an' a troop of mounted officers came in ratt over there." Lucius gestured to the southwest corner. "Gen'ral Sherman in full dress marched ratt up the steps here. The drum corps of the army band sounded off a roll ratt here where this pew is.

"Sherman pulled out two sheets of paper and announced, 'People of Savannah and visitors from roundabout. I have two announcements to make. The first is a proclamation by the President of the United States, Abraham Lincoln, effective January first, 1863, or just over two years ago.'"

Zachariah whistled through his teeth. "So that was ratt here where we're sittin'."

"Mm hmm, ratt here," Lucius echoed softly. "He read it through slow, stoppin' after each long piece. Over there on the no'th side a whole lotta preachers was explainin' all the hard words to folks. When Sherman said the line that ended 'henceforward and forever free' there was laughin' and weepin' on the no'th side, an' lotsa folk was doin' both at once. On the south side folks was hangin' their haids, an' some ladies was skeered. One lady's voice said, 'Oh Lawdy, Lawdy. You mean they can go anywhere an' do anythin'? By day or natt? Oh it can't be, it can't be.' Other watt folks called out, 'Save us, save us.'"

Zachariah frowned. "Who were they askin'? Sherman? The Almighty?"

Lucius shrugged in reply, "Don' mattah. Neither one answered 'em."

After digesting this for a moment, Zachariah unknit his brow. "Go on."

"Well, Sherman finished readin' the Proclamation. The band played that hymn that starts off 'Now Thank We All Our God.' Then Sherman said, 'For the President's freedom to mean somethin' every man needs three things: the will to work, a chance to work, and reward for work. Until now the labor of the black race was slave work that unnaturally rewarded white folk. But now, as freemen they will have the chance to earn a free livelihood. So, as General of the Army of the Tennessee I have issued Special Field Order Number 15 for all troops and officers under my command and it affects the civilians in these areas as well.'

"Then he read out the plantations on the islands an' coast would be divvied up into forty-acre plots an' any black family that wanted to farm it could git an' army mule to hepp do it. You shoulda heard this square then," Lucius grinned.

"I'll bet," Zack answered.

"On the north side, folks was cheerin', whistlin', stompin', even dancin'. On the otha side was a wail of lamentation. Old men was sayin', 'No, no it cain't be', an' 'We've come a cropper now'. A lot of the womenfolk were cryin' or fannin' themselves.

"I was standin' ratt 'bout there watchin' the crowd." Lucius pointed to the peach carts. "There was a flock of the carriage trade women an' this one started carryin' on ratt at me. She said, 'What do you know 'bout farmin'? What do you know 'bout workin' without an overseer keepin' you movin'? It isn't ratt, I say, it isn't ratt. Negroes ownin' property 'stead o' bein' property.' Then she started goin' on 'bout ungrateful, lazy niggas an' their thievin' ways, an' how the damned Lincolnites..."

Here Zachariah gave a skeptical look. Lucius nodded and said in a quiet voice, "Yep, she said 'damned.' In all my borned days only time I heard a woman say it in public." Zachariah whistled in awe.

"She kept on an' the boodle o' watt folk 'round her was gettin' egged up. But then Lieutenant Bingham came over good an' riled. He went up to her so close their hat brims was touchin' an' says, 'You secesh cow! Any more talk like that and I will personally enforce General Butler's New Orleans order against you an' all you biddies here.' She went as watt as her blouse an' fainted away, along with two or three others. But the fatt went ratt outta them."

Zachariah chuckled. When he sobered he was thoughtful. "Ya know, I knew a differ'nt kinda faintin'. In the Petersburg lines, men was turnin' to skin an' bones for lack o' food. One time on picket duty I sat down by a tree watchin' fo' blue bellies, an' next thing I knowed it was near sundown. Cap'n Bidwell woulda strung me up by my thumbs, but he didn't know."

Both men sat in silence for a time, wrapped in separate thoughts. Then Zachariah brightened. "Course we found a silver side to it as well. Our colonel had jes' gotten' a Fraynch book that a blockade runner had brought in. The name on it in Fraynch was *Les Misérables* and the fust section was called, 'Fantine.' Well some o' the boys saw him readin' it an' axed him to read it to 'em. He explained it was all in Fraynch. They said, 'But its 'bout us. Ratt there on the cover an' fust section it says, "Lee's Miserables, Faintin."' So you read us 'bout us.'"

Both men's easy laughs were cut short by the quick step and sharp tongue of Rachel Collins who emerged from the group of shoppers.

"Zachariah Hampton!" Both men automatically rose to their feet at the sound of a woman's voice. "Zachariah, of all things! Talking with one of them right here in the open? And sitting with one of them here in public on an integrated bench? You are shaming Emily and the Cause. You're runnin' down every white man and puttin' ideas in their dark heads. Don't be such a scalawag!"

Zachariah stood in unhappy silence between Lucius and Rachel. He looked from one to the other, thinking hard. Then he nodded in salute to Lucius, turned his face toward Rachel, and very deliberately sat back down. He tugged at Lucius's sleeve to join him in snubbing Rachel but Lucius had another idea. In a Lieutenant Bingham moment, he pointed to the "Sinners Welcome" sign and stepped up to Rachel's hat brim. With a broad smile, he locked eyes with her and said, "Beg pardon, ma'am. I didn't know this sign didn't apply to you."

Rachel's eyes went wide in shock at both Lucius' nearness and his words. She managed an "Oh!" as she turned sharply, then scurried off as quickly as she'd arrived.

Lucius rejoined Zachariah on the pew.

Sunday, August 24, 1913

Rutland

Rutland's Paramount Theater had been jammed to capacity for Marian Anderson's concert and consequently, the steps coming down from the balcony, the lobby, and the sidewalk in front were all aswarm with milling people. Calvin, Eleanor, Anna Louise, and Sam had been left shaking their heads in wonder at Marian's singing. The Salisburys maybe handled it a bit better because they had been shaking their heads in wonder for a week over the idea of Sam Wentworth actually courting Anna Louise McCloud. Yet they had seen them chuckling over dinner, holding hands on the front porch swing, or having soft, earnest talks in the Salisburys' flower garden.

"Well, what about a bit of ice cream at the parlor?" Calvin boomed. "My treat." Sam looked a trifle embarrassed and then said, "Um, not to be impolite, but, ah, I wonder if you two wouldn't mind if Anna Louise and I went for a walk?" His eyes twinkled as he teased like a young swain, "I'll be sure to bring her home at a proper hour, Mr. Salisbury."

All of them gave off great laughs. Eleanor shook her finger at Anna Louise and pretended to scold, "Now mind your manners, young lady. No arch looks at Mr. Wentworth, because after all, he is a gentleman." The women exchanged warm smiles while Calvin said, "All right, we'll see you later at the house."

In the lobby, Sam and Anna Louise had to detour around a mass of men and women dressed in their Sunday best but obviously living hard-working lives. In their midst, Father Mason from St. John's Catholic was enjoying a hearty round of thanks and congratulations from his parishoners. "Grazie, Padre" alternated with "Thank you, Father" and "Shoor now that was a voice to hear" was answered by "Bellisima" and "Marvelosa."

Josiah and Abigail Trimble were coming around the mass, heading for the door as Sam and Anna Louise also jostled close by near the street entrance. Josiah shook his head. Although he dropped his voice a bit so just Abigail would hear, it was still fairly strong in the noisy lobby. "Do you hear them, Abby? 'Shoor' for sure and 'bellisima'? Why, hardly half their words are English. Father Mason bringing them to such a concert and thinking he's doing them some good? Hmph. And yet from that stock we're supposed to make Americans?"

He happened to look right at this moment into the face of an elderly, bright-eyed woman with salt-and-pepper hair under a bolero-style hat.

"America stooped to your ancestors and made them into you," she snapped over a fiery smile. Josiah recoiled and scowled at a mere woman speaking to him like this, but she held her gaze steady at his eye until the crowds swept them apart.

The ice cream parlor on Merchant's Row swarmed with the after-concert crowd. Eleanor perched at a little table with bent-wire legs while Calvin ordered two chocolate sundaes at the counter. He maneuvered through the crowd and neatly landed a cut glass dish in front of Eleanor. Taking the opposite seat, he set to work on the other dish with his spoon.

"That was a wonderful concert, Calvin. Thank you so much." Her tone and smile were so warm Calvin blushed.

"You're very welcome. My stars, that Marian Anderson is the bird." He took a spoonful. "I think the crowd not only enjoyed it but their eagerness helped her along. I recognized Reverend Stanton and his flock, and they seemed to hang on every note."

"Oh, they were out in force," Eleanor agreed. "In fact, I see the Reverend and Dahlia over there near the door. You know, Mr. Boyle is bringing in all sorts of delightful entertainment to the Paramount. Do you think he'll get that Thomas Ince motion picture, that hour-long one?"

"Ayup, I'll wager he does. That's the sort of thing Boyle does to sell out his theater."

A few minutes later, another couple landed at the next small table, barely two feet away.

"Why, hello Eleanor. Calvin. Good to see you here," exclaimed Abigail Trimble.

"Yes, indeed," Josiah added, bowing slightly toward Eleanor. He settled his ample form onto the less than ample bent-wire parlor chair. Like the Salisburys, the Trimbles were having sundaes, although their choice was caramel instead of chocolate.

"No, no, don't get up," Abigail said quickly as Calvin started to his feet. "It's too crowded for all that and you might spill something."

Calvin settled back as greetings went around.

"Been to the concert, Abigail?" Calvin asked.

"Yes, indeed," she replied. "Josiah ran into Mr. Boyle the manager a few weeks ago and got us some excellent seats." In a lower voice hardly necessary in the clamor, she added, "Josiah paid one dollar and seventy five cents each for them."

"For that money, they must have been excellent," Eleanor agreed. Calvin noticed her brief annoyance at Abigail's boasting about expense rather than bargains. She asked Josiah, "So what did you think of the concert from that close range?"

"Remarkable," Josiah responded. "Even colored, that girl has a gift. It was unfortunate she needed to play to such a mixed crowd."

"Oh, it looked rather like the usual crowd to me," Calvin said carefully.

"Well, yes I suppose up in the balcony it was," Josiah replied. "I was thinking more the pieces she sang. You expect a spiritual like 'Deep River,' from them, although it was beautifully done. But putting in 'Ave Maria' was something Mr. Boyle and his Irish Catholic crowd probably insisted on."

"Oh, Josiah," Eleanor remarked, "those pieces were chosen to show her voice at its best, not to play to certain members of the audience."

"I think Josiah's onto something," Abigail piped up, gesturing with her spoon. "He's very good at seeing the political angle in such things."

As Calvin and Eleanor absorbed this Josiah weighed back in. "You must agree the piece from Mendelssohn's 'Elijah' was playing to the synagogue flock from Merchant's Row."

Calvin was grateful the cool of the ice cream offset his rising temper. "Not many singers attempt that piece because of its difficulty. I hardly think religion enters into the calculation."

"It's all part of the same trend, Calvin. Every immigrant group erodes the essence and goodness of what is here." Abigail nodded vigorously as Josiah held forth. "First it was the Germans, but at least they were Saxons. Then it was all those Africans the Southerners had to start civilizing... and doing a poor job of it to boot." Eleanor's spoon stopped still and she squared her shoulders toward Josiah as he went on. "Then came that Irish race, tamed a bit by the British. But now come Catholics from Italy and Jews fleeing the czar. I just read a few thousand last year were admitted from the Levant! Think of it! Ottomans bringing Mohammedanism here."

"We all came here from somewhere, Josiah," Calvin answered, finishing his sundae.

"The Indians might have thought we were eroding their goodness," Eleanor added.

Josiah looked at her hard, trying to assert himself, but for the second time tonight a woman met his gaze so steadily he had to look away. He shook his head. "I hardly think so. Nothing there to erode."

Eleanor moved to cut off an annoyed Calvin. "Everyone comes for the promise of America, Josiah. Liberty. The chance to work and worship."

"But it has to be the right work for the right people and it has to be the right worship," Abigail said earnestly.

Calvin hard-eyed Josiah. "Remember at Gettysbaag when we camped up the street from the 61st Pennsylvania Cavalry? They were Jews to the last man. When they elected a rabbi as chaplain, it took two years and an act of Congress so the rabbi could get paid to bless and bury his men."

"In an American army," Josiah persisted, "chaplains should all be good Christian men with no use for rabbis or Latin-mumbling priests. We Anglo-Saxons need to keep it pure from other races and false faiths so American power stays in righteous hands."

Calvin and Eleanor both stared as Josiah swallowed a spoonful. "You're serious," Eleanor breathed.

"And he's quite right too," Abigail chimed in, with a smile that went all the way to smug.

Calvin wondered, "So you don't think the Vermont GAR should support a USCI monument in Washington, condemn lynching, deplore Griffith's Klan film, or..."

"Worst mistake the GAR has made since the War," Josiah pronounced. "All caught up in Camp Lincoln's minstrel show in Gettysbaag's square when they left town."

Calvin and Eleanor exchanged glances and both rose.

"Oh, must you be off?" Abigail asked.

"Ayup. I'm afraid we both need to get some rest," Eleanor said honestly.

Josiah rose for Eleanor. "Well then, good night. Pleasure to see you again." He held out his hand. "Calvin."

Calvin took it, shook it, but then held it. "Tell me, Josiah," he said in a low tone. "Is there any person you actually approve of that doesn't show up in your shaving mirror?" He turned, offered his arm to Eleanor and headed for the door. Calvin planned to just walk out, but Eleanor steered him wide. He looked at her, and she gave him an arched eyebrow.

"Blast the Trimbles," she said softly through the sweetest smile. Calvin's stomach dropped at her use of such language. As they came to a table near the door she burst out, "Reverend Stanton! Dahlia! So good to see you again."

The black couple stood reflexively, and Homer bowed. Eleanor put her arms in greeting around an amazed Dahlia and said, "Wasn't that a wonderful concert? What singing! Look, we've already had our treat but could we sit with you and talk?"

"Well, uh, yes, but there are no extra chairs," Homer stammered.

From across the parlor, the Trimbles threw dark frowns at the amalgamated quartet talking and laughing and spooning ice cream. All four were having a delightful time while the Josiah and Abigail talked furiously to each other, Abigail in particular making her points by tapping her spoon on the lip of her dish. Even when the Trimbles left about twenty minutes later, firing off hard faces at the four and cracking wise to each other, all they heard in reply were snatches of friendship and remarks at the wonder of Marian Anderson's voice.

Labor Day
Monday, September 1, 1913

Savannah

August ended in Savannah on the back of a storm up from the Caribbean. Tropical scents mixed in among days of rain. On Monday, September first, the downpours were such "frog downers" – as Zachariah put it to Emily and Lee – the city cancelled the Labor Day parade. The rare double break of Sunday and Monday was not cancelled, giving working men a five day week instead of the usual six, but there was a lot of grousing just the same both indoors and on front porches.

Monday evening a cold front pushed the storm out to sea. The front ignited a string of spectacular thunderstorms that crashed across the city, blazing with lightning. A forked bolt arced from cloud to ground south of Franklin Square. One prong blasted an electrical transformer, knocking out telephones and power to the streetcar system, businesses and homes that were wired for about a third of Savannah. The other prong leaped across the street into the bell tower of John C. Calhoun Elementary School. The charge crackled through the center hall where long tables were stacked with reading and copy books ready to be passed out the next morning to grades 1-6. The bolt ignited all the paper explosively and burned to ashes the two flags ready to hoist in the morning, the Georgia ensign and the Stars and Bars. Even if the fully motorized Savannah Fire Department had arrived in ten minutes rather than the twenty-five it actually took them, they could not have saved the school.

Next morning, the ruin still smoked, a blackened crater with two wings. The left wing consisted of a back wall and a piece of the side that remained, while the right wing was rooms gaping open toward the center. First day school bells rang across town but school superintendent Preston Hill and other members of the school board stood on the Calhoun sidewalk with other gawking spectators.

They were watching city engineer John Howard and his assistant Lee Thompson examine the ruins, take measurements, and push and shake walls and columns among the debris. The engineers reported that even the right wing was structurally unsound and that the building was a complete loss. The board asked Howard and Thompson to visit West Broad Street School as possible temporary quarters and make a report. Without waiting for their return, the board held an impromptu but official meeting right there on the sidewalk. Mr. Hill gave a hand-written decision to Lamar Simpson of the *Savannah Tribune*, which ran the notice in their afternoon edition.

> *John C. Calhoun Elementary School was destroyed by lightning Monday night and declared a total loss. Although insured, a new school will take several months to build. During the rebuilding the Savannah Board of Education has designated West Broad Street School a white school, and ordered all white children grades 1-6 enrolled at Calhoun school begin attending there on Friday, September 5th. While West Broad Street School is technically on the west side of town, beginning Friday the colored children will be dismissed, the Calhoun children will be taught by their white teachers from Calhoun, and the Savannah police department will provide protection.*
>
> *The board will hold a special meeting tomorrow night, Wednesday the third at 7:00pm sharp to answer questions and concerns from the public. Due to the interest and numbers expected, this meeting will be held in the main hall of the Cotton Exchange Building on Factor's Walk.*

Hannah and Sherman brought the news home with them from the first day of school at West Broad. Sherman was trying hard to understand over supper as he said, "The Calhouners could come to our school. We'd move ovah and share our chalk slates and books with 'em. I'll bet those Calhoun chillun like learnin' as much as me and Hannah."

"But that's not what they're sayin', Sherman," Hannah answered in a big sister way. "The grown-ups don't want us to share."

"They don't?"

"No!" she cried. "Those white grown-ups want to take our whole school for their children and leave us with nuthin'. That's not sharin', that's takin'!"

Sherman's eyes went wide, then watered as he swung among surprised, upset, and horrified. "Mama? Daddy? Grandpops? You won't let them take our school, will you? Will you?"

Beulah reached over to hold his hand, then looked him in the face and promised, "All the West Side grown-ups and some friendly white grown-ups are going to do everything we can to make sure you and Hannah and Ralphie and Abner and all God's children, black and white, get all the schoolin' they need."

Then everyone listened closely over bites of supper while Rufus read to the table from the *Savannah Colored Tribune* extra edition. Phillip Yancey's story reprinted the school board notice and confirmed rumors that colored children would be sent home for the year. He quoted Preston Hill as promising to "make every effort to provide alternate arrangements for colored children in the near future so they might find a way to learn for part of the year."

"There you have it," Beulah snapped when Rufus had finished reading. "'Separate but equal' all ovah again. Our children are separated out so white children can have a school building equal or even more equal to their burned down one. You know those high-toned families on the west squares have wanted West Broad Street School for years." She put on a fine air and her voice went to a combined British and Southern lady accent, "Ah declare, that old merchant man Scarborough built it in the 1820s, even brought in a genuine London architect to design it. That place should belong to us of the uppah crust and not those dahkies on the west side." She went back to her normal voice, dripping with contempt. "They've been lusting for that building like a bunch of fresh-docked sailors in a Bay Street bawdy house!"

Rufus and Lucius were astounded at her language when Hannah began, "What's a bawdy house?" Rufus answered quickly, "Never mind that. But something has to be done. I went by what's left of Calhoun school and there's barely one stone on another, like Jerusalem laid waste."

"Well they's got to be a way," Lucius chimed in. "All the colored chillun need their learnin' and so do white chillun. But it's a head-scratcher ratt now." Talk, sadness, anger, and head scratching went on far into the night on the West Side.

Wednesday, September 3, 1913

Savannah

All West Savannah could talk about Wednesday was the school board meeting that night, but their excitement remained almost unknown to white Savannah or the police department. The *Tribune* had no reporters on the West Side and the police had no officers who walked a regular beat there. Colored men jawed about it over work. Their wives, daughters, and mothers chattered about it in homes, in shops, and across fences. Fancy Porterfield, the pastor's wife at the Second African Baptist Church on Franklin Square, presided over a raucous midday meeting of over a hundred church ladies.

Citywide, two petitions were in circulation door to door, on street corners and at streetcar stops. One supported the school board's seizing West Broad Street School to educate the Calhoun children there. The other called for the West Broad Street School to remain all black – a petition that picked up a certain number of signatures which noted "White" after their names.

The Rufus Saxton GAR post held a special morning meeting at Second African.

"New battle, same War," Lucius said at one point in the cross-talk.

"We need a strategy," Charlie Gibson said, "and we need one quick."

"This is harder than escorting Abe Lincoln through Richmond," Reuben Keyes confessed, his brow knit. Then his eyes suddenly lit up with an idea. "We can't have Lincoln visit, but how 'bout someone almost as good?"

"Who you got in mind?" Lucius asked.

Reuben grinned and said, "What about a certain GAR gentleman from Beaufort, South Carolina?"

The dozen men slapped the table. "That's good!" "Yes sir!" "Oh that'll out flank 'em." "Yeah! Bring him in."

"Okay, gotta move fast then," Lucius said. "We're gonna need a telegram and we gotta pay for it and rail fare to boot."

A former railroad porter who had gone all the way through eighth grade said, "Gimme a paper and pencil. I'll work up the message."

"Attaboy, Quincy," Lucius said gladly. A couple of pencil stubs and a wrinkled envelope from somebody's pocket skidded to the end of the table in front of the Pullman retiree as Lucius said to the assembled, "Ever'body else ante up. Anybody got an idee of rail fare both ways and the wire cost?"

Coins jingled on the tabletop as men dug in their pockets. Charlie carefully untied an oblong leather pouch and pulled out several limp dollar bills saying, "I move the Post Treasury commit six dollars to this worthy cause." The motion carried swiftly, the men giving the typically penny-pinching Gibson second looks and a few back pats.

Reuben Keyes and Quincy left for the Western Union on Factor's Walk. The rest of the men went home with orders to write down thoughts and ideas, put on their Sunday best, and meet back at the church at half-past two. Lucius volunteered ("special duty for the sergeant" the men jibed) to meet the 2:07 Coast Line train from Beaufort and bring former Navy veteran Robert Smalls to the second GAR meeting of the day.

The Cotton Exchange Building closed for business as usual at five o'clock. For the next hour, custodians set up scores of folding chairs on the main floor. Superintendent Hill had arranged for a couple doors to be unlocked and for some Savannah police to be at tonight's meeting. Sergeant Caldwell and two patrolmen arrived promptly at six, and the four colored men on the night crew opened the two side doors to the officers and the Reverend Elijah Porterfield of the Second African Baptist Church.

"Where all do we sit, suh?" Porterfield asked.

Sergeant Caldwell frowned and said, "Superintendent Hill didn't say nothin' 'bout segregatin', so I guess it's first come, first served."

"Thank you, Sergeant," Porterfield said with an elegant bow, but his eyes were dancing. It took less than two minutes for several of Porterfield's flock to fill the first three rows wall to wall. The Rufus Saxton GAR men held the center of the line in the fourth row, with Captain Smalls on the aisle. Colored workmen like Rufus arrived steadily, many toting a second midday dinner for supper, which they ate while waiting. In twenty minutes every seat was taken. The officers hastily designated standing room areas while the custodians hustled to set up more chairs. Mr. Vernon Blakely, the math and science teacher at the white junior high, set up and tested a loud-speaking machine.

By half-past six the first-arriving white parents were limited to parts of the last three rows or to standing. A few, seeing the hall filled with dark faces, turned and left immediately. Others fussed and whined, complaining to the officers or to each other about the noise, or that some of their house servants and cooks had front seats, or "the whole idea we have to sit or even stand back here." But mostly the white faces were shocked that so many West Siders were out for a school board meeting and only three police officers were present. Yet as seven approached, they had to admit the crowd was orderly and polite.

Just before the meeting began, Mr. Hill entered with the rest of the board. Lamar Simpson of the *Tribune* and Phillip Yancey of the *Colored Tribune* trailed in behind them and set up shop as a two-man press section.

"Meetin' is in session," Hill declared. Reverend Porterfield immediately waved his hand and Hill called on him.

"Mistah Hill? I see the custodians have set up an American flag next to y'all. Might we all stand and recite the Pledge of Allegiance to set a propah tone for this meetin'?"

Applause burst out and folks were standing up all across the room before Hill could respond. Flustered but overwhelmed by the room's momentum, the board rose and led the Pledge. All except Porterfield resumed their seats. The Reverend said, "Mr. Hill? Membahs of the School Board? Since the West Broad Street School children are the most affected by the notice printed in the papers, we would like to go first to address the board through a spokesman."

"You'll get yo' turn," Hill answered, trying to reassert control. Some low rumbling and chair shifting came from the center section. "But fust the parents of Calhoun Elementary will be heard." A thin smattering of white applause greeted this from the edges of the room. "Yes, you, suh?" he said, pointing his gavel at a distinguished, white-haired gentleman somewhere about sixty.

"Thank you, Mr. Hill. If I might introduce myself, I'm Clayton Loomis, an attorney practicin' law heah in Savannah for ovah thirty years. I congratulate the board for calling this public meetin' and for their courage in goin' forward with it despite the obvious effort of certain dangerous, immoral, and unAmerican people to fill the room and intimidate the board." A smattering of applause and a couple whistles of support came from the white edges of the crowd. "The board made a ratt, propah and wise decision in its notice that ran in yesterday's newspaper. The West Broad Street School is indeed an excellent facility for the education of white students." Rumbles filled the air, but Hill gaveled them down. Loomis continued.

"I hope the board in its wisdom will review the petitions in public circulation. One of these calls for the West Broad Street School to remain colored only. There are white parents and citizens who say this is a not a good idea."

Someone shouted from the edge of the crowd, "Let's swap buildings. West Broad for Calhoun with a circus tent. White for colored." The main floor erupted and a policeman bravely placed himself in front of the shopkeeper who had called out the idea. Mr. Hill gaveled the meeting back to order and said to the edges, "If you want Mr. Loomis to speak for you then let him speak. Otherwise y'all keep quiet, ya heah?"

Loomis resumed. "All the school buildings owned by the board are equally good for educatin' students so it's just by custom that they are separated, some used by white children and some by colored. But in this instance, custom should yield to the necessity of the white children." There was small applause and larger hissing.

"If I might dispose of another idea. Some people have suggested white and colored children share the West Broad Street School." Several boos and catcalls echoed on the Cotton Exchange floor from parents of both races.

"From this reaction, members of the board can see this is not a popular idea. Neither is it a good idea for colored children. Mixed schools like those up North give colored children ideas of equality, the notion they might rise above their station instead of being content with the station in life God designed for them." Strong applause from the edges of the crowd and a "preach it, Mr. Loomis" was drowned out by boos from the rest of the room.

"The board has every right to use the West Broad Street School for educating white children. The building itself, former home of a gentleman, designed by the distinguished London architect William Jay, borders on a genteel neighborhood of refined homes. The well-to-do neighbors of Mr. Scarborough's old mansion would welcome the sound of the children of Savannah's upstanding citizens using the building for a noble use such as educating their own kind."

"Told you they wanted the building," Beulah said quietly to Rufus as angry comments flowed around them.

"In closing I would remind the board that the Supreme Court has established 'separate but equal' as the law of the land. This wise ruling preserves both God's orders of mankind and the social order built upon it." The room became very still and the silence deepened so Loomis had to struggle against its thickness.

"This is why white children and colored children are educated separately, to fit each of them for their separate places in life. Educating white children in a former mansion and in a genteel neighborhood, taught by excellent white teachers, surrounded by wholesome influences, would help fit them for living future lives in such settings just as God intended. This is nothing unusual. Outside school walls, all adults likewise encounter signs in daily life that say "Whites Only" or "Colored Only." These are merely friendly reminders to everyone of the natural and social orders ordained by God and the Supreme Court. The board should go ahead with its plan. I thank the board for its attention."

Applause for Loomis was thin but enthusiastic. Board members shifted uneasily in their seats at the hard expressions and powerful quiet from most of the room. Mr. Hill took a deep breath and pointed his gavel at Reverend Porterfield. "All right, who's yo' man?" Porterfield nodded and then signaled Robert Smalls. As Smalls moved toward the microphone in front, Porterfield said in his preaching voice, "For those of you who don't know, our spokesman tonatt is Captain Robert Smalls. I say captain because that was his rank in the United States Navy, the first colored man ever to command his own ship."

"Musta been a garbage scow of a ship to give to a nigga," came a raspy call from the side. Laughter cackled, then died suddenly under the hard stares from the room.

Unshaken, Porterfield resumed. "Not only did he bring twenty slaves and himself to freedom by sailing a ship out to the Union blockade, but he was made second in command of a ship because he was obviously a leader. When his ship came under enemy fire and his captain wanted to turn and run, he put the captain under arrest, ordered his ship to fight, and captured a blockade runner carrying supplies to the enemy."

"No supplies is part of why you lost the War," said a brawny workingman from his seat to the section where the earlier crack had come from. Several other colored men rose and pointed fingers and made remarks in support of this answering crack. Sergeant Caldwell made a point of strolling between the two sections, his nightstick prominent.

Porterfield pleaded, "If I might finish? In honor of this sort of leadership, Captain Smalls was awarded a yet higher honor. Five times the voters of his South Carolina district elected him to the United States Congress. And while he could have stayed in a quiet retiracy he has agreed to come tonight and speak for the education of colored children of Savannah."

The board grudgingly accorded Smalls a modest respect. The West Siders burst into chants of "Smalls, Smalls" and cheers for "our congressman." Phillip Yancey of the *Colored Tribune* wondered if certain facts he had provided the congressman at the GAR meeting might figure in his remarks.

Smalls bowed to the room and Mr. Hill. "Thank you, Reverend Porterfield, for that introduction. This board is charged with a solemn responsibility, the education of children, which is an American tradition since the days of the Puritans. As Thomas Jefferson once said, "If a nation expects to be ignorant and free in a civilization, it expects what never was and never will be." Mr. Jefferson and the Puritans earned a nice round of applause.

"Tonight's turnout shows how much all these parents, both white and colored, love their children and want the best for them. Now, Mr. Loomis spoke handsomely for the Calhoun children and parents but in his eloquence he forgot something. He gave the board no help with your responsibility to educate all of Savannah's children, including the ones now attending West Broad. The West Side parents believe the board, in its understandable hurry to deal with the sudden loss of Calhoun school, was hasty in its decision regarding both Calhoun and West Broad. We admire the wisdom of the board in calling tonight's meetin' to give itself a chance to consider with grace and full knowledge what might be done.

"Now West Broad Street School has, for over thirty years, educated colored children and only colored children..."

"Let 'em keep doin' it," came a twangy, nasal voice from a lean white man in worn overalls and a battered hat from the far side. "Bad 'nuff chillun got to go to school 'tall, 'stead of workin' an' earnin' their keep. If the coloreds want their young-uns wastin' time larnin' ABCs, let 'em waste it." A storm of protest met this from both black and white, putting fear into the man's face, and he edged toward the door.

Preston Hill rolled his eyes at the man and sighed at his aggressive ignorance. Then he gestured to former Congressman Smalls, who resumed.

"As the distinguished Mr. Loomis put it, West Broad exists as a colored school because of 'separate but equal.' Four years ago, this board bought fourteen hundred new McGuffey readers to replace copies that were old and torn. Fourteen hundred white children used these new McGuffey readers. Meanwhile, fourteen hundred colored children were made to learn out of the old and torn McGuffeys that the white schools had thrown away. We recognized this was separate but believed this was not equal. This board ruled that it was." A couple board members looked uneasy at this while the others tried to put on an impassive air.

"Two summers ago, this board hired four new fifth grade teachers fresh out of teacher's colleges, two of them white and two colored. The white teachers earn $160 a year and both teach twenty-two students apiece. The colored teachers earn $105 a year and both teach thirty-one students apiece. We recognized this was separate but believed this was not equal. This board ruled that it was." Board members shifted uneasily in their chairs. Reporter Phillip Yancey took an inner satisfaction in all those boring school board reports he had read regularly every month.

"Mr. Loomis made reference to the friendly reminder signs across town noting 'White Only' and 'Colored Only' as expressions of 'separate but equal.' Now as I understand it, in the past several weeks the people of Savannah who wish to sit while they wait for a streetcar have had occasion to ponder not only how separate they find the seating but also how equal they find it." Chuckles ran around the room. The GAR men found their moustaches all seemed to itch at the same time and every one of them had to raise a hand to their face to scratch – or hide a smile.

"The West Broad Street School building was the home of a bankrupt man, whose house carried that stain and shame through several owners and was allowed to decay. The school board acquired it in this dilapidated condition, has not spent a penny on it for repairs, and yet sent colored children to be schooled there. For over thirty years, colored children have learned there despite leaking roofs, broken windows, inadequate books, and hard-working but often under-trained teachers. We recognized this school was separate from Calhoun school, its nearest neighbor, but believed it was not equal. This board ruled that it was." Preston Hill found it hard to look Smalls in the eye.

"Now this board has given notice it wants to take this so-called separate but equal school for colored children and use it to educate white children. But if the board seizes the building for the use of white children it tears down the separation between the races. Do the white parents of Savannah really want the school board to have that kind of power? Just willy-nilly say one day this school or that is going to be white? Or colored? Would you want your children walking into the wrong school some morning?"

"Then too, if the board makes white children learn under leaky roofs and behind broken windows, learning in a place where who knows what black diseases or African rituals might be haunting the rooms, I doubt Mr. Loomis and the white parents from Calhoun will believe this is the equal of Calhoun school. But if the board makes repairs on West Broad, it then admits the school was not equal to Calhoun. Even Mr. Loomis would have to agree the board would be violating both separate and equal." The board squirmed under the weight of 'separate but equal' turned against them.

A hatless white woman in a ragged dress called out, "My Alice won't go to a school like that unless it's been scrubbed clean from top to bottom with lye soap!"

One of the maids in the second row stood and snapped back, "Which of you white women is going to scrub it like that?" In the uproar that followed, both women were escorted out by the police, and by separate doors. Mr. Hill banged his gavel in exasperation at this outburst and at the bind he was feeling. He said to Smalls, "You 'bout done?"

"Yes, Mr. Hill, after one final point," Smalls said with a nod. "When the board's notice was published, several black churches made offers of their space if necessary to educate the colored children of West Broad. I am surprised Mr. Loomis has not reported similar offers from white churches to the children and parents of Calhoun school. Since those churches preach a generous, forgiving Christ of the Bible just like the black churches I am mystified by their silence. But thereby the board can see the simple solution to the issue of the loss of Calhoun school. West Broad can remain unaffected, or perhaps even repaired with board funds, while the Calhoun students can call upon their churches, pastors, and deacons for blessèd classroom spaces as ordained by God."

The room buzzed with talk. The few whites were now sharply divided whether they wanted their children to attend West Broad. Many colored parents were standing firm on keeping West Broad a colored school, getting a certain satisfaction from turning around the usually demeaning language. The board thrashed about trying to assert white privilege while not being blatant about it, particularly with the make-up of the room.

To stall for time, Mr. Hill banged his gavel and announced, "The board will now hear a report from Mr. Howard, the Savannah city engineer, on the official condition of both the Calhoun School and the West Broad Street School. Mr. Howard?" He looked for the stocky form of John Howard, but could not pick him out. A lean, pale-skinned man with dark hair and matching sharp, dark eyes stepped forward.

"Mr. Hill and members of the board? Mr. Howard has taken ill and has sent me to make the report you requested. I am Lee Thompson, Mr. Howard's assistant."

"Very well, Mr. Thompson, and welcome," Hill answered.

Lee nervously cleared his throat. "Thank you, sir." He spoke carefully in a rather soft but intense voice that made people lean forward just slightly to listen, yet his manner seemed the calmest in the room. "Mr. Howard and I personally examined Calhoun School. The destruction was extensive, and after some tests we determined the remaining walls are not sound. We recommend they be knocked down before they fall down and cause injury." He was so matter-of-fact that the idea of using the Calhoun site for anything except new construction became ridiculous.

"We have also examined and measured the West Broad Street School. Calhoun was a moderately-sized space with seven classrooms and 123 children enrolled. West Broad has 212 students in a somewhat larger space. After calculation, the Calhoun children will fit into West Broad without displacing the colored students, and with more space than they had at Calhoun, with one exception: the thirty-two seventh and eighth grade boys currently at West Broad would need to have class somewhere else. I've spoken with Reverend Elijah Porterfield of the Second African Baptist Church on Franklin Square about three blocks away. He said his church is willing to rent classroom space to the school board for one dollar per student per month. Also, West Broad does not have a math teacher for these classes and asks the school board to have Mr. Blakely teach them that subject at the church."

Conversations popped across the room among both spectators and board members. "We should get the whole West Broad Street School jes' like Mr. Loomis said."

"Let those boys go to that church. Keeps them black bucks away from our little girls."

"Why do black boys need any 'rithmetic past countin', addin', and subtractin'?"

"Let them white children take the year off. It's our buildin'."

Mr. Hill and the board huddled at the front as their secretary took speedy notes. A string of people were waved over to the board one by one: Reverend Porterfield, a workman or two, Mr. Blakely the math teacher, Mr. Loomis, Mr. Smalls, and Mr. Thompson, while the conversations around the room rose and fell. Finally, everyone could see the board members raise their hands and Mr. Hill count. He gaveled the meeting back to order as everyone fell silent.

"After due deliberation, the Savannah Board of Education has reached the following decision: A work crew will be sent to the West Broad Street School to construct panels on the stairs and within the halls... and to fix any roof leaks. The colored children will continue their studies for the rest of the school year" – applause boomed out – "on the north side of the building. While some may disagree, the board feels colored children who are educated will become bettah workers in the future and are less likely to engage in crime, be a burden to charities, or to misbehave in general." The grumbling over this was both white and black.

"The white children from Calhoun school will begin school as previously ordered on Friday, September 5th on the south side of the West Broad Street school." There was uncertain growling from both black and white parents.

"Signs designating 'white' and 'colored' will be posted but will hardly be needed since both sides of the building have water fountains and plumbing facilities for both teachers and students." There was silence at this, but only grumpy. "The seventh and eighth grade colored boys will indeed be taught at the church mentioned" – a smattering of applause – but the board cannot pay Mr. Blakely to teach them math. Under Georgia law a white teacher cannot teach colored students." A short round of boos was drowned out by Hill's voice: "However, Mr. Blakely has agreed to teach them without pay after school each day on a volunteer basis." Colored parents cheered a blushing Mr. Blakely.

"Education on this temporary mixed basis will last only until a new Calhoun white school is completed. By a vote of 5-2 the board feels this is the best decision under the circumstances. The fact that both Mr. Clayton Loomis for the white parents and Robert Smalls for the colored folk are both strongly opposed to this idea tells us we got it right. As Assistant City Engineer Mr. Thompson so kindly reminded us, "Blessed are the peacemakers, for they shall catch it from both sides."

A nice chuckle ran around the room as people considered this. Hill banged his gavel once more. "So ordered. Meeting adjourned."

Thursday, September 18 through Monday, September 22, 1913

Savannah, Chicamauga, and Gainesville

Zachariah rode in front with Hugo while Emily and Lee shared the Thomas' back seat. He wore his old uniform and carried a lightweight valise on his lap. As Hugo waited at an intersection, he idly watched some school children crossing under a policeman's friendly wave, headed up toward West Broad Street School. The four in the Thomas chatted casually but each wondered about the station scene today. A repeat of the Encampment carnival atmosphere was most unlikely, but how much would it be scaled back?

Hugo turned onto Broad Street and the station loomed gray against a slate sky. There was a good crowd, a big Saturday one happening on this Thursday. As Hugo parked, their spirits rose as they heard a band. In the main hall a company of vets crowded together among family and friends. The Fire Department band was playing "The Bonnie Blue Flag." A color guard sported the Stars and Bars, the Georgia flag, a couple old regimental flags, and a banner proclaiming "Chickamauga!" The UCV was holding an encampment at the South's last great victory.

The younger men and families erupted in several yips and Rebel yells. Zachariah joined the band of comrades and shook hands with Bob Bidwell, Jim Calhoun, and Turner Hawkins. A moment later, Dooley Culpepper pushed himself to the cluster.

Zachariah stepped up to the ticket window. Payton Colby's window. He sighed and pulled out his pass. The young clerk read it over and said, "Jes' a minute, suh." and took the letter with him. A couple minutes later, he was back with a supervisor who had the clerk copy down Zachariah's name, destination, and travel dates in a ledger. He issued a three-part ticket, changing cars in Augusta and Atlanta.

The Savannah crowd grew larger and louder. Everyone remembered the Gettysburg sendoff and did their best to invoke that spirit.

Emily threw off her airs and kissed Zack goodbye. "I know it won't be Gettysburg but I'm hoping…" and smiled.

Zack finished. "Every day'll be a good one, I'm sure." His eyes were warm and soft upon her.

The train ride improved as it went on. At Augusta, several cars coupled onto the Savannah train and a huge swarm of whooping Carolina veterans raised the general mood. In Atlanta, the station scene for the change of trains was festive and sprawling. Bands, flags, streamers, confetti, Rebel yells, and back patting were spread over the platforms. The mayor of Atlanta gave a speech, and the lieutenant governor added a few remarks before boarding the train himself for the run to Chickamauga.

The whole event was smaller than Gettysburg—it could hardly be otherwise—and shorter by several days. It was a whites-only affair with Southerners setting the tone. The Union men were outnumbered about three to one but were mostly Sherman's men. They had not suffered like the eastern army from bad leadership and had scored mostly victories over these same Confederates, with Chickamauga a big exception. Zachariah noticed the only black faces in camp were those handing out blankets and scrubbing pots and pans behind the field kitchens. Their dirt-watching shoulders and deferential whimpering gnawed at him. When he'd seen Dooley Culpepper lead a group of vets in pitching watermelon slices at four black dishwashers, he'd managed to duck behind a tree, and then got away between a couple tents without anyone asking him to join in.

The Savannah men were at a big, Friday night campfire chewing the fat with some Kentuckians and three or four Tennesseans. Early on, they'd been divided over news from the California UCV. President John Mosby had pushed through a statement recognizing that colored men had been Union soldiers. Most of the men wanted to keep their reactions to themselves but it wasn't easy. On the one hand, Dooley Culpepper and a vicious Louisville man were loud and proud about the old Klan and hard-case nasty at Mosby's move. On the other hand, a Memphis vet kept pushing everyone around the fire to at least admit there had been colored soldiers on the other side of the firing line and that was all Mosby's statement was saying. Like the rest of the men in the middle, Zachariah kept as quiet as he could, but he found his heart was with Memphis.

Tensions eased as they moved from Mosby to talking over their old commanders. Hood earned some bitter remarks while Johnston and Beauregard got the best of it. But on and on went the jawing about Braxton Bragg. That sour martinet was the butt of all kinds of jokes, insults, and tales. They hooted approval as Bob Bidwell recounted Joe Johnston's complaint: "Jefferson Davis tried to do what God had failed to do. Davis tried to make a soldier out of Braxton Bragg."

A Bluegrass corporal who had been on headquarters duty told about how Bedford Forrest had told off Bragg after Chickamauga, "'If you were any part of a man, I would slap your jaws and force you to resent it.' Thought I'd see a saloon brawl ratt thar," he added.

"Wouldn'ta gone half a minute," the others agreed. "Forrest woulda taken him apart."

Tennessee private Tom Perry was nearly hoisted on the men's shoulders when he told his Bragg tale: As the Union army staggered off in retreat from Chickamauga, Forrest, Longstreet, and Polk urged Bragg to order pursuit. Bragg was not sure the Federals were retreating. "Them gin'ruls couldn't budge Bragg," said Perry, "so I thought I'd have a go at it myself. I poked my head in the wrangle, saluted all of 'em and said, 'I seed 'em runnin', gin'rul, all broke up, ever' man fo' himself.' Bragg put his nose up to look down at me and said, 'Private, do you even know the characteristics of an army in retreat?' I gave him both barrels. I said 'I oughta, gin'rul. I've been with you your whole campaign!'"

On Sunday night, Zachariah was lying in his cot in the dark. A shade lantern on the center post dimly lit the interior for later arrivals. He'd turned in early but couldn't sleep. He missed the magic from Gettysburg but other thoughts pulled on him too. The vets at this gathering struck him as old: old talk, old campaigns, old grudges, old hat. He found himself almost grateful for the set-to over Mosby, and Perry's tale from Friday, because otherwise these past two days he'd been...bored. Images of Lee and Emily rose in his mind, Lee sighing and staring off and Emily rolling her eyes when she thought Zack wouldn't see it. No wonder. Dang, he thought, how had they stood him for so long?

Outside, men said "Good night" to each other in various volumes and levels of slurring. Then the tent flap fluttered open and there was an uneven shuffle of brogans across the plank floor of the eight-cot tent. Dooley Culpepper was doing a "Virginia fence," staggering in a letter "Z" and pretending it was a straight line. His broken voice blathered out, "Trick or treat!" He tried singing, "There'll be a hot time on the west side that night." His last zigzag brought him down in a heap across Zachariah's legs.

"The South forever," he croaked.

"Phew!" Zachariah exclaimed, sitting up and then recoiling.

"Hurrah, hurrah, hurrah for Southern rights," Dooley sang back.

"Lawdy," Zachariah groaned. Dooley sang worse than he smelled, and his stink tonight could make a pig cry. "C'mon, let's git you laid out."

"Too late," Dooley grinned. "Jack Daniels already did."

"I can tell," Zachariah replied, getting a pry on Dooley's shoulder, "but I meant in yo' own bed." With a grunt, he managed to pull his legs out. Getting up, he got his hands under Dooley's arms and made to drag him across to the next cot. Nothing doing. Dooley was only about ten pounds lighter than Zachariah, and he needed more leverage. After a thought, he took a deep breath, held it, pulled up Dooley's arm, stuck his neck under, wrapped that arm across his own shoulders holding it with one hand. He put his left arm across Dooley's back to the far armpit, got a grip, and then straightened up by his back and legs. Dooley's deadweight rose enough that Zachariah got a foot in place under the two of them. He balanced for a moment, then took a couple steps in a duck walk crouch toward the next cot. As he strained, he had a flash and took advantage of their momentum to part-drag, more-carry Dooley to that empty cot two away from his own.

Zachariah's aim was pretty good under the conditions. Dooley's rear swung around as Zachariah hoped and headed for the middle of the cot. But at this moment, Dooley had a burst of consciousness, opened an eye, found himself in motion without use of his legs and got scared. Instinctively his hands clenched, and Zachariah couldn't let go as he'd planned. Dooley's hips hit the cot center and his shoulders went slanticular toward the far edge. His head banged hard against the wooden side pole inside the canvas. The bump made him loosen his grip on Zachariah, who managed a fairly soft landing on the floor, only bumping his knee. Zachariah gained his feet and looked down at the stretched-out Dooley. Then he reached down, picked up one of Dooley's feet and worked the shoe loose. Although his nose warned him not to, he did the same for the other. Then he pulled a blanket up over the old coot and sighed. Dooley groaned and turned his face toward Zachariah.

"Zat you, Zack?"

Zachariah flopped into a canvas camp chair. "Yep." He took a pull from his pewter flask for the first time since leaving home.

"Yore a good man, Zach'riah."

"Mm-hmm."

Dooley panted, fighting off a heave. "Yep, you are."

Zachariah sat silent.

"By my lights you've had a good life, Zack."

"Oh I don't know..."

"You have," Dooley insisted. "Got through the Wah without gettin' shot. Got married. Have a daughter. Had a good life conductin' on the railroad. Comfortable retiracy."

"I guess so."

"Not ever'body does, ya know," Dooley whimpered. "Take me, fer instance. I had a good life growin' up in S'vannah. I can see it now, but not then. Always felt like them planters an' boss dog merchants was lookin' down nose at us." Zachariah shook his head but Dooley insisted. "They did. Big houses. Lotsa hosses. Ownin' all them slaves. Buncha swells livin' the... the high nose life." He gripped Zack's sleeve with a surprising strength and whispered intensely, "But all that was gonna change on my twenty-fust buthday. I was gonna become one o' them."

Zachariah squinted. "Whaddya mean?"

Dooley smiled. "My momma and daddy promised me on my twenty-fust buthday, bein' o' legal age, I'd go down with my daddy to the auction house and we'd look over the stock that day. Then as the house auctioneer, he'd use his privilege to buy one Negro fo' personal use an' I'd be the owner."

Zachariah chewed this over, Lucius in his thoughts. "Well didja?"

Dooley's eyes were closed and Zachariah wondered if he'd fallen asleep or passed out. Then the cot started shaking and Dooley's face scrunched up as he blubbered out tears.

"My twenty-fust birthday was December 20, 1860!" Zachariah started at the date. "We went down to Factor's Walk an' all Savannah was there. South Carolina had seceded. Ever'body celebrated the whole day an' the auction house was closed. After that, with the secession in Georgia an' musterin' the militia I never got my nigga. Never got the chance. Never did…" His voice cracked and then petered into whimpering.

Zachariah stared off into the dark. After a time he said in a low voice, "Then the War came. And finally Sherman came to Savannah, an' read the Proclamation."

Dooley nodded. "Ended slavery. Put an end to our family bidniss. He didn't burn Savannah but some o' his men found out who owned the auction house and who worked there. Some o' them came…" here he choked, coughed violently, and then recovered. "Some o' them came one natt and rifled the house, then burned it to the ground. Wouldn't let the fire department get near until all they could do was protect the houses next door."

"I'm sorry, Dooley. I never knew."

Dooley stared vacantly. "They found my daddy's body in the auction house, hanging from a rafter. His note said twern't nuthin' left to live fo'. Set my momma off out o' her haid. Her family tried carin' fo' her, but they finally had to put her in a county home…" here he croaked out a whisper, "…fo' the insane." A fresh wave of tears and shame shook him. He went on in a strangled whisper. "I asked Bidwell for a furlough. He bucked it up to the colonel, an' he took it to Longstreet. He said, 'I'm sorry as can be, but we cain't spare a man, not even fo' this tragedy. Furlough denied.' I was hot 'bout it an' thought o' goin' home anyway. Turns out wouldn't a mattered, an' the War ended three months later."

Zachariah stirred. "Men deserted fo' less than that, Dooley."

"That's what stopped me. Didn't want to be a deserter from Gen'rul Lee."

"You stuck, Dooley. To the end. Remember that. You stuck when others deserted."

Dooley's eyelids fluttered shut. "I stuck. To the end. The bitter end. Bitter end. Burned our house down? Burn some o' theirs. Trick on them. Treat fer me."

Dooley slept but Zachariah couldn't. It was after curfew, but he pulled on his shoes, stepped out of the tent in his shirt and suspendered pants, and put on his jacket. He avoided the various campfires around and finally found a spot, a log near a creek, with a fair moon giving some light. He used the log as a backrest and had a couple cigars to smoke over Dooley's tale. A lot fit together now: black freedom, Longstreet, the string of mudsill jobs he reported every regimental dinner, hating Yankees. He sipped from his flask, then lay down, staring up at the stars. Soon after, the stars covered the sleeping man.

Bob Bidwell watched Zachariah heft down his valise from the rack as the train pulled into Atlanta.

"Gettin' off, Zack?" he teased, figuring Zachariah was going for his traveling flask.

"Yep. Gonna look up an old friend."

"Izzat ratt?" Bob said in surprise. "Anybody I know?"

Zachariah smiled in a far-off way. "Reckon you do."

"Like some company?" he asked, somewhere between joshing and serious.

"I b'lieve I would," Zachariah answered with a strange earnestness. "That'd be nice. We'd jes' be a few hours."

"OK, I'm game." Bob said, pulling down his own bag as the train hissed to a stop. They joined the large carloads of Atlanta graybeards stepping onto the platform. As they pushed through, they heard snatches of reunions. "Hi Daddy!" "Welcome home!" "Didja have a good time?" answered by various phrases "Great time there," and a mock-formal "How are ya, Miss Peggy Mitchell? Didja miss yo' old grampa?"

They checked their bags at the baggage room, but Bob was surprised when Zack studied a timetable and then showed his pass at a window to get himself a free ticket and bought Bob's to Gainesville. They got lucky as a train was leaving soon from the next platform.

As the local pulled out, Bob asked, "So who you goin' to see in Gainesville?"

"I'm feelin' a powerful urge to visit Longstreet's grave."

Bob whistled softly, but they talked of idle things until they pulled into the depot. They asked directions and walked about a mile to the Alta Vista cemetery. They stood in silence a long time, heads uncovered. At last Zachariah saluted and they trudged back to the depot. Zack's walk showed every one of his seventy seven years. They sat quietly on a bench at the platform. Bob passed over his flask and Zachariah took a pull.

"I guess I needed to see it. Say goodbye like I wanted to."

"You been here before?"

"Almost. I was here fo' his funeral. January, '04."

Zachariah sipped meditatively. "Matilda was in bed with a bad cold but was on the mend. I didn't want to leave her, but she said I should go. Emily did too. We was formin' ranks for the procession to the chutch when the Westun Union boy came by with the wire." Woodenly he recited. "'Momma much worse. Please come home ratt away. Emily.'

"She died when I was on the train. Emily chafed that I'd been here when she'd passed over. Took her a long time to hear the name Longstreet again. Pains her to this day, I think."

Robert nodded and put his arm on Zachariah's shoulders. "Couldn't be hepped. You was caught between two millstones."

Zachariah nodded. "Yep. Felt that way. Sometimes I still feel like they're grindin' on me. Like today." With a trembling sigh, he added, "I don't know how to git out from 'tween 'em. Cain't seem to make it ratt with Emily although lately there's been some sweetness."

Robert kept an eye on Zack for the rest of the trip. He seemed all right chatting with other veterans but Bob saw a cloud about him until they parted in Savannah.

Wednesday, September 24, 1913

Savannah

Zachariah and Lucius were winding up a back porch chat a couple days after Zack got back from Chickamauga. As Lucius collected his hat, he said, "Say, Zachariah, remember Calvin wrote a couple letters ago 'bout him goin' to a concert?"

"I 'member," Zachariah drawled. "He an' Ellie went to the concert an' he had a tiff with that Josiah feller after."

"That's the one," Lucius nodded. "Well, I jes' heard that same singer is commin' to Savannah. She sang at Camp Lincoln." He looked him square on. "Zachariah, I wanna tell you: Marian Anderson is one in a million. Her voice makes birds give up on singin'. Even watt newspapers say good things 'bout her singin'. She's comin' to the Grand Savannah Theater on Thursday an' Friday natt the ninth and tenth o' October. Jes' sayin' iffin' you an' yo' family likes music she's one to take in."

"Izzat ratt?" Zachariah ruminated. "You know, jes' to stay even with you an' Calvin, I might have to show up. Thank you, an' thanks fo' comin' by. I'll get our letter off to Calvin later today."

"Sounds fine." Lucius held his hat in his hand, stepped across the porch, turned and nodded toward Zachariah for the sake of any watching eyes among the neighbors and headed for Fahm Street. But he took the long way around on Tattnall, as had become usual for him.

Zachariah found Emily in the parlor. She looked up from her letter and smiled. "Daddy, here's your latest to Calvin and Eleanor. I'll have Lee mail it when he goes back to work."

Zachariah smiled. "No need. I'll drop it off myself. Thank you for rattin' it out for us." He folded it into an envelope.

Emily wondered. "Thank you, Daddy. I'll get a stamp on it."

"No, thanks. I'll do that too."

"Hmm," Emily wondered a bit more. "Well, all right. Goin' to take it up 'round the corner this mawnin'?"

"Yes. Uh, wait, no," he stammered, "but I'll get it mailed. Got to go next door fust an' see Hugo."

Emily blinked in surprise. "Hugo?"

"Yep," Zachariah said hurriedly, tucking the letter in his jacket pocket. "I'll be back soon," came his voice from the front hall. Emily stood in time to see him pluck his yard hat off the rack and stride out the front door. "What on earth has gotten into him?" she muttered.

"What on earth has gotten into him?" Emily repeated about a half hour later on the front porch. Zachariah had returned by the back door about ten minutes later. He changed into his good suit and dug out his bank book from the nightstand drawer. While sitting in the parlor he kept tapping his jacket pockets every few minutes and deflecting all Emily's questions with variations on "I can't tell you ratt now, but I will soon." His pocket watch earned several inspections until he rose and went to the hat rack. Instead of his battered yard hat, he put on the light gray planter's hat Emily had bought him for everyday.

The capper had come a couple moments later. Emily had followed him onto the front porch when Hugo pulled up in his burgundy Thomas. Her father turned to her suddenly, doffed his hat, gave her a peck on the cheek and said, "See you fo' lunch, honeybunch," went down the steps to the path, and climbed in next to Hugo. Emily stared after him, her nose still twitching from his hair pomade. It smelled full strength to her, but seemed odd somehow, until she realized it was unmingled with the scent of bourbon.

Lee came home at midday and found the table set for three but only Emily waiting. She had just told him about Zachariah's behavior when the old gent came springing in by the back door. He nearly tossed his hat on the rack and sat down as the hall clock began chiming noon. "Ratt on time," he proclaimed. "Call me a vet. Call me a reb. Call me old. But don't call me late fo' dinner."

After grace, Lee asked innocently enough, "So, Zachariah, how was your mawnin'?"

"I guess I'm in high feather, thanks, Lee," Zachariah returned. Emily and Lee smiled at one of Zack's Gettysburg phrases. "Lucius was over fo' a spell early on. Then I took a ride downtown with Hugo."

Emily slid into the talk. "I saw you leave with Hugo, Daddy. Time was you didn't care much fo' motorcars."

"Well Hugo likes to run 'round in it, an' it's time fo' me to get used to the twentieth century, doncha think?" He finished gently while dipping his spoon into some of his fruit salad.

Emily and Lee raised eyebrows. Lee came back, "Well, yes, of course we oughta be progressing. Any place in particular you an' Hugo progressed to this mawnin'?" Emily loved his little way of turning a word or two.

"Matter fact we did. He took me down to bankin' square. Then he took me over to the Grand Savannah Theater on Bull Street to see the manager."

"The Savannah?" Emily noted in surprise. "On a Wednesday mawnin'?

And what did you need to see the manager about?"

"These." Zachariah pulled an envelope out of his jacket with a flourish and passed it across to Lee and Emily, who both peered inside. "I'd be honored iffin' the three o' us could attend this concert on Thursday the ninth. My treat. The manager showed me these seats an' they're purty good."

"Why, thank you Daddy. That is so kind. I'm sure we could repay you fo' these tickets."

"That's right, Zachariah," Lee chimed in. "You didn't need to go to the trouble to get them." Both of them were touched by his effort and knew what $3.75 for three main floor seats meant to Zachariah's funds.

Zachariah looked steadily at both of them, spoon poised with the last of his fruit. "I know you two could pay yo' own way, but please." Emily almost started in her chair. "I'd like this to be my treat." The silence was broken only by tableware tinkling against the china.

After Alma cleared the fruit cups and brought in the ham and scalloped potatoes, Lee picked another line. He looked at the tickets and said, "This here Marian Anderson. Does she sing or play? Can you tell us 'bout her?"

"I jes' know a little bit," Zachariah answered as he took a bite of ham. "She's in high school in Philadelphia. She sings. But she's head an' shoulders 'bove the common. The papers think she's the real McCoy, even if she is colored."

"Really," Emily remarked. "Hmm. How is it she's able to sing at the Grand Savannah?"

"I asked the manager 'bout that," Zachariah said between chews on his scalloped potatoes. "Her singin' is such the bird that places like the Grand Savannah are puttin' aside their restrictions even in the South." He winked at them. "Green an' silver trumps black fo' theater managers."

"Well, if that's the case," Lee put in, "she must be first water. It's once in a blue moon the Savannah has coloreds on its stage, except fo' vaudeville on Saturday afternoons."

Both Thompsons worked to adjust their thoughts to this chipper, hearty Zachariah, who would take an upsetting motorcar ride, generously spend his few dollars on concert tickets for them, and carry on about a singer, and a colored one at that. "Well, all right," Emily said, still a bit amazed. "Daddy, Lee and I would be delighted to accept. How did you hear about her?"

"From a couple friends," Zachariah replied as Alma began clearing the table. "Calvin in Vermont, an' Lucius here in Savannah."

Conversation over the peach cobbler dessert dawdled across ordinary topics. Lee and Emily had heard Zachariah call his companions in the regiment 'men' and 'boys' and even 'soldiers'. Old Peyton Colby had been a 'pal.' But try as they might, they couldn't remember him using 'friend' until right now, and for a colored man and a Yankee.

Thursday, October 9, 1913

Savannah

Thursday morning was cool in the Laurel Grove cemetery. Two men and a woman stood reverently by a grave. Fresh cut flowers lay up against the tombstone. After a time Emily said, "Well, I think I'm ready."

She was surprised when Zachariah turned to her with brimming eyes and said, "Emily? Yo' mother was salt o' the earth. She meant the world to me. Her birthday today was always full of smiles an' presents an' singin'. Iffn' she was still here, goin' tonatt to the Savannah would tickle her fancy."

Hugo Ratzinger smiled. "Yo' ratt Zack. I remember Aunt Matilda an' my mother always singin' round the house, playin' the piano, makin' us sit still through recitals."

Emily smiled at the memory. "They were two singing sisters, weren't they?"

Zachariah took a deep breath fighting for control and asked, "You remember Bob Bidwell an' I got home on the late train from Chickamauga?"

"Yes?"

"We took a side trip in Atlanta to Gainesville. I went to visit Gen'rul Longstreet's grave. It was a good visit, Emily. I said my piece to him, an' gave him my final salute like I couldn't back in '04." He looked at her steadily. "That man kept me alive through…through ever'thin'. I tried to live up to him. Yo' mother knew his passin' was like losin' a father. We were goin' to his funeral togetha till she caught cold, but she told me I had to go. I told her goodbye and she told me she'd wait for me as usual, 'hopin' every day.' That she passed at the same time ain't somethin' we could see comin'." Emily could not hold back her tears. "As much as Longstreet meant to me, Matilda meant mo'. An' now you mean the most to me. I'm sorry I wasn't by yo' side fo' her passin' but not a day goes by I don't miss her. I want you to know I think the world of you. I'm proud as a jaybird to have you as my daughter."

"Oh, Daddy," Emily said, putting her head on his shoulder.

After a time, as the three walked away from Matilda's grave, Emily asked, "Tell me again how you met Momma."

Zachariah smiled. "There was a concert at the Salzburger church on Wright Square. You know, the one they call Ascension Lutheran nowadays? Well afterwards, dippin' out lemonade at a punch bowl were Matilda an' Greta Ratzinger…"

The Thursday night leaving crowd was thick in front of the Grand Savannah, segregating itself as best it could on the sidewalk, but black and white kept mingling. Some in the crowd were still grousing at the Savannah's signs apologizing for not segregating the lobby that night and a phrase was heard, "With all this mixin' it's like we all are attendin' West Broad Street School or somethin'." Zachariah beamed proudly at the pleasure glistening on Lee's and Emily's faces.

"Daddy, that was such a treat. That girl has a voice that is truly topnotch," Emily said delightedly.

"The highest caliber," Lee added excitedly. "Just astounding."

Around them they could hear echoes similar in nature, though mixed with the occasional crack, "fo' a colored girl" and even "'iffin' only she were watt."

Zachariah put in, "Well, Calvin and Eleanor were really pleased, an' you'd think a judge could judge a voice." He grinned at his own wit.

Lee's height let him see a bit further than many. The faces coming through the doors were increasingly Ethiopian as the balcony emptied. Suddenly he nodded toward the doors and touched his hat brim. "I can see Alma and some others with her over there, headin' this way." Zachariah beamed. At the same time, the crowd flow deposited Libby Pocklington and Rachel Collins alongside the three. Emily's face showed a mix of worry, propriety, and a half-smile. A moment later, Alma, Lucius, and a man and woman whose age was in between the two appeared.

Emily began on her safest ground. "Why, Alma. What a surprise to run into you here, although it is your night off."

"Yes, ma'am," Alma said, appropriately submissive. Libby and Rachel were within earshot, looking for their husbands' carriages. All was proper, lady to servant.

Zachariah turned to Lee and said, "This is Lucius, the one I've told you 'bout. Lucius, this is Mistah Lee Thompson, my son-in-law." Lucius looked at him closely, trying to remember where he's seen these calm, dark eyes over pale skin before, and said, "Pleased to meet ya, suh." He held out his hand. Lee decided in a flash and shook hands under the four arched UDC eyebrows. Unusual but still acceptable, they decided, although Rachel let a glare fall on Lucius.

Zachariah went on. "Lucius, that was some singin'. Best I ever heard. Thankee fo' lettin' me know 'bout her comin' to Savannah."

"Glad ya liked it, suh," Lucius said softly and Zachariah's heart fell as Lucius took to studying the sidewalk. "Now, Lucius, don't you be like..." Zachariah stopped and his face fell, realizing Lucius had to. But he also wondered and he reached across to take Lucius' shoulder. Lucius straightened noticeably and raised his face.

Emily had noted Lee's handshake and saw her father's pain. She glanced at Libby and Rachel and saw their bully stares at the Robinsons. In her mind flashed an image of a northern woman in a barn with a sword. She lifted her chin. "Daddy, I'm so grateful you treated us tonight. Miss Anderson" – the title arched the UDC eyebrows to the hairline – "is a God-gifted talent. She's of the very highest quality and any person alive is privileged to have heard her."

Although crowded in together so most folks wouldn't see anything, Emily squared herself to Lucius and said, "Thank you, Lu... Mister Robinson, for givin' Daddy the idea." Libby and Rachel turned away tossing their heads, so they never saw if Lucius actually shook Emily's outstretched hand there on the sidewalk in front of the Grand Savannah Theater.

Thursday, November 27, 1913

Savannah

The slanting beams of the setting sun came from their left as Emily, Lee, and Zachariah crossed the tracks. It had been a drizzly Thanksgiving morning but it was ending in gold.

"Go on ahead, Lee. Sling the knapsack for new fields," Zack said as the sidewalk narrowed. "Emily will be ratt behind an' I'll bring up the rear."

"Honestly," came Emily's voice, protesting one last time. "Are you sure we should go? There's been one every Friday since Halloween." Alma had come to work wide-eyed once a week. What had first seemed an accidental house fire on the West Side on the 31st had become a weekly story in the *Savannah Tribune.* The paper reported that police detective Miller had turned up hints of arson, but the details were a police secret.

They tramped a few blocks and turned onto Fahm Street. A burned ruin stood on the corner and suddenly Zachariah remembered Dooley's drunken tent singing from the Chickamauga encampment. They passed by quietly until Zachariah said past the lump in his throat, "It'll be the fourth one on the left. It's new, one o' them kit homes from Sears n' Roebuck."

"I've read about those kit homes," Lee said. "There's several on the south side, but this will be my fust time inside one."

"And this'll be my first time on this side of town," said Emily in an edgy tone.

Lucius saw them through the parlor window as they paused to let Zachariah take the lead up the walk. "They's here," he called to the family. Hannah and Sherman scampered up.

"You both ready with yo' company manners?" he asked. They both nodded excitedly.

"Lemme see yo' courtesies." Sherman bowed carefully, then stuck out his hand to Lucius and said, "How do you do, suh?"

"Jes' fine," said Lucius, approving. Hannah dropped a little curtsey with her skirt held just high enough to show off her footwork and Sunday shoes.

"Pleasure to meet you, suh," she said sweetly. Lucius tweaked her cheek and then moved to answer the ring.

Pulling the door open, he smiled and said, "Mr. Hampton, welcome to our home. Would you and yo' family please come in?" Zachariah stepped in with a soldierly stride as a board squeaked under his shoe. Rufus and Beulah stepped up beside Lucius as he closed the door. Zachariah nodded to them all, then helped break some of the tension by offering his hand to a surprised but clearly delighted Lucius.

"Mr. Robinson," he began – Lee and Emily blinked as Zachariah used the title – "this is my daughter Emily Thompson an' my son-in-law Lee." Lucius truly felt the world turned upside down. This introduction overturned all the rules: black folk were presented to white folk, and white folk had titles, while black folks had first names.

"Pleasure to meet you," Lucius said a bit dazed, holding out his hand to Lee. Then he remembered something. "We shook hands before, outside the Grand Savannah the natt Marian Anderson sang."

"Good to make yo' acquaintance, Mr. Robinson," Lee replied, and he gave a hearty shake. "I remember that concert and I was pleased to thank you then for giving the idea to Zachariah."

Lucius dropped his hand and slowly bowed toward Emily while keeping eyes on her face. She found herself at a loss, honored by the rather courtly bow but unnerved by the eye contact.

Lucius turned and said with a small flourish, "Miz Thompson, may I present my son Rufus and my daughter-in-law Beulah?"

"A great pleasure, Mrs. Thompson," Beulah said with a perfect curtsey. "Very pleased," Rufus added with a bow. Zachariah, Emily, and Lee all felt unaccountably like nobility. Rufus suddenly snapped his fingers. "I've got it, Pops. We've been tryin' to place you, Mr. Thompson, apart from the Grand Savannah. I think it was you at the school board meetin' back in Septembah that came up with the savin' idea fo' the West Broad Street School."

Lee dropped his eyes and said, "Well, I just reported on a few measurements. Congressman Smalls was the real hero."

"But you did your part," Beulah answered, "and it's worked out pretty well. In fact, here's two people very happy your idea helped them stay in West Broad Street School."

There was a scurry of quick feet as Hannah and Sherman hurried in. "These are my grandchillun," Lucius said with a wide smile. "May I present Miss Hannah Marie and Mastah Sherman Howard?" Hannah picked up her skirts and swung toward Lee, showed off her long-practiced curtsey, and said, "I'm delighted, suh."

"The pleasure is mine," said Lee dazed, with a short bow.

Hannah pivoted toward Zachariah. "And you too, suh," she chirped. Zachariah came to military attention, then bowed with a snap of the neck.

"An' finally," Hannah said, swinging back part way to face Emily, "I'm tickled to tears to meet you, Miz Thompson." She wanted this curtsey to be deep and spectacular, but as she began she wobbled and pitched to her right. Just as her eyes opened wide in panic at her coming stumble, Emily bent over quickly and reached out and caught both Hannah's elbows and steadied her. Her heart melted at Hannah's face and she gave a small curtsey in return and said, "Miss Hannah Marie, I hope all your tears will ever be from tickles."

Sherman went through his bowing routine with all three visitors, and then Lucius said, "Now that we've done all the introducin', let's move into the parlor fo' some visitin'."

On one parlor wall were several frames. One held a copy of the Gettysburg Address with a picture of Lincoln. Another held a copy of the Emancipation Proclamation. Lee squinted at a third one to make out "Special Field Order #15." There was also an oval photograph of a determined-looking young Lucius in a sergeant's uniform and a black, curly Grant beard.

Zachariah recognized a smaller-framed pencil sketch. "I know that face. That's a fried chicken prisoner."

Lucius laughed. "Yep. A narrow-nosed New Englander."

"A rogue's gallery of one, Your Honor."

"You're ratt," Lucius said half-serious as he turned and poked Zachariah with his finger. "I should add another rogue's picture up heah. Know where I can find one?"

Zachariah looked at him startled. "Really?"

"Yep."

"I'll see what I kin do."

As they sat down, Emily noticed the modest but pleasing furnishings. Lee took in the fine woodwork and the built-in bookcases and cupboards and said, "I understand this is a kit house. I had no idea they were this well trimmed out."

Rufus suddenly found the rug pattern particularly fascinating as Beulah said, "That'd be Rufus' doin'. He's mighty handy with a saw, a miter box, and a varnish brush."

"Are you now?" said Lee to Rufus.

"Well," Rufus answered with only a trace of a stammer. "I makes a livin' at it."

Emily noticed the ceiling crown molding and the gleaming chair rail. "You know, I hadn't noticed before, but Lee is ratt. This is nicely done. It reminds me of the trim I've seen at the Green-Meldrim house on Madison Square when I was there recently for a social."

"Uh, well, yes'm," Rufus said with a real stutter, staring rigidly.

"Don' be that shy, son," Lucius said. "Go ahead an' tell her."

"Tell me what, Mr. Robinson?" Emily said with only a slight stumble at using "Mister."

"Uh, well, you see ma'am," Rufus stumbled, "um, I was the finish carpenter fo' the Green-Meldrim house 'bout three years ago."

Emily was taken aback. "You were the… the finish carpenter for the Green-Meldrim house…" her voice faded.

"Oh, he's got a real gift fo' it, ma'am," said Lucius. "He's done finish work on the Mercer House, the Davenport House, and Magnolia Hall."

Emily was bowled over by the thought that this colored…no, African… no, Ethiopian… bother, what to call him?… that this *man* provided the elegant touches to some of Savannah's most renowned houses. Indeed, he had been in some houses that she could still only long to visit.

"Some iced tea fo' you, Miz Emily?" said Alma, who had noiselessly appeared with a tray-full of glasses.

"Yes, thank you, Alma" Emily said, woodenly, reaching mechanically for the nearest glass. "Alma," she said suddenly, "why, yes, thank you," sputtering with embarrassment as she tried to change her tone from lady to servant to one of friend to hostess. She felt like every eye in the room was on her and she blushed slightly. Recovering, she said to Beulah, "Might I do something to help with dessert? I can be pretty handy in the kitchen."

Now everyone *was* looking at her. Beulah inhaled and said, "That is so kind of you to offer. Why don't we leave the menfolk talkin' 'bout pointless things," here she smiled at Rufus, "and we'll call 'em to the table?" Rising she said, "Alma, would you show Miz Thompson where we keep our company spoons?"

Despite the last moments, Emily already felt more welcome than at any number of socials and teas with the "right" women of Savannah. As she rose to go, the men also stood politely. Emily froze everyone in the room with her next words.

"Beulah," she said, and then turned to make eye contact with others in succession, "Rufus, Mr. Robinson," and after a pause, "Alma? I would be honored if for the rest of the evenin' you would please call me Emily." Beulah's eyes went wide and Alma took an involuntary step back. Rufus, Zachariah, and Lee all wore expressions of amazement. Lucius finally broke the spell with a wide gesture of his hand. "The dinin' room an' kitchen are this way… Emily."

"Thank you, Mr. Robinson," she said with charm as she moved toward the rear of the house. Alma and Beulah trailed after her, exchanging a long glance.

Before the four men could get fairly far along talking, they were summoned to dessert. Pecan and pumpkin pies along with lemonade and iced tea put everyone at ease. Hannah made sure each man had seconds on pie and Sherman kept popping up between bites of his own slice of pecan to refill everyone's glasses. Conversation warmed and the glow of the electric lamps seemed to grow stronger as evening overtook the windows. Beulah and Emily ended up at a corner of the table chatting like old friends. Rufus took Lee on a small house tour and they had a long look at the construction manual. Zachariah and Lucius went onto the front porch for cigars. Neither noticed a figure in the next yard approaching the shadow of the camellia bush at the end of the porch.

"Now you sit here in my rocker," Lucius was saying to Zachariah.

"All ratt," said Zachariah, settling in and finding the rocker quite comfortable. He held his cigar to his mouth as Lucius produced a striker match and flicked it lit with his thumbnail. Zachariah made two or three pulls until the business end glowed a bright orange.

"You wait ratt here. A cigar don't taste ratt lessen it's washed down with some whiskey."

Zachariah snorted a chuckle and nodded to Lucius as the old vet went back inside. Zachariah took a long draw and rocked back and forth slightly, as though the smoke of his exhale had blown him backwards. He saw the door open and Lucius bringing a small tray with two glasses and a flask. He heard a floor board creak as Lucius stepped out, but he never heard the shot.

Lucius did. He heard the pistol roar and the glass of the window crash in shards as the bullet passed through the back of Zachariah's head and lodged in the parlor ceiling. He saw the flash light up the leaves of the bush, some directly and some in silhouette. For an instant he also saw the profile of a face cut up by the leaves and a left eye squeezed shut after aiming. Zachariah's cigar dropped and rolled to a stop between two boards, melting some of the spar varnish into a scorch. As first one, then two screams erupted from inside, Lucius made out a bowlegged shadow heading away from the bush, but still in line with it.

No one had been in the parlor at the moment of the shot. Hannah and Sherman were crying somewhere in their room. Rufus and Lee were in the doorway of Alma's room and Emily and Beulah were holding each other in shock and tears in the dining room. "Was that a gun shot?" Emily wailed. "O God, help us." She made to stand, but Beulah held her down and whispered urgently, "Put yo' haid down on the table. There might be mo'." Lee was about to bolt through the parlor to be with Emily, but Rufus grabbed his arm and pulled him down into a half crouch. "Wait a spell," he said, scared. "We don' know if they's done shootin'." This struck Lee as fearfully reasonable. Emily's wail choked down to frightened sobs from the dining room, now mixed with Beulah's low voice telling her to try to keep quiet so a shooter wouldn't know where to shoot. The crash of a dropped dinner plate from the kitchen announced Alma, too, was not herself.

Lucius' voice boomed from the front hall, "There was jes' one an he's run off. I think we'll be all ratt fo' now."

Lee and Rufus came into the parlor and saw a slowing rocker through the shattered window. Powdered plaster fell in a tiny, lazy column, marking where the bullet had plowed through before lodging in one of the attic rafters.

"Rufus," said Lucius quickly, "you've got to go up to Bay Street lickety-split and fetch the poh-lees. Tell 'em careful-like that an old watt man's been shot over on Fahm Street. Go ratt now." Rufus nodded and rushed out the front door. He hesitated on the porch and his eyes darted around the gloom. He cocked his head, listening for unusual sounds, but there were only neighbors calling out and asking each other what had happened.

Lee stood in shock at Lucius' words to Rufus. Lucius called back into the kitchen, "Alma, stay with Hannah and Sherman for a spell, would you?" Then Lucius stared hard at Lee. "Zachariah's dead. Haid shot." Lee's stomach reeled and a wave of nausea swept to his throat. Lucius saw him paling rapidly and gripped his arm. "Settle down, Mistah Thompson. You've got to be strong now fo' Miz Emily. We gotta tell her best we can an' then we's got to hepp her."

Lee swallowed hard and used a deep breath to beat back the nausea. "Okay," he said, and Lucius saw the strength welling back in him. "Let's go."

The two entered the dining room grim-faced to find Emily sobbing in fright, both hands clutching a handkerchief by her nose, her eyes screwed shut and her elbows pinned to her sides. Beulah was also shaking and had her hands on Emily's elbows, trying to console her.

Lee moved over to Emily's chair and knelt in front of her. Lucius moved behind Beulah. She leaned back and reached up one hand to her own shoulder where Lucius' hand rested.

"Emily," Lee said softly, putting his arms around her, "it's Lee. Look at me, sweetheart." After one more shudder Emily slowly opened her eyes to see Lee's troubled face.

"Emily," and his voice soothed her some more, "I have to tell you. That shot you heard, the one that frighted you so much – Emily, that shot just killed yo' father."

Emily stared, searching his eyes for some sign, some hint, she hadn't heard what he'd just said. Beulah gasped and her tears flowed freely. A tear rolled down Lucius' face as well. Emily looked from Lee to the others, then back to Lee. She let out a hopeless wail, rocked forward in his arms, and fainted.

Tuesday, December 2, 1913

Savannah

Tuesday came in gloomy with a stiff wind. The First Baptist Church filled for Zachariah's funeral, not only with family and friends but with strangers too. City Engineer John Howard sat with old Nicholas Symington, retired president of the Central of Georgia Railroad. Despite personal feelings, Libby Pocklington and Rachel Collins came with their husbands, along with Pauline Meldrim and Juliette Low. Hugo and Katie Ratzinger sat kitty corner from Lee and Emily, unconsciously matching the relation between their houses. Several of Payton Colby's relations came, as did several retired Central of Georgia conductors in uniform. Emily recognized a little man in a tan suit but couldn't place him since he was outside the brass bars of his teller's window.

The service was done in high style and the music was beautiful. As everyone followed the casket outside across the Greek temple porch, they could see the clouds were thinning and the wind had fallen off. It was about a mile and a half to Laurel Grove Cemetery and the processional was long. The UCV Longstreet Post honorary pallbearers refused kind offers to ride and instead walked alongside the horse-drawn hearse. The muffled drums of a band beat the walkers the distance and through the cemetery gates. Several gravediggers waited respectfully by the fence. A band and a Confederate rifle squad waited at the freshly dug grave next to Matilda's. Behind the rifle squad, a color guard held a Confederate flag, the Georgia flag, the UCV Longstreet post ensign, and the new forty-eight-star Stars and Stripes rippling overhead.

Emily and Lee sat down on a short bench as the mourners assembled. The band offered a mournful rendition of "Dixie." The Reverend McWilliams offered his final prayers and benediction. After the coffin was lowered, Emily rose and moved to the edge of the grave. She nodded to McWilliams who stepped forward with his strong voice.

"Miz Emily Thompson has asked me to explain. Sergeant Hampton attended the National Peace Jubilee Encampment in Gettysburg this summah. He met a certain Union soldier there. A telegram was sent to Vermont with the news of Zachariah's death and yesterday a special delivery letter arrived in return."

Here McWilliams unfolded a small piece of paper and read the precise, steady lines.

I wore these brass letters, 'VT' for Vermont, all my days with the Army of the Potomac. I wore them with great pride to all the functions of the Grand Army of the Republic. I wore them to Gettysburg this summer where I met Zachariah Hampton of the 8th Georgia. They are a sign of my devotion to duty and to a cause, the cause of America. My brief but deep friendship with Zachariah Hampton was part of healing what some called 'an irrepressible conflict' and others 'an impassible gulf'. I would be honored if these letters could be buried with my comrade from the South, my fellow soldier, my friend.

Major Calvin Salisbury,
14th Vermont.

Emily bent down and gently tossed the old brass letters onto the flat lid. Lee moved to her side as the rifle squad came to attention. Three old fashioned, black powder volleys cracked toward the sky. Emily moved to the mound of fresh piled earth and tossed in the first handful. Lee threw in the second. As they circled back to the bench and the other mourners came forward, the band softly played "When Johnny Comes Marching Home."

The line of mourners past the pile of earth was almost done when the band finished playing. Everyone was gathering themselves to leave when they saw a small group approaching. Four men walked, no, marched in a single rank, trailed by a man and two women. They stopped about fifty feet short of Zachariah's grave. Emily rose and lifted the black veil from her face to see more clearly. Yes. They were in matching dark blue uniforms.

The first man in line turned his long pole and unfurled a shot-torn American flag, stitched with place names on its white stripes. The second man likewise unfurled a dark red silken banner stitched with white letters: "Rufus Saxton Post, Grand Army of the Republic, Savannah Ga." The third man pulled a bugle out from under his arm and began to play. And on the right, the post of honor, First Sergeant Lucius Robinson, 2nd South Carolina Union Volunteers, saluted and wept. "Taps" was written by a man in McClellan's army, but its bittersweet ache made it a favorite of both sides before the War was half over.

Beulah, Rufus, and Alma stood at Lucius' side with civilian salutes, holding their right hands over their hearts. Emily curtseyed toward them, turned toward the grave and also put her hand on her heart. The rest of the mourners followed Emily's example. The rifle squad and pallbearers from the Longstreet post matched her with military salutes.

When "Taps" ended, Lucius' friends from the GAR post withdrew. Emily and Lee, shepherded by Hugo and Katie, went over to the Robinsons. Low murmurs came from the mourners at the easy familiarity and apparent bond between the Thompsons and Robinsons.

A tall, square-shouldered man wearing a dark overcoat and sporting a handlebar moustache made his way casually around the gravesite. He appeared to be lost in thought, looking down at the casket, but he was listening carefully to various snatches of conversation. Henry Miller had joined the Savannah police department in 1903. He had made sergeant in his fourth year and detective two years later. A careful, thorough man, his one quiet passion was anything from the pens of Arthur Conan Doyle and Georgia's own Jacques Futrelle. His captain was often surprised by Miller's success in solving cases, but then the captain thought Sherlock Holmes and Dr. Van Dusen were only for boys.

Those two literary detectives made Miller wonder about Hampton's case. The physical evidence was scanty, motive or suspects obscure. Hampton had no known enemies, was not powerful or wealthy. Playing a hunch, Miller came to the funeral.

Turner Hawkins, Dooley Culpepper, Jim Calhoun, and other UCV men were talking with many headshakings. "Cain't b'lieve it," Dooley was saying. "Zachariah dead."

"Awful. Jes' awful," Calhoun agreed.

"A heavy loss," Robert Bidwell added.

"Dang shame," Hawkins muttered.

After a pause, Dooley asked, "I ain't heerd how it happened."

Bidwell glared at him. Dooley probably hadn't heard because he'd been on a three day bender in honor of Thanksgiving. Bidwell had found him yesterday in his little shack of a house with a barbed wire hangover. He'd written down the time and place for the rifle squad and stayed until he'd fed Dooley a cup of coffee. Today Dooley was upright but still sported a pair of red-rimmed eyes and some deep-etched drinking lines by the corners of his mouth.

"Died over on the west side," Calhoun was saying, "on somebody's front poach."

"Visitin' friends?" Dooley asked.

"Friends!" Hawkins spat out. "Like hell. I ain't heerd rhyme o' reason why he an' his fam'ly was at his maid's house."

Dooley looked at him sharply. "Maid's house?"

"Yep," Bidwell said with a head shake. "On Thanksgivin' natt most folk stay in. Never heard no one visitin' a servant's house fo' Thanksgivin'."

Dooley swallowed dryly as, nearby, a woman on her husband's arm sobbed loudly. The pair walked past Rachel Collins and Libby Pocklington and a dark-coated man with a handlebar moustache. Dooley shifted uneasily and said in a voice halfway between hungover and afraid. "Thanksgivin' natt. Terrible natt to keel over."

Jim Calhoun frowned at him. "A bullet to the haid sho' will keel ya over."

"Dang!" Turner said, smashing his fist into his palm. "Why cain't them colored robbers take a natt off like Thanksgivin'?"

Calhoun sighed heavily. "Who knows what they think, or even iffin they do."

"'Inferior race,'" Dooley agreed dully.

"Say, Bob, you need some hepp gettin' the flags back to the post?" Jim asked.

"Thankee, Jim. I'm 'bliged." The color and rifle squads dispersed.

Dooley walked slowly out of Laurel Grove, the ten pounds of his rifle heavier than usual. He took a streetcar up Broad, then waited on a "white" bench under a "colored" sign for a few minutes. He took an eastbound on Bay Street to the edge of town where a neighborhood of down-luck houses clung to the Savannah riverbank. He didn't notice the mustachioed stranger at the far end of the car who rode along from the cemetery to his stop.

Dooley trudged into his tin-roofed shanty, put away his rifle and changed out of his uniform. He flopped down on a worn sofa and lifted a flask of Kentucky's finest off of a slip of paper. The paper read, "Tuesday, 10:30 am. Laurel Grove Cemetery. Zachariah."

Henry Miller wrote down the Dooley's house address in his little notebook, then took a streetcar back to the West Bay Street station.

Tuesday, January 27, 1914

Savannah

"The state calls Lucius Robinson," Bailey Taggert announced. A compact man of forty-five, Taggert was clean shaven, with jet-black hair slicked down and carefully parted. Lucius walked through the courtroom gate in his dark blue Sunday suit and white-striped tie as the crowd hummed. Colored testimony often weakened a case, but Taggert hardly had a choice. Lucius was the only eyewitness.

Lucius stood by the witness stand as the bailiff picked up a shopworn Bible from a bare plank shelf and said with a bored air, "Put yo' left hand on the Bible. Raise yo' ratt hand. In yo' testimony do you sweah to tell the truth, the whole truth, an' nuthin' but the truth, so hepp you God?"

"I do," Lucius replied earnestly. The bailiff looked like he didn't believe a word. "Take the stand and state yo' full name," the bailiff said. Without waiting for Lucius, he turned and indifferently replaced the Bible on its shelf.

"Lucius Greene Robinson."

Taggert began. "Lucius, what is yo' current address?"

"305 Fahm Street."

"Is that address a rooming house, hotel, boarding house, or what?"

"It's my house since 1888."

"So you've been a homeowner for twenty-five years?"

"Yes, suh."

"Do you live there by yo'seff?"

"No, suh. My son Rufus, his wife Beulah, an' three granchillun all live there."

"I see. Now Lucius, were you at home on the evening of Novembah 27th, 1913?"

Yes, suh. We were all home."

"Will you tell the cote what happened that natt?"

Lucius recounted Thanksgiving evening up to the moment of the shooting. Taggert summarized, "So you were standin' in the front door, one foot on the poach, holdin' the tray with the glasses and the flask, is that ratt?"

"Yes, suh."

"Describe what you saw and heard next."

"There was a shot. The flash lit up the camellia bush at the end of the poach. Mistah Hampton slumped in my rockin' chair. The front window of the parlor broke real loud."

"Was there any smoke from the gun?" Taggert prompted.

"Yes, suh. Some of the smell of it drifted into the parlor."

"Would you say there was a cloud of smoke?"

"Yes, suh, quite a cloud."

"How large a cloud would you say, size wise?"

"Oh, maybe three o' four feet across."

"I see. And you say you smelled the gunsmoke?"

"Yes, suh."

"Anything in the smell remind you of anything?"

"Objection," Clayton Loomis called from the defense table.

"Overruled," Judge Crawford said crisply.

"Go ahead, Lucius."

"Well suh, the smoke was black powder smoke, like from the Wah."

"Objection!" Loomis was on his feet. His silver hair showed more of his fifty-nine years than his unlined face. "Hearsay evidence. Witness cannot know the smell of black powder smoke from the Wah Between the States. No foundation for this claim."

"Sustained," came the word from the bench. "Jury will disregard witness's last answer."

Taggert doubled back. "Lucius, you are retired, is that ratt?"

"Yes, suh."

"Retired from what?"

"I was a harness maker 'round town fo' some of the livery stables. Also did a lot of carpentry work."

"Do that yo' whole life did you?"

Lucius caught on where Taggert was going. "Well, yes, suh, after I got mustered out of the army."

At the defense table, attorney Loomis and defendant Dooley Culpepper froze. Several members of the jury sat up as Taggert asked, "And what army was that, Lucius?" The spectators were still with surprise.

Lucius pulled himself up and said with a crisp fire, "I was Fust Sawjint, 2nd South Carolina Union Volunteers, Fust Brigade, Second Division, Howard's XI Corps, Army of the Tennessee, General Sherman commandin', suh." Up in the colored balcony, after each piece of the identification, one or two more old bearded men stood, shoved their heels together, stuck out their chests and did their best to pull in their stomachs. As Lucius reached "Sherman," salutes snapped into place. Younger men in the gallery looked around in shock while women covered their mouths in wonder, and not a few tears of pride rolled down cheeks.

Most of the white folk on the main floor missed the muster upstairs but the courtroom buzzed. Juror Number Three blanched like a first-day recruit at the steel in Lucius' voice. Over Judge Crawford's banging gavel, Taggert called out, "And where did you learn about the smell of black powder gunsmoke?"

Lucius punctured the shaky hopes of those imagining him a ditch-digger or cook. "Gettysburg. Lookout Mountain. Missionary Ridge. Resaca. Dalton. New Hope Church. Kennesaw Mountain. Ezra Church. Chattahoochee Creek. Jonesboro." He looked up at the balcony and swept his eyes across it, then gave a crisp nod that said "dismissed" as surely as if he'd ordered it aloud. The men dropped their salutes and sat back down.

Taggert's quiet voice tightened the intensity. "So you know the smell of black powder gunsmoke, then?

"Yes, suh." Defense had no objection.

"So that's what you smelled on yo' front poach and in yo' parlor?"

"Yes, suh."

"What happened next?" Lucius recounted events from the arrival of the police to the removal of the body.

Taggert sat down, satisfied. Lucius had been calm and matter-of-fact. His speech had shown some signs of education but not too much. "Solid, reliable testimony," he thought to himself. "Yo' witness," he said out loud.

Clayton Loomis stood and tugged the lapels of his black suit. He walked halfway to the witness stand. "Lucius Greene Robinson. How old are you, uncle?"

"Objection!" Taggert snapped, annoyed that it had started with the first question. "Counsel is demeaning and intimidating the witness."

"Jes' tryin' to be friendly, yo' honor," Loomis said with innocent eyes.

"He's not a witness fo' yo' side. Jury will disregard counsel's 'friendly' remark. Witness will state his age."

"I'm seventy-three, yo' honnah."

Loomis continued. "So how well do yo' seventy-three-year-old eyes see?"

"I have some spectacles to hepp me read."

"Oh. So you say you can read. Could you demonstrate yo' ability to this cote?"

"Objection yo' honor. Witness did not testify to reading anything."

"Sustained."

"All ratt. Lucius, you said it was Thanksgivin' evenin' all this happened. 'Bout what time was the shootin'?"

"'Bout quarter to eight, suh."

"Pretty dark by then, wasn't it?"

"Yes, suh."

"How could you see what happened in the dark?"

"Well, suh, we had the latts on in the parlor, and the parlor window faces that side of the poach."

"Were the parlor latts gas or kerosene?"

"Neither one, suh. They's electrical."

"And did the parlor window have curtains?"

"Objection," came Taggert's voice. "Home decoratin' yo' honor?"

Loomis turned. "Defense is tryin' to 'stablish how much or how little latt was on the poach fo' the witness to see by."

"Overruled."

"Now, Lucius. Curtains?"

"Yes, suh. They's watt cotton curtains, jes' one layer."

"And were the curtains open or closed across the window?"

Lucius thought for a time, trying to remember. "I don't know, suh."

"You don't know?"

"No, suh. I know they was open when the police came but I don't remember iffin' they was open or closed before then."

Loomis gave the jury a long look. "Now, Lucius, you said when the shot came you were standin' in the doorway, one foot on the poach, holdin' what again?"

"I had a tray with two glasses an' a flask of whiskey. Zacha... ,uh, Mistah Hampton an' I was goin' to have some with our cigars."

"An' was this flask of whiskey full? A new bottle?"

"No, suh. It was partway gone."

"An' did you make it partway gone before you put it on the tray?"

"No, suh."

Clayton suddenly roared at Lucius. "Ain't it a fact that you'd been drinkin' with supper, drinkin' after supper when Mistah Hampton and the Thompsons came over, and had another nip before you loaded the tray? Ain't that the truth?"

"No, suh," Lucius said firmly.

"Weren't you as loaded as that tray?"

"No, suh."

Loomis pounded ahead. "You weren't standin' there in the doorway. You were leanin' 'gainst it to keep yo' seff from fallin' down, ain't that the truth?"

"No, suh," Lucius answered firmly, mostly looking annoyed and remembering Woolworth's in Gettysburg.

"You were drunk as a skunk that natt, weren't you?"

Lucius took a breath and slowed his reply, making Loomis march to his tempo. "No, suh." His tone almost dared Loomis look him in the eye. After a glance, Loomis looked at the jury.

"Yo' own family sent you out on that poach 'cause you were drunk an' they didn't want you 'round, ain't that ratt?"

Lucius set his jaw. "No, suh."

"Uh huh, so you say," Loomis remarked to the jury. "You in the habit of keepin' liquor in yo' house?" Lucius let the silence grow to fit around his scorn.

"We keeps some on hand."

"And how often do you need to restock?" Loomis asked pointedly.

"Whenever we run out, suh," came the answer in a near growl. A few giggles rose from the spectators.

"An' that happens how often? Ever' few days, maybe?" The pause lingered so that Loomis looked Robinson in the eye for a moment and quailed slightly.

"No, suh," Lucius answered with a deliberate pace. "Around holiday time we have mo' of it, but that flask had been 'round fo' several months."

"So you say. No mo' questions, yo' honor." As Lucius stepped down, Loomis took an extra long drink of water at the defense table.

"Emily Thompson, please step forward," the bailiff called. Emily rose from the second row and stepped past her husband. She wore her dark green Sunday skirt and a pleated white blouse. Her eye was steady but perhaps a bit wetter than usual. The bailiff lifted a handsome, leather-bound Bible from its velvet-encased shelf and held it before her. Without prompting, she removed her left glove, put her hand on the book and raised her right hand for the swearing. Taggert was brief and pointed in his direct examination.

For cross-examination, Loomis was in a tough spot. Emily's testimony as a white woman had corroborated Lucius' and partially offset the taint of his color. He had to untie Emily's testimony from Lucius', but a direct attack on a woman was risky.

Clayton stepped forward. "Miz Thompson, as we begin, let me say I'm deeply sorry fo' yo' loss. I'll try to keep this short."

"Thank you," Emily answered in a whisper.

"Now then, yo' fatha, yo' husband, and yo'seff went over to the Robinsons' house on Thanksgivin' natt. Had you been there before?"

"No, sir."

"How does a lady like yo'seff know a West Side colored family like the Robinsons?"

"Alma Robinson is our maid. Turns out her grandfather, Lucius Robinson, came to know my father, Zachariah Hampton."

"How did they meet?"

"At Gettysburg last summah."

"I see," Loomis responded, holding his lapels. "So yo' fatha met Lucius handin' out blankets or cookin' at that Encampment an' got friendly with him?"

"No, sir."

Loomis looked up confused. "No?"

"No, my father attended the all-white Encampment at Gettysburg as a veteran of the War and of that battle. The colored folk put together their own Camp Lincoln fo' their own, that is, the rest of the veterans." Whispers ran through the room. Discrimination and segregation were assumed and practiced, but it was somewhat impolite to directly point them out. "The blue, gray, white, and black veterans got along quite well, accordin' to my father."

The look in Emily's eye made Lee unconsciously clench the arm of his chair two rows back. It made Loomis waver, but he took it as a dare. "So yo' fatha an' yo' family are in the habit of associatin' with colored folk?"

"My father and..." she took a deep breath, "Mistah Robinson," she continued as whispers rose, "were veterans of the same War. The Encampment was for reconciling the veterans, No'th and South, and through them, the nation. By all accounts, including a speech from President Wilson, there *was* a reconciling and reunion. My Confederate father and Union Sergeant Robinson are...were, an example." A tear streaked her cheek but her gaze remained steady.

Loomis was game. "Perhaps that accounts fo' yo' father. Fo' what reason would a woman of yo' standin' associate with them?"

Emily blinked and a tiny smile creased her lips. "By reason of faith, Mistah Loomis. My Bible teaches me 'in Christ there is neither Jew nor Greek, slave nor free, male nor female, but all are one in Christ.'"

On shaky ground Loomis countered, "So' yo' Bible tells you to go visitin' folks 'neath yo' station?" counting on Emily's ambition and pride.

She almost imagined those Port Royal women smiling down on her as she spoke quickly so Loomis could not interrupt, "It's not a matter of station but a matter of being an American. Jefferson declared 'all men are created equal.' Are you opposed to Mr. Jefferson and his Declaration, Mr. Loomis?" She raised her voice slightly over the murmurs running around the room. "Madison wrote our Constitution to 'secure the blessings of liberty upon us and our posterity.' Would you oppose the liberty of Mr. Madison's Constitution, Mr. Loomis? I must say I stand with the Founding Fathers, Mr. Loomis. Whom do you stand with?"

The courtroom erupted. Lee heard comments ricocheting around like, "She's right, you know," "Pretty feisty for a woman" and "A real lady wouldn't talk like that to a man in public." Taggert wore a broad smile. Loomis looked like a sick tomcat. The colored gallery was all smiles and handshakes and ladies' handkerchiefs waved in salute of Emily. Judge Crawford gaveled some time for order. "Spectators will conduct themselves in silence, or I will clear the courtroom! Y'all understand that?" he glowered over his gavel. "Mistah Loomis, you may continue."

Loomis wondered if he should, or even if he could. "If we leave aside politics and return to the case," he opened gamely, "would you say yo' late fathah was on good terms with Unc... uh, Lucius?"

"Yes, suh."

"And were you were on good terms with this black man as well?"

Emily dodged. "He was a fellow veteran and companion to my fatha."

"Do you consider him a friend of yo's?"

"He is my maid's grandfather. He was a comrade to my fatha. I consider him... a good acquaintance."

"An acquaintance who regularly visited yo' house."

"Yes."

"An acquaintance who had refreshments at yo' house."

"Yes."

"An acquaintance you prepared iced tea or lemonade fo'?"

"Yes."

"An acquaintance who you wrote letters fo'." A murmur ran around the room.

"Yes."

"An acquaintance you visited in his home on Thanksgiving?"

"Yes."

"An acquaintance whose family was introduced to yo' family?"

"Yes."

"An acquaintance in whose house you ate and drank on Thanksgiving natt?"

"Yes." More whispers fluttered.

"An acquaintance who you invited to call you by yo' fust name? Not 'Miz Emily' or 'Miz Thompson' but simply 'Emily' ain't that ratt?"

Emily paled and swallowed. "Yes."

"Miz Thompson that's quite an acquaintance with a Negro man." The crowd squirmed. "Negro" was only used for slaves before the War or for insult. It was as close as Loomis could come to using another word beginning with "N".

"An' as a woman of faith, an' of yo' word, you want to stick up fo' yo' acquaintances, don't you Miz Thompson? Take their side, ratt Miz Thompson?" Another tear rolled down Emily's cheek.

"No further questions, yo' honor."

Emily rose and stepped down. A look of resolve came over her and she strode purposefully through the gate. Lee rose to greet her back to her seat, but she walked on down the aisle. Confused, Lee picked up his hat and followed.

As Taggert called out, "State calls Henry Miller to the stand," a commotion stirred in the courtroom balcony. The bailiff picked up the velvet-shelved Bible. As he turned to swear in Miller, he could see a white couple sitting over on the left side of the colored gallery by a similarly aged black couple. The bailiff recognized Lucius Robinson welcoming Emily and Lee Thompson, sitting next to Rufus and Beulah.

Henry Miller answered the bailiff, "I do," and sat down. Bailey Taggert stood and swept his soft gray eyes over the jury on their way to the stand.

"Now Detective Miller, we have heard Savannah Police officers retell the events of November 27 at the Robinson house on Fahm Street. When did you fust visit the scene of the crime?"

"The next mawnin', November 28. I got there about eight o'clock," Miller answered.

"Please describe what you found outside the house."

"Yes, suh," Miller answered, pulling out a small, flip-over notebook. "The front poach runs 'cross the whole house. On the ratt end there was a rockin' chair. Also at that end there's a big camellia bush 'bout fourteen feet high and maybe five feet through."

"Did you examine the ground around the bush, Detective?"

"Yes, suh. I found a set of footprints with the toes pointin' toward the poach. I went 'round back and found a crate box an' put it over the footprints. Later that mawnin' I came back with some plaster mix and made a cast of the prints."

Taggert lifted a pair of ghost white plaster squares from the prosecution table.

"Are these the casts, Detective?" handing them to Miller.

Miller peered at one corner of the casts. "Yes, suh," he answered. "As the plaster set up I put my initials and the date here on the corner. After I made the cast, I made this second slab from the fust one showin' how the footprints looked in the ground."

The slabs fit together perfectly, and both were admitted into evidence.

"What else did you find outdoors at the crime scene, Detective?"

Miller continued. "In among the leaves, on the ground, an' on the poach side of the bush, there were small bits of papah. Lookin' at them under a magnifyin' glass I could see their edges on most of 'em were burned."

Taggert handed him a small envelope. "Would these be those bits of paper, Detective?"

"Yes, suh. This is my envelope, my initials, and the date here. I also wrote, 'Robinson case, paper bits' here on the flap." The paper bits were admitted.

"Detective Miller, these are small bits of paper," Taggert remarked, looking in the envelope. "Did you handle them with your fingers?"

"No, suh. They're frail, so I used tweezers."

"What kind of paper this is, Detective? Butcher paper maybe, or newspaper?"

"None of those, suh. It's latt weight, some sort o' tissue paper. Look here." Miller produced a pair of tweezers and plucked out a piece smaller than a postage stamp.

"If I hold this and wave it a bit," he said, fluttering the piece toward the jury, and then turning, toward the judge, "it waves ratt easy." He placed the sample back in the envelope, then tore off a bit of paper from the back page of his notebook close to the same size.

"On the other hand, "he said, taking this piece in the tweezers, "this paper, held the same way and bein' the same size, but which I know is writin' paper, it doesn't wave near as much." Once again he waved toward the jury and the judge, and this piece of paper was definitely stiffer. The judge looked suitably impassive, but three or four members of the jury nodded unconsciously.

Taggert noted these jurors and went on. "Now, detective, what else did you find at the scene of the crime?" Taggert carefully repeated "scene of the crime" to build up a certain image in the minds of the jury.

"Well, suh, the top back of the rockin' chair is woven cane. An oblong chunk of it was missin'. There were bits of cane weave on poach. Some of those bits, and a whole lot of the cane weave on the rocker, and a splotch of the poach floor about eighteen inches across was dark red with dried blood. Also on the poach was a fair bit of broken glass. The parlor window had been broken and bits of it were still everywhere."

"Detective Miller, cane weave bits and broken glass bits. Did you find either of these anywhere else at the scene?"

"Yes, suh," Miller answered. "The window facin' the poach is a parlor. A whole lot more glass bits and bigger shards were inside. There were a few cane weave bits too, but most o' them were outside on the poach."

"Like the bullet that broke the window came from the outside?"

"Objection."

"Sustained."

"Like whatever broke the window came from outside?"

"Yes, suh."

"Did you find anythin' else in the parlor inside?" Taggert asked.

"Yes, Mr. Taggert." Miller said. "Toward the back o' the room up in the ceilin' was a gouged out hole 'bout as thick as yo' finga, but taperin', with the shallower end angled toward the window."

"What else did you discover about the angle of this gouged hole?"

"Well, suh, I had Rufus Robinson get up on a ladder an' hold one end of a long piece of string I brought with me. I told him to hold the string in the deepest end of the gouge. Then I took the otha end through the winda frame onto the poach an' pulled the string tatt in a straight line."

"And where exactly did this string line go?" Taggert prompted.

"The string line went ratt through the top of the rockin' chair on the poach an' into the camellia bush where the box was over the foot prints."

"Like whatever made the gouge came from the camellia bush."

"Yes, suh."

"Did you discover what caused this gouged hole?"

"Yes, suh. Usin' some o' Rufus' tools, we cut through the plaster at the hole. There's a big rafter above the ceiling and small hole in it in line with the gouge. With a bit an' brace we drilled out around the hole and pulled out a bullet."

Taggert was ready with another envelope. "Would this be the bullet you found?"

Miller went through his identification ritual again. Taggert presented the bullet to Loomis and Culpepper at the defense table. Dooley looked away and Loomis glanced at it with disdain. The bullet was passed among the jurors and returned to Taggert.

"Now, Detective Miller," Bailey said, "what can you tell the jury about this bullet?"

Miller consulted his notebook again. "Well, sir, the bullet is flattened out on one side, the side that hit the raftah. The back side is round as round. I had Dr. John Foster at Gaylord's Pharmacy, just down the street from the police station, test it for any sign of copper or brass. He said…"

"Objection," Loomis boomed. "Hearsay."

"Your honor," Taggert responded, "Dr. Foster has often assisted the Savannah police this way and is beyond reproach. However, if the defense would like us to call Dr. Foster instead of relying on the lettah he wrote the court and the defense, we will do so."

Judge Crawford eyed the pharmacist's letter and Foster's signature at the bottom. He said, "In view of Dr. Foster's limited addition to this case, and his common practice of helpin' the police in these matters in the past, I will overrule the objection. Prosecution will call Dr. Foster as a witness if you go beyond this heah lettah."

"Thank you, yo' honah," Bailey said. He turned back to Detective Miller. "You may continue."

"Well, sir, like Dr. Foster writes, the bullet is all lead and there's no trace of any other metal. He said it weighs 128 grains or 3 an' 4/10 ounces. The measure of the diameter makes it a .42 caliber."

"What else can you tell us about this bullet?" Taggert urged.

"Given what Dr. Foster told us, and its shape, it can't be from a modern gun. It's too big to fit an Enfield rifle or a Navy Colt pistol, and too small for a Smith & Wesson. Given it's a ball and the little bits of paper I found, this would have been fired from a muzzle loading gun, with a paper cartridge and black powdah."

"Objection!" called Loomis, scrambling to his feet. "The detective cannot know this for a fact."

"Either a bullet fits in a gun barrel or it doesn't," Taggert answered. The two attorneys argued the point vigorously, but the court ruled for Taggert.

"Now then, Detective Miller," Taggert said at last, "when were guns that used paper cartridges and round lead bullets common?"

"Until recently," Miller answered. "Factory-made metal cartridges for the Yankee cavalry's Spencers were made toward the end of the War. Colt started making six-shooter bullets couple years later. Smokeless powdah was invented in 'bout 1887 and has been used evah since."

"So would it be fair to say," Taggert boomed, tugging at his lapels, "that the younger a person is, the less likely they would be to be familiar with homemade ammunition?"

"Objection," came from Loomis.

"Sustained," said the judge. "The jury will disregard the last question."

"Detective, to your knowledge, did soldiers in the War Between the States make ammunition for their weapons?"

"I've read that much of the ammunition was made in shops and factories, even though it was paper cartridges. But a lot of fellers knew how."

"Thank you, Detective," Bailey gave Dooley a long look at the defense table. He led Miller through his visit to Hampton's funeral, tailing Dooley home, and later interviewing some of the rifle squad. Accompanied by a patrolman, Miller had gone to Dooley's house.

"Did the defendant object to you searching his house?"

"No, sir."

"What did you find at defendant Dooley Culpepper's house?"

"Well it's jest a porch, front room, bedroom, and a bit of a kitchen. Out back, there's an outhouse and a shed. In the shed I found some latt weight tissue paper and some black powder gunpowder. In the front closet we found a .42 caliber LaMatt revolver, recently fired."

"Objection," Loomis called. "Calls for a conclusion."

"Sustained."

"Detective, could you describe the condition of the LaMatt revolver?"

"There was a strong gunpowder smell to it and black powder residue in the barrel. Five of the six chambers were loaded with paper cartridges. The one jes' past the hammer was empty with black powdah residue inside it."

"Did you find anything else in the house?"

"Under the bed I found an old pair of high-topped shoes, men's size six, with dried mud on 'em. The left heel on the outside is worn down at an odd angle. The sole on the ratt one is wearin' through by the toe and is missin' five little nails, two on the inside of the foot and three on the outside."

Taggert brought Miller the high topped old shoes and then the plaster cast made at the Robinson's house. Miller fit the left shoe in one cavity for a perfect fit. He indicated the five open nail holes in the right shoe and the matching tiny peaks in the cast of the right footprint, as well as the matching shape and location of the wear hole. The jurors took their time studying these as they passed along. Several glanced under the defense table at Dooley's prison-issued black brogans.

"Having found these items in the defendant's house, what did you do?"

"I had him arrested an' charged with murder."

"Thank you detective. Your witness."

Thursday, February 12, 1914

Rutland

It was mid-afternoon and Calvin was about to start dressing for the GAR Lincoln Day dinner when Eleanor answered the doorbell and helped Sam off with his hat, coat, and scarf. "Why, Sam," Calvin exclaimed. "Good to see you... although I thought it'd be later tonight."

Sam's face was so somber Eleanor blurted out, "My heavens, Sam. Has someone died?"

Sam sat down at the dining room table and took out several letters as Calvin and Eleanor joined him. His freshly cleaned dress uniform added extra weight to his words. "After John Franklin's funeral last month, I went home and looked through my souvenirs from Gettysburg to see if I had something to remember John. I didn't, but I came across a sheet of four sketches of Josiah I'd forgotten about. I'd told the artist to go ahead and draw them from the old regimental photograph because I was sure Josiah would buy them. Well, he didn't, so I paid the man myself."

"Ellie, I remembered what you'd said about Josiah after his discharge, working around New England to get enough money to marry Abigail. I wrote letters to the GAR posts of the 91st New York of Albany, the 36th Massachusetts of Worcester, the 18th Connecticut of Norwich, and the 6th Connecticut of Hartford. I put Josiah's sketch of what he looked like fifty years ago in each letter and signed it formally as 'Acting Secretary, Stannard Post.'"

"'Acting Secretary?'" Calvin asked. "I'm the Post Secretary."

Sam smiled. "Well, the bylaws say since Post Commander Franklin has died and no elections have been held, Josiah right now is the Acting Commander and you have moved up from Secretary to Acting Junior Post Commander."

"And how did you get promoted to 'Acting Secretary?'" Eleanor wondered.

Sam winked at her. "By acting like one. The last of the replies came yesterday. Read for yourself." Calvin and Eleanor read first with curiosity and speed, then slowly, sick at heart, passing them back and forth.

Calvin took a deep breath. "These look irrefutable. This extra sheet here from Hartford is an affidavit, sworn out in court."

Eleanor looked at both of them. "What are you going to do?"

Calvin broke a heavy silence. "For now, nothing. We keep this to ourselves, think about it, even pray about it. We need to weigh this carefully." He looked at his friend solemnly. "It will be hard tonight, but Sam, I promise you I'll keep this quiet. Will you help me and will you promise as well?"

Sam stood at his seat, a shaft of afternoon sunlight making his polished buttons gleam, and said, "I will, on my honor as a soldier."

After Calvin dressed and left with Sam, Ellie felt empty, not wanting to believe bad news about anyone, not even someone as cantankerous as Josiah Trimble.

The GAR Stannard Post annual Lincoln Day dinner talk flowed around the national ruckus in the UCV. Calvin and Sam found themselves only half-listening to what otherwise would have pleased them greatly. The California UCV had voted that Yankees had found colored men to be useful soldiers, although it didn't say anything about courage or honor, and had asked the UCV as a whole to agree. "It's a start," the Vermonters told each other.

Acting Commander Trimble asked Sam to serve as temporary secretary for the business meeting. He then gaveled for order, posted an agenda on the chalkboard with elections, and announced, "Before elections, I believe it wise and fair we settle who will vote since three veterans recently moved here have applied to join our post. That is why I propose as the first item of business, 'Voting on New Members', followed by the elections. Any questions or motions from the floor?" Silence.

"May I have a motion adopting the agenda? Second? All in favor of the agenda say aye. Opposed? The agenda for February 12, 1914 is adopted."

Josiah nodded to Sam, "Mr. Secretary." Sam pulled out several papers tucked in the front of the ledger-sized minutes book for the post. "I have membership applications from Amos Wilson and Quinton Odoms, both from Roxbury, Massachusetts, and Taylor Smith from New York City. Each has the endorsement of his post commander and is a member in good standing of their respective posts."

Ordinary procedure now took a turn. "Sam, will you tell us which GAR posts these men are currently members?" The post commander typically sat silent in these routine matters, so Trimble's question was odd. Men made allowances for his first time presiding. Calvin thought that while this approach was unusual, he found he liked it. Generally only the post officers read through an entire application, so this was a way to let the members know a bit more about the men wanting to join. "Ah, yes, sir. Smith is, um... is a member of the Frederick Douglass Post, Harlem, in New York City. Wilson and Odoms are both members of the Robert Gould Shaw Post of Boston."

"And in what regiments did these men serve?" The men wondered at Trimble's question but again Calvin found himself liking this. He saw several men's heads tilted with interest and he guessed they might like this too. Sam scanned the letters and applications. "Private Wilson was with the 2nd

Louisiana Native Guards. Corporal Odoms was with the 4th U.S. Colored Cavalry. Private Smith was in the 21st U.S. Colored Infantry."

"I see," Josiah said, pursing his lips. "I'm not sure the members would want to increase the mixed nature of the Stannard Post. We are, after all, Vermonters first. Of course as a courtesy any veteran is welcome at our meetings and events, but membership is another matter." As the men chewed this over in a low hum of conversation, Josiah tapped his gavel. "Order please."

A voice came sharply, "Move to reject all three applications." Calvin stared to spot who had moved this and half-stood out of his chair. Not in forty years could he remember an application being... a "second" arrived over the top of the word "applications." Heads jerked around to see who had spoken. Calvin sat heavily as the "second" cut his legs from under him. In a daze he heard Josiah call, "Motion made and seconded to reject the three applications before us. Discussion?"

A strong round of conversation rose up, immediately gaveled down hard by Trimble. "Any *discussion*?" he said pointedly.

A private from West Rutland asked, "Is there any doubt the men served hon'rably?"

Sam scanned the letters. "No black marks or unkind things in any of these."

"To be expected, supporting their own kind," Josiah said softly enough to be heard by the front row or so. More loudly, he called out, "Further discussion."

One annoyed, front-row private who had heard Josiah, spluttered, "That's not fair. You can't do this."

Josiah looked at him haughtily and said, "Decide to accept or reject an application? Of course we can."

Calvin wondered if this was true, the shock wearing off of him. He whispered to Sam, "Bylaws." Sam slid the sheets from the back of the minutes book across to Calvin as the discussion rolled.

As the front-row private began to say back to Trimble over the hubbub, "That's not what I meant and you..." a much louder voice came from the left side.

"This is about race, isn't it? All three of them are colored, right?"

Many turned to hear Josiah respond, "This is about the heritage of this regiment and post, and the legacy of those who wish an endless mixing of races. If the GAR gives sanction by receiving just anyone, it gives certain people entry into arenas unfit for them." Calvin heard him with one ear as he skimmed the bylaws until he came to the section marked "Membership."

The private at the left side persisted, his voice as hard as the marble company he once headed. "They were fit enough to bleed and die for their country."

A corporal from Proctor stood and answered, "Because they knew it would get them out from under those slave drivers. But they haven't done anything deserving since, sittin' around waitin' for 'forty acres and a mule.' Why should we just hand them something we earned for them?"

The uproar continued as Calvin sat unhappily at the head table. The bylaws stated each member had to be voted in by the post members but it was always routine, almost boring. He had read: "Any applicant rejected by vote of the post may re-apply after sixty days for a fresh vote." Amid the hubbub, Calvin thought back and remembered a few times a man had applied to join and had actually had some votes against him. But not once could he recall anyone flat-out moving to reject an application.

Calvin and Sam not only sat together miserably at the head table, they sat silent. Post officers were banned from joining in a general discussion – there were too many echoes of "pulling rank" – but Josiah could run the meeting as he saw fit. Calvin saw his aim and detested his tactics. Josiah had obviously set friends in the room and the turnout tonight was good. Indeed, it was too good. Some of the occasional members, the ones who came for the parades and not much else, were here. The argument was turning on race all right, but in such a serrated way that Calvin half-expected someone to say, and then that corporal from Proctor *did* say, "Would you want your granddaughter to marry one of them?"

Pandemonium erupted. Men were on their feet, gesturing and pointing, pounding their palms with fists. Tears streaming, Ashton Melo went from group to group pleading for the applicants, but the men's blood was up and he often got rudeness for his pains. Sam was livid, and at one point gave Calvin a glare, followed by an imploring set of arched eyebrows. He even broke the silence rule and leaned over quickly to whisper, "The letters?" Calvin took a deep breath and shook his head "No."

Josiah's gavel clacked limply for quiet. Calvin gave him a hard look – for Judge Salisbury knew from gavels – and saw Trimble not much distressed, giving his beard a backhanded rub. Actually, for this level of intensity he was overly calm. Trimble gaveled listlessly. As his tapping gained ground, he loudly cleared his throat, theatrically shook his head with downcast eyes and said loudly to the table top so his voice carried further, "They are always the cause of such friction. If only we could have peace."

Men in the front rows began resuming their seats, sympathizing with their heavy-hearted, apparently beset, commander. They did not want their cozy post and all their friendships bruised by this sort of controversy. Sympathy for Josiah won over several hearts.

The gavel continued clacking for quiet and now with success. Calvin watched as Josiah sighed heavily and then asked almost tremulously, "Further discussion?"

A voice from the rear half-squeaked, "Call the question."

Josiah appeared relieved. "Very well. All those in favor of rejecting these three applicants as members of the Stannard Post of the GAR please raise your hand. The Acting Junior Commander will count. Calvin?" Woodenly, Calvin rose and counted. "All opposed?" Calvin counted again. Eighteen to accept. Twenty-six to reject. He sat down sadly. An image of Lucius Robinson crossed his mind.

Josiah said in a routine business tone, "Any further membership matters?"

That half-squeaky voice said again, "Move to release Ashton Melo from membership so he and those other three can form their own post." Calvin was staggered. Snatches of conversation from the Louisiana tables at the Dobbin House Tavern flashed through his mind, followed by the image of the heavy-set restaurant man Mueller leaning against the ribs of a waiter in the kitchen.

"Second," came the word in a suddenly still room. Ashton was still reeling from the past twenty minutes of fury. He looked up in a mix of grief and horror. "But I don't want to…"

Manners and "pulling rank" be damned, Calvin thought. "Point of personal privilege, Commander," he snarled. Sam looked alarmed and reached over to touch Calvin's arm.

"Um, well, yes," Josiah stumbled. He'd never heard this tone before from Calvin. "Point recognized. I mean, the junior commander is recognized but I must remind you, Calvin, as a post officer the rules prevent you from speaking on such a matter."

"Understood, *Corp'ral* Trimble," Calvin shot back. "I hereby resign my position as junior post commander. Does anyone object?" He looked out over a stunned room and a voiceless Josiah. "Sounds unanimous to me," and with that he stood, picked up his wooden folding chair and strode around the head table to the end of the first row. He set down the wooden chair with a crash and said savagely, "Now as a member of the body, I rise to speak against the motion to release Ashton Melo. He is a member in good standing. He's a faithful attendee of these meetings when others are only casual." He glared at that Proctor corporal over by the potted fern and looked for the owner of the squeaky voice in the back.

"A member can only be released at his own request, by death, or by conduct unbecoming, *none* of which applies here. Ashton's case and the case of all colored people is the case about liberty. Americans promise each other, and everyone who becomes an American, liberty. We call on everyone who wants liberty for himself to defend liberty for all. It was a colored man, Crispus Attucks, who was among the first to give his life for the liberty of the thirteen colonies."

Here he broke into verse, reciting by heart a part of James Weldon Johnson's poem from last year's Emancipation Jubilee.

> *That Banner which is now the type*
> *Of victory on field and flood*

Remember, its first crimson stripe
Was dyed by Attucks' willing blood.

Coloring slightly, he went on. "Now after a great civil war, it is for us the living to be dedicated to the great task remaining before us." Men caught themselves recognizing Calvin's slightly changing Lincoln's line from the Address.

"This GAR post has a heritage of liberty, which we defended with our blood. And yes, we have a legacy to leave. I say that legacy is one dedicated to the proposition that all men are created equal, endowed with life, liberty, and the pursuit of happiness. Our white and black comrades died, so others after us could live, and allow all God's children to pursue happiness and secure the blessings of liberty for ourselves and our posterity." Veterans nodded in awe. Calvin was touching all the greats: Lincoln, Jefferson, Madison, the Address, the Declaration, the Constitution. Ashton's ear caught the cadence in "all God's children," unknowingly hearing a moment from Obadiah Jones.

"This motion should be defeated." Calvin sat down, and his hunched back dared anyone else to speak. No one did.

After an awkward stretch, Josiah asked, "Call the question?"

"Yes" came several calls from around the room.

"Um, all in favor of releasing Ashton Melo from the post hold up your hand. Sam, would you count? Sam?"

Sam glared and said through gritted teeth, "Count 'em yourself."

Calvin and Sam stood with Ashton on the sidewalk afterwards, their breaths rising in ice clouds in the night air. Ashton wrung Calvin's hand. "Thank you, Major. Thank you for your words." Sam patted Calvin on the back. "Hear, hear. Great speech. And hearing Josiah say 'thirty-three to nothing' was a pleasure."

Calvin nodded modestly. "You're welcome. But this isn't over. We'll tell those three men to try again in sixty days. Gives us time to block any other moves by Josiah." He paused, then added, "And Ashton? Please call me Calvin." He looked at him with a piercing stare. "I mean it. Call me Calvin. Any time. All times. And any place."

Ashton caught the import of his words and the significance of the first name. He pulled himself to attention, saluted, and said with a twinkle, but seriously too, "Yes, sir, Major Calvin." Calvin laughed heartily, pulled off his hat, and lightly swatted Melo's kepi. "As you were, you old coot."

Sam pulled off his hat and gave Calvin a playful tap. "You officers are always abusing us non-coms. C'mon Ashton, give him a lick. We got him outnumbered."

Civilians at the Merchant's Row ice cream parlor didn't know what the three old veterans in the corner were laughing about over their hot chocolates. But everyone noticed their hats all got quite a workout.

Monday, February 16, 1914

Savannah

A noisy crowd pressed around the two bailiffs on either side of Dooley Culpepper, both leading him along and shielding him from the mass of bodies. Several Savannah policemen led them in a wedge calling, "Make way. Get back. Move out of the way, please." The chatter of the onlookers echoed and multiplied off the polished stone of the corridors.

As police and prisoner drew near the tall, brass courthouse doors, Police Sergeant Caldwell ordered, "All ratt boys. Swing 'em open." As they did, the noise inside was redoubled by outdoor shouts of "Here they come!" from the Bull Street steps. A double line of policemen had cleared an aisle down the steps. They locked their elbows together and held back the surging spectators. With Caldwell leading the way, the wedge of policemen, bailiffs, and Dooley crossed the courthouse porch and started down the steps toward the waiting paddy wagon.

A newspaper reporter fired off his flash powder for a picture. The crowd spilling down to Wright Square noised excitedly when Dooley appeared, but then quieted at the sight of Captain Robert Bidwell, commander, Longstreet Post UCV. Members of the 8th Georgia were moving into place just inside the still-struggling police lines.

Dooley's eyes misted over. The regiment had come out. In all the nightmare and catastrophe of these past weeks, the long nights in his cell and the humiliation by day at meal tables not sorted by color, he had remembered the regiment. The wrong man had died, a haunting that would never leave him, but here were old comrades and old scenes playing out in his mind. A lump rose in his throat that the old boys had come to see him off. In his watery eyes he thought the uniformed veterans looked solemn.

As police Sergeant Caldwell neared the bottom of the steps, Captain Bidwell solemnly held up a hand. "Sergeant, and detail, halt!" Although Caldwell didn't know him and had no reason to obey an eighty-one-year old Confederate, Bidwell's tone stopped them. "A moment of your time, sawjint. This is the convicted prisoner, Dooley Culpepper?"

"Yes, suh," Caldwell answered. "Twenty years for murder."

"The murder of a fellow soldier," Bidwell answered. He read carefully from a slightly trembling sheet of paper. "Private Dooley Culpepper, 8th Georgia, having been duly found guilty in a court of law of murdering a fellow soldier, indeed, a fellow member of the regiment, is hereby discharged from the ranks of the 8th Georgia regiment with shame, dishonor, and opprobrium. Signed this 16th day of February, nineteen hundert an' fourteen. Ordered by the unanimous vote of all members of the Longstreet Post, UCV Savannah."

Dumbfounded silence fell on the crowd at these words, but the shock on Dooley's face was one of true horror. Bidwell called out to the two lines of grim-faced veterans on either side, "Company, at-ten-shun! About face. Eyes down." The twenty or so old men pivoted and turned their backs, casting down their eyes, and Jim Calhoun wept. Dooley swayed, threw back his head and wailed inhumanly. He sagged between the two set-faced bailiffs. They followed Caldwell to the paddy wagon, half-carrying the rag-doll limp Culpepper through the back door. The door swung to with a clang that sounded extra loud in the still air. Dooley's wail from the depths of wagon keened out through the barred windows over the clop of the horses' hooves far down the block out of the square.

Sunday, February 22, 1914

Savannah

A cold, wind-whipped rain beat the windows of the Robinson house all through Sunday dinner. Beulah and Alma washed up in the kitchen and set a tea kettle to boil for later. Lucius took it easy in the parlor, drowsy from the meal and the steady rainbeat. He only thought he heard a tramping on the front porch but startled full alert as the doorbell sounded.

Pulling open the front door, he was amazed at the raincoat-clad, dripping man folding an umbrella in front of him. "Mr...Mr. Thompson, suh. Why come in, come in." Lee nodded gratefully but stepped aside to let a wrapped figure enter first. Rufus, Beulah, and Alma came to the hall in time to see Emily Thompson shed Lee's borrowed slicker.

"My stars," Beulah exclaimed, "Miz Thompson! Let me help you."

Emily tucked a stray strand of her hair behind her ear and said with a warm smile, "Thank you, and... call me Emily, Mrs. Robinson."

"Yes, yes," Beulah answered, beaming, hanging up the slicker. "Come into the parlor, Emily. You too, Lee."

"Nasty day to be out, you two," Rufus said.

"Would you like some tea to warm up? Kettle's ready." Alma chimed in.

The Thompsons exchanged a glance and Emily said, "That sounds lovely, Miss Robinson, but please hurry back."

Alma grinned as she turned toward the kitchen. "Lickety-split, Emily."

The adults took chairs in the parlor as Hannah and Sherman peeked in from the kitchen. Alma set up several teacups on the counter, set the teabags steeping, and headed back to the parlor. As Lee crossed to a chair, he handed Emily a book-sized package he'd pulled from his raincoat. Emily gestured toward the parlor wall with the framed family treasures.

"Mr. Robinson," she began to Lucius, "when we were here last, before things went horribly wrong..." she broke off and bowed her head. Lee reached over to pat her arm and Beulah crouched down next to her and put an arm around her. Emily nodded, took a deep breath and straightened up. "When we were here last, you and Daddy stood over by those frames and joshed about you two and Calvin Salisbury."

Lucius nodded. "I 'member." He pointed toward the wall. "That thar's the 'Rogue's Gallery.'"

"Precisely," Emily answered. She handed him the package. Lucius looked at her, then pulled the tail end of the bow. The ribbon fell loose and he pulled out a frame and turned it over. He broke into a smile, then a chuckle, dampened by a tear from each eye. Lee explained.

"We had Zachariah sit for a formal photograph about two years ago. I took the picture to the art department at Thunderbolt School and paid one of their students to do a quarter sheet pencil sketch, adding some of details from his old uniform and the hat." The Robinsons all clapped in delight as Lucius gave off a sound that was both a laugh and a sob. He wiped his eyes and said softly to the picture, "You old coot. Rufus, would you fetch me a hammer and a little nail? This old rogue is goin' up on that wall."

Rufus also brought a carpenter's level and the three men fussed over the placement with the other items. Meanwhile, the women relayed teacups and fixings to the dining room table and everyone reassembled there after admiring the men's handiwork. Rufus got the name of the art student.

Lee straightened with pride and said, "We have something else for y'all."

"Well, bless your heart, Lee," Rufus exclaimed, "this is turning into Christmas in February. Stop by anytime!" and laughter ran around the table.

"Night before last, Emily and I went to the motion picture show at the Grand Savannah. It's that one in all the papers, *A New Birth of Freedom*. It's quite a story, well-told and easy to sit through, even at an hour and a half."

"They's been stories 'bout it in the *Savannah Colored Tribune*," Lucius noted.

"Well then, you probably read that late Friday natt after the last showin' there was a fire at the Savannah. Somebody burned a cross like in the bad old days and part of the theater was damaged." All eyes were hard at this except Alma's, who looked worried.

"Word's gone 'round the West Side 'bout that," Beulah said.

"Well, it's a damned shame," Lee snapped and they all recoiled at this quiet man's language.

Emily piped up, "Lee and I have fond thoughts about the Savannah, especially since Marian Anderson's concert. I had an idea." Lee reached inside his jacket and pulled out an envelope and passed it across to Lucius as Emily went on.

"Daddy treated us to Marian's concert after you gave him the idea. We found out yesterday the Savannah's going to be closed a week or more for repairs. The manager agreed to rent the picture show to the Majestic Theater over on West Bay Street. So Lee and I would like to treat y'all to the six-thirty show tomorrow natt."

Lucius peeked in the envelope as Lee added, "There's six in there so Hannah and Sherman can go too, even bein' a school natt. Good seats."

"Thank you, suh," Lucius said, shaking hands, "thank you very much." Hannah and Sherman had been eavesdropping and scampered in with excitement and handshakes too. Rufus, Beulah, and Alma all followed so Lee felt like a pastor after a sermon.

They all talked deep into the afternoon, hoping the rain would let up, but it didn't. After getting wrapped up and saying goodbye, Lee paused in the doorway. He gave Lucius a strange look and said, "Toward the end of the picture show there's some scenes from the Encampment."

"Really, now," Lucius said with excitement.

Eyes twinkling Lee said, "I'm sure you'll want to watch those scenes real careful."

Monday, February 23, 1914

Savannah

So it was that the Robinsons wore their Sunday best on a Monday night, riding the streetcar to a block from the Majestic. Rufus noticed as they got off that not only were there matching benches for waiting but that the sign by each of them said simply, 'Streetcar' instead of 'white' or 'colored.' As promised, the theater seats were excellent, fourth row on the piano side. Word had got around about the Majestic's coup and probably three-fourths of the seats were sold on this Monday, even the twenty-five centers in the first eight rows.

Ince's work gripped the crowd from the first frame and they provided a running response along with the piano. They cheered General Washington and nodded along sagely with Ben Franklin signing the Constitution. They winced at a plantation overseer lashing a slave and booed lustily at Jefferson Davis and any shot of the Stars and Bars. Abraham Lincoln was warmly applauded and cheers rocked the hall at USCI troops in battle and as Sherman's men chased down and flogged the overseer. Murmurs swept the seats at the man playing Frederick Douglass; one of Ince's controversial innovations was using black actors to play black roles.

Toward the close, Ince showed off two technical achievements that would mark him as the first great filmmaker and leave Griffith in obscurity. Gettysburg's Encampment came into view, not just from the ground, but from the air. People shrieked and stomachs churned as Ince's white-knuckled footage swooped and careened in front of them.

Then to booming cheers came a ground scene from Camp Lincoln, with many veterans passing along a wood-paved street. The camera panned from a musical troupe on a stage to men filling the audience benches. Suddenly men moved in slow motion. Three veterans approached, obviously friends, two white, one black. Two were in dark uniforms, one in light gray. Two sergeants, one officer. And clearly visible on their collars were state badges, two 'GA' and one 'VT.'

"Grampa!" screamed Hannah and Sherman together, jumping up pointing.

Reporter Phillip Yancey's story in Tuesday's *Colored Tribune* noted both President Wilson and Senator Lodge – political opponents but fellow scholars – rated the work excellent history and great entertainment. "It's like history written with lightning," they agreed, ironically quoting D.W. Griffith's brag about his now-forgotten film. Yancey's story finished,

Majestic Theater patrons were given an extra treat by the presence and tales of USCI veteran Sergeant L. Robinson, who appears briefly in the film, shown here among family and well-wishers in the lobby following the 6:30 showing. (See photo right.)

Tuesday, April 14, 1914

Savannah

Alma was running hot water from the boiler into the sink to do the noon dishes when Emily came in and put on an apron.

"I'll get the dishes done ratt away, Miz Thompson, soon as I get this water soaped up."

Emily's eyes twinkled. "Oh, I wasn't thinkin' of that, Alma. I was thinking you should take the rest of the afternoon off. Don't fret, I'll still pay you for the day. I'd like to fuss over supper myself. Here now, take off that apron and we'll call it done. Remembah, Mr. Ratzinger will call 'bout quarter past five."

Alma took off her apron, a bit dazed. Dazed hardened into stunned as Emily took the apron and then held out her hand. "Thank you fo' this morning. We'll see you tonatt." With a slow nod, Alma limply shook hands then fetched her purse and hat from their cupboard. "Iffin' yo' sure now, Miz Emily."

"I'm sure. Thank you. Off you go."

"All ratt, an' thank you, ma'am." She closed the door, crossed the porch and went down the backyard path past the old outhouse to the alley. Her walk home was a pondering one.

As promised last week, just after five o'clock, Hugo Ratzinger pulled up in front of 305 Fahm Street. The Robinsons were in their Sunday best. Beulah and Alma had fussed with Madame C.J. Walker's various preparations, and even Hannah had been given a touch of Beulah's lipstick. Rufus and Sherman were in matching black suits with white shirts and string ties. Lucius made three tries until he liked the knot in his blue striped tie.

Hugo bustled around seeing to everyone's comfort. Everyone got settled into the Thomas, with Rufus up front peppering Hugo with questions. Hugo was happy for a new audience and described each of the knobs and levers.

In this excited mood, Hugo turned onto Tattnall Street the roundabout way so he stopped with the Thompsons' house on their right. Rufus glanced back at Lucius and Beulah, then turned and said softly, "Uh, Mistah Ratzinger? It matt be better iffin' you'd pull up 'round back in the alley."

Hugo grinned. "I cain't do it. I'm under orders from Miz Emily, you understand?"

Rufus was puzzled, but not Lucius.

"I understand, suh. When Miz Emily gets that fire-eyed look about her..."

"...that's what I'm talkin' 'bout." Hugo nodded. "An' she said pull up ratt here an' fo' me to tell you from her," imitating some of Emily's tone, "have the Robinsons come up the walk to the front door."

The Robinsons all froze. After a pause, Hugo prompted them with a smile, "Y'all don't wanna cross Miz Emily do you?"

"Uh, no, Mistah Ratzinger, we don't," Beulah said slowly, "but we don't wanna get her on the outs with her neighbors neither."

Hugo twisted around. "She also said, 'Don't mind the neighbors. Except fo' the Ratzingers all half of them have ever done for twenty years is complain, so we matt as well make 'em real happy.' Now, come on. It's 'bout five-thirty, so it's time."

He turned back and opened his door. Rufus did the same curbside. Hugo leaned the driver's seat forward and handed out Beulah, elegant as a footman of old. Lucius followed Rufus out with more of a scramble. Alma and the children assembled themselves with the men as Beulah walked around to join them.

"Okay," Lucius said, head high. "Let's go see the Thompsons." He crossed the sidewalk and swung open the wrought iron gate for Beulah. Rufus came next, then Alma and the children. As Beulah reached the bottom porch step, the front door swung open. A beaming Emily came out with arms open in welcome. Lee was right behind wearing a big grin. Hugo and any watching neighbors saw a well-dressed black family walk through the Thompson's front door.

Emily had done up the dining room in patriotic bunting. To the special delight of Hannah and Sherman, over each plate was an arc of seven shiny Lincoln pennies. The sideboard held a framed picture of President Lincoln, draped with a bit of black ribbon and a small candle burning in vigil.

After they'd taken in the dining room Emily said, "Today is April fourteenth, the day President Lincoln died." Lee raised an eyebrow at her use of "President." "Lee and I have invited you here for supper tonight in his honor. But not in sorrow. I would like this to be a wake for Mr. Lincoln, to celebrate his life.

"I could use your help on one thing. I've made supper for us all," she looked at Alma and said, "which will be served family style. But I'm not sure a supper is a wake. Then too, I didn't know if you'd want a houseful of mostly white folk for a wake, or you'd feel more at ease with just Lee and myself. How do y'all feel about it?"

The Robinsons paused and exchanged glances and quizzical looks. All the looks finally ended up on Lucius, who cleared his throat. "You know, there's been plenty of dinners and suppers for Abraham Lincoln, even his birthday set aside, lots of speechifyin' 'bout him and quotin' his words. Iffin' anybody ever deserved a wake it was President Lincoln but you know, I've never heard tell of one fo' him. I think I speak for ever'body in mah family, as grand as a supper can be, and I have no doubt you can put on the dog, Miz Emily, a wake needs mo' people. They need to be sittin', standin', jawin', drinkin', toastin', cryin', eatin', shakin' hands, even holdin' each other or dancin'. The mo' folks the bettah the wake iffin' you see my meanin.'"

"I do indeed, Mister Robinson. So we'll use what I cooked and baked as a starting point. I did say a word or two to some of the neighbors but I wanted to make sure it was all right with all of you."

"That is so understandin'," Beulah exclaimed. "What a lady you truly are." She held out both hands to Emily and everyone watched the two women share four hands and a warm look eye to eye.

"All ratt," Lucius resumed, "we'd best get goin'. Lee, somebody needs to invite over that Hugo Ratzinger, his wife, an' any other neighbors who can drop ever'thin'. Tell 'em to bring supper an' a bottle. Tell em' it's the day of Mr. Lincoln's end. That should cut ice with some of 'em."

Lee frowned. "Cut ice?"

Emily giggled. "That's a Vermont phrase, Lee. When they go out to cut blocks in the winter, if their tools are dull they make no impression, or 'cut no ice.' Right, Mr. Robinson?"

Lucius grinned. "That's how Calvin taught Zachariah and me. Okay, after that, everybody's gotta hepp lay out food. Hannah and Sherman need to pocket that emancipation money and then start gettin' in ever'body's way, plunkin' the piano or windin' up the Victrola. I'll set up glasses an' open the liquor cabinet iffin' you'll show me where it is."

As the neighbors started arriving by both doors, Lucius found himself by Emily in the dining room. "You know what'd make this sideboard complete? Iffin' you'd add a picture o' Zachariah."

Emily clapped her hands in delight. "Of course." She dashed to the back room and came back with a hinged frame. Both were Zachariah, one not long after he enlisted, and the other from a couple years ago, which Lucius recognized immediately.

"It's a good photograph, but I like the pencil sketch better. Thank you... Emily."

Emily blinked in surprise, then blinked a tear down her cheek. "You're so welcome...Sergeant Robinson." Lucius' tear was a perfect match of hers.

A most unusual wake followed under the watchful eyes of Abraham Lincoln and Sergeant Zachariah Hampton. Food and drinks flowed with conversations and good spirits. Emily smiled with an inner satisfaction as Hugo arrived with another motorcar of guests, Elijah and Fancy Porterfield with Reuben

Keyes and Charlie Gibson from the GAR. "Now the Robinsons won't feel so outnumbered."

There was a touchy moment when one of the neighbors who hadn't been tipped off by Emily but came along for the party mistook Lucius for a bartender hired for the evening.

"I'll have a gin rickey, boy," he said with a grin and a practiced condescension.

"Yes, suh," Lucius said, mixing up the gin with the lime juice. He spooned in some sugar and added the seltzer, then passed the glass over. As the man took it with a polite, "Looks good, boy. Thank you." Lucius calmly reached over for his own tumbler, down to its last third of a corpse reviver, looked the man square in the eye, and offered up a careful toast, "To Abraham Lincoln. May he never be forgotten."

The man sputtered toward a fast-arriving Lee Thompson, "What kind of uppity...? Lee! Yo' boy heah is drinking yo' liquor and spoutin' nonsense."

"Walter!" Lee exclaimed smoothly, reaching out to shake hands. "Haven't seen you in too long. Thanks for comin'. I see you've met Zachariah's old friend Lucius Robinson. I'm sorry I didn't get ovah here earlier to introduce you to our guest of honor for this wake." Walter stared as Lee clinked his glass against Lucius', who was still holding his glass out in toast position. "To Mr. Lincoln."

Walter looked back and forth between Lee and Lucius, thinking hard. Then he raised his glass and ever so lightly touched it against both Lee's and Lucius' and said carefully, "Rememberin' Lincoln" and took a sip. His eyes lit up at the flavor and he blurted, "Dang, b... uh, Robinson. This is real good." He eyed Lucius' concoction and added, "Say, what's that yo' drinkin'?"

Lucius downed the last of his drink as he drawled, "This heah is a Georgia Corpse Reviver, which is maybe the rightest drink to drink at a wake." A chuckle ran around between not only the three but several other nearby men. "Can you show us how to make one?" someone asked.

"Sure, in jes' a minute" Lucius answered, "but fust I wanna try makin' somethin' a Vermont Yankee showed me. Never tasted anythin' like it." Just then, Alma happened by and he asked her to get something from the kitchen. He started measuring two parts bourbon and one part lemon juice into a shaker. Alma came back with a breakfast bottle and to everyone's wonder he added one part maple syrup. As he poured all these together with some ice chips and mixed them up in the shaker he said, "This is called a St. Lawrence, like the rivah up by Canada. My friend the Vermonter showed me how last summah at Gettysburg." St. Lawrences flowed among the men carrying on about favorite drinks and the Encampment.

The wake was not as big as the soiree that had welcomed Zachariah home last summer, but perhaps that made it more fun. The Victrola played music into the evening and the conversations rattled and giggled through the house. A couple hours along, Ray Younger rosined up his bow. While he tuned up his fiddle, the menfolk moved furniture back to the walls and rolled up the carpets. While the fiddler played, folks cakewalked and two-stepped, fox-trotted and waltzed, even showed off a schottische or a hambo.

Lee and Emily were dancing gaily when they turned up near Rufus and Beulah. Lee suddenly stopped and tapped Rufus on the shoulder. He made a short bow and said, "May I cut in?" Rufus' face went from stunned to delighted in a flash. "Of course, suh. And may I return the favor?" looking at Emily.

"By all means, suh," Lee answered, taking Beulah's hand. "After all, I'll be dancing with the prettiest lady in the room..." he said with a wink as Emily blinked in surprise, then finished smoothly "...who doesn't actually live here." Both women laughed heartily.

As Rufus rather nervously took Emily into dance position she managed to stammer out to Beulah, "What a silver-tongued devil he is!"

Beulah nodded back with a chortle saying, "Light on his feet in mo' ways than one!" The two mixed couples had such an obvious good time turning across the floor that Hugo and Katie Ratzinger decided to join them. They pulled a protesting Lucius and Alma out of their seats and paired off with them across the floor. The neighbors cheered in delight while Hannah and Sherman giggled themselves to the floor.

The hard-case neighbors on Tattnall Street who had turned down Emily's invitation could only cluck their tongues at the fiddling and revelry at the Thompson place. The food lasted, the dessert was wonderful, and the drinking, chatting, and visiting went far into the night. Looking through the family album was a high point, especially the pictures of Zachariah.

Far into the night the last guests helped put back the rugs and the furniture. It was almost eleven when the Robinsons left. Emily's last words to Alma before the Thomas pulled away were, "Let's call ten o'clock tomorrow morning startin' time."

In the front hall, Emily put her arms around Lee and buried her head in his chest. "That was so good, Lee. What a wonderful evening. Thank you for all your help tonight."

He bent his head and kissed her. "So what are you going to do, now that you've sealed your dismissal from the UDC and are banished from the 'right circles' in Savannah?"

Emily thought a moment, then playfully took his hand and led him down the hall toward their room. "Well, tomorrow I think I'll call on Juliette Low and see how she and the Girl Scouts are getting on."

Lee threw back his head and laughed.

"Who knows?" he teased. "Maybe you and Juliette will teach them how to use swords."

Emily closed the door behind them and teased back. "Or how to vote."

Lee tweaked her cheek. "My very own suffragette."

Monday, May 25, 1914

Rutland

On a soft May morning, Calvin stood facing the statue reading again from today's *Herald*.

> *One of Carson McKenzie's many soldier statues graces the Center Street park facing Rutland's Courthouse. A local man, Lieutenant Michael Salisbury, served as McKenzie's model. Working from photographs of Salisbury taken just weeks before his death at Spotsylvania Courthouse, McKenzie created several dozen Union monuments across New England. McKenzie, 98, died after a long illness...*

Michael would always look this jaunty and young, both in copper and in photographs. "Good," Calvin thought. "At least they'll know we were young once, not just crippled up old geezers." Passersby saw an old man with a chestnut cane come to attention and salute the statue fifteen feet taller than himself. Thoughtfully he wandered past the courthouse toward Merchant's Row. A whistle-accented voice broke in. "Judge Salisbury?"

Calvin looked up at a silver-haired man in a stiff bowler hat who looked a bit younger than himself. He frowned and then said in recognition, "John. John Higgins. How are you?"

Higgins shook hands. "Just fine, just fine. And you?"

"Oh, not too bad," Calvin answered. "Say, are you on a case? Aren't you retired? Or is this 'once a detective, always a detective'?"

"You're close," Higgins answered from under his silver moustache. "Captain asked me in for a two-year old case. Seems a young lout serving thirty days for public drunkenness talks in his sleep. His cellmate listened in. The fella talked about he and a partner beating up an old Union vet right here in Rutland. The captain finally remembered assigning me to look into it."

"Is that right?" Calvin said keenly, alive to a possibility. "Any luck?"

"Oh, it's all settled. Fella made a full confession just now and will plead guilty."

"He say why they did it?" Calvin wondered, trying not to sound too interested.

Higgins dropped his voice. "Well it's odd. Seems his great uncle had been doin' some drinkin' and rantin' 'bout having coloreds in the army and he didn't care for them at all in the GAR here in Rutland. The nephew was drinkin' with him and took it on himself to make points with his uncle."

"Any idea who the great uncle was?" Calvin asked in a conspiratorial way.

"That's why the guilty plea and so no trial," Higgins said. "Keeps Josiah Trimble's name out of it. 'Course bein' a fellow vet and a judge you're probably in on most of it already."

Calvin shook his head sadly and bent the truth. "I wonder how ol' Josiah feels about his black sheep nephew."

"Well, I suppose every family has its troubles." Higgins shifted his tempo. "Say, Calvin, I'm sorry but I've got a couple appointments that won't wait. Would you mind?"

"Not at all, John. Go on. We'll have another chance soon. See you."

"See you too, Calvin. Greet Eleanor from me."

Calvin walked toward Merchant's Row thinking hard. As he neared the Rutland State Bank, he could see that just up past the corner, Josiah was sweeping his shop's sidewalk. A horse-drawn wagon pulled to a stop alongside him on Center Street. The driver jumped down from his bench and pulled on a pair of gloves as Calvin approached. "Morrnin' Judge.".

Calvin stopped and looked curiously. "Mannin'. Have we met?"

"No sorr," the man answered, "I joost know you're Judge Salisbury from here in Rutland. I'm Rory O'Sullivan from Green's hardware store."

Calvin nodded. "You know my job. What job are you going to?"

"I'm goin' up there to Trimble's jewelry store. He's got a case with a cracked glass top and I'm going to replace it."

"Is that right?" Calvin asked. An idea leaped into his mind, a mad, irresponsible, utterly justifiable idea. Judges shouldn't think like this. But justice demanded something be done. But the law was clear. But Trimble deserved it. O'Sullivan studied his face until Calvin asked him, "When are you due at the store?"

"Right now, I'm aboot fifteen minutes 'arly."

"Aha," Calvin said softly. "And how much will you charge Trimble?"

O'Sullivan grasped the straps of his overalls. "Well the glass'll be two dollars and fifty cints. My labor will be another dollar and a quaartar, so three dollars and seventy-five all togayther. Why air ya askin'?"

Calvin smiled and said quickly, "Never mind. Now Rory, I have a favor to ask that I'll pay you fifty cents for. Just wait here for the next twenty minutes until you're due at Trimble's. Will you do that?"

"Fifty cints? Just for sittin' here?" The idea appealed, but he hesitated. "What'll I tell Mr. Green? How will I explain the extra four bits?"

"Rory," Calvin replied, looking at him closely, "you need say nothing to

Green. This is a private contract between us for twenty minutes of spot labor. Is it a deal?"

Rory smiled. "You bein' a judge it shoor sounds legal to me."

With that, Calvin turned and headed up the steps into the bank. O'Sullivan could see him at the first teller's window. The teller took time, but eventually Calvin pocketed something and came back down the steps.

Calvin handed him two quarters, flipped open his pocket watch and said, "All right. There's the depot clock showing eight minutes to ten. Our contract expires in thirteen minutes. Be sure to go back on Mr. Green's time at five after. I'll expect our contract to remain private," he finished, winking. O'Sullivan pocketed the silver and muttered, "Mumm's the waard." He watched Calvin trying to appear casual as he walked away.

Calvin entered the shop with his heart pounding. Josiah was showing some rings to a young couple obviously planning their wedding. Calvin looked around idly and found a certain showcase over on the side. The young couple said they would come back later, leaving Calvin and Josiah alone across the cracked top case. They both glared at each other.

"Calvin."

"Josiah."

"Something you want?"

"Yes," Calvin hissed. "Satisfaction."

Josiah's puzzled look changed to alarm as Calvin pulled his sword from its chestnut scabbard. He brought it down by the flat with a tremendous crash onto the cracked glass top. In the tinkling quiet Josiah roared, "You'll pay for that! Do you know how much that'll cost?"

"Yes, I do! Three dollars and seventy-five cents. Now here." He reached in his coat pocket and thrust a small piece of paper in Josiah's face. It was a Rutland Bank slip, dated, signed, and the time noted by the teller stating, "Paid to Calvin Salisbury, $3.75."

Calvin flung the slip into the case among the jewelry and shattered glass. He stepped back, reached in his pocket again and produced a small cloth bag. He tossed it in the air over the case and swung his sword. The blade sliced the light fabric cleanly and a shower of copper sprayed down.

He shouted, "Paid in full! $3.75. All pennies. Lincoln pennies. Emancipation money. And you get to pick them all up!" Josiah cocked a fist, sword or no sword. Calvin lowered the blade and said in a low, singsong voice, "'Tote that barge and lift that bale, beat up Ashton, your nephew's in jail.'"

Josiah's eyes widened in shock until he pasted a scowl on his face. "The brat deserved what he got. Beating up one of them just gets sympathy from pant-wearing petticoats like you." Calvin snapped the sword back into its cane.

Josiah began picking at the pennies among the glass fragments in the case and snarled, "You chipped the wood here."

"Gives it character," Calvin shot back. "More than you'll ever have."

"Well, your character will be mud after I get through with you and that prissy little wife of yours. A real man would never have let his wife go off for years with a pack of half-human animals in Port Royal." Calvin's knuckles holding his cane whitened as Josiah looked up with a savage grin. "Why are you two so soft on them anyway? Eleanor do some horizontal dancing in those lonely months? Is there some fifty year old 'Little Black Calvin' or 'Eleanor Sambo' running around with a permanent suntan?"

Calvin started to draw his sword but Josiah sneered. "Don't bother. No way to explain away sword cuts or a murder. I'll just go home for lunch, mention a few of these things to Abigail and say to her, 'By the way, dear, just keep that to yourself.' It'll be all over town by sundown."

Calvin fought back the bile in his throat, pale with anger, staggered at the depths of Josiah's hate. He said shakily, "You'll do no such thing. Your friends will stop you."

Josiah gave off an evil chuckle. Josiah gave off an evil chuckle. "My friends? My friends are all right-minded white men. We're tighter than a drumhead to each other against those sub-human niggers."

Calvin closed the sword back in his cane and steadied himself with it. His heart was still pounding but his voice came out fairly calmly. "Actually, not only will your friends keep you quiet, but they'll see to it Wilson, Odoms, and Smith will be voted into the Stannard Post as members this month."

Josiah frowned, dry-mouthed, trying to read Calvin's eyes for madness or danger. "What friends could you mean? None of my friends would stop me. You're raving. You're insane. You should be locked away."

Calvin's voice came back rock steady. "Your friends will do it. You and they have two things in common. First, all of you have the same initials: Josiah Trimble, 14th Vermont; John Temple, 91st NY in Albany; Jonah Treptow, 36th Mass in Worcester; Jeremy Tipton, 18th CT in Norwich; and Joshua Tilton, 6th CT in Hartford." Josiah went ghost pale, gripping the case in front of him as Calvin finished. "Second, all of you are bounty jumpers."

Rory O'Sullivan saw Calvin come out of Trimble's shop and put on his hat at a rakish angle, his chin proud. He walked, no, strutted up the street, his cane almost dancing along at its own pace. O'Sullivan thought Calvin looked for a moment like an old knight who had just slain a dragon.

Wednesday, June 3, 1914

Georgia Penal Quarry

"So that's it," a burly guard said over at the long table. "Remember a few nights back that southeast light? Says in the paper, *'A light seen over Atlanta an' fo' many miles was a large cross, burnin' on top o' Stone Mountain. A group of several dozen men announced they are re…"* …he squinted. *"…reconstituting the Ku Klux Klan.'"* Table thumps and whistles greeted this, from both guards and white convicts as he continued.

> *Mrs. Helen Paine of the United Daughters of the Confederacy said, 'I hope this act will be a sign that white women can rest easy, knowin' they will be defended by these champions of Southern manhood.'*

Breakfast over, the day's heat already hung like a damp blanket. After the convicts broke loose a block of marble from the quarry face, they dragged or carted it in the manner of the pyramid builders to the open-sided, wide-roofed block shed.

In consideration of his age, Dooley Culpepper's job was measuring the blocks. Then he painted a number on it and recorded the number and dimensions on his clipboard. Monument architects nationwide wrote to the quarry to order blocks of marble, specifying their approximate dimensions.

Dooley looked up around midmorning and saw two civilians and a guard walking his way. Dooley looked twice, since one man was the warden. The other was a stranger.

"Hoo, it's gonna be a hot one today," Warden Addington exclaimed, taking off his hat and wiping his brow. "Hope it's tolerable fo' you Mistah Fraynch."

"Quite warm, surely," answered French. Trickles of sweat ran down from both sideburns, and tiny sweat beads pebbled his upper lip. But even as he fanned himself with his hat, his eyes took in the marble.

"Dooley," the warden said, "Mistah Fraynch is a customer. He's gonna buy several blocks, so you show him 'round an' write down ever' one he wants."

"Yassuh," said Dooley, his eyes switching between Addington and French. What kind of customer came to the Georgia Penal Quarry? Regardless, one thing quickly became clear. French knew marble. Certain blocks he gave hardly a glance. Others he would study closely, even pulling out a small magnifying glass. Some he would feel over with his hands. Sometimes he produced a small chisel and hammer and tapped off a chip. Then he would fit it back into its former home, squinting at the remaining crack.

When he was satisfied he would step back, note the number and say to Dooley, "Number 68, please, or "Number 236, please." His accent marked him as a Yankee, but to Dooley's surprise, the "please" came every time. Dooley appreciated his manners over the next hour as French picked out over thirty blocks. The novelty of a visitor caused the guards to find reasons to visit the block shed in twos and threes.

"How many do we have?" French asked the warden as they roosted on a low oblong block marked 402. Addington looked at Dooley, who made a quick count on his sheet. "Looks like thirty-six, no, thirty-seven blocks."

"Hmm," French calculated. "That's enough. However," here he turned to Addington, "I'll need to check for veining and crack lines. This project needs very clear, white marble. The one's I've picked look pretty good, but I need to see the sides resting on the ground."

"Well you can look at 'em all you want, suh," said Addington. He put two fingers in his mouth and fired a whistle toward a cluster of guards. The shrillness startled French into wondering if the sound could cut marble as well as his chisel. Two guards came up fast.

"Go get 'bout seven or eight hefty cons an' bring' 'em here," said the warden.

When the squad assembled, Addington addressed them. "Men, Mistah Fraynch here has come down from Noo Yawk City to buy some marble. He needs to have several blocks turned on their side so he can see their bottoms. He 'n' Dooley will show you which ones."

A bit flustered by a team of well-muscled and presumably dangerous convicts, French stammered, "Uh, thank you, Warden. Dooley, what's the first one?"

"Ratt over here, suh," Dooley answered, pointing. "Numbah 48." The warden, Dooley, several guards, and French, watched the convict gang assemble around the block. With a heave or two it tumbled over with a ground-trembling thump. French stepped forward and knelt to examine the newly exposed face. He produced a small whisk brush to clear out dirt. He turned to Dooley and said, "This is good. Please circle it on your list."

For most of the next hour the group moved around tumbling blocks and waiting for French's inspection. Mostly these were positive, but occasionally he would tell Dooley, "I don't think so" or "Please cross this one off." When the crew strained at block nine – the largest French had picked out – the block turned with a thump and then a crack. A third of the block split away and fell flat like a massive coffin lid.

"Well, I think both of these can stay," French said drolly.

"Ratt," Dooley answered. "Numbah six and numbah three, formerly numbah nine, crossed off."

French rode off before noon. Later in the week, Dooley saw French's twenty-eight blocks loaded onto a flatcar on the quarry spur siding. A switch engine pulled the car onto the main line so the marble followed French to New York by about a week.

There were quarry rumors for several months about French and the day he visited. That he was a sculptor was established fairly quickly, but the twenty-eight-block project remained only rumors.

One day the guards stirred at their end of the mess hall. "Here, take a look at that," said one of them to a table of convicts, tossing down an Atlanta newspaper several days old. Dooley was finishing his breakfast with an old man's gummed chewing motion. An article and photo datelined from Washington DC read,

> *Under the watchful eye of artist David Chester French, workers today began assembling his latest sculpture of twenty-eight blocks of white Georgia marble. When finished they will form a nineteen-foot high statue of President Abraham Lincoln, the centerpiece of the Lincoln Memorial. The statue will be in a sitting pose, looking down the Mall toward the Capitol Building.*

There was more, but Dooley couldn't read it. He was throwing up.

Tuesday, June 30, 1914

Savannah

Lucius sat rocking on his front porch by the camellia bush. The Atlantic breeze carried some wayward seagulls across Savannah. He'd read the *Colored Tribune*'s story about several men at Stone Mountain, Georgia, attempting to revive the Klan. The state had arrested them for inciting to riot, and there was talk the federal government would try them by the anti-Klan laws from the 1870s. Lucius' eye had just caught a headline noting the assassination of Austrian Archduke Ferdinand when the postman delivered the morning mail. Lucius sifted through the envelopes and found one addressed to him in a gentle, unknown hand. He squinted through his spectacles and saw that the postmark read "Vermont."

He opened the flap and unfolded several close-written pages.

"My dear Mr. Robinson" it began.

> *Thank you for your letter and handsome pencil sketch of you from your War days. Calvin said, 'He looks like a soldier determined to be free.' We both recognized Mr. Thrash's style from our Zachariah sketch.*
>
> *Although I have never written you before and we have never met, I have the sense of knowing you. Your many letters this past year to Calvin have introduced you. Mr. Robinson, Calvin cherished your letters. Any day a Savannah postmark arrived from you, or, in earlier days, from Mr. Hampton, was a red letter day.*
>
> *I don't know if Calvin told you, but the name Savannah was a trial for him. In 1859 we went there for our honeymoon. We also visited a plantation called Mulberry Grove where his uncle Eli had served as a tutor. Calvin's uncle was a clever man, and he invented a machine to comb seed out of cotton bolls. It was Calvin's everlasting shame that Eli Whitney's invention strengthened the bonds of slavery. I believe it fueled his devotion to the Union cause. His devotion also gave me the courage to travel with Amanda Fairchild to Port Royal and teach freedmen. (I was their 'Miz Ellie.')*

Lucius inhaled sharply.

> *But your letters were a healing and tonic for him. He would read each one through several times. Then, before he would write you a reply, he*

would favor me with a reading as well. We so enjoyed the experience. Each time it was like having you in the room.

I am writing you now, Mr. Robinson (and if I may be forward, may I call you Lucius?) because a week ago this Saturday my dear, dear Calvin passed away."

Lucius' handkerchief needed several turns before he could read on.

He had been ill with a fever for a few days but he seemed to be rallying. On the evening of the twentieth I went to check on him. He was worse, a bit delirious. He looked at me and knew me, but he said, 'Eleanor, what are you doing here? A battle is no place for a woman. Come quickly.'

I went over to the bed, wondering about 'battle.' He gripped my hand with a strange strength and pulled me down into a chair by the bed saying, 'Stay down behind this wall.' As I sat still for him he seemed mollified, for he loosed my hand and then said, 'I must find Michael over on the left.' (Michael was Calvin's younger brother who was killed at Spotsylvania Courthouse.) Then he slept for a while.

When he woke he looked at me and smiled as sweetly as he ever did. He pointed to an old photograph and a framed sketch on the wall and said, 'Michael is safe, and so is Zachariah, but now I must find Lucius.'

Mr. Robinson, he fell back asleep and passed over a short while later. Those were his last words.

Lucius' nose needed several attempts before it was clear.

His burial day was a crisp, blue-sky day. All but one of the members of the GAR Stannard Post turned out. As he asked, we laid him to rest in his major's uniform. By his request, Ashton Melo, a member of the 54th Massachusetts who lives here in Rutland, delivered the closing remarks at the graveside. The band played both 'The Battle Hymn of the Republic' and 'Dixie,' and an amalgamated choir from several churches delivered a powerful rendition of 'My Lord, What a Morning' that left us all in tears. I don't know how I could have gotten through it except for the comfort and support of my old friend Anna Louise and my new friend Dahlia. I could cry with them and they shared their tears with me.

Yet these were good tears, Lucius, tears that water the heart and soothe the soul. I wanted you to know about Calvin's end, his love for his country, and his friendship with you. I hope your days will be peaceful and your faith will comfort and strengthen you.

Lucius, may I have the honor to be your friend up North?

Gratefully, Eleanor Salisbury

Lucius laid his head back and held the letter in his lap.

Beulah came through the front door with iced tea. The floor board by the door creaked as she stepped out and said, "Papa?" She saw Lucius' hand fall limp as the letter slipped to the floor. His face was wet but his mouth sagged open and his whole body slumped small. Alarmed, she quickly balanced the two glasses on the porch rail and knelt by the rocker.

"Papa?" she asked anxiously, patting his hand. "Are you all ratt Papa?"

Lucius stood over her trying to say something. A voice said to him, "She can't hear you, Lucius." Lucius looked up toward the front door. "You've moved on, Lucius," said Calvin.

"Moved on?" Lucius asked. "How d'ya mean?"

"Lucius, life is an encampment, and there comes a time to strike the tent and move on."

"You've gone and joined the majority," said Zachariah, appearing suddenly next to Calvin. His collar sported a pair of brass letters, VT. "Time to be movin' on."

Beulah caught her breath between sobs and looked up. She distinctly heard the board creak by the door, although no one was there. As she doubted her hearing, she thought she caught a tramping sound, like three shoes stepping onto the first step off the porch, very nearly as one. A seagull wheeled over Fahm Street and keened as it turned toward the Atlantic.

The End

Chronology of Dates and Facts

1733   February 12: Savannah founded. James Oglethorpe lays out a grid of interlocking squares with blockhouses for defensive purposes. 23 Squares remain.

1735   October 30: John Adams born, Braintree, Massachusetts

1743   April 17: Thomas Jefferson born, VA

1744   Salzburgers found Lutheran Church in Savannah.

1751   March 16: James Madison born, VA

1770   March 5: British troops attempting to keep order fire on Boston civilians killing Crispus Attucks and four others. Samuel Adams (older brother of John) calls event, "Boston Massacre"

1773   First African Baptist Church established. Eventually buy land on Franklin Square, Savannah.

1776   July 2: Philadelphia, Second Continental Congress, adopts Jefferson's Declaration of Independence. Public proclamation, July 4.

1778   December 29: British capture Savannah and occupy entire Georgia colony.

1780   October 14: George Washington sends Nathaniel Greene as commander to defend Southern colonies.

1781   October 19: Washington accepts Cornwallis' surrender, Yorktown.

1782   British evacuate Savannah (July 11) and Charleston (December 14) to Greene's troops.

1785   October 14: For deliverance of the South, Georgia presents Mulberry Grove Rice plantation to Gen. Nathaniel Greene, wife Kitty and family.

1786   June 12: Nathaniel Greene dies.

1787   September 17: Philadelphia. Madison's proposed Constitution presented to public and states for approval.

1789   April 30: New York City, George Washington sworn in as first President, John Adams as Vice-President.

1791   March 4: Vermont admitted to US.

   May 12: George Washington as President visits Savannah & Mulberry Grove to call on Kitty Greene.

NOTE: Names in bold appear as characters in the novel.

1793 Eli Whitney, serving as tutor for children of Kitty Greene (widow of Nathaniel) at Mulberry Grove invents cotton gin. Receives patent March 14, 1794

1796 John Adams elected President.

1798 Kitty Greene and husband sell Mulberry Grove plantation.

1800 Thomas Jefferson elected President.

1802 First African Baptist Church acquires land on Franklin Square, Savannah

1807 January 19: Robert Edward Lee born, VA

1808 June 3: Jefferson Davis born, Fairview, KY

1809 February 12: Abraham Lincoln born, Hodgenville, KY

1818 February 14: Frederick Douglass born, Easton, MD

December 4: Savannah Theater opens; the US oldest continuously operating theater. Building designed by London architect William Jay

1819 January 25: Jefferson founds University of Virginia, Charlottesville

William Jay designs mansion for Savannah merchant William Scarbrough at 41 Broad Street

1820 February 8: **William Tecumseh Sherman** born, Lancaster, OH

1821 January 8: James Longstreet born, Edgefield, SC

1822 April 27: Ulysses Grant born, Point Pleasant, OH

1823 September: President James Monroe travels to University of Virginia to meet with Jefferson regarding Monroe Doctrine Proclamation

1826 July 4: Both Jefferson and Adams die, 50th anniversary of Declaration of Independence

1828 Jefferson Davis graduates from West Point

1829 Robert E. Lee graduates from West Point

1835 Jefferson Davis becomes cotton planter along Mississippi River at plantation "Briarfield"

1836 June 28: James Madison dies

1839 April 5: **Robert Smalls** born, Beaufort, SC

1840 St. John's Episcopal established, Madison Square, Savannah. Parish House is the Green-Meldrim House, Sherman's headquarters in 1864-65. **Sherman** graduates from West Point.

1842 Longstreet graduates from West Point.

1843 Grant graduates from West Point.

1844 January 30: **Joseph Clovese** born, St. Bernard Parish, LA

1846   Abraham Lincoln elected to Congress. Serves one 2-year term.

Mexican War begins; Lee, Grant, Davis, Longstreet, **Sherman**, all serve as junior officers

1847   August 10: Jefferson Davis named Senator from Mississippi

December 23: **Pleasant Crump** born, Crawford's Cove, AL

February 11: **Albert Woolson** born, Antwerp, NY

1856   April 5: Booker T. Washington born, Hale's Ford, VA

1857   March 30: Dred Scott decision; Supreme Court says neither Congress nor states can confer citizenship on African Americans.

1860   45 trains/day serve Rutland VT. Connecting point between Atlantic seaboard and Canada.

December 20: South Carolina secedes from the Union (6 others follow until Feb. 1)

1861   February 18: Jefferson Davis named President of Confederacy. Alexander Stephens of GA named Vice-President.

Rutland Herald Newspaper goes to daily

March 21: Alexander Stephens in Savannah gives famous "Cornerstone" speech: "...the Negro is not equal to the white man; that slavery – subordination to the superior race – is his natural and normal condition."

April 12: Firing on Fort Sumter, Charleston SC begins US Civil War. Lincoln calls for 75,000 volunteers to put down rebellion. Four more states secede.

April 25: New York 7th reaches Washington DC, parades past White House

June 18: Balloon ascension over White House. Prof. Lowe sends history's 1st air-to-ground military report.

July 21: Battle, Bull Run/Manassas, VA Confederate victory. Thomas Jackson holds off Union attack at critical point, earns nickname "Stonewall."

September 12: Lincoln approves plans for ironclad USS Monitor over Navy objections with the story about girl putting her foot in a stocking and remarking, "It strikes me there's something in it."

October 31: **Juliette Gordon** born in Savannah, GA

1861   November 7: US Navy bombards Forts Walker and Beauregard in Hilton Head, SC harbor. Both forts and town of Port Royal surrender about 2:30pm & occupied by Union troops. Major Rufus Saxton a member of the Quartermaster Corps in these occupation troops. Major civilian panic in Savannah, 25 miles away.

1862 Early Union Black enlistments. Col. Thomas Higginson commands 1st Negro regt. in Union army, raised in Port Royal, SC

April 6-7: Battle, Shiloh, MS. A.S. Johnston surprises US Grant but unable to defeat him. Grant throws back Johnston's army next day. Total casualties more than all US war casualties combined since 1607.

May 8-June 9: CSA General Stonewall Jackson conducts Shenandoah Valley campaign. Through hard marching and hard fighting with 17,000 men he fights and wins 4 battles, 6 skirmishes in the face of 60,000 Union men assigned to catch him. He captures 3500 prisoners, 10,000 rifles, 9 rifled cannons, and a double column of captured wagons piled with supplies (from Gen. Banks) 8 miles long. Tactics are still required reading at West Point.

May 13: **Robert Smalls** (an experienced pilot) leads 12 other slaves to take control of Confederate ammunition ship *Planter* and steers it to Union blockading squadron off Charleston Harbor.

Late June : Robert E. Lee drives off McClellan's army from Confederate capital at Richmond in battle of Seven Days. Union General O.O. Howard loses arm in fight

September: Lee in Maryland and Bragg in Kentucky attempt two-pronged invasion of North to conquer a peace. Lee defeated at Sharpsburg/ Antietam Creek, Sept. 17 – single deadliest day of battle in US history.

October 9: Bragg defeated at Perryville.

December 1: For heroism under fire, **Robert Smalls** promoted to captain of *Planter* (now a US Navy vessel), first black captain in US Navy.

1863 April 20: **Helen Dortch** born in Carnesville, GA

May 1-3: Lee defeats Hooker at Chancellorsville. Stonewall Jackson accidentally shot by own troops and dies.

June 4: 1000 Union troops, mostly black, burn 34 homes and buildings in Bluffton, SC

June 9: CSA General Taylor attacks Milliken's Bend, LA to disrupt Grant's plans on Vicksburg, MS. Attack repulsed. First action by 2nd LA Native Guards – African American unit.

July1-3: Battle of Gettysburg.

July 1: CSA General James Archer captured by **Private Patrick Maloney**, 2nd Wisconsin. Lee's army drives Union I and XI corps through town onto Culp and Cemetery Hills and Cemetery Ridge. Meade concentrates Army of Potomac.

July 2: 3:00pm Union general Sickles moves off Cemetary Ridge to form salient on Union left.

1863 4:00pm Longstreet attacks Sickles, tries to take Little Round Top hill. Union hangs on to Little Round Top. Sickles wounded and III Corps overrun.

5:00pm CSA Ewell attacks Union right on Culp's Hill with artillery support from Benner's Hill.

6:30pm Longstreet momentarily reaches Cemetery Ridge but driven off by Hancock's II Corps.

July 3: 1:00pm Lee begins 2 hour bombardment of Union center (Hancock II Corps)

2:00pm CSA Stuart attempts to ride cavalry around Union right. Fended off by Custer-East Cavalry field

3:00pm Pickett's division leads assault column on Cemetery Ridge. Gen. Armisted at Union wall carries hat on sword tip as a guide; dies by a Union cannon. Hancock repels Pickett, but wounded.

September 19-20: Battle, Chickamauga, GA. CSA Bragg, with Longstreet's 1st Corps transferred from VA, defeats Rosecrans. Thomas' stand saves Union army from disintegration. Howard's and Slocum's Corps transferred to Chattanooga to reinforce Thomas. Remain in western theater for rest of war.

November 24-25: Battle, Chattanooga. 24th Thomas, **Sherman**, Howard and Slocum, all under direction of Grant, storm Lookout Mountain and Tunnel Hill. 25th, Thomas attacks base of Missionary Ridge but attack overpowers Confederate center on top of Ridge.

1864 March 3: Congress passes law equalizing pay, bonuses and benefits between whites and blacks in US military

May-June: Grant and Lee duel across VA: Wilderness, Spotsylvania, Cold Harbor, Petersburg. **Sherman** and Johnston/Hood tangle across northwestern GA.

July 12: CSA Gen. Early turned back from attempted capture of Washington. Abraham Lincoln observes skirmishing at Fort Stevens--only US President to come under hostile fire while serving as President.

September 2: **Sherman** captures Atlanta.

November: Lincoln re-elected, defeating anti-war candidate McClellan. Sherman marches across GA to Savannah.

December 20: **Sherman** captures Savannah

1865 January 16: Savannah **Sherman** reads Emancipation Proclamation Greene Square opposite 2nd Baptist Church, with black clergy explaining meaning. Also issues Special Field Order 15, which provides 40 acres of land and a mule for each freed family.

1865 April 9: CSA General Lee surrenders to General Grant at Appomattox Courthouse, effectively ending the War.

April 14: Abraham Lincoln assassinated at Ford's Theater.

May 12: Jefferson Davis captured, imprisoned for 2 years

Autumn : President Andrew Johnson revokes Special Order 15.

December 6: 13th Amendment, prohibiting slavery, ratified.

1867 December 23: **Sarah Breedlove** born, Delta, LA

1868 February 23: **William Edward Burghardt (W.E.B.) DuBois** born, Great Barrington, MA

July 9: 14th Amendment ratified giving citizenship to all persons born or naturalized in US. Equal protection under laws regardless of race, sex or creed.

November: US Grant elected President

1870 February 3 : 15th Amendment ratified, giving black men the right to vote.

October 12: Robert E. Lee dies

1871 **James Weldon Johnson**, poet, born Jacksonville, FL

1875 March 1: Congress passes Civil Rights Act prohibiting racial discrimination by public entities or businesses. Law is challenged immediately in Federal Courts.

1876 Savannah, *The Colored Tribune* (newspaper) begins publishing

March 27: Supreme Court rules United States vs. Cruikshank: federal government could not charge private citizens with violations of state laws. Allow white mobs in South to assault blacks almost at will. Rare court cases tried by white judges and juries.

1876 **Robert Smalls** elected to US Congress from South Carolina. Serves 5 2-year terms.

1877 March 3: Last Federal troops withdrawn from SC and LA. In exchange these states' Presidential electors make Rutherford B. Hayes the 19th President. Withdrawal ends "Reconstruction" in South. Whites begin imposing legal restrictions and segregation – the beginning of "Jim Crow"

1878 March 31: **Jack Johnson** born, Galveston, TX

Savannah Board of Education acquires Broad St. School for education of colored children

1882 November 6: **Thomas Ince** born, Newport, RI

1883 October 15: Supreme Court (8-1) overturns 1875 Civil Rights Act; 13th and 14th Amendments do not empower Congress to legislate on racial matters in private sector.

1885 July 23: Ulysses Grant dies

November 11: **George Patton** born, San Gabriel, CA.

1886 June 25: **Henry "Hap" Arnold** born, Gladwyne, PA.

Summer: Former CSA general John Gordon runs for governor of GA. Jefferson Davis gives campaign speech in Atlanta and publicly reconciles with Longstreet.

December 21: **Juliette Gordon** marries William Low

1889 December 6: Jefferson Davis dies

1891 February 14: **William Sherman** dies

October 7: Georgia State Industrial College for Colored Youth opens in Thunderbolt, GA (Savannah suburb). Later becomes Savannah State College.

1893 Gettysburg Power plant opens, providing electricity to 34 street lights and for an electric rail line to Big Round Top Park

1894 Rutland replaces horse-drawn trolleys with electric cars.

1895 February 20: Fredrick Douglass dies.

September 18: Booker T. Washington gives famous "accommodation" speech in Atlanta

1896 May 18: Supreme Court (7-2) Plessy vs. Ferguson: "separate but equal" laws providing for racial separation were legal. Public accommodations, facilities, schools, and private businesses could all operate on this basis.

1897 February 27: **Marian Anderson** born, Philadelphia, PA

1897 September 8: **Helen Dortch** marries James Longstreet; he is 76, she is 34.

1898 April 25 to June 12: Spanish-American War. Savannah major embarkation point for troops going to Cuba.

November 10: Wilmington, NC. White mobs, aided or ignored by police, kill over 100 and burn many black-owned businesses and homes.

1900 US Census reports average annual life expectancy for Americans to be 46, 48 for whites, 33 for black Americans.

Sarah Breedlove begins developing hair care products for black women

November 8: **Margaret "Peggy" Mitchell** born, Atlanta, GA

1901 McMillan Commission chooses site in "West Potomac Park" as site for Lincoln Memorial

1902 Mobile, AL streetcar boycott against segregation by black population

1904 January 2: CSA General James Longstreet dies, Gainesville, GA

1905   Thomas Dixon publishes *The Clansman*, a book of white supremacy

Georgia establishes separate parks for blacks and whites.

1906   January 4: **Sarah Breedlove** marries Charles Joseph Walker, a newspaper sales agent; styles herself as "Madame C.J. Walker"

January 9: **John Fitzgerald** becomes first American-born Irish Catholic mayor of Boston

February: Rutland's Bates House (hotel), much of Merchant's Row destroyed in largest fire in city history

1908   December 26: African-American boxer **Jack Johnson** wins world heavyweight title by defeating Canadian Tommy Burns in 14th round in Sydney, Australia. (Johnson had to agree to let Burn's manager referee the fight.) Defends title over next several years against a series of "Great White Hope" contenders.

1909   US Army buys first US military airplane from Wright Brothers. Orville Wright comes to Fort Myers, VA to teach Army pilots to fly

Lincoln Penny first issued.

February 12: **W.E.B. DuBois** instrumental in forming National Association for the Advancement of Colored People (NAACP).

College Park, MD - Army opens first military airbase. Orville Wright teaches **Frederic Humphreys, Frank Lahm** and **Benjamin Foulois** to fly here.

Groundbreaking in Washington for Grant Memorial statue on west side of Capitol facing down National Mall.

George Patton graduates from West Point. Assigned to 15th US Cavalry

1910   July 4: Boxer **Jack Johnson** defeats former undefeated and retired champion Jim Jeffries by TKO in 15th round in front of 22,000 at an outdoor ring in Reno, NV. Collects over $100,000. Reporter for *Variety* magazine is Al Jolson. Blacks across America celebrating win with spontaneous parades and gatherings are frequently attacked by angry whites in their towns, then blamed for "rioting."

November: First issue, *Crisis* magazine. **W.E.B. Dubois**, editor

Madame C.J. Walker moves to Indianapolis to build factory and training school for her products. National sales force grows to over 1,000.

1911   February 12: President Taft signs Lincoln Memorial Bill, establishes a Lincoln Memorial committee and appropriates $2 million for construction. (Final cost: $3 million)

College Park, MD – First military aviation school opens. **Henry Arnold** instructor.

1913   Planning begins for National Encampment in Gettysburg by US Army. Colonel Lewis Beitler appointed as chief planner and coordinator for 1913 Encampment.

Savannah - first motorized fire department of any city in US

Helen Longstreet lobbies legistlature to establish a state park at Tallulah Gorge and protect it from Georgia Power Co.'s effort to build hydro-electric dams. State park not established until 1993.

1912   **Thomas Ince Studios** established; Ince builds 18,000-acre studio near Malibu, CA

Spring: Savannah- **Juliette Gordon Low** organizes first troop of "Girl Guides." Name changed in 1913 to "Girl Scouts."

June 18: Savannah Earthquake; mild to moderate damage

Summer: US Army Corps of Engineers and Quartermasters visit Gettysburg.

Summer: **Capt. Chandler** and **Lt. Henry Arnold** fly from College Park to Frederick, MD and perform "flyover" for National Guard encampment.

Summer: **George Patton** travels to Stockholm for Olympic Games. Patton finishes 5th in pentathlon, due to scoring error in pistol shooting. Army assigns Patton to French fencing academy for nine months.

July 31: Feature length film of **Johnson**'s boxing win over Jeffries is so popular with blacks and upsetting to whites, Congress enacts national ban on prizefight movies. Ban lasts until 1940.

August 26: Congress grants $150,000 in matching grant to state of PA for expenses.

October 11: Frederick Eells flies a biplane from a Gettysburg field, circles town and lands again. 6 miles.

Autumn: College Park, MD - Aviation School moves to San Diego.

November 5: VA Democrat **Woodrow Wilson** (President of Princeton University) defeats both former president Theodore Roosevelt and incumbent William Taft. 1st Southern Democrat elected president since before the Civil War (Zachary Taylor, LA,1848)

1913   **Thomas Ince** releases Battle of Gettysburg, one of 98 films about the Civil War that were made this year, and one of over 150 films produced by Thomas Ince Studios.

PA legislature votes to pay rail fare for all veterans attending Encampment from inside PA

George Patton named US Army's youngest ever Master of Sword. Invents new saber for cavalry.

1913 January 11: Vermont legislature unanimously votes $10,000 to pay rail fares for VT veterans to attend GB13.

February 4: **Rosa Louise McCauley** born Tuskegee, Alabama to James, a carpenter, and Leona McCauley, a teacher.

March 10: Harriet Tubman dies

May 13: **Jack Johnson** convicted in federal court of violating the Mann Act "transporting a woman (his fiancee **Lucille**) across a state line for 'immoral purposes'."

Spring: Regular US army troops at Gettysburg put up thousands of tents, picnic tables, benches and boardwalks. 7000 tents, 280 acres, with 47 miles of avenues and company streets, lit by 500 electric arc lights. Installed 32 bubbling ice water fountains. Each tent held 8 men, each with cot and bedding. Also 2 hand basins, 1 water bucket, 2 lanterns and several candles.

Two Battalions of the 5th US infantry served as security force (MPs), along with 15th US Cavalry. Several hundred Boy Scouts served as various messengers and helpers. 2000 Army cooks and bakers in 173 field kitchens put on 3 squares a day for the vets. Each veteran was issued a mess kit: cup, plate, knife, fork & spoon (with embossed stuff of GB13) which each could keep as souvenir.

June 25: **Jack Johnson** skips bail and meets wife **Lucille** in Montreal. Couple spend next seven years abroad.

June 25: First veterans arrive for Gettysburg Encampment
9,980 vets treated by medical personnel during Encampment. 9 died (better than statistical avg. would suggest for time, era and ages of men)

June 29: Encampment begins with supper. Several hundred reporters cover story including *London Times, London Evening Telegraph.* The *New York Times* sends regular reporters to cover the event and hires **Helen Longstreet** to file daily reports as a special correspondent.

July 2: Gettysburg. Temperature over 100 degrees. Heavy Thunderstorm late afternoon

July 3: Gettysburg, 15th Cavalry reports restoring order in local tavern. A slurring remark about Lincoln was met with argument and fists. Attributed to "too much drink" among the septuagenarians.

July 4: **Pres. Wilson** gives speech in "Great Tent" – focus on reconciliation of sections. Two references to race. Fireworks display shot off from Little Round Top

July 6: "Every porch, every window, was filled with women, from all parts of the country, waving flags and handkerchiefs, throwing kisses to the gallant old Confederates, and bidding them Gods speed on the homeward journey." Article by John C. Hill, *Roanoke (VA) Times.*

1914   January: Rutland – Paramount Theater opens. Seats 1000

February 12: (Lincoln's Birthday) Groundbreaking ceremony as construction begins for Lincoln Memorial

> Statue of Lincoln Sculptor: **Daniel Chester French**.
> First plan: bronze, standing pose, 12' tall.
> Final statue: 19' high, sitting pose, made from 28 blocks of white Georgia marble.

1915   **Marian Anderson** takes first long concert trip, Washington to Savannah, riding Jim Crow rail cars

February 18: DW Griffith releases history's first full-length movie: *Birth of a Nation.* based on Thomas Dixon's *The Clansman,* Premieres in White House for **President Wilson** and staff.

February 23: **Robert Smalls** dies.

June 21: Supreme Court (8-0) Guinn vs. United States: "grandfather clause" declared illegal (only allowed registered voters whose grandfather had been eligible – ie, not a slave)

November 14: Booker T. Washington dies.

November 25: Thanksgiving Day evening, KKK revived with cross burning on top of Stone Mountain, GA

1916   John Wright invents and patents "Lincoln Logs" building toy. Wright is son of architect Frank Lloyd Wright.

1917   May 29: Boston - Mayor **John Fitzgerald** has a grandson. They name him after the mayor: John Fitzgerald Kennedy.

Madame C.J. Walker delivers anti-lynching petition to **President Wilson** at the White House.

1919   **Madame C.J. Walker** dies

1920   Spring: 28 blocks of Georgia Marble assembled on site of Lincoln Memorial to form Lincoln's statue.

July 20: **Jack Johnson** and wife **Lucille** return to US. Johnson surrenders himself to serve prison term of 1 year. Released July 9, 1921.

August 26: 19th Amendment ratified, giving women the right to vote

1922   US House passes anti-lynching bill. Defeated by Southern filibuster in Senate.

April 27: Grant Memorial dedicated, 100th birthday of Grant

May 30: Lincoln Memorial dedicated by President Harding. Robert Todd Lincoln attends. Theme of dedication: Lincoln as Savior of the Union. Keynote speech by Dr. Robert Moton, President of Tuskegee Institute. Segregated ceremony.

1924   November 19: **Thomas Ince** dies

1927 January 17: **Juliette Low** dies

1929 January 20: Martin Luther King Jr. born, Atlanta, GA

1932 December 18: **Rosa Louise McCauley** marries Raymond Parks.

1933 **Marian Anderson** begins two year European Tour. Aurturo Toscanini declares "A voice like yours is heard only once in a hundred years."

1936 February 19: **Marian Anderson** gives White House concert; first black artist ever to perform there.

1936 June: **Margaret Mitchell**'s *Gone with the Wind* published, becomes bestseller.

1937 **Marian Anderson** gives 70 concert US tour. US House passes anti-lynching bill. Defeated by Southern filibuster in Senate.

1938 June 26: **James Weldon Johnson** dies.

September 29: **Henry "Hap" Arnold** becomes Brigadier General and Chief of Staff, Army Air Corps.

December 12: Supreme Court Gaines vs. Canada: state must either admit Gaines to all-white University of Missouri law school, or establish a comparable law school (ie "separate and equal"). Gaines admitted.

1939 April 9: **Marian Anderson** scheduled to sing in Washington's Constitution Hall, run by Daughters of American Revolution. DAR refuses to let a black singer use Hall. DAR member Eleanor Roosevelt resigns in protest, arranges site for outdoor concert. Easter Sunday, 75000 in audience (including 200 Texas DAR members) at the Lincoln Memorial. Nationwide radio broadcast and newspaper coverage.

December 15: World premiere of movie *Gone with the Wind*, Atlanta, GA. A week of events precede opening, including an evening of "plantation songs" concert. One of the children's choir singers is 10-year old Martin L. King.

1940 US House passes anti-lynching bill. Defeated by Southern filibuster in Senate.

1941 Rev. A. Philip Randolph calls for African-American "March on Washington" to desegregate US military and defense industries. Estimated 100,000 will attend. President Roosevelt has White House meeting with Randolph, reaches compromise: defense industries will be desegregated and federal government will enforce. March on Washington canceled.

1945 December 21: **George Patton** dies

1946 June 10: **Jack Johnson** dies

1947 June 29: President Harry Truman first President to address national convention of the NAACP. Address delivered in Washington, outdoors, on steps of Lincoln Memorial.

1948 July 26: President Truman issues executive order to end of segregation in US military

1949 August 11: Author **Margaret Mitchell** dies

1950 January 15: Gen. **Henry "Hap" Arnold** dies

1950 At age 87, **Helen Longstreet** stands for election of Governor of Georgia as a write-in candidate. Loses to Herman Talmadge.

1951 July 13: **Joseph Clovese**, oldest surviving black Union veteran, dies, Detroit, MI (age 107)

December 31: **Pleasant Crump**, best-documented, oldest surviving Confederate soldier, dies, Lincoln, AL (age 104)

1954 May 17: Supreme Court Brown vs. Topeka, (9-0) overturns Plessy vs. Ferguson, ruling under the 14th Amendment that separate but equal in public education is inherently unequal.

1955 December 1: Montgomery AL black bus boycott begins with arrest of **Rosa Parks**. Boycott, led by GA minister Martin Luther King, Jr. receives widespread news coverage. Boycott successful and busses integrated.

1956 August 2: **Albert Woolson**, oldest surviving Union soldier, dies in Duluth, MN (age 109)

1957 September 24: Little Rock Arkansas. Governor Faubus uses National Guard troops to prevent school integration. President Eisenhower sends in regular US Army troops to enforce court integration order, first time since Reconstruction federal troops so used.

1962 May 3: **Helen Dortch Longstreet** dies in Milledgville, GA, and buried in Atlanta.

1963 Summer: Savannah, On Greene Square where Sherman read Emancipation Proclamation Martin Luther King gives speech, featuring catch phrase, "I have a dream."

August 18-25: "March on Washington" for civil rights. On 25th, Rev. A Philip Randolph gives keynote address. Crowd estimated at 250,000. Later that afternoon, on steps of Lincoln Memorial. Dr. King delivers "I Have a Dream" speech to nation.

1964 July 2: After several weeks, Southern senatorial filibuster is closed off and Congress passes Civil Rights Act banning discrimination and segregation in education, voting, and public and private facilities.

1968 April 4: Martin Luther King assassinated, Memphis, TN.

1993 April 8: **Marian Anderson** dies

1998 January 28: US Postal Service issues stamp honoring **Madame C.J. Walker**

2005   January 27: US Postal Service issues stamp honoring **Marian Anderson**

October 25: **Rosa Parks** dies. The first woman in US history to lie in state in the Rotunda of the US Capitol. 30,000 mourners file past her casket in one day.

2008   November 5: Barack Obama is the first African American to be elected president of the United States.

About the Author

Ohio native Carl Eeman has had an array of life experiences: ski lift operator, Dad, Lutheran pastor, shoe salesman, wine merchant, and now author. Previous books include *Generations of Faith*, a book on generational issues affecting ministry, and *Recounting Minnesota*, a rollicking, insightful blogging account of the Al Franken Senate recount from 2008. *Encampment* is his first novel. Carl currently resides in Minnesota.